THE HUNTSMAN'S AMULET

*Dear Robert
Best wishes
Duncan MacPherson*

ALSO BY DUNCAN M. HAMILTON

SOCIETY OF THE SWORD TRILOGY
THE TATTERED BANNER

Copyright © Duncan M. Hamilton 2013
All Rights Reserved
The right of Duncan M. Hamilton to be identified as the author of this work has been asserted.

All of the characters in this book are fictitious and any resemblance to actual persons, living or dead, is coincidental.

THE HUNTSMAN'S AMULET

SOCIETY OF THE SWORD, VOLUME II

DUNCAN M. HAMILTON

PART I

Chapter 1
THE WATCHING ASSASSIN

Macchio Ferrata stood atop a building that provided an unobstructed view of the street below. There was only one person visible, walking slowly as though he had nowhere in particular to go, but Ferrata knew there were two others concealed. He stroked his thin moustache.

Of the man in the street, Ferrata knew only two things for certain. The first was his name and the second was that he had made some very powerful enemies. How or why, Ferrata did not know. The price he was being paid to kill this man did make him curious though. For a man with no titles or fame to warrant the bounty of a duke or a prince was a very unusual thing. Ferrata had killed a duke, but he had not been paid nearly so much for that.

All of the evidence suggested that one way or another, this man was very dangerous. Ferrata had not lived this long by being reckless, so his first act — which saw him standing atop the building — was to see for himself just how dangerous.

He gestured with his hand and one of the two concealed men moved out of his hiding place and aimed a crossbow. The thrum of its string was barely audible in the evening air as Ferrata crouched to watch the little show he had arranged for himself. If it resulted in the man's death, Ferrata would have made himself a great deal of money for very little work. If it didn't, he would know exactly what he was dealing with.

◆—◆

Soren had called a halt to his search long after darkness had descended, as he had each evening since he arrived in Auracia. The optimism with which he had initially approached his task, telling himself each day that this was the day that he would find her, had long since waned. Now he forced himself from his cot each morning, progressively later, and made his way out into the city expecting to find exactly what he had the previous day: nothing.

He had spent every waking hour walking the streets, hoping to catch sight of Alessandra or find some clue as to where she might be. He had been inside every tavern, inn, whorehouse and religious house in the city, but it was as though she had never been there.

As he made his way through the streets back toward his inn, he began to wonder how much city remained to be searched. He was already beginning to fear a reality he did not want to accept.

A clatter behind him tugged at his attention. He didn't pay it much thought at first, but its source invaded his mental lethargy. It had been the sound of the metal tip of a crossbow bolt striking the brick wall of the building behind him.

With the connection finally made he dashed toward the entrance to an alley a few paces further down the street. Once in he pressed himself against the building's wall. It was several stories high, and he hoped it would put him out of sight of whoever had fired. There was only one person who had any reason to want to kill him, but Soren had hoped that he had gone far enough to be free of that danger.

He strained his ears for any sound of movement, but whoever was attacking him seemed to be content to wait for him to come out. At least it meant that, wherever they were, they couldn't get at him.

'We can wait all night,' a voice called out.

It was an Ostian accent, a lilt that Soren had not heard in many weeks.

'Don't see why I can't do the same,' Soren shouted back. He cursed himself. It would have been better to have said nothing. Unless they had both ends of the alley watched, they wouldn't have known if he was still in there. The only question that remained was if they genuinely were prepared to play a waiting game. If they were hired assassins, he doubted that.

Soren glanced down the alley. A few paces further along, it turned sharply to the right. Any bowman would have to turn it to get a clear shot at him, which would put them within reach of an energetic lunge. The same was the case for the end Soren had entered through. Short of firing down on him, they would have to come in and face him down with steel.

He tried to still his breathing as much as possible to listen for any movement. There was still silence and he began to wonder if the assassin — or assassins — were content to sit and try to wait him out.

Finally he heard movement, the sound of feet hitting the ground, then footsteps. Soren drew both sword and dagger and pressed his back against the wall, silent and motionless.

A figure appeared at the end Soren had entered, holding blades rather than a bow. Another appeared around the corner opposite, with blades also.

'He said you'd be best taken out from a distance,' the one at the entrance said.

'Who's "he"?' Soren said.

The figure was silhouetted against the light of the mage lamps on the street. The alley itself was dark. Soren could not see if the man was smiling, but he imagined him to be doing so.

'Guess we're going to find out if he's right,' the man said.

No sooner had he spoken than his partner pounced. Soren felt the tension that had been building snap like a branch.

He parried the first strike with his dagger but kept his sword ready: an attack on the other side would not be long in coming. The other man came at him, forcing Soren to fight in two directions at once.

It had been some time since he had been in a fight, and longer since he had considered using the Gift. He'd been reluctant to try since proving to himself that he couldn't control it. However, control was not an issue now; if he didn't kill, he would be killed. He tried to focus on the blue glow, imagining it everywhere as he knew it was — even if normally he couldn't see it and it was permanently invisible to the vast majority of people.

It was difficult to imagine it right now. His concentration was needed just to fend off the attacks, which left little to be desired in terms of the skill of their execution. They were not hired thugs, and the only thing that stood in Soren's favour was that they were being careful. As the talker had indicated, they knew he was dangerous at close quarters and were doing little more than sounding him out, hopeful that the dual assault would be enough to overwhelm him.

Soren was not able to concentrate enough to see the energy that fed his Gift. There was nowhere for him to retreat, to get the momentary respite that he needed to focus. With tentative, probing attacks against him Soren was holding his own, but as soon as they began their assault in earnest he could be in trouble.

The man at the entrance took a step back and straightened. 'Not so dangerous, I don't think,' he said. 'Time to finish this up.'

Soren parried the strike from the man behind him with his dagger and took advantage of the few seconds that had been given to him. He forced all other thoughts out of his mind and the world flashed with a benign blue glow. It wasn't particularly strong, but it was enough. As soon as he released the thought everything returned to normal. The man at the entrance attacked again, committing his full body, not just his arm. Despite moving far faster, he appeared slower. Soren turned his body square to the attack, not worried about anything coming at him from behind: there would be plenty of time to deal with that. He parried the attacker's sword to his left and thrust. The sword blade punched through the man's chest, a fatal strike. His eyes were just beginning to widen with surprise as Soren pulled his sword free and turned to face the second attacker.

He was in the process of striking at Soren's back, but in the grip of the Gift he appeared to be moving at less than half pace. Soren parried with sword, thrust his dagger into the man's chest and finished it with a slash of his sword that cut the man's neck almost to the backbone.

Soren sheathed his weapons. He thought of inspecting the bodies, but he was certain he knew who had sent them, and while any coin they were carrying would have been useful he didn't want it. He jogged out onto the street and returned to walking pace when he got there. Auracia was a violent city and the discovery of two well-armed men's bodies would not cause any great fuss. Nonetheless, it would be better for Soren if he were nowhere near them when that discovery was made.

Aside from that, once the effects of the Gift faded he would be exhausted. Not having called upon it for so long he had no idea how debilitating it would be, but he did not want to be in the open street when he found out. He was already beginning to feel a little nauseated, not something he had felt since his early days experimenting with the Gift. It was not a good sign.

◆—◆

The man walked out of the alley shortly after the sound of clashing metal stopped. He looked none the worse for the episode, and

Ferrata sighed. The men he had hired came well recommended. They had not lasted long, but he'd never expected that they would. Nevertheless he had allowed himself to get his hopes up for an easy job and a large payday.

There were more pleasant ways to spend one's time than chasing a man across the world and killing him, but it seemed that he would have to continue for a little time yet. Despite the inconvenience, there was something about this one that fascinated Ferrata. He wondered what it would be like to fight him one to one.

Chapter 2
THE CITY OF AURACIA

NICCOLO'S INN WAS QUIET; none of the groups of sailors that often congregated by the bar were there. Soren slumped down on a bar stool in relief and waited for the waves of fatigue to wash over him. By the time the innkeeper had put a mug of ale in front of him, Soren was barely able to lift it.

Niccolo's was usually quiet; one of the reasons Soren chose it. The waterfront district of the city had seen better days but had never been the most desirable of places to stay, and Niccolo's was right in its centre. It was a solid brick building, but old, and Soren doubted if anyone living would be able to recall when it was last decorated. The furniture was old and worn but functional, and there was a damp, musty smell about the place.

There was never anyone to bother him, apart from the innkeeper, but even he ignored Soren most of the time. On a typical day, perhaps a dozen people would pass through the inn, sometimes more in the evenings, but they tended to keep to themselves.

'You gonna pay for that?' the innkeeper said. He stood on the other side of the bar wiping a glass, looking out the corner of his eye at Soren. It was clear that he would not stop without an answer.

'I've coin. I'll pay when the rest of my bill is due at the end of the week,' Soren said. His coin was close to running out, and he was still no closer to his reason for coming to Auracia than he had been when he arrived.

He stood and picked up his mug before shuffling over to a table at the other side of the large room that made up the lower level of the inn. It was as much distance as he could put between him and the innkeeper without going outside, and about as much as he thought he could manage without further rest. Even that short distance caused his legs to burn and his mind to swim in dizziness. He hoped the signal that he wished to be left in peace was clear.

Some men came into the bar. Soren sighed. Men meant noise, and more often than not they would be looking for conversation. Perhaps they would not see him in the dim taproom, but it was unlikely. He could always hope though, he thought.

'A round of drinks please, innkeeper; whatever you have on tap!' one of the men said. 'Ho there, friend! Can we get you a drink?' the man shouted in Soren's direction.

Soren held up his still half full mug and sloshed it for them to see, forcing a smile as he did, not wanting to appear completely ungrateful.

'Perhaps later then, my friend.' He turned back to the bar, and his companions.

Soren felt a little churlish. They were just trying to be friendly. He could tell that they were not Auracian, but he could not place the accent.

'We've been at sea for two weeks, and not in this city for more than three months. What's been happening in this part of the world?' the generous man said to the innkeeper.

'Not much of anything — usually the case these days. Your

news of the north is probably fresher than our own. There's more fighting between the other cities of the Principalities in the south, but there's nothing new in that.'

Soren let the chatter of the men drift into the background as he fell back into his thoughts, a place he spent much of his waking time these days. He had been in Auracia for nearly two weeks. His initial elation at having escaped a prison cell and the headsman's block in Ostenheim had flagged as his days melded into what felt like a purposeless existence. He'd come to the city expecting to find Alessandra, naively it seemed.

When he thought of it he realised his recent actions sounded like a ridiculous romance story; the brave and heroic swordsman finally reunited with his great love. The main difference was that Soren didn't feel brave, and he certainly wasn't heroic. Of the two factions in Ostia, he was disgraced with one and it now seemed the target for assassination by the other; the one that was currently, and for the foreseeable future, in power. It could only have been Amero who sent those men to kill him.

Auracia wasn't a large city. Smaller than Ostenheim, so he had thought it would be easy to find her. His expectations proved sorely misplaced. He was rapidly running out of places to search, but what looked to be his best and possibly last hope of finding her would come the next day. Despite the fatigue, the nausea and the headache left behind by the Gift — as much a sign of his neglect of it as of its recent use — the thought made him feel better than he had in some time.

The Harbour Master of Auracia, who professed himself too busy to answer Soren's questions whenever he had called unannounced, had finally agreed to meet him. The other workers around the harbour had been of little help, but he hoped that the Harbour Master would be different. They were always hazy on the coming and goings of ships more than a week or two previously. The titbits of information they offered up rarely agreed and were often contradictory. The only thing of use they had been able to tell him was that the Harbour Master kept extensive records and knew each and every ship that was a regular visitor to the harbour as though they were old friends.

Soren stood next to the counter in the Harbour Master's office, doing his best to contain his impatience.

'From Ostenheim, y'say?' the Harbour Master said. He was lounging in a captain's chair behind the counter, and it did not look as though he got out of it very often.

Soren nodded. 'Ostenheim.'

'Sailed five weeks ago, y'say?'

'Five weeks.' The conversation was grindingly slow, but he needed this man's help and had to remain polite.

'Your wife?'

Soren nodded again.

'Sure she wants to be found?'

Soren smiled, but it was difficult to conceal just how desperate he was for this information.

The man scratched his chin and thought for a moment. 'A ship that takes female passengers travelling alone between Ostenheim and Auracia. Not every ship will take passengers, fewer still lady folk. Won't have the facilities to see to a lady's... needs. Some captains won't even have women on board at sea. Sailors' superstitions. They bring bad luck. So that narrows things down a bit. You're sure you can't remember the name of the ship?'

'No. I had to get her out of the city fast. The way things are in Ostenheim now...'

'Aye, more and more people coming through here every day from Ostenheim, Ruripathia an' all parts between. I just hope that bastard Duke doesn't set his sights on the south. They say he might when he's done with the northerners.'

'The ship?' Soren said, hoping to keep the Harbour Master on track. He had been waiting too long to allow the conversation to go off in another direction.

'Yes, right, the ship. Sailed from Ostenheim 'bout five weeks ago, so shoulda been here 'bout a week, ten days after that.' He took a black ledger book from a shelf behind the counter and began flipping through the pages.

'Four weeks ago,' he muttered. 'Right, here we are. Three pages for that week.' He ran his finger down each page. 'A few of 'em were out of Ostenheim.' He started listing off names and dismissing them. Then he frowned.

'What is it?' Soren said.

'There was bad weather that week. I've three local ships listed as overdue here. I can tell you off the top of my head that none of 'em have arrived since. By now it's safe to say they're lost.'

'And they're the only ones likely to have been carrying a passenger?' Soren felt a wave of nausea pass over him. After all that had happened, to think that she might be lost at sea seemed like a cruel joke, and was too difficult to believe.

The Harbour Master nodded. 'Reckon the *Wind Sprite* was the ship we're lookin' for. She's the only one doin' a regular passenger run up and down the coast that's likely to take a lady on board. Twelve sailors on her, not counting any passengers.' He grimaced.

'What if she wasn't on a local ship, if she came south on an Ostian one? How would I find out about that?' Soren said, trying to grasp onto any hope. He had convinced himself that he would find what he was looking for here. It had never occurred to him that he would discover something like this.

The Harbour Master shook his head. 'Haven't had an Ostian ship stop here since the war started. Not for six weeks. All the warships are fightin', and the merchants have gone north with supplies and to bring home the plunder. If she came south it was on an Auracian ship. If it was an Auracian ship, it was the Wind Sprite.'

'There's no way she was on one of the others?'

The Harbour Master shook his head again. His demeanour had changed from curiosity to sympathetic condolence, and Soren felt as though the room was spinning around him.

'They have to declare passengers in their custom duty check. I make note of it in the ledger.' He tapped his finger on the page. 'No female passengers that week at all. There've been a number of them the last two weeks, but they all came here on ships that were still here when your wife would've left Ostenheim. I'm sorry, lad, but ships are lost. It's the way of the sea.'

His words faded into the distance. All Soren could hear was her voice.

Soren went back to the inn, ordered a mug of ale and retreated to the darkest corner of the taproom. His mind raced with conflicting thoughts, and despair threatened to swallow him up whole.

Alessandra had fled their home city of Ostenheim shortly before he had at his suggestion, as guiltless as he in the assassination of the old Duke, but just as heavily implicated. She had been headed for Auracia. He had not expected to get away or be able to keep his promise that he would find her. She knew that it was unlikely he would survive when they parted, but thinking she would be safe was enough for him.

Despair was mixed with anger when he allowed himself to dwell on the reality that she was dead; lost to the sea. The fear she must have felt, the loneliness. He had to fight back sobs of anguish. The same person who sent men to kill him the previous evening was responsible for her having to flee, for tearing them apart and manipulating their lives as though they were little more than tools or playthings. Grief turned to fury as he thought of everything that had gone wrong in his life, of the terrible things that had happened to Alessandra and how they could all be traced back to Amero and his lies, intrigues and manipulation.

Now the bastard was sitting on the throne of Ostia, comfortable in the palace while he sent thousands of men to war and had hundreds more that opposed him murdered, or as it was being called, 'executed for treason'. That Amero sat there at all was in part down to Soren. Even when he had thought he was making his own choices, Soren had only been playing along with Amero's master plan, contributing to its forward momentum in his own small — and sometimes not so small — way. Amero was sitting there, smug in the belief that he had destroyed his enemies and could relax as he reached out to tie up any loose ends with no thought to the consequences for the people involved.

Alessandra was the cause of the only true happiness Soren had ever known. Amero had taken that from him, had taken so much from so many. In that moment, Soren decided he was going to kill him for it.

Soren's thoughts may have been directed by anger, but that anger was not blind. Walking into the Ducal Palace in Ostenheim fuelled with rage would achieve nothing. He had rushed into things in the past and paid the consequences. If killing Amero meant dying himself so be it, but he would not squander his life without achieving his purpose.

His Gift had given him an advantage many times, but he didn't understand how it worked, or why he had it. He had developed a rudimentary method to bring it on, but as the episode in the alley had shown, his method was not good enough. It was overly involved and unreliable. Even when he did manage to bring on the Gift, he had no way to control it. Each time he reached out for it felt like he was leaping into the unknown. As powerful as it promised to be, right now it was all but useless as a tool to help him kill Amero.

If he was to be successful, he needed to know more about it. As sleep finally came to him, he made his second decision of the evening. He would seek out more knowledge on the Gift. He would seek to understand it and he would seek to control it. Then he would use it to kill Amero.

Chapter 3
A Futile Search

SOREN CERTAINLY WASN'T CHEERFUL the next morning, but he had a sense of purpose. Focus and clarity directed his movements, but he felt nothing else. He would visit the library at Auracia's Academy. He was due some luck and he hoped he would find it there in the form of information on the Gift, or at the very least a clue of where to look next.

The academies had once been the home away from home to the Society of Mages, one in each of the former provincial capitals of the Empire. It was not as simple as walking in and picking the relevant book off a shelf, however. After the mages were defeated in the wars that fragmented the Empire, the victorious swordsmen, the bannerets, took over their former homes and converted them into schools of swordsmanship: the academies. They also destroyed every trace of magery they could find.

All objects, documents and traces of their existence had been hunted down in an effort to prevent the influence of magic from ever rising again. This included the contents of the libraries in Ostenheim and Auracia, along with every other academy around the Middle Sea.

Going there was a slim hope, but Soren did not need much; enough to keep his search moving forward was all he wanted. Perhaps an innocuous volume on a different subject, overlooked by the bannerets, would give him what he sought.

There was a hypocritical qualification to the purge that always irritated Soren when he tried to learn about the Gift, as not everything had been eradicated. If it made life a little more convenient in many cases it remained untouched, so long as it could not serve a role in the creating of magics. The mage lamps found in most cities were a prime example of this, but there were other, less visible things.

In his darker moments, Soren thought that it was unlikely he would find much that would be of help to him. He had to try though.

He had briefly tried to search out information in the Academy at Ostenheim when he was a student there, but it had turned up nothing. The irony was that in destroying the mages' libraries, the bannerets had wiped out all information concerning themselves, the one-time servants and bodyguards of the mages. The result was that now the stories about them were little more than legends, with perhaps the faintest seed of truth at their centre.

White stone was the building material of choice amongst the mages. Like his own Academy in Ostenheim, the Academy in Auracia stood out in the city as one of the few buildings not constructed from bricks of brown or dark red and capped with rust coloured tiles. The Academy was built with finely cut stone, off-white in colour, and its buildings stood taller than those around it.

The streets of Auracia tended to be tight and twisting, lined with tall buildings on either side. This changed as he drew near the Academy, where the streets widened into spacious boulevards culminating in a small square outside the front of the Academy itself.

Soren was admitted to the complex with little scrutiny; bannerets tended to carry themselves in a certain way that was easily recognised to an experienced eye — not to mention he was carrying a rapier, something that was illegal for anyone other than a banneret inside the city walls. Once inside he was given directions by a student, and quickly found the library.

It looked very much like the library in Ostenheim; all of the buildings he had seen in the Academy so far were similar to their Ostian counterparts. It was a long hall with an apex roof high above the wooden floor. There was a dusty scent in the air that was strangely calming. Shelves jutted out from the wall at regular intervals, creating little alcoves that were home to desks and chairs. A mezzanine ran around the room above the shelves, which gave access to another row of shelving that lined the wall above, their continuity interrupted only by the large windows that allowed daylight into the room.

Without any clear idea of where to begin, he started by wandering slowly along the shelves, scanning the titles on the spines of the books as he went. The vast majority related directly to the day-to-day curriculum of the Academy; illustrated guides of fencing positions, treatises on physical training, tactics and suchlike. He would have headed straight for the history section, were it not for the fact that it would surely have been one of the first stops for the men who had purged the library. If he was to find anything of use, it was going to be tucked away in a less obvious tome. He'd need to make a thorough and careful examination of far more books than he would have liked.

※

After several hours of searching, the skin on his face and hands was grimy with the dust that gathered around large numbers of books. His back ached from stooping down to reach lower shelves, and his hands bore the stinging marks of half a dozen paper cuts. All he had to show for his efforts were two books that were so old all the writing on the spine had worn away. He thought that age and anonymity might have allowed them to escape the purges.

With almost one quarter of the library surveyed and dismissed, it was time to take a look at what he had. He retired to one of the desks to leaf through his two selections. He opened the first, causing a small plume of dust to twist up into the air, and flipped over the first few pages, which were blank. He turned a dozen or so before he went straight to the middle of the book. All blank. It seemed the years had been as unkind to the ink on the inside as they had been to the writing on the spine. Perhaps there was some magic concealing the text, but that seemed a little too fantastical for even his imagination.

Nonetheless, he was tempted to concentrate on the blue glow to see if it had an effect, but after the previous night, he had no desire to put himself through the post-Gift recovery again so soon. It mattered little. If there was anything concealed there, it would most likely have taken something more complex than his tenuous connection to a magical world to reveal its secrets. It was just as likely an old book faded by the passage of time as a magically protected text. His imagination did seem to get ahead of him from time to time, and he was confident that this was one of those occasions.

He pushed the blank volume to the side and opened the second. Happily it had retained its contents in a legible state. Sadly they were entirely on the subject of victualing a force of men in various climates. He sighed and pushed the volume aside. Was he wasting his time? His high spirits had ebbed and his hands were so covered in greasy dust that he could think of nothing more than a frustrated desire to wash them.

There was so little to go on it was hard to know where to

begin. The large gaps on the shelves betrayed just how many books had been destroyed in the purges; even centuries later the library had not accumulated enough new works to fill them. The library might have been so ruthlessly censored that there was no mention of those times when magic had still been practised, and when all bannerets had allegedly enjoyed the Gift of which Soren now seemed to be the sole beneficiary. The worrying thought was that he knew every library around the Middle Sea would be the same; it stood to reason.

Searching the universities would most likely be a waste of time as they all post-dated the break up of the Empire. The libraries of the academies were the oldest repositories of information available. A search of the other libraries would take a great deal of travelling and time, and he knew it would be equally futile.

He wondered where to turn next. The options available filled him with feelings of such futility that he couldn't view them as reasonable. He got up and went to the geography section. He had no real idea of the distances involved between all of the cities that were once provincial capitals of the Empire, and wanted to satisfy his curiosity on that before giving up for the day.

He pulled a large atlas from the shelf and opened it. The spine creaked in protest; the book had clearly not been read in a long time. Each page revealed a beautiful map of a region or a city of the Empire. In the middle of the book, covering both of the facing pages, there was a map of its entire territory.

Spread across the centre was the Middle Sea, vast but surrounded by the coastline of the mainland that hemmed it in on all sides. The only break was in the far south, where, amongst a littering of small islands that stretched between the coastlines, the Middle Sea met the Southern Ocean.

Soren traced his finger along the eastern coastline from north to south, looking for places he could identify to gain a sense of scale. Ruripathia, which he had visited what seemed like a lifetime before, sat in the north east. Ostia was to its south — where he had lived before fleeing — and then farther down the coast, Auracia, where he was now. It all seemed so vast to Soren, who had spent most of his life unaware of everything beyond the walls of the city in which he was born.

Auracia was once the largest province of the Empire, but now it was a loosely affiliated collection of petty principalities often at war with one another. Its southern edge marked the limit of the Empire with the deserts and rivers of Shandahar beyond. On the left hand page on the other side of the Middle Sea there were the other former imperial states running down the western coast: Venter, Humberland, Mirabaya and Estranza, but those places were little more than names to Soren.

There was so much of the world out there of which he was almost completely ignorant. It was daunting. His eye was drawn to the two large islands in the centre of the Middle Sea. He had ignored them up until now. While all of the other states were illuminated with brightly coloured inks, and marked with tiny, immaculately neat labels indicating the names of towns, rivers and mountains, the islands had been given no attention; merely shaded with grey lines and devoid of any labels bar one: 'The Shrouded Isles'.

It told Soren that the atlas had been made after the fall of the Empire, since prior to that the Isles had been home to its capital. Soren knew of the Isles; everyone did. They formed part of the various legends that were told of the Empire and the days that followed its fall, and were often used as the home for all sorts of monsters in stories told to frighten children.

The city of Vellin-Ilora had sat on either side of the Straits of Saludor, the channel of water that divided the two islands and had been used as a shortcut for ships crossing the Middle Sea. The city became enormously wealthy as a result and eventually gave birth to the Empire. Terrible things were said to have happened there during the Mage Wars, and anyone who had been able to flee the city did so. It had been avoided ever since, with ships' captains preferring to take the longer route around the islands rather than venture into the straits and anywhere near the cursed city.

Nobody ever went back after the wars, so the stories said. If nobody had ever gone back, perhaps nobody had destroyed what was in the city or, more importantly, its library. He stared at the greyed out blobs, lurking ominously at the centre of the map. After so much time it seemed a slim hope, but could it be that the answers he sought were still there?

Chapter 4
THE HONEST CHRISTOPHE

SOREN ADOPTED A CHATTIER demeanour that evening back at the inn. A handful of sailors drank there most evenings and they came from all over. He couldn't think of any group of people better qualified to update his old wives' tales and legends about the Shrouded Isles.

He walked up to a group of three sailors standing at the bar.

'Just arrived?' he said.

'Aye,' said one of the sailors, turning from his friends to look at Soren.

'Where are you out of?'

'Brisham.'

Soren nodded. It was the capital of Humberland, on the other side of the Middle Sea. 'Long way.'

The sailor shrugged.

'Fair voyage?' Soren said.

'Aye, we've had plenty worse,' one of the other sailors said.

'Must be annoying having to go all the way around the Isles to get home again,' Soren said.

'No option,' the first sailor said, shrugging again.

'Ever think about trying to go through the straits?'

The sailor turned back to his friends and they all burst into laughter.

'Not a chance,' the first sailor said, turning back to Soren. 'Even a landsman like you must have heard the stories?'

'Heard 'em. Always wondered if there was any truth to 'em,' Soren said, hoping to wring some more information from them.

'Plenty of truth. Too many stories for them not to be true; ships wrecked, sailors drowned. They're the lucky ones. The ones that end up on the island have it worse. No one's ever made it off them alive. Things that happen there? Horrible things.' The sailor shook his head in knowing dismay, a gesture mirrored by his two friends.

'If no one's ever made it off them alive, how do you know what happened?' Soren said, jumping on the obvious hole in their story.

The sailor opened his mouth to reply but closed it again. He hesitated before responding. 'If you think they're just stories, why don't you go there yourself to find out.'

The other sailors started to laugh as though the idea was the most ridiculous thing in the world, and Soren was the most naive fool.

'Well, enjoy your time ashore, lads,' Soren said, before turning to head for his room.

'Yeah, you too. Good luck finding a ship to take you to the Isles,' the sailor said.

The others chuckled with renewed enthusiasm.

First thing the next morning, Soren went to the harbour. Someone had tried to kill him in the city once already, and he had no desire to dally there for whomever it was to try again. The port area of Auracia was smaller than the massive harbour at Ostenheim, but it was still busy. Soren intended to find a ship that would take him close enough to the coast of the Shrouded Isles to row ashore.

He cast a glance at the Harbour Master's office as he went and felt his stomach tighten into a knot. He tried to push the memory from his mind, but it was enough to leave him feeling unsettled.

He spotted a ship flying a Ventish ensign and approached.

'Ho there,' Soren called out. 'Is the captain available?'

A wiry looking sailor with a deep tan looked him up and down and with a jerk of his head indicated toward the stern of the ship. Soren thanked him and made his way up the gangplank. He didn't like ships, or the sea. He never had, but now it made him think of Alessandra. The thought of a voyage of any length made his stomach twist in protest. It couldn't be avoided though. It was a means to an end.

'Might you be the captain?' he asked a man sitting at a small portable desk poring over a ledger.

'I am,' the captain said. 'Captain Gheert. Who's asking?'

'I'm Banneret of the Duke's Cross Soren,' he said. The captain's demeanour improved slightly. He was dealing with a man of some status and possibly wealth, rather than another out of work landsman seeking work.

'What might I do for you, Banneret?' His tone was less gruff, but was still far from anything that could be called congenial.

'I'm seeking passage on a ship. I was hoping you take passengers,' Soren said.

'I'm amenable to the idea. It's not our usual practice, so the accommodation won't be anything special, but it should suffice if you're willing to forego the luxuries of city living a few weeks. Is it just yourself that will be travelling?'

'It is,' Soren said.

'And it's to Venter you're wanting to go? We set sail for Voorn in the morning.'

'Actually, no. I was hoping you could have me rowed ashore on the way. I want to land on the Shrouded Isles.'

'Get the fuck off my ship before I have my lads throw you off.'

Soren wasn't looking for trouble. He did as he was ordered. It was a discouraging reaction. He didn't have the coin to make a large enough offer of payment to tempt a captain, so if they were all of a similar mind, his plan could be over before it started.

He got much the same reaction from the second captain he tried, and another after that. He was about to wait for some fresh ships to arrive on the next tide when he walked past a ship that he had discounted earlier, the *Honest Christophe*.

She was far smaller than the others, and they were not particularly impressive when compared to the enormous oceanmen that sailed from Ostenheim. He had discounted her purely on the basis of her appearance; she was ungainly and not as orderly looking as the other ships. He was unhappy enough with having to take a sea voyage and he certainly had no inclination to take one on a less than well-appointed ship. However, now he was becoming desperate and it was worth talking to the captain to keep his options open.

'Ho there,' he called. His voice had considerably less enthusiasm in it than it had a few hours earlier. 'Might I speak with the captain?'

A man appeared at the bulwark and looked down at Soren standing on the dock. 'You're speaking with him. What do you want?'

Soren squinted to make out what he looked like, but the captain was silhouetted against the sun and he could not.

'I was wondering if you take passengers?'

'That depends,' the captain called back. 'On who the passenger is, and if they can pay.'

'The passenger is me,' Soren said, 'and I can pay.'

'Come aboard then, and we'll talk.'

Soren tottered up yet another gangplank and onto the ship. As befitted its size, it was quite cramped and the disorderly appearance from the dock was carried over onto the deck. It did not make for a promising start. The captain walked forward and offered his hand.

'Captain Christophe, I presume?' Soren said.

'Nah.' The captain laughed. 'That name was on her when I bought her. Bad luck to change it. Don't think the fella I bought her from was Christophe either. I'm Captain Joris. Pleased to meet you.'

He offered his hand, thick, coarse and covered with smears of tar. Soren took it and shook it firmly.

'Banneret of the Duke's Cross Soren. Pleased to meet you,' he said. He looked around him and noted the absence of any crewmembers.

The captain spotted his curiosity. 'I let the lads into town for the night. They'll be back in the morning, like as not. We didn't have the easiest trip over; that's why the deck's in a bit of a state. This tub doesn't take too many hands to run though, so they know I'll leave without 'em if they're not back in time. So, you want passage to Venter then?'

'Not exactly,' Soren said. 'And that's where the problem may lie. I want to disembark on the way. I want you to drop me off on the Shrouded Isles.'

The captain barked out a laugh. 'Did that old prick Gheert put you up to this?' He continued to chuckle, but when Soren did not react he cut his mirth short.

'Come on now, someone put you up to this. You're making fun of me, aren't you?'

'I'm not,' Soren said.

'You're mad then.'

It was going better than Soren had expected; the other captains had told him where to go by that point. 'I'm not.'

'You do know the Isles are cursed? Anyone who goes there

is never seen again. Any ship that strays too close? Never seen again. Even the birds won't fly over them.'

'Do you actually know anyone who went missing there?'

'Yes.'

Soren raised an eyebrow.

Joris frowned. 'No, but there are too many stories. People I have spoken to know people who went missing.'

'I'm not so sure that I believe anything I don't know first hand. Do you?'

'I believe the stories well enough to stay away. Well away. Only once have I strayed close enough to even lay eyes on them.' He leaned forward as he continued. 'You know why they're called the Shrouded Isles? There's a thick grey bank of cloud that sits above them, hanging there like a shroud. A mourning shroud for all the poor souls that met their end there.'

Soren was determined, and wasn't going to be put off by Joris's tales of doom. 'If you were able to make passage through the straits, it would take days, or even weeks off your journey. Let me off just close enough to row ashore. You don't need to go any closer. I'm taking all the risk. If I make it back to the ship, then you'll be the only captain who knows the straits are safe to navigate. If not, you've only gone a day or two out of your way.'

'You're best advised to drop this idea. If you're really serious about it,' Joris said.

'You haven't told me to fuck off yet. All the other captains had well before now,' Soren said, his hopes rising. 'Perhaps you don't believe all the stories quite as strongly as you say.'

Joris sighed and frowned again. 'You're right on one thing. Making passage through the straits would cut weeks off my voyage. Take a look around.' He gestured about the haphazard state of the ship. 'Business is hard and the time that shortcut would save me would be a gift from the gods. But nobody goes near those isles; it can't be without good reason.'

'Take me close enough to row your small boat there to the island. Continue on your way, and stop off for me again when you're on your way back. If I return safely, you'll know that there's no danger, that all the stories are baseless superstition, and that you can use the straits between the Isles. Keep it to yourself and you'll have a big advantage over every other merchant crossing the Middle Sea. If I don't make it back, it's no loss to you, but you'll know that the stories are true once and for all. All the risk is mine.'

Soren could see the captain was interested, but kept his excitement to himself.

Joris sighed deeply and stroked the greying stubble on his chin. 'Your point's well made. But I just don't know. We sail on the morning tide, come back then. I'll have made up my mind by morning, one way or the other. Be ready to depart if I decide to take you.'

Soren headed back to the inn to pack his things. He knew Joris was on the hook, even if the captain had not quite admitted it to himself. There were so many stories about the Isles that it was difficult to dismiss them completely, but Soren didn't care. The potential reward was too great for him to be held back by rumours and old wives' tales. If the information he needed to master the Gift was there, any risk was worth taking. It was the key to killing Amero.

Chapter 5
THE VOYAGE

There was little that needed doing to prepare Soren for departure from Auracia. He'd arrived there with nothing more than his sword and dagger, a purse of coins and the clothes on his back. In the time since, he'd added little to this; no more than the additional clothing he needed so as not to appear completely down and out.

He arrived at the docks shortly after dawn. The tide was not due to turn for another couple of hours, but he didn't want Joris to have an excuse not to take him.

He was pleased to see there was more activity on the ship than there had been the previous day. It was not quite the hive of activity that the larger merchantmen were, but she showed signs of being ready to go to sea. The deck looked ordered and neat and men moved about with a sense of purpose.

'Captain Joris,' Soren shouted.

A moment later Joris appeared at the bulwark. 'I was hoping you wouldn't show.'

Soren shrugged.

'You're insane. You realise that?'

'It's been said before.' He knew he had his berth and smiled.

'If I think my crew or ship are in danger at any time, I'll turn around.'

'All right. I understand,' Soren said.

'If I think you are a danger to my crew at any time, I'll throw you overboard.'

'That's fair,' Soren said.

'You'd best come aboard and get your kit stowed away then,' Joris said.

There was not much enthusiasm in his voice, but he had agreed and that was enough for Soren.

Ferrata felt his anger threaten to flare as he watched the sails drop and the ship accelerate away from the harbour. A few deep breaths were all he needed to quell the rage, but his displeasure would be harder to shift.

'You.'

The rough looking dockworker Ferrata directed his call at stopped. He did not appear to take kindly to being spoken to so harshly. One look at Ferrata clearly convinced him that his irritation would be better taken out on someone else.

'That ship.' Ferrata pointed out at the ship Soren had boarded. 'Where's it headed?'

The dockworker looked out to where Ferrata was pointing. '*Honest Christophe*? Sails between here and Venter,' he said, before continuing on his way.

Ferrata looked back at the ship and swore.

As Captain Joris had promised, there was not much in the way of luxury to be found on board the *Honest Christophe*. Soren's berth was a hammock on the lower deck, slung from the wooden beams above. The air had a putrid tang of bilge water and the stench of the rotting remains of whatever loose bits of cargo had ended up in the bilge. The smell, coupled with the rolling of the ship meant that Soren could only spend a couple of moments below before he became nauseated. It wasn't so bad when he remained up on deck, but there was little or no chance to get any sleep there.

He had taken a sea voyage several years before and the memory of it still made the bile rise in his throat. This time around he seemed to be coping better, but the sea was far more placid than it was in the north. A gentle and regular swell rolled across from the west, giving the ship a slow pitching gait as she ploughed her way toward Venter. He hoped the conditions would remain similar for the rest of the voyage.

The ship looked very different under sail than she had tied up at the dock. It reminded Soren of the difference in a tree between winter and summer. The once bare, skeletal masts, sprits and yards were now alive with billowing cream coloured canvas. While she could never be called a thing of beauty, the *Honest Christophe* was no longer an inanimate hulk tied to a quayside; she felt lively and spirited under a full press of sail.

They had been at sea for a few days before Soren began to relax into life on a constantly moving surface. He found that his feet began to meet with the deck when he expected them to. To alleviate boredom, he had even taken to pitching in with one of the watches, and although he would not contemplate going up into the rigging, he liked to think that he was useful to have around.

He stood for a while at the bulwark each evening after supper, looking out to sea in the direction that the Isles lay. Usually he was left in peace, as the few men of his watch went below to rest and those on watch went about their duties. It was not the case on that night however, as Captain Joris made his way over with two mugs of steaming tea.

'Staring won't make them appear any sooner!' he said, as he handed Soren one of the mugs.

Soren nodded in appreciation as he took it. 'I know.'

'You'll see the bank of cloud long before the Isles anyway. Still determined to go ashore?'

Soren nodded, but he felt his certainty was less now; it seemed to ebb ever more the closer they got.

'I want to convince you to stay on board. I'm only going to do it the once. You're a decent young man. You've pitched in when others wouldn't have and all the lads like you. If you were to stay aboard you'd be a rated seaman by the time we reach Voorn and you'd have no trouble at all finding work if you wanted to move ship. I'll even offer to keep you on myself if you want it.'

'It's kind of you,' Soren said, 'but I have to go ashore. I'm not going to explain why, but I'm going.'

'I thought you might say that,' Joris said, 'but I had to try. I expect we'll be seeing the cloud by tomorrow.'

'Land ho!'

The call came from one of the top-men, perched at the junction of the yard with the mast far enough off the deck to make Soren feel dizzy every time he looked up.

As Joris promised, they had been able to see the cloudbank since the previous day, a thick grey blanket sitting above the sea, out of place in the otherwise clear sky. The mood on board had changed as soon as it was spotted. The men's spirits sank and they all started to treat Soren a little differently, as though he were a condemned man.

The winds had been fair up until that point, blowing across the side of the ship and allowing them to continue in a straight line, but the next leg of the voyage would not be as easy and part of Soren was glad that he would not be on board to endure it. After doubling back to clear the Shrouded Isles, the crew of the *Honest Christophe* would have to beat against the wind as they made their way north to reach Venter. This meant zig-zagging back and forth, with every ten miles sailed only getting them four or five miles closer to home. It seemed like a very frustrating way to travel and the value of being able to pass safely through the straits was obvious.

The Isles were much as Captain Joris had described them. Where the ship sat, out in the open sea, it was a fine, clear day, the late winter sun strong, but not hot. The dark grey blanket of cloud hovering low in the sky over the Isles was ominous and ugly.

Joris joined him at the bulwark and surveyed the Isles. 'I wasn't much more than a child when I saw this place. Hoped I never would again. Gives me a chill just looking at them. They're just as I remember. Grey, empty, dead. Seems nothin' has changed.'

'It's bleak,' Soren said, feeling a little reluctance to continue.

'You're still sure you want to go ashore?' Joris said.

Soren nodded. 'You'd best prepare the boat. I'm sure you want to get underway again as quickly as you can. I can tell the men don't like being this close.'

'They don't and neither do I. Superstition or not, there's something not right about that place,' Joris said. 'It'll take us about twenty-five or twenty-six days to get home, if the winds remain fair. We'll need two days there to unload and take on a new cargo, and to give the lads some time to relax. The trip back'll be faster, two weeks maybe. When we get back, I'll hold station off the point where you go ashore. I'll wait from dawn to dusk for three days before I continue on to Auracia. Start watching for us forty days from today. If we get back sooner, I'll only start counting the days from then. It's up to you to be back on that beach looking out for us. If you don't signal during those three days, I'll consider you lost to the curse of the Isles. I won't be sending anyone ashore to look for you. If we're late by more than ten days, you may consider us lost to the curse of the seas.'

He laughed, but Soren could hear the tension in his voice. He felt the same.

'There won't be any other ships coming this way. I've given you my word that I'll be back for you, which means I'll be back if it's in my power to do so, but if the worst happens you'll be stranded here.'

Soren felt a twist in his guts, but he trusted Joris. Soren would just have to hope they'd have fair seas and winds until they met again. There was no turning back now. There might not be any answers there, but if there were any to be found at all, this was his best chance.

The boat was prepared quickly and the crew loaded it with dried meat and biscuits, along with several skins of wine and water. If strictly rationed, it would last the forty days and more. Soren didn't find the prospect of eating dried rations for that long attractive, but it didn't look like there would be much opportunity to forage for fresh food on the islands.

With no reason for further delay, he shook Captain Joris's hand and made his way down the rickety boarding ladder and into the boat. It pitched unexpectedly as he set foot in it. He caught his breath, balanced and sat down carefully. Eventually it steadied and he was ready to go. As he pushed off he saw the crew lined up at the bulwark watching him. They all shared the same expression: that of watching a man going to his certain death.

Chapter 6
THE SHROUDED ISLES

As Soren pulled on the oars, he was reminded of a day when he and Alessandra had rowed to a small island not far from the shore in Ostenheim bay for a picnic. How different the world had seemed then; so full of hope and opportunity. Now all of his dreams had been cast to the wind.

The day grew ever duller as he went, as his small clinker built rowboat passed fully beneath the blanket of cloud that sat unnaturally still over the Isles. When he grew closer to the shore, the small breaking waves drove him in with no further effort needed from him, other than to keep the boat pointing in the right direction.

There was a scraping sensation as the bottom of the boat came into contact with the sandy bottom, before finally it ground to a halt. He hopped out, hoping to make it to land completely dry, but one of his boots let in a flood of cold water. He cursed quietly as he dragged the boat completely clear of the water and pulled it up the beach until it was above the high tide line.

He sat down on the sand for a few moments to catch his breath. It was grey, unlike the light golden grains found in Ostia or Auracia. He took a handful of the damp sand and let it crumble from his palm as he tried to decide what his next step would be. He was still far from the straits and had a long walk ahead of him. It was late in the day, so he decided it would be best to make camp there for the night and set off in search of Vellin-Ilora the following morning.

He unpacked the boat and made a quick mental inventory. There was plenty to get him by which he was thankful for, as a cursory glance around suggested foraging would not just be poor, it would be non-existent. Rather than lush forest or grasslands beyond the beach, there seemed to be little more than sparse scrubland; small, stunted vegetation clinging on to life. He had survived a long time without food on a previous occasion, but had no desire to repeat the experience.

He tipped the boat on its side and propped it up with an oar to provide some shelter before heading up the beach to gather firewood. He knew lighting a fire there was probably not the best of ideas, but he was simply too damp and cold to care. Wild animals were more likely to be frightened off by it, and he was happy to take his chances against any people it might draw. As for anything else, he would just have to take what might come.

◆—◆

He slept fitfully and woke early. The chill in the air had penetrated all the way to his bones, and he had a headache that was strong enough to be an irritation. He ate a little and packed food and water to last him for three or four days before burying the rest beneath the boat in an oilskin — hopefully deep enough to protect it from anything that might be alive and hungry. He set off in search of the capital of the Old Empire.

The *Honest Christophe* had dropped him on the eastern shore of the southern island, as close to the straits as Joris was willing to go. The city of Vellin-Ilora sat on both sides of the strait, but the Emperor's palace was said to have been in the part of the city on the southern isle, Vellin. Soren thought the mages would most likely have built their college there.

He walked all day, and by the end he had sore feet but no indication that he was getting closer to what had once been the greatest city in the world. There was something about the island that was unsettling, but for most of the day he could not put his finger on it. It was only when he stopped for the night and lit a fire that he realised there was an absence of sound. Other than the breeze, the gentle lapping of waves against the beach and the crackle of his fire, there was no noise. No animals, no birds, no insects; none of the sounds that he'd expect anywhere else. It was strange, and incredibly unsettling.

He spent the night on the edge of the beach, huddled next to a small, smoky fire in a vain effort to keep out the damp and cold. Perhaps this was an adventure that would have been better left to the height of the summer, although with all the cloud above he wondered if the Isles were ever warm and dry.

The discomfort of sleeping in the open on a desolate beach resulted in another poor night's rest. He gave up as soon as the first hint of dawn appeared on the horizon. Once again he began his walk, hoping that it would not be much farther.

His hopes were realised in the late afternoon — or what he thought was late afternoon; without the sun to give some indication it was difficult to tell. As he made his way around the base of a rocky bluff, Vellin-Ilora came into view.

Soren had expected to find ruins, with perhaps a few of the better constructed buildings extant enough to protect what was contained within. What he saw far exceeded his expectations. Laid out in front of him was what looked like a completely intact city. Vellin-Ilora, and the hinterland of the Isles had been abandoned during the Mage Wars, hundreds of years earlier. Although he could not see any movement from that distance, the city looked pristine; as though it was still being maintained.

High walls surrounded Vellin-Ilora, interspersed with square, octagonal or round towers, obscuring most of what was on the other side. Here and there, tall, slender towers reached up from behind the walls, breaking the skyline. The wall extended out into the sea on the right, presumably creating a harbour on the other side. Toward the seaward end of the wall, two of the large towers were closer together than the others. They looked like a gate to Soren, so he headed in their direction

As Soren got closer to the walls, his initial impression of them proved correct. The crenellations were crisply outlined against the sky. It felt surreal being so close to such an ancient city, the place where so much of the world as he knew it had originated. It was even stranger to find it in such good condition. The picture he had of it in his mind was not of an intact city. Piles of rubble and some occasionally intact walls, but little more. Certainly not this.

His main thought as he approached the walls was that a city in such good condition could not be uninhabited. Everything he had read over the years relating to the city said that it had been abandoned because it was cursed. Could things have changed since then?

It had become noticeably darker in the time it took him to reach the walls. Night was not far away, and Soren had no desire to take his first steps in a city that was quite possibly inhabited with gods only knew what, in darkness. He would camp beneath the wall and enter the city in daylight the following morning. He was incredibly tired and the headache that had nagged him since arriving on the island refused to go away, so he was glad of the break. Next to the wall, he was sheltered from the breeze, but this was a hollow benefit, as so close to the city, there was no way Soren was willing to risk lighting a fire.

Sheltered from the wind, away from the water, and without the comforting crackle of a fire, the island was completely silent. Soren huddled against the wall and did his best to sleep.

Chapter 7
A DEAD CITY

Soren woke the next morning, stiff and sore. His headache had eased, but it was still there. After stretching his stiff limbs, he made his way along the base of the wall to the gate he'd spotted the previous day. The stonework was intact, not looking at all as though it had stood there for over a millennium. The wooden gate had not fared quite so well; the thick planks had faded, dried and splintered over the years and in places Soren could see daylight between them. There was a smaller wicket door set into one of them, which Soren pushed. It was stiff and the hinges squealed, but it opened with a little effort, giving him his first glimpse of the capital of a long-dead empire.

He had seen a dead city once before, but it had been reduced to little more than gravel. That city, Rurip, had been rumoured to be haunted. Stories were told that no man who entered the city would return alive, much like the tales about the Shrouded Isles. Soren had encountered the ghosts of Rurip and they had turned out to be nothing more than bandits and looters, hoping to find something of value among the ruins. The stories of that city had proved to be just that, and he saw no reason for those of Vellin-Ilora to be any different.

Like the walls, the buildings of Vellin-Ilora looked to be perfectly preserved. They were cream and ivory in colour, with faded brown tiled roofs. The buildings were tall, and bore all the hallmarks of years of use, but also years of maintenance. There was nothing about them to indicate they had been abandoned centuries ago.

There was something chilling about looking down a city street in daylight to see it completely deserted. The absence of people was so unnatural that it put Soren on edge. He refused to give any credence to the stories, he had already rationalised them in his head, but it was difficult to completely dismiss the fears that they caused. He could not help but feel a degree of reluctance and trepidation as he stood on the threshold of the city. He had taken his sword and dagger from his pack and strapped them around his waist before setting out that morning, and as he stepped through the wicket gate he realised that his hands had found their way to the hilts without him thinking about it.

He looked around, constantly expecting to see movement. He felt as though there were people there in hiding, watching him, and it sent a tingle down his back. He could see nothing but empty buildings and deserted streets, though.

Soren had not been able to make any worthwhile plans before getting to the city. There was not enough solid information available; so much from when the city was still alive had been destroyed. The earliest books that he found had been written decades after the wars ended and the city was abandoned. These were based on second and third hand tales. Even to an uninformed reader it was clear that they were mixed with so much hyperbole that it was difficult to know what was useful and what was mere fancy.

Soren knew that the bannerets of old had been closely tied to the mages and had been created for the purpose of being their bodyguards. It stood to reason that they would have shared a headquarters, or at least be based close to one another. If he were to find anything useful, it would be there. He was certain the mages' headquarters would stand out, but in such a large city that didn't mean it would be any easier to find.

Finding the mages' headquarters was only a small part of his task; once discovered, his true search would begin. There was no way of knowing how long that would take. Suddenly, coming all this way seemed very foolish. He was there though, and standing still staring at empty buildings would not achieve anything.

He started off along the street with the sea to his right and the city ascending a hill to his left. As he walked, he tried to reason out a method for his search. If they had been one of the most powerful institutions in the Empire, the mages would have based their headquarters near to the administrative centre of the city, amongst the other buildings of power and influence. To Soren, that meant size and height. In Ostenheim, the castle and the palace both sat near the top of the hill overlooking the city. The homes of the wealthy spread out from their walls. He saw no reason for it to be any different here; the air was clear higher up and the views were better.

He couldn't see much of the city inland from where he was, as it was uphill and blocked out by the buildings that lined the road. He decided to make his way to the highest part of the city and look for a cluster of tall buildings. If luck favoured him, they would be on this side of the straits.

The road he was on led north in the direction of the straits, roughly following the line of the eastern shore. He stopped to take a look around when it reached a wide quayside.

Large iron rings sat where they had been left, the traces of where ropes had worn against them still visible. They looked as though they could still perform their original task if put to it, and showed only minor patches of rust. The water lapped against the large cut stones of the quayside and Soren wondered how long it had been since a ship had last berthed there. By appearances, it looked as though it might have only been the day before, but he knew that it had been far, far longer. It was all so eerie.

The city wall stretched out into the water and curved around like a protective arm, creating a large harbour. There was another wall extending out from farther along the shore, which stopped short of meeting its counterpart, leaving an opening large enough for a behemoth oceanman to pass through. Stone piers reached out into the water in various places, which once must have been busy with crews and harbour workers. It was strange to see them deserted; unsettling.

He looked directly inland. With the open space around the quayside he could see farther than previously. The southern part of the city, Vellin, was built on the slope of a hill that rose away from the water. The part on the far side of the strait to the north, Ilora, was still obscured by buildings.

He started off toward a street that seemed to lead uphill. The buildings that lined the street varied between plain and ornate and started to reach higher than three stories with greater frequency. The stone window frames were often carved with ridges and curves that made them pleasing to the eye, and they all seemed to still have their glass intact.

The cobbles of the street had been worn smooth by the passage of thousands of feet, but the years in which they had lain unused had not marred their surface with weeds or moss. Now that Soren thought of it, there was no vegetation growing anywhere in the city that he could see. He walked on, curious as to what might be found in each of the buildings he passed, but aware of the limitation on his time. At some point he would need to go back to his original campsite to get more food, so he forced himself to ignore the distractions all around.

As he walked up the hill, the buildings took on a less residential look and it seemed that the ground floors had been home to businesses. There was much about the city that reminded him of Ostenheim; the tight, winding streets, the tall buildings looming above. In Ostenheim the buildings were usually made of brick, but there were a number of more important ones that had been built with cut stones. Most notable among them was the Academy, and it had been built out of the same cream coloured stone as Vellin-Ilora, in a style similar to the buildings now before him. It gave the strangeness of the city an odd familiarity.

He reached a cross-section with a larger road, but continued with the street he was on as it was still taking him in the direction he wanted to go. He wondered what the city must have been like filled with thousands of people. Noise, colour and movement, rather than silence, pale cream stone and stillness; a living place rather than a petrified monument to a forgotten way of life. Had things been any different for them than they were for people living now? It was easy to forget that magic had been practised legally and extensively then. What difference must it have made to their lives?

As he walked, something caught his attention; something familiar. He was flabbergasted when he gave it a proper look. The building was not huge, nor did it display the trappings of power, wealth and sophistication he would have expected. In neatly chiselled lettering over the doorway, set in a carved cornice that jutted out from the building's face were the words 'Austorga's Banking House'.

He looked more closely at the inscription, but the word 'Austorga's' was definitely in the singular. The bank he knew was run by the Austorga dynasty, a close-knit family that kept the management of the organisation within its confines. This must have been where they started, a not particularly remarkable building on a not particularly remarkable street. It was a far cry from the palatial banking house that they had in Ostenheim, where the name above was simply 'Austorgas". Everyone knew what business was conducted there, so there was no need to advertise it any further.

Despite his earlier decision not to go into any of the buildings to explore, this was too great a temptation. He had never been wealthy; destitute in his youth, and entirely reliant on the beneficence of his sponsor at the Academy when his fortunes did change. Could there be any money left inside? There was only one way to find out.

He pushed on the door and it groaned gently under the pressure. It was gloomy inside. He stepped through a small foyer and into a larger room. As soon as he walked in, the previously dark room illuminated. The sudden change gave Soren a start and he found himself in a low crouch with his sword and dagger out in front of him scanning for an attacker.

The light came from several mage lamps suspended from the ceiling. He took a deep breath to calm himself and stood straight; they had been activated when he walked in. Mage lamps were common in Ostenheim, but those that responded to the presence of a person were rare and enormously expensive. He thought about pulling them from the ceiling and stashing them in his pack, but they were too bulky, nor were they what he had come in for.

There was a counter by the wall opposite, and a layer of fine dust that covered everything. As he moved about, his boots kicked up little swirls that revealed the polished floorboards hidden beneath. He felt a pang of guilt at his intentions, but surely abandoning property for several centuries would extinguish any other claims of ownership.

He went behind the counter. It looked as though that side had once housed a number of drawers, but they had all been removed and the same layer of dust that covered every other flat surface had also found its way into the drawer frames. He checked each one, blowing a cloud of dust into the air in the hope of revealing even a single coin, but it was not to be. Despite the disappointment, he was enjoying the experience of not knowing what he might find.

A door behind the counter led into another room. Soren opened that and peered in. It was dark, but once again a number of lights went on as soon as he stepped across the threshold of the door. A few paces back from the door, there was a steel cage that lined the rest of the room, the entrance to which was open. The cage contained a number of extremely sturdy and heavy looking safes, all open, all empty. The drawers that had been pulled from the counter in the other room were there too, carelessly piled in a heap and also empty. Soren shrugged. Nothing ventured nothing gained, he thought, but he would not become rich that day.

Chapter 8
THE SURPRISE

He walked out of the bank, still amused by the fact that he had been in a branch of Austorgas' Bank in a city that had not seen a living soul in a thousand years. The direct link to something he was so familiar with made him see the city in a different light, less a faceless monument and more a place that was connected to the world he lived in. It was only some instinct of self-preservation that allowed him to drop into a shoulder roll and avoid the sword that whistled through the air toward him when he stepped out of the doorway. The blade clashed against one of the faux pillars of the portico with a clang and crumble of stone, the only sound in the street.

Soren rolled twice more before springing back to his feet and turning. Full of silent menace, a drone hovered a few feet away from him, long blades gripped by each of its four appendages. He was momentarily surprised to see something so well known to him and unexpected.

In the Academy, he had spent more hours training against drones than he could count, but had never faced one armed with sharp blades before. With blunt blades they were menacing, their inanimate character capable of inspiring fear on a primal level. Knowing this one had sharp blades made it truly terrifying.

The drones were one of the creations of magic to escape the purges, as they did little more than they were bid by whoever was controlling them. It made them ideal training tools for student swordsmen. Soren wondered if someone was controlling this one.

There wasn't time to give that much consideration. The drone came toward Soren, rotating as it moved to reorient its weapons for attack. At the Academy the drones had been armed with whatever swords were being trained against, usually rapiers, but this one was carrying weapons created with far less artistry; they were little more than long metal bars with a sharpened edge. Despite their ugliness, they looked truly wicked and added to the intimidating presence of the tall, soulless leather cylinder.

It hovered above the ground and was a head's height taller than Soren, who was taller than average himself. It attacked with two blades simultaneously, hacking inward with both as though to slice Soren in two. Had he not seen the attack coming and jumped back, it would have succeeded. It repositioned its blades and started moving toward Soren again.

At the Academy, each drone had six patches, usually more worn and scuffed than the rest of the leather cadaver. These were the contact points that would deactivate it. This drone had no such patches. Their absence was of little consequence, as Soren had spent so much time striking at them he knew where they were. His only hope was that this drone had deactivation points like those he was used to. As soon as the drone was in range he lunged forward, firing the tip of his sword into a spot he thought to be a deactivation point.

He felt his sword pierce the leather and strike something solid on the interior, but the drone appeared unaffected. For the first time Soren felt a kernel of doubt in his gut. Could drones have been built purely for combat? He backed away, down the street in the direction he had come from. He cast a glance over his shoulder and was relieved to see that the street was empty. Was there more than one? Had he simply been unfortunate in having this one stumble upon him?

The drone moved forward again to follow Soren, matching his pace. He could see the neat hole where he had punctured it and wondered if a second strike at the same spot would be worthwhile. The drone moved forward with greater speed and slashed down with its two blades. Soren parried them both with sword and dagger but was pressed to the wall behind him. He hacked at the appendage blocking his way up the street. There was little skill behind the strike; it was intended purely to clear his path. In all the time he had practised against the drones, he had never struck at the arms, only the target points.

His sword made a horrible shrieking sound as it clashed with the metal of the appendage and sent a numbing jolt and vibration into his hand, arm and shoulder. Part of him had hoped his blade, made from the very finest Telastrian steel, would cut through. The blow knocked the arm out of the way and allowed Soren to move back into open space. As he passed, he jammed his dagger into one of the other deactivation spots. He plunged it in until it struck whatever solid framework lay behind, but it did nothing.

As soon as he had struck the arm to spine tingling effect, it occurred to Soren that it might be his blade, Telastrian though it was, that had come off the worse. He sighed with relief when he saw it was intact. He was certain a lesser blade would have shattered with the impact.

The drone responded to his changed position. It moved in his direction and accelerated, slashing high and low with the two arms facing him.

He ducked under the high strike and parried the low with his sword, using the force of the attack to drive him in closer to the drone's body where he struck again with his dagger, hitting what he hoped was a third deactivation point.

The drones in the Academy had six spots in total where they could be deactivated; the number required to turn it off could be varied, so the fact that hitting them had done nothing did not mean his logic was flawed. He would have to follow it all the way to its conclusion to know one way or the other.

As well as moving faster, the drone increased the intensity of its attacks. They lacked the finesse of the drones he had fought before; these were savage strikes, any of which would cleave him in two should they connect with flesh.

Soren moved back under the barrage of attacks in an effort to maintain some distance. As he parried between sword and dagger, stepping back with each attack, he tried to visualise the blue glow that brought on the Gift. Fighting drones was one of the occasions where the Gift had descended on him most readily in the past; he couldn't understand why that wasn't the case now.

Faced with death, Soren was always grateful for small mercies. In between parrying and retreating it occurred to him that the headache that had dogged him since not long after arriving on the island had gone.

Soren was fast naturally, a fact that had served to his advantage even without the aid of the Gift, but he was being pressed to his limits. Already the drone was attacking at a far higher pace than he had ever experienced from a person. If its rate of increase intensified, things would go very badly for him. The attacks were coming in too quickly for him to have any chance to try to bring on the Gift. Unless it descended on him of its own volition, he was going to have to do without it.

Such was the rate of its assault that Soren could not consider a counterattack. It was all that he could do to continue diverting the deadly metal blades from slicing him asunder. Sweat began to bead on his forehead and his arms started to feel heavy. It had been some time since he had trained intensely with any regularity, and even when he had he would have been hard pressed to keep up with the drone without the aid of his Gift. When he felt as though he could take no more, the thought and the act came almost in unison; he turned and ran.

He had never run from a drone before and had no idea of how fast they could move. Soren had a good turn of pace, and if he could avoid running into a dead end he might get away. Sticking to the street he had been on seemed the best bet; taking random turns in the hope of shaking the drone off like he would a person seemed futile considering it had found him in the empty city in the first place. The city was simply too big for their meeting to have been a coincidence. It also brought him back to the question of who had given the drone its order, and more pertinently, when.

Soren had gone some way before he dared to look over his shoulder to see where the drone was. His heart sank when he realised that it was keeping pace with him, perhaps even moving slightly faster. There was no way he would be able to maintain his own pace for much longer. Even had he been feeling in peak form, which was not the case, he was subject to limitations that didn't affect the drone.

His mind raced as he tried to think of a possible means of escape. There must have been rivers running through a city of that size. Perhaps if he could make it to one and dive in, the drone would be unable to follow. The sea was another option, but that would require trying to circle back in the direction he had come, along an unknown route, and run the risk of getting caught in a dead end. He didn't even know if the drone would be able to hover over water.

It was all moot however. Another drone appeared from an intersection ahead. Approaching drones now blocked both ends of the street. As Soren stopped in his tracks, the original drone slowed to a walking pace, mirrored by the new arrival, and they both closed in on him. In the Academy, the drones would work in harmony when more than one was commanded to attack, rather than getting in each other's way. It was one of the eerie qualities of the magic that powered them, but in unison they were more coordinated than any two men and far more of a challenge.

Soren looked to the walls on either side of him in desperation, but they were too smooth to allow him to try and climb up. Perhaps the curse of the Isles would claim him after all. He crouched in a low balanced position in preparation. If he were to die, then it would be amidst the finest swordplay that he could muster.

The drones drew closer and Soren tried to control his breathing and maintain his calm. Perhaps there was a chance he could hit all six of the deactivation points on both of them; perhaps that would still work. He thought of Alessandra, and of how his own stupidity and hubris had pulled them apart, of how things could have been so very much different if he had only been a little smarter. He wished he could see her one last time.

Soren watched the drones move toward him, concentrating deeply, trying to decide where to strike first. It took a moment for him to notice that his body felt refreshed and energised. Not one to over-think good fortune, Soren burst into movement. He had already hit three of the points on the original drone, so he made for it first. Its blades moved so slowly now that Soren didn't need to parry them; he could move between them at leisure. He pierced two points on his first pass, and weaved his way back between the steel blades to strike the final one.

All fear and uncertainty fled as soon as the Gift had begun to take its hold on him. He almost had time to watch the first drone's appendages drop to its side as its body sank down onto the cobbled street before turning his attention to the second. He repeated his dance of steel around the other drone, revelling in the pleasure of superhuman speed, strength and agility. The relief at having escaped death was such that the consequences when the Gift faded were of no concern.

Chapter 9
IMPERIAL MAJESTY

Soren fell to his hands and knees and retched on the cobbles, before the second drone had even touched back down to the ground. He had been eating little since he arrived at the island and there was not much to bring up. His head swam and it was several minutes before he felt up to standing again. He was tired, more tired than he ought to be; the hangover from the Gift was as strong as he had ever experienced — and stronger than he would have expected from such a short time in it. It had come on so quickly, and left such punishment in its wake that Soren was curious as to why, but that curiosity would have to wait.

Despite his fatigue he was concerned about being caught by another drone, so he forced himself to keep moving. Once he found the College of Mages, he could barricade himself in and rest before he began his search. With luck he would be safe from attack there. All he had to do was find it before he encountered any more. The questions of how they'd found him and if anyone was controlling them would also have to wait until he was safe.

He walked up the street until it levelled off and opened onto a wider road. To the north, the buildings seemed to remain consistent with those he had seen already, similar in size and design with nothing to make any of them stand out. To the south however, they seemed to grow larger. He headed in that direction.

The first building of any significance that he came to was a very large church, perhaps a cathedral. A tall campanile abutted it, which presented a good opportunity to get a better view of the city. He was exhausted and his legs felt like they were made out of lead, but he forced himself up the steps. He had no idea of how many more drones were hovering around the city, or how many might already be heading in his direction, but the longer he spent wandering around the streets the greater the chance of encountering one.

The ascent was torture on his legs, but the vantage point would make it worth the effort. Eventually he reached the top and made his way around the huge bronze bell that was still intact in its fittings. He was careful not to disturb it for fear of bringing all sorts of unknown unpleasantness in his direction. The roof was supported by an arch on each side of the square tower, each archway affording a spectacular view across the city.

He looked out in the direction he had just come from. The city was situated on promontory and had the sea running along its northern, eastern and western sides. In the north eastern corner there was a great bowl harbour with a small outlet into the sea. It was octagonal in shape and bore some resemblance to the inner harbour at Ostenheim, being enveloped by the land rather than having walls jutting out into the sea.

To the north he could just make out the stretch of water that separated Vellin from Ilora, along with the tops of two great towers that stood on either side of the strait. It was a vast city, and if his suppositions proved unfounded it would take far longer to search than he could remain on the island for. That was without even taking Ilora into consideration.

He made his way back around the bell to look to the south. He could see the gate through which he had come in, leading into the lower part of the city along the coast. He was now much higher, and in places the sloping hill looked as though it became sheer faces, often with buildings constructed up against them. Had he continued following that lower road, it would have led him to a castle built at the end of the far harbour wall that he had seen from the quayside. The castle looked far older than the other buildings around it, and considering how old they were it must have been very ancient indeed.

The campanile was on the plateau of a hill that extended to the south, while it sloped gently down to the strait in the north. The area he was looking for was spread out on that plateau. Gone were the tight and twisting streets lined with buildings, replaced by broad avenues, a central square and monuments, surrounded by majestic looking buildings. Imperial was an even more appropriate description.

He moved around the south-facing archway to try and take in as much of that part of the city as he could. The large buildings obscured much, and it was difficult to see anything but walls, roofs and towers. It didn't matter though; he was certain this was where he needed to go and there was no time to be wasted. He scanned the city quickly as he was about to step back into the trapdoor. His eyes locked onto movement, distant but visible. Another drone.

He swore under his breath and debated what to do. Staying in the campanile and hiding was not an option. The drone was a long way off and moving slowly, so not of any immediate threat, but he had now seen first hand how quickly they could move when necessary. He would just have to go back out onto the street and take his chances. If he had to, he could take refuge in another building until he was more rested. The fact that the Gift had proved so elusive for the start of his fight bothered him. If it failed him again, or at least took as long to descend on him, the result of any confrontation would be far too heavily balanced against him for his taste.

The drones, the way he felt, and the way the Gift had behaved raised more questions. Perhaps the information he sought would answer these ones also.

He tried to summon up a little more will to push himself on faster. The truth of the matter was there were limits to what his body could do, and it desperately needed rest. Usually so long after experiencing the Gift, he would have begun to feel better. He'd still need to rest, but the initial impact and all it brought with it would have faded somewhat. That wasn't the case this time, and Soren was concerned that he would not be able to keep going for much longer. The headache that had gone when the drone appeared was back with a vengeance. Another question to add to the growing list.

He exited the campanile and broke into a pace that was faster than a walk but not quite a jog. It was as much as he could sustain — and even then not for long. He headed along the street in what he took to be a southerly direction. It had been difficult to tell if the drone had been going anywhere with any purpose, but it was safest to assume that it had detected him and proceed on that basis.

He passed by the large building that had obscured his view from the top of the campanile and found himself in the square that he spotted when straining to peer around the building's edges. The building was one of several magnificent constructions surrounding the square, each with beautiful and imposing façades of columns, decorated windows and arches.

The road passed beneath it, through an exquisitely decorated arch, before heading toward the strait. The other buildings were large and impressive, statements of power and wealth befitting the capital of an empire. On the far side of the square, behind a low wall topped with iron railings, was what could only have been the Imperial Palace. To see it so perfectly intact after so many years was awe-inspiring. Soren had read histories of the Empire while studying at the Academy, but he had never thought to find himself standing in front of the seat of the emperors, nor to find it in as pristine a condition as it would have been during those times.

Soren couldn't afford to allow his fascination to delay him, for his heart sped up when his eyes fell upon the building on the right hand side of the square. There were too many familiar features, too many similarities to the Academy in Ostenheim for it to have been anything other than the College of Mages.

Chapter 10
THE COLLEGE OF MAGES

While the other buildings on that square were impressive, the one that Soren took to be the College of Mages made them all pale by comparison. There could be no doubting where the real power in the Empire had resided, at least when this building was constructed. There was a large central rotunda with an arched portico in front. Wings extended out from either side of the central rotunda, both four stories high with gabled roofs that merged into the verdigris dome atop the rotunda.

Soren could not stop himself from hoping that the answers he was looking for would be there. Each day that he lived with the Gift raised more questions and to be faced with the prospect of being so close to having them answered was tantalising. He stepped forward quickly, remembering the drone he had seen from the campanile.

A short flight of steps beneath the portico led up to the doors, massive and wooden. As with the others, this building was in perfect condition. The door of the College looked as though it was freshly varnished, and it made him wonder. The city gate had been badly weathered; this door was pristine. Why would that be?

He touched the surface of the door gently at first and then with more confidence. It was smooth and solid, and most certainly not just his eyes playing tricks on him. Could these doors really have gone untouched for nearly a millennium and remained in such perfect condition, despite all those years of wind and rain?

As he pushed, the door moved as though its hinges had been recently greased. His mind raced. His natural curiosity was piqued to a point of mania, but he was also nervous, afraid, and exhausted. His head pounded and fatigue made it difficult to order his thoughts. He stepped inside and closed the doors, shoving across a large iron latch to secure them. He had never heard of a drone being able to open a door. Smashing them down was an entirely different question, which he preferred not to dwell on.

From there he passed through a large vestibule, which was painted white. It was austere but there was something serene and beautiful about its simplicity. He continued through another set of doors and into a room that had clearly been designed to overwhelm every person who stepped into it for the first time; perhaps every time.

It was the central room of the rotunda, one vast open space beneath the dome that bore the mottled greens and blues of verdigris on the exterior, but was highly polished bronze on the inside. Like the vestibule, the walls were white; no trace of colour anywhere. The room was lit by an oculus in the centre of the dome, which allowed enough light in to see, but little more, bestowing a calm and peaceful atmosphere. The majority of the room was occupied by a circular pool of still, clear water that was surrounded by a low stone wall. The light from the oculus made the water appear as though it was glowing.

He walked around the edge of the pool, his gaze still locked on the dome above and the opening in its centre. He felt an enormous sense of peace, a marked contrast to the way he had felt before entering the building. Even his headache had eased a little.

Feeling safe for the first time since encountering the drones, Soren sat on the wall surrounding the pool, allowing himself a moment's rest. The water was utterly still, the surface like glass. He dragged himself away with reluctance when the ache in his legs subsided to a bearable level.

There were four large and ornately carved archways equally spaced around the room, one of which he had entered through. Each archway contained a pair of chestnut coloured wooden doors. Soren walked toward the nearest pair and pushed them open. He was not sure what to expect, and his hand hovered over the hilt of his sword. As the door swung open his heart was in his throat and he wondered what would be on the other side. Would it be another architectural marvel to rival the one he had just been in, or would it be a drone brandishing savage weapons?

It proved to be neither. There was only a long straight corridor on the other side that ran parallel with the front of the building. One side was lined with windows, each pane of which was intact, while the other side was lined with more modest doors, which one would expect to have offices behind them. The floor was of highly polished wood that also appeared to have received its last buffing only hours before. It made him wonder once again if there were people hiding from him. It seemed unlikely, but no more unlikely than the condition the building was in if it had lain empty for so long.

The library was what he was looking for and it didn't seem likely that it was to be found behind any of these doors, so he returned to the domed room. He took the next exit, that opposite the doors he had first entered through. It led outside to a large, cloistered quadrangle, enclosed by four story buildings. A path leading away from the doorway and on to the buildings on the opposite side divided the quadrangle. There were two towers on the opposite side of the square, on either side of the path.

Soren walked toward the marble monument in the centre of the square. The two towers were the tallest buildings there, half as high again as the surrounding buildings and at least as tall as the campanile he had climbed, perhaps taller. On either side of the path there was the same dead, grey soil that he had noticed as he had neared the walls of the city. It appeared that they had once been lawns or gardens, but now were devoid of life, much like the city and the island.

The monument proved to be a circular fountain with a statue of a heroically stylised mage at its centre. Any water had long since dried up but there was a stain along the inside showing where it had once been. Walking around the fountain, he made his way toward the opposite side of the quadrangle. The towers did not appear to have any entrance until he had passed them. Covered bridges, two stories up and similar in style to the quadrangle's arcades, connected each tower to the building closing off the quadrangle's far side. The bridges curved gracefully through the air and appeared to be the only means of access. Ahead of him, an arch passed underneath the building giving access to another quadrangle on the other side.

A large hall dominated the centre of the next quadrangle, jutting out from the opposite side. It made the quad seem more like three connected courtyards forming a 'u' around the hall. There was a door on the narrow side facing him. In his mind there was only one purpose this building could serve. He approached the doors and pushed them open, to be greeted by a familiar sight.

Chapter 11
The Library

THE LIBRARY OF THE College of Mages was similar to the libraries in the academies in Ostenheim and Auracia. The only real difference was the scale. The library in Ostenheim where Soren had studied would have easily fit into this one four or five times over. Additionally, where there had been great gaps along the shelves there, the consequences of the purge, here, the shelves were packed to capacity. He felt a shiver run along his spine. So much forgotten knowledge lay on the shelves, and perhaps also the answers to all of his questions.

There were book-filled shelves everywhere. There was a central block of them splitting the room in two, and they lined the walls on three levels. Metal spiral staircases provided access to the two mezzanine levels, where windows were the only interruption to the rows of books. Shelves also extended out from the walls, creating bays in between, which were filled with desks and chairs. Hundreds could study there at any one time. It was much like the other libraries he had been in, but on a far larger scale.

The windows filled the room with light, but there were also ornate chandeliers hanging from the vaulted roof, containing hundreds of small mage lamps that would have ensured work could continue there long after sunset.

As he looked at the shelves on the three levels, packed with an array of different coloured book spines, the enormity of the task struck him and he wondered if the time he had until the *Honest Christophe* returned would allow him to scratch the surface of the information there.

He set his pack down on the desk in one of the bays on the central block and began to look around, wondering where to begin. The one thing he could be certain of was that the purge had not reached this library; there were simply too many books. He did not know what value there was on those shelves in monetary terms, but he had no doubt that there were those who would pay handsomely for the secrets contained within.

There was something about the prospect of that knowledge being out in the world once again that sent a shiver down his spine. All the secrets of the mages, good and malevolent alike. There was no doubting that he could use the money, but some things would never be worth it.

The legends of a curse over the Isles were clearly successful at keeping treasure hunters and looters away, but if his presence there led to the sea route between the islands being reopened it would only be a matter of time before greed, desperation or ill luck led to someone making landfall and exploring the city, despite the fear and superstition surrounding it. It would not be long after that before someone managed to avoid the drones, or perhaps even destroy however many were left and all that forbidden knowledge would make its way out of this prison. Perhaps as a banneret, and the only one possessed of the same skills as the original bannerets, it was his responsibility to ensure that this knowledge was destroyed once and for all, as soon as he had found what he was looking for.

He returned to the desk and began to lay his things out. First was a small mage lamp that he brought to allow him to continue working into the night, although it would clearly be redundant with all of the chandeliers above. Next, his parcels of dried food, a notebook, pen and ink. There seemed to be little reason to look for anywhere else to sleep. He would need to work every moment that he could, so he laid his blanket on the wooden floor beside the desk.

He was about to begin exploring the shelves when he heard a sound at the far end of the library. He had bolted the doors shut after he had come in. Could a drone have gotten in by some other way? He drew his sword and dagger and peered out of his bay and down the aisle. He felt the slight tingling on his skin that often indicated the presence of large and unnatural concentrations of the energy that seemed to bring on the Gift. More than he would have expected from a single drone. More than he would expect from two. His heart raced as he waited for several drones to hover into view. For the second time that day he found himself in expectation of death.

He stepped out of the bay as quietly as possible. Did drones respond to noise as they did voice commands? He slowly made his way down the left hand side of the aisle, crouched in a low fighting stance. He cautiously peered around each bookshelf before proceeding past until he finally came to the last bay in the library. There was a sound of a page being flipped over. He took a deep breath and stepped past the shelf and into the bay.

An old man sat at the desk, which was covered with stacks of books and pieces of paper. He had a neat grey beard and equally grey, swept back hair that receded at his temples. The most striking thing about him was a pair of crystal blue eyes. He held up his index finger, indicating that he was aware of Soren's presence but too busy to address him. Soren opened his mouth in bemusement. The old man did not lift his head from the book he was reading. There didn't appear to be any immediate threat, so there was nothing to be gained by killing the man. Still though, Soren did not know how to proceed.

Eventually the old man spoke. 'Take a seat. I'll only be a moment longer,' he said, with a smooth, rich voice and unaccented Imperial. In the absence of any better ideas, Soren sheathed his weapons, pulled a chair out from the opposite side of the desk and sat.

The old man continued studying his book for a moment longer before closing it and switched his attention to Soren.

'Well,' the old man said, 'I suspected someone had entered the city, but it's been such a long time; I wasn't sure.'

'You seem to have the advantage of me, sir,' Soren said.

'Indeed I do.' The old man looked at Soren, his blue eyes scrutinising him intensely. 'My name is Berengarius. While I have an inkling of what you are, I'm afraid I don't actually know who you are…'

'I'm Banneret Soren.'

'A banneret. As I thought. Are there many of your kind remaining?'

'Yes, of course,' Soren said. 'A great many.' He wondered how long the old man had been there.

'Really?' Berengarius said. 'I had thought that after so long there would not be many of you left. None in fact. Surprising. Very surprising indeed.'

'I think perhaps the title of "Banneret" as you know it, has changed,' Soren said, suspecting now that the old man had been there for a very long time.

'That might be the case,' Berengarius said, nodding his head slowly, but not breaking his intense stare. 'Not with you though, I think.'

This came as a shock to Soren. He could not fathom how this man knew anything about him, or his gift.

'And just what is it that you think I am?'

'Well, a banneret of course. But a banneret of my meaning,' Berengarius said. 'Which I think you understand.'

Soren was reluctant to reveal anything. This stranger already seemed to know far more about him than he was comfortable with. 'I'm not sure if I do.'

'Why don't you explain your understanding of the term to me then and mayhap we will clarify things,' Berengarius said.

'A banneret is a trained swordsman, who has studied at an academy of swordsmanship and has the right to carry their own banner into battle.'

'Ah. What are these academies? And there are many such men?'

'They're schools for a martial education. There are many men trained in the sword and entitled to call themselves "Banneret".'

'I understand. But how many of them are like you?' Berengarius said, emphasising the last word.

'Again, I'm not sure I understand what you mean.' Soren felt his grip tighten on his sword.

'Yes, I think you do,' Berengarius said. 'I also think a mere treasure seeker would have found his way to the Palace before ever seeking out a dusty old library,' Berengarius said. He held Soren's gaze with the faintest hint of a smile on his face. 'Perhaps you don't know. Only suspect. Interesting.'

It was cryptic and tantalising, but Soren wanted to know more about this man before he revealed anything. 'And you?' he said. 'You're a mage?'

Berengarius laughed. 'No, not a mage. Just a librarian; tasked with the custody of this library many years ago and for some reason affected by the same power that keeps this place and everything in it from falling apart, but in my case perhaps not so well as I'd like.'

It was a reasonable explanation, but Soren was not convinced. Berengarius could be a malevolent old mage, controlling the drones. Equally, they could be rogues and the old man might be prisoner to the safety of the walled college campus. There was no way to know, but Soren would have to keep his guard up.

'Walk with me,' Berengarius said. 'I haven't had the opportunity to speak with another person in a very long time.'

He stood and walked around the desk, stretching his back as he did so. 'This way, please,' he said, gesturing toward the door.

Soren followed.

※

Chapter 12
A New Friend

'You're here for answers then?'

Soren wasn't sure if it was a question or a statement. He was already uncomfortable with how much the old man seemed to know, but if he was the librarian, then he would be able to help Soren with his search. He had no reason to trust the old man, but the assistance he could provide was too valuable to dismiss. He'd have to play along.

'Yes,' Soren said. 'But I'm not exactly sure to what.'

'Well, it's the right place for that. Those seeking out an affinity to the science of magic came from all over the world to study here, the College of Mages, to learn how to shape and wield the power that makes magic a possibility.'

'How is it all in such good condition?' Soren said.

'The library was the centre of the world for the mages. All their knowledge was stored there, so they crafted powerful magics to protect and preserve it. The magic is so strong it has extended across the city, but it weakens as you move away from the library.'

It explained a lot, including why the city gate had been in poor condition while the door to the college looked new. That the magic was still in effect after so long was impressive. They exited the library and continued on through the archway and into the square on the other side.

Berengarius stopped and surveyed the grey soil between the paths and sighed. 'This was once such a beautiful garden. A quiet and restful place for contemplation. Nothing will grow here anymore, despite my best efforts. I struggle to remember what it once looked like,' Berengarius said. He gestured to the left. 'We're headed this way.'

Soren hesitated. 'I saw some drones when I was coming through the city. Is it safe here? I mean, can they get into the College?'

'Oh, I'd forgotten about the drones. You were lucky to avoid them. You don't need to worry about them in here.'

It didn't answer the question of whether Berengarius controlled them, and Soren wanted to ask why he needn't worry, but he feared pressing further would reveal that he had destroyed two of them, and he had no idea what kind of reaction that would provoke.

They walked in silence for a while before the old man spoke again. 'When did you first notice that you are different?' he asked.

'I'm not sure really. It's just normal for me. It was only when one of my instructors at the Academy commented on my level of ability that I thought there was something unusual about it. He suggested it might have something to do with what he called the "Gift of Grace",' Soren said.

Berengarius nodded. 'Describe to me how it manifests itself.'

'It's always there to some degree. I've always been fast. I thought that was just the way I was, but the masters at the Academy watch hundreds of young men pass through there, and I was the fastest they had ever seen. Then there were some incidents where the effect became very noticeable, even to me. Everything around me seemed to slow down, but I kept moving at my normal speed,' Soren said.

'It's what I thought. What you have experienced is indeed called the "Gift of Grace". Your master was correct in this. Once there were many men who had this gift. These were the men that I knew as bannerets, and this is where many of them lived and trained,' he said.

They stopped at the arch on the left side of the front square, which led underneath the building and into another quadrangle.

'This is Bannerets' Square, home to the Order of Knights Banneret. They were the finest warriors of their time. They served as bodyguards, protecting a mage from physical harm while they shaped magic and while they were exhausted by the effort it required.'

Soren looked around and tried to imagine it full of people, training, returning home, or preparing to depart for adventures around the empire. It sent a tingle across his skin to think he was connected to all of this.

'In return for their services, the mages gave the bannerets the Gift of Grace. It made them far more potent than they could ever be alone. It was of course in the mages' own interests to enhance their bannerets; by ensuring that their protectors were better warriors than their enemies, they were also ensuring their own safety.

'When one became a banneret, one was given an affinity with magical energy, the source of which was known as "the Fount".'

Soren immediately thought of the blue glow. Was that the Fount?

'The Fount is not any one thing as its name might suggest. It's nebulous, as much an idea as a reality, and despite centuries of study it was never truly understood, but it is the spring from which all magical power flowed, so that was the name the energy came to be known as.

'After many years of considering the matter, I've come to believe that none of the explanations were entirely wrong, they were simply never able to go far enough to fully explain the Fount or any of its effects. Perhaps it was that the minds of men are not capable of ever fully appreciating its intricacies. Not that it matters anyway, enough was known to utilise it and shape it — and as this knowledge grew, so too did the power of the mages.'

Soren's mind raced with possibilities. How far did his affinity with the Fount go? 'Does that mean I can use it also? Shape it?'

'No. Bannerets didn't use it. They derived benefit from it, unlike ordinary people, but that is all. The affinity bestowed upon them enhanced their speed and strength generally. When a mage channelled the Fount into them, this enhancement became more pronounced. In its most extreme form, "the Moment", bannerets became truly fearsome.'

Almost everything Berengarius said raised another question for Soren. Without any mage to channel the Fount into him, how had Soren experienced the Gift, and the Moment also? He was ravenous for answers.

'To the surrounding world, they appeared to gain incredible strength and speed. To the bannerets, it appeared as though all around them became slow and weak. This gift was also an important component in the bond between a banneret and the mage he served. In order for a banneret to continue to enjoy the benefit of the Gift of Grace, he required an on-going connection to the Fount that was facilitated by his master. In this, the mages were able to manipulate their servants and ensure their continued loyalty. In the event of a banneret turning on his master, his connection to the Fount would be severed.'

'How is it that I've experienced these things if there are no mages left?' Soren said, unable to contain his curiosity.

'That's where things become complicated,' Berengarius said. 'As much as I'm enjoying talking with you, it's been a very long time since I have spoken with anyone, and I must admit that I'm tired; too tired to start on that topic. We can continue in the morning.'

Soren wanted to press Berengarius to continue. The thought of stopping now was difficult to accept, but he realised that he had already learned far more than he would have with a week in the library on his own. He quelled his impatience and nodded in agreement.

'There are rooms on this square that were always kept prepared for visitors, and they have not been disturbed. You will find one of those more comfortable than the floor of the library. If you are hungry, there is food in the dining hall.' He gestured to the building opposite the archway before leaving.

Food in the dining hall? Soren wondered if the years of isolation had caused Berengarius to go a little mad. What food was he likely to find in a dining hall that had been unused for hundreds of years?

Soren fetched his things and returned to Bannerets' Square. As he walked across it with his pack slung over his shoulder, he considered the situation. On the one hand, there was a sense of homecoming. This had been the centre of the world for men like him for hundreds of years. On the other hand, there was a feeling of loneliness knowing that he was the only banneret there, and perhaps the only true banneret as Berengarius described them, alive in the world.

His mind still raced with questions. How had he become a banneret if there were no mages to give him the affinity to the Fount? How had he experienced the Gift if there were no mages to channel the Fount to him? He was excited, agitated and impatient, but exhausted also and still suffering from a nauseating headache. He had forgotten all about the drones as he listened to Berengarius, but could not discount the possibility that the old man had sent them to attack him and he needed to stay on his guard.

He found a room on the ground floor of the building beside the dining hall. Like the other two squares, this was cloistered. Inside the arcaded walkway there were a series of doors and windows. These led to private rooms, once homes to bannerets. He picked one at random, which was small, but comfortably appointed. He dumped his pack unceremoniously on the table by the window, kicked off his boots and collapsed onto the first proper bed he had seen in some time.

He worried that if Berengarius had sent the drones to attack him, he might seek to do Soren harm while he slept. It was a danger, but Soren was so exhausted he knew he wouldn't be able to stay awake for long. If the old man was a mage, as Soren still suspected, he could have already killed Soren with little difficulty. They were the only comforting thoughts he could come up with before he fell asleep.

CHAPTER 13
THE GIFT OF GRACE

Soren awoke abruptly. It took him a moment to remember where he was, and he'd have sworn that he had only put his head on the pillow moments before. Nonetheless it was bright outside, and it had been near dusk when he had arrived at the room. He felt confused for several minutes, with brief flashes of dreams that were so vivid he had difficulty separating them from reality.

It took enormous willpower to get up. He sat on the edge of the bed for a moment to gather his wits. He was absolutely ravenous, as though he had not eaten in weeks. He took a little food from his pack and ate it quickly, not a full meal but enough to quell the hunger pangs in his stomach. He thought of Berengarius's parting words and wondered if it was worth taking a look in the dining hall. He couldn't see any way there would be food there. However, his curiosity about what was in the dining hall was tempered against his curiosity for what Berengarius had to say. His hunger for that was far greater.

He was about to leave his room when he realised his sword belt was still hanging where he had left it the night before. He went back for it; he couldn't allow his eagerness for knowledge to cause him to drop his guard. Berengarius was still a stranger, and despite his seeming friendliness and eagerness to talk, there was still too much about him that Soren did not know.

When he arrived at the Library, the old man was sitting at the same desk he had been at when Soren first encountered him, albeit with a larger accumulation of books in front of him.

'Good morning, Banneret,' he said. 'I trust you slept well?'

'Yes, very well, thank you,' Soren said.

'I thought we might walk again while we talk.'

Soren wondered why the old man was telling him all of this — starved of company and conversation probably — but he was too eager to hear more to question his good luck.

They left the Library and made their way through the College in silence until they reached the domed room.

'Impressive, isn't it,' Berengarius said, as they circled around the pool. 'It's called the Hall of Reflection, perhaps because of the mirror surface of the water or the reflective mood it puts most people in when they enter; I'm really not sure. No vibration or impact will disturb the water's perfectly smooth surface, nor will it evaporate or develop any organic growth.'

Soren looked at the illuminated water and suppressed the temptation to throw something in to see what would happen. They stepped out of the cool, shady Hall of Reflection into the dull daylight outside, and beyond the confines of the College. The heavy cloud hung in the sky overhead, as it had the whole time Soren was there, without so much as the slightest break to afford a glimpse of blue sky. Berengarius noticed Soren's skyward gaze.

'It's been like that for a very long time. It seems to be worse over the city, and I think it goes some of the way to explaining why nothing ever grows here. I don't recall the last time I saw blue sky or sunlight.'

'The drones?' Soren said, seeing the chance to discover if the

College walls kept them out, or if Berengarius could influence them.

'No need to worry. They won't come near us.'

Soren forced himself not to frown. It was still not the answer he was looking for, but he felt confident now that Berengarius had some influence over them.

'I thought I would show you the Imperial Palace, which is over there.' He pointed to the building on the left-hand side of the square.

'The eighth emperor designed the layout of this part of the city. He left the greatest mark on Vellin-Ilora. Before him, the heart of the city was over that way,' he said indicating the direction with a gesture down toward the harbour and the ancient looking castle. 'This square was intended to be the centre of power of the entire Empire. All of the institutions fundamental to the running of the Empire were given a home around the square.'

Berengarius stopped for a moment and looked around, as though seeing things that Soren could not. Soren wondered what the place must have been like with powerful magic being used all around. It was difficult to imagine now, in that empty, silent place.

'The use of magic grew rapidly with the rise of the Empire. Of course it had been used in various forms and places before then, but never on the same scale or with the same ambition and confidence. It was not long before the mages started employing bodyguards, to allow them to concentrate on their magical endeavours without fear for their physical safety.

'The first bannerets were merely soldiers who excelled in their profession. They were chosen from the ranks of the Imperial Army, those who had proven themselves brave, competent and physically capable. Each banneret protected a mage, and carried their banner. The College perfected a way of giving them an affinity to the Fount by bombarding them with magic during a process that took a full day. That was the Gift. After a time, bannerets became a class of their own, and service became a tradition in families of that class.'

After so long speculating about the Gift with no way of knowing if he was right, Soren felt giddy to hear it being talked of in such a casual way.

'The Gift was an amazing thing. The residue of the magic used to give it to bannerets made them faster and stronger, but when a mage channelled the Fount into his banneret, they really became a class apart. For them the world seemed to slow.'

Hearing Berengarius describe the things that Soren had felt as though they were common occurrences nearly made him laugh with bemusement.

'There was a danger however. While under the Gift's influence, they could place far more strain on their bodies than they were intended to take, literally tearing muscle and breaking bone through exertion. The more of the Fount channelled in, the stronger the influence of the Gift, until the banneret went into the Moment, a truly devastating state. It required the banneret to be completely flooded by the Fount. If the state was allowed to continue for too long, it would burn the banneret out, whether they exerted themselves or not. When the Moment ended, they would simply drop dead.'

The giddy excitement Soren was feeling was replaced by anxiety when he remembered that he had already experienced this state. How close had he been to the point of no return?

'The Moment was so named, because that was as long as it could be maintained. Even when used within comparatively safe limits, the banneret would fall unconscious when the Fount was cut off and the Moment ended. It was an extreme; rarely used, and only when the mage and his banneret were in mortal peril.

'Once granted, the Gift of Grace could never be completely taken away, but there would be no way for the banneret to bolster it on his own. Those with power always guard it jealously, if they have sense that is, and while the mages wished their protectors to be powerful, there was always the danger that they would create the instrument of their own destruction. So long as the mages controlled access to the Fount, they retained this ability to de-claw the bannerets when needed. Eventually, the bannerets found their own way to the Fount, and that is what led to the wars and the fall of the Empire, and, ultimately, you.'

Chapter 14
A TRUTH REVEALED

THE PALACE'S FAÇADE WAS long and three stories high. The lower two levels had large arched windows, while the top level had smaller square ones. A colonnaded portico concealed the entrance. Soren and Berengarius walked up the steps that led to the doorway to the Imperial Palace.

'The palace was a statement of wealth, power and permanency. In the same way the Hall of Reflection at the College was intended to provoke a reaction among all who entered, the Imperial Palace was intended to send that message to all who laid eyes on it.'

It was certainly that. It was the most impressive building that Soren had ever seen, and it was difficult not to stop and stare at its proud and imposing magnificence.

Their heels clacked on marble floor as they walked. The hall was lined with columns that reached up to an ornately plastered ceiling high above. Dome shaped skylights filled the hall with light and busts on pedestals sat between each of the columns, which Soren took as being likenesses of the emperors. They continued through the hall and on into the next room.

'This is the throne room. It's where generations of emperors held their court and it's where the fifty-seventh was killed, along with his family. Just there,' Berengarius said, pointing to an innocuous spot on the floor.

'Murdered by the sorcerers,' Soren said, thinking aloud.

'We were not sorcerers,' Berengarius roared. His voice rose like a winter gale and blasted through the throne room, sounding as though it came from many different places at once.

His voice reverberated in Soren's chest and ears and seemed to tug at his very essence. It was the first time Berengarius had shown any sign of bad temper, but his change in demeanour was insignificant compared to the way he had displayed his displeasure.

Soren didn't know how to react. What happened could only mean that Berengarius was a mage, and to Soren that meant danger. His initial response was defensive and to reach for his sword; he was now very glad he'd turned back to get it that morning, but Berengarius showed no further signs of hostility.

The old man took a deep breath and calmed himself. 'I apologise. That was uncalled for. I dislike the use of the word "sorcerer". It carries with it many negative connotations, which are not appropriate. The term was used for a very specific type of mage and even then sparingly, but you weren't to know that. Remember also that it is the victorious that write history, not the vanquished, and that victory in affairs as significant as those that followed the killing of the emperor rarely leaves one with clean hands.'

'You are a mage then,' Soren said, his hand still near to the hilt of his sword.

'Yes, I don't suppose that there's any reason to deny it now, although I did not lie to you entirely. I was charged with the custody of the Library a very long time ago, but perhaps not in the role that I might have implied. There will be time to correct any misconceptions I may have created later. It will be easier if I explain everything in sequence.'

'Why are you telling me all of this?' Soren said, unable to ignore the question any longer.

'To help you understand. Because you are a throwback to an era long passed and that must be difficult for you to comprehend. Because I and my kind bear some responsibility for that, even though so much time has passed.

'So, where was I? Ah yes, Saludor the Fifty-Seventh. His death marked the start of the Mage Wars. We decided hereditary leadership was the cause of the Empire's problems. Corruption, profligacy, incompetence, and dynastic wars were the characteristics of the later Empire. We knew we could do better, but not everyone agreed.

'Perhaps we were arrogant, but there was no risk of a member of the Council seeking to establish their own dynasty, as the affinity to the Fount needed to shape magic renders men and women sterile. Unable to have children.'

Interesting, but Soren didn't see what it had to do with him.

'In order to learn to create a close enough affinity with the Fount, a mage had to begin his training at a very young age; no later than ten years old or so. It seemed like a reasonable price to pay for the power and longevity one gained,' Berengarius said.

There was a grave, sympathetic tone to his voice, which puzzled Soren. 'Could they not have had a family and then started their training later?' Soren said, now realising the implication this might have for him.

'No, that wasn't possible; it would be too late to develop any real connection or skill, beyond the ability to conjure up base parlour tricks.

'At some point before this all happened, I don't know when exactly, some of the bannerets developed the ability to draw from the Fount on their own. Not all of them, you understand, but enough. You see, normal bannerets didn't have the same limitation imposed on them that we did. They were simply recipients of the Fount, rather than conduits for it. They remained fertile. I believe exposure to the Fount caused an accumulation in them over the generations, with son following father into the ranks, eventually leading to those who were born with the ability to connect to the Fount. It was something that had never been experienced by mages as we could not, cannot have children. How were we to have known?

'Indeed, we did in fact create the instruments of our destruction, as we had feared we might.' Berengarius paused, and looked fatigued. 'I'm sorry, Soren, but I'm very tired. I'm simply not used to speaking so much, or even walking about as much as we have today. We can continue tomorrow.'

Soren nodded, disappointed, realising that he was also exhausted. He had become accustomed to the constant headache, and was able to ignore it for the most part, but he'd only been awake for a few hours, not nearly long enough to explain why he was so tired.

'In the meantime, I really do recommend you visit the dining hall. I know that your need for food is not as normal men's, but I think you will be pleasantly surprised. The Fount is very weak here, but there are still some things that can be achieved with what there is.'

◆--◆

Intrigued, Soren went to the dining hall after they parted in the College's front quadrangle. True to Berengarius's words, there was a table at the head of the dining hall laden with platters of all sorts of food, hot and cold cuts of meat, fruits, vegetables, breads and desserts, a product of magic that Soren was too tired to consider. It wasn't the massive buffet he would have found at the Academy, but there was certainly more than could be eaten by one person.

Despite feeling hungry, he had little appetite. That was unusual for him but he was too tired to want anything other than a bed, and his headache was making him feel nauseated again. He forced himself to eat a small meal, surprised at himself for having to do so. When he reached his bed, he didn't have time for a single thought before falling asleep.

※

Chapter 15
THE TEST

THEY MET AGAIN EARLY in the morning. Soren had to drag himself out of bed once again, feeling as though he'd been pressed into the mattress. His first waking sensation was one of extreme hunger, despite having eaten the night before. He disliked the hollow feeling; it brought back too many bad memories. He went straight back to the dining hall after dressing and was greeted with a table full of food more suited to breakfast; entirely different to what had been on it the previous night. He ate well.

Berengarius appeared fresh and rested when Soren arrived at the Library, a little later than he had intended. They walked to the Hall of Reflection in silence and stopped once they got inside. Berengarius stood next to the pool, staring down at the still water. He had his back to Soren, who looked around, starting to feel impatient.

Without warning, Berengarius turned, twisting his right hand in the air as he did. A blinding streak of light flashed through the air toward Soren. He flinched as it hit, but it wasn't solid and it passed over him. He felt a warm, tingling sensation as it did, and could hear the air sizzle. He took a deep breath, but as soon as the shock of the incident subsided he realised that the light had no effect on him.

Soren was about to demand an explanation for what he had done when Berengarius clenched his right fist and pulled it toward himself forcefully. Soren felt a strange tugging sensation, as though something was pulling at the very essence of his being. It reminded him of something from years before, a feeling he had experienced when fighting a shaman in the east. The feeling passed quickly though, and once again he felt no different, and seemed unaffected by the experience.

'What in hells was that?' Soren said, drawing his sword.

'A test.' Berengarius held up his hands defensively. 'It confirms what I thought, but I needed to be sure. You can put your sword away. I've done all I needed to do.'

'A test for what?' Soren said.

'The type of banneret born with the ability to connect to the Fount had unusually high resistance to magic,' Berengarius said. 'Magical attack in particular. We needed so much energy to affect them that the Fount around the Isles was completely drained. Even now, there's barely any.'

'What would have happened if I wasn't born like that?' Soren said, still too shocked to decide how to react, but dangerously close to cleaving Berengarius in two.

'The light would probably have incinerated you. If it hadn't, the second attack would have ripped whatever life remained from your body. I was certain the result would be as it was. There was never any real danger to you.'

Ferrata had been watching the docks every day. That he had arrived before the ship he was following came as something of a surprise, but it was a long voyage and there were many variables. Voorn had been cold, wet and grey since he arrived, and he was not in any way charmed by the city. The cold and the damp brought out a variety of aches and pains; old wounds and injuries reminding themselves to him.

It came as a relief when the *Honest Christophe* finally did arrive. He was eager to be gone from Voorn and back to the more clement weather in Ostia or Auracia, but patience was not so much a virtue as a necessity in his line of work. He continued to wait and to watch.

Nobody went far from the ship while she was being unloaded, but he didn't see the face he was looking for on board or on the dockside. When the cargo was completely unloaded, the crew made their way into the city in twos and threes, but still there was no sign of the man he was waiting for. Once he felt he had satisfied the requirements of patience, Ferrata went to the ship for a closer look.

At first glance there was no one on board, but sailors tended to get all out of sorts when someone set foot on their ship without permission.

'Ho there. Anyone on board?' He waited for a reaction for a moment before vaulting over the bulwark and looking about.

'Who are you?'

Ferrata turned to the source of the voice, a man who had just come out of the companionway beneath the poop deck.

'Apologies,' he said. 'I did call out, but got no answer.'

The man glared at him, but said nothing.

'I'm looking for a friend. I was given to understand that he would be arriving on the *Honest Christophe*.'

'Who might your friend be? A sailor?'

'No, a passenger. He's an Ostian by the name of Soren.'

The man's eyes narrowed. '*Honest Christophe* ain't a passenger ship. You must have been told wrong.'

'I don't believe that I was,' Ferrata said. He had seen Soren board the *Honest Christophe* with his own eyes, and had watched the ship sail out of the harbour in Auracia.

'Ain't no one called Soren on the *Christophe*. Didn't bring any passengers into Voorn. Is there anything else you're wanting?'

Ferrata smiled and tipped his hat, but felt his temper rise. 'No, thank you. You've been very helpful. Good day.'

The sailor nodded, but said nothing more.

Voorn was not yet a dead end. There were other men who had sailed on board the *Honest Christophe* from Auracia, and they all had tongues.

Chapter 16
THE FOUNT

When Soren woke he felt tired and stiff, as though he had spent the night training rather than in bed. His mind was fresh with memories of his dreams, all centring around Alessandra, of cold, dark water; things he had no desire to think about. It was light outside when he woke, so he pushed the troubled thoughts from his mind and headed to the library. There were still so many questions.

True to form, Berengarius was sitting at his desk, barely visible behind stacks of ancient leather bound books and pages of handwritten notes.

'You're finally awake. Good morning,' he said. 'Let's go out into the city again, I find a walk is a nicer way to discuss these things. Shall we?'

Soren nodded in agreement and once more they went out into the city.

There was one pressing issue in particular that Soren wanted an answer to, but he couldn't bring himself to ask it outright. 'What happened to the bannerets that were like me?'

'I can't say for certain, as I haven't left the city in a very long time, but I expect that they died out. When the bannerets developed the ability to connect to the Fount, they took on the same burdens that were imposed on the mages. The connection would have made it impossible for them to have children and pass their ability to the next generation. With the mages wiped out, there was no one to give the Gift to new bannerets. By wiping out magic, the bannerets doomed themselves. An interesting irony, don't you think?' Berengarius said.

'That makes it difficult to explain how I've come to have these abilities, so long after,' Soren said.

'You're right, it does. I'm fascinated by it, and I've been giving considerable thought to it since you arrived. Might I ask what your family name is?'

'I'm afraid I don't know. I was raised in an orphanage.'

Berengarius nodded with a mixture of condolence and disappointment. 'That is a shame, but while it would have been nice to know who your ancestors were, my theory isn't contingent on that knowledge. The best explanation that I can come up with is that your ancestors were bannerets. The quality has remained latent in your family's blood for all the generations since. Why it has chosen to manifest itself now, with you, is hard to say. Perhaps your mother's family had a similar history of service in the bannerets, and when the two bloodlines converged, it was enough for the trait to manifest itself. It is impossible to know for certain.'

Soren nodded. It really wasn't important when he thought about it. All that mattered was that it had happened. 'It means I'll never be able to have children, doesn't it.'

'Ah, yes. I'm afraid it does seem likely that you won't,' Berengarius said. 'I am sorry.'

It was strange. Soren had never given any thought to having children of his own before. For most of his life just surviving from day to day had taken up all of his consideration. However, now that he was presented with the fact that he would probably not ever be able to, he was filled with the most profound sense of loss and regret.

'Those towers you can see,' Berengarius said, breaking the silence, 'on either side of the strait are the houses for the Chain of Saludor. It could be raised or lowered to control the passage of ships through the strait.'

They reached the nearest tower. It sat atop a walled quay overlooking the narrowest point of the strait and he could see the chain dropping away into the water from its far side. Each link was at least as large as his body and as Berengarius had said, there was no trace of rust; each link looked as though it was freshly forged.

'How does this all work? How do I tap into the Fount?' Soren said.

'That's probably the only question that I cannot answer with any certainty,' Berengarius said. 'Even among the mages, everyone's method differed slightly. I know little about how it worked for bannerets born with an affinity, so can only tell you of how it worked for those we created and for the mages.

'The Fount is everywhere, an ambient energy that is stronger in some places, weaker in others. When you connect to the Fount, you can draw on that energy to use it as you choose. It's given off by all life, much like how a flame gives off warmth, and how that heat is strongest closest to the flame. The Fount is also inside us, like a reservoir, which can be used and replenished. The most important thing to know in this regard is that it can be drained completely. Doing so is always fatal. It's difficult to do though. You'll use ambient energy before you draw from your reservoir.'

More danger, Soren thought. For something that was referred to as a gift, it brought a great many ways to kill its beneficiary.

'In the ordinary course of things you'll be very aware of when your own reservoir is being depleted; exhaustion, headaches, physical pain the like of which you would not have thought possible. The Moment may mask those warnings, which is another one of its dangers. Sleep will allow your body to replenish its reservoir most quickly by passively drawing on the Fount. The more drained you are, or the weaker the Fount, the longer you'll need to rest.'

Soren nodded. It explained the headaches and the speed with which he was tiring.

'As a general rule,' Berengarius said, 'the greater the concentration of life the stronger the Fount will be, and the easier it will be to draw on. It's what made Vellin-Ilora such an ideal site for the College of Mages. At its peak, there were over a million people living here. The Fount was limitless. It allowed us to shape some of the most breath-taking and important magic you could possibly imagine. Now, the city and the Isles are dead. It's a struggle to draw even a small amount.'

Mention of the word 'dead' led Soren to an uncomfortable memory. He had seen a shaman kill someone, and seem to gain energy by doing so. 'If I were to kill someone...'

'No, that never worked for the bannerets, and I am certain some tried it. It was only the mages, the sorcerers, who could use that energy, and even then only for destruction. Only a few did, but they blackened all our names.

'I tap into the Fount at will, but that skill took many years of training and practice. The greatest difficulty is accepting that it is everywhere. Once you can do that, to draw on it is as easy as reaching out to touch it.'

'It's a gentle blue glow that surrounds things?' Soren said.

'You've seen it then. Yes, that's how it manifests itself to human eyes that are open to it. Seeing it is the first and most difficult step. And you say that you are able to see it at will?' Berengarius said.

'To a degree. It needs a huge amount of concentration. That can be difficult to achieve in a fight.'

'I see,' Berengarius said. 'It really just comes down to practice once you have reached the point that you have. Eventually it appears quickly and with little effort. Accept that it is there when you want it, and it will be. The danger is that the Fount might rush in and overwhelm you. It was something that had to be practiced carefully, breaking the connection quickly and at will, until the desired amount of energy could be drawn without danger of being flooded.'

'That's something I've wondered about,' Soren said. 'A number of times, when the Gift has been stronger, things that I didn't intend to happen have happened. At least, things I intended to do went farther than I meant them to.'

Berengarius bent down and picked up two similar sized pebbles from the ground.

'Take these,' he said, handing them to Soren. 'Now throw one of them out into the water.'

Soren did as he was asked. He watched the pebble as it sailed through the air and plopped into the water.

'Very good,' Berengarius said. 'Now, throw the other one, but don't do anything differently.'

Soren felt a tingle on his skin as he threw the pebble. It went farther, despite him not throwing it any harder.

'I channelled some of the Fount into you when you threw the second stone. Not very much, but does that explain to you why that happened? If I channelled more, the stone would have gone farther again. It's about controlling the flow of energy. With the Moment though, there is no control. Everything you do will be with absolutely maximum effort, everything you attack will be destroyed.'

Soren nodded. It made sense, but he had no idea of how he could ever hope to master it.

'How close do I need to be to draw on the Fount?' Soren said.

'That depends on a great many things,' Berengarius said. 'How far away you are from the source, how strong the source is and how skilled you are at drawing from it. The Fount accumulates more around living things, so there is more of it close to larger amounts of life, a city for example. With more skill, or more focus, more energy can be drawn from weaker concentrations. Certain things can dampen, or block a connection. Stone, for instance will dampen, and water will block it.'

'What about magical objects, like mage lamps? Can I draw from those?'

'No. We could imbue objects with magic, but not draw it back out again. We could never find a way to store the Fount for later use.'

Soren nodded, but didn't contradict Berengarius. It was interesting and gave Soren pause for thought, but he saw no reason to reveal that to Berengarius. He was certain that he had drawn from the drones, both in the Academy, and again when they attacked him in the city. Perhaps it was something peculiar to bannerets born with the Gift that mages were never aware of.

Chapter 17
A Shocking Discovery

'My ship won't be back for another thirty-five days or so,' Soren said. 'I was hoping you would help me practice with the Gift.'

'Thirty-five days? From when?

'Well, forty since I arrived on the island, a few days before I met you.'

'Soren, it's been nearly forty days since we met.'

Soren looked at him as though he had lost his mind. 'I've only been here six days, including the days it took me to get to the city.'

Berengarius shook his head. 'I didn't think to mention it. With an affinity to the Fount, your body is also more dependent on it. It's so weak here, it takes you longer to restore your reservoir. Your first night here, you slept for six full days. I was beginning to wonder if you would ever wake.'

Soren couldn't believe what he was hearing, but when laid before him, it made sense; the extensive and vivid dreams, the ravenous hunger when he woke, the unusual tiredness. Then he realised what it meant; he could miss his rendezvous with the *Honest Christophe*.

'I have to go,' Soren said. 'If I miss that ship, I'll be stuck here.'

Berengarius sighed. 'I had hoped that we could avoid this for a little longer; it's been so nice to have company. I can't let you leave.'

'What do you mean?' Soren said. His hand drifted to the handle of his sword.

'After the war, bannerets came here to destroy the library, to wipe out the last trace of magic. They couldn't manage it; the spell protecting the library made it impossible. I made an agreement with them and swore an oath to watch over the library and prevent its secrets from ever escaping. I've kept that oath ever since. It's not a task I've enjoyed, or one I would ever have wished upon myself, but it is necessary. The few deaths I cause here prevent countless more if these secrets returned to the world.'

The reason the myths about the Isles had lasted so long. It should have occurred to him before. 'You told me that you don't have the power to kill me,' Soren said. 'When you tried, it didn't work.'

'You're right of course,' Berengarius said. 'The Fount isn't strong enough here for me to be able to do a banneret of birth like you harm. I regret the fact; it would have been fast and painless if I could. The alternative, I fear, is unlikely to be so. The Fount is too weak for you to put up much of a fight. It will be over faster if you just accept it.'

Soren caught movement out of the corner of his eye and turned his head slightly. There were two drones behind him, and another two approaching. He was not sure if the headache had already gone before he spotted them or if it happened at the same time, and fought to suppress a smile.

'I really am very sorry about this. If there was any other way… But the risk is simply too great. I hope you can understand that. I'm sorry we didn't have longer to talk. Goodbye.'

Berengarius turned and started to walk back toward the College, leaving Soren alone with the drones.

As the drones surrounded him, Soren felt stronger and more positive than at any point since arriving on the island, confirming what Berengarius said about the effect the Fount had on his physical well being.

Flushed with the energy for the first time in days, he felt almost euphoric as he fought off the drones and deactivated each one. Soren wondered if Berengarius really did not know that he could draw on the energy stored within the drones, or if he was simply paying lip service to the oath he made and never really intended Soren to be killed. One way or the other, Soren had no intention of staying in the city long enough to find out.

As soon as he deactivated the last of the drones, he turned in the direction of the city gate he had come in through and started to run. Fatigue would be hitting him soon, perhaps also the headaches and nausea. The discomfort they would cause paled in comparison to the notion that he could be stuck on that dead island for the rest of his life.

The night closed in quickly; it was difficult to tell when the evening was drawing in with all the cloud above so it went from dim and murky to dark with no warning.

He moved more slowly than during the day, but still making better progress than if he had stopped for the night. The darkness was complete. The clouds above, which did so much to hide the light of the day, completely choked out moonlight. His eyes adapted, but not enough to allow him go much faster than a crawl. A twisted ankle, or worse a broken one, would destroy any chance he had of getting to the spot where he would meet the

Honest Christophe, if it was still there. He had no real sense of how long he had been on the island, but he refused to accept that he had already missed his rendezvous; the prospect was simply too terrible to contemplate.

The darkness allowed him to develop a sense of tunnel vision, with nothing else existing other than his goal. It allowed him to block the thoughts of what he would do if they were gone by the time he got there, which he knew was a very real possibility.

He continued on relentlessly, despite fatigue setting in. One foot carefully placed in front of the other, tentatively looking for a safe place that wouldn't cause him to slip and fall and take away any hope of him getting off the island. Occasionally the going was easier, smooth sand rather than pebbles and rocks, and he was able to increase his pace. He couldn't let it make him complacent however, as there was always another patch of rocks looming in the darkness.

He had no way of knowing how far he had managed to go during the night. When light finally began to appear, it brought with it despair when he realised he had not travelled anywhere near as far as he needed to. He suspected that day was the last that the *Honest Christophe* would wait for him and he still had a great deal of ground to cover.

Being able to see his route helped him increase his pace once again, but not nearly so much as he would have liked. Fatigue, which had been a nagging strain, was now a severe problem. His thighs and calves threatened to cramp any time he pressed too hard on them. The lack of sleep was beginning to affect him also. He found his mind wandering from periods of clarity to ones where he was not sure if he was awake or dreaming.

Had the Fount been stronger, he knew it would have sustained him enough to keep pushing on with the certainty that no matter how awful he felt he would be able to keep going. He had experienced that once before, and although he had not then known what the Fount was, it was what had kept him alive and moving toward safety. Here, with nothing, he had no idea when his body or his mind would give up. He had never been separated from the Fount for so long, even though he was only now aware of how important it was to him.

He felt thirsty and nauseated. His head pounded as though he had spent the whole of the previous night drinking cheap booze. His joints ached and his muscles burned, but still he had to force himself on. To be trapped on that island was not a fate he could contemplate.

Chapter 18
THE LIE

SOREN MANAGED TO KEEP moving for the whole day. One step at a time, he pushed himself toward the rowboat. Even when his mind drifted to near delirium, part of him still kept his body moving in the right direction. However, as the day began to darken, he had still not spotted the upturned boat.

He knew how quickly the first hint of sunset became the black of night on that island, and started to panic. All he could think about was being stuck on that grey, damp island, sleeping half of his life away. What made it even more terrifying was the thought that the spells that had kept the city in such exceptionally good condition would keep him alive for an eternity also, stuck in that lifeless prison.

It was fully dark when he walked straight into the boat. He had been so caught up in the panic of his worst-case scenarios that he had been stumbling forward without any care or caution. His momentum carried him over the boat and head first into the sand, which filled his mouth and nostrils.

He got to his hands and knees and stared out toward the water. He could see nothing but the occasional phosphorescing wavelet. No sign of a ship. If Captain Joris had departed at nightfall, he would be long gone. That was assuming he had ever come back at all.

Soren was beyond exhausted and chilled by the cold, damp air. There was a pile of wood lying by the remains of the fire he had lit on the first night. There was also the food that he had buried. If he was going to be miserable, he could at least be warm and fed.

He had some dry tinder in his pack, but the wood was damp from having been left lying on the shoreline for over a month. It took several attempts, but eventually he got the flame to take, and it slowly grew into a proper fire. The warmth was welcome, and after allowing it to wash over him for a few minutes, he turned his attention to digging out the food buried under the boat.

It was still there, untouched by the imagined wildlife he had feared might take it. The oilcloth he had wrapped it in kept it from getting too wet, but it didn't make for good eating even as hungry as he was. He chewed on a piece of dry biscuit without any enthusiasm when he felt his mind drift into another one of its bouts of waking sleep. His eyes grew heavy and his head was filled with strange and nonsensical things, pieces of memories, inventions of his imagination, all rolled together making it impossible to tell what was real and what was not. He forced himself to stay awake, not knowing how long he would sleep if he allowed it take him.

Somewhere in the midst of the desolation in his mind, he heard a bell ringing off in the distance, the campanile of some great cathedral in his imagination or the bell of a village signalling danger to its inhabitants, or the bell of a ship…

The bell of a ship. Soren snapped himself from the daze and listened carefully, his senses alert and sharp for the first time in hours. He could hear the sound of the waves lapping against the shore and the crackle of the fire, but nothing else. Had he imagined it? Had it just been a product of his delirious, dreamlike state? No, he heard it again, drifting across the water, no more tangible than the fantasies that had been running through his mind only a moment before, but he was sure it was there. Then again. He was certain he was awake. He was certain he was not imagining it.

He looked out into the darkness, straining to see anything. The bell rang out again, three distinct clangs. Then he thought he saw a flicker, faint, but he had definitely seen it. Just a tiny twinkle in a sea of darkness, no larger than a star in the sky. It flashed three times, and he heard the bell again, three more clangs. They were signalling him. They must have seen his fire. The *Honest Christophe* was still out there.

He flipped the boat back over onto its hull and shoved it down the beach toward the water's edge with newfound energy. He drove hard with his exhausted legs, but they answered. He realised that he was laughing like a madman and as soon as he heard the hull splash into the water, and felt it float off the sand, he hurled himself in and lay flat on his belly in the bottom, panting from the exertion. He sat up as soon as he had caught his breath and with every ounce of will that he had left in him, he put the oars in their locks and began to pull away from the beach and the dead island.

He kept glancing over his shoulder to make sure he was still heading in the right direction. He was so tired that he was throwing his body backwards with each stroke. The pressure on his oars was not equal and he realised the boat was corkscrewing along erratically, like a drunk stumbling down the street after a heavy night's drinking.

His strength was fuelled by the elation of not having been left behind. When the little rowboat finally clunked into the side of the *Honest Christophe* he slumped back into the bottom, too tired to do any more. He could feel the abrupt movement of the boat as somebody jumped down into it. He was barely aware of a shape standing over him, and only just registered the sound of his voice.

'Think he's passed out, Captain. Still alive though. Looks awful.'

There was another voice from the ship, but Soren couldn't hear what it said. The man in the boat with him moved about doing something, and then there was a jolting upward movement as it was hauled back on board the Honest Christophe. As it swung sideways over the bulwark and onto the deck, Soren let the exhaustion swallow him whole.

Soren sat in silence opposite Joris in his stateroom at the stern of the Honest Christophe. He had a blanket draped over his shoulders and sipped hot broth from a mug held in shaking hands.

Eventually Joris broke the silence. 'You don't look like you've had the easiest few weeks.'

Soren shook his head.

'So, the stories about the isles are true?' Joris said.

Soren's appearance said more for the lie he was propagating than anything that would come from his mouth. He made the decision as soon as he woke up. Berengarius was right; the information in the library was too dangerous to ever allow back out into the world. Nonetheless, he needed to be sure that his message got across. 'They are, and more. It's a hideous, dead place. Even the few plants that grow there are twisted and evil looking things. There's no food to be had; were it not for what I brought with me, I'd have starved days ago.'

'Aye, you look like you could use a couple of decent meals. We'll soon solve that. I've a hold full of Ventish apples and pears. I'll have one of the lads bring you up some. A bit of fresh fruit will set you up again.'

Soren nodded and smiled in thanks.

'Was there anything else of interest there? Did you find the city?'

Soren nodded again. 'Yes, but there was hardly anything of it left. Piles of rubble, the remains of the city walls. Whether it was the years or the wars, the city was destroyed. I couldn't help but feel there was something wrong about the place. About the whole island, but it was worse in the city. Can't say what it was, but I couldn't wait to be away from it. There were noises in the night. I never saw what made them, and I count myself lucky.' He was concerned that he might be overdoing it, but sailors were a superstitious lot and Joris seemed to be accepting Soren's story.

'The straits then, they're not passable?' Joris said.

'No, I don't think so. I saw them from a distance and there was lots of debris in the water. The passage was narrow to begin with, but it looked like it was intentionally blocked. Some of the harbour walls and towers had collapsed into the water, but there was more to it than that. The straits were blocked for a reason. There's something wrong about that place. Only a madman would try to take a ship through there. But then I suppose only a madman would have ventured onto those cursed isles in the first place.' He forced a chuckle, but it was not intended to be convincing.

Joris stood and walked over and gave him a reassuring pat on the shoulder. 'I thought it would be the case. There's a good reason people stay away. You're a brave lad, but don't worry yourself any longer,' he said. 'You're safe away from there now.'

Soren felt guilty for lying to Joris; he was a good man, but the myth of the Isles needed to be maintained. The consequences of its secrets getting out were too terrible to contemplate.

PART II

Chapter 19
Gathering Clouds

It seemed that Soren was finally coming to terms with life at sea. It had been a full twelve hours since he had returned aboard the *Honest Christophe* and he had not yet vomited. He hadn't even fallen over — usually a regular occurrence in his first few hours on board. In fair breeze and clement weather he was even beginning to see the appeal of a life at sea. It was also nice to see the sun again. He hadn't realised the effect the constant gloom in the Isles had had on his morale.

For Soren, the most interesting thing was what he had learned about the Fount since coming on board. Berengarius had told him that the sea, or water in general, would cut off access to the Fount underneath. With whatever energy was created by and accumulated in the presence of the nine people around him, he found that he already felt far better than he had at any point on the island. He had only needed a few hours of sleep after arriving on the ship before wakening refreshed and he was not tormented by the shadowy memories of dreams that were so vivid at times they seemed real.

He stood next to the bulwark watching a large flock of birds pass overhead, flying south, the first he had seen in many days. He was wondering how much longer it would take them to get back to Auracia when Joris approached him, also looking at the birds.

'A fine day,' he said. 'But not so fine everywhere. Those birds. They're flying away from a storm.'

'A storm?' Soren said. 'The weather seems fine.'

'Aye, here it is. But there's a storm out there. No more than a day to the north I think,' Joris said.

'Will it affect us?'

'I hope not,' Joris said, with a laugh. 'But it might; it's still too early to tell.'

'That's a cheery thought.'

Joris laughed again. 'Anyone who tells you Ventish sailors are optimists is a liar. But listen, I've been meaning to say something to you. When we arrived in Voorn, there was a man there asking about you. Said he'd been told you were due to arrive there with us. You've friends in Voorn?'

'Not that I know of,' Soren said. 'That's odd. Even if I did have friends in Voorn, there's no one who could've known I'd taken passage on this ship. I haven't been in contact with anyone in… months. Did he say what his name was?'

'No. I didn't think to ask. I didn't like the look of him and wanted him off the ship fast. I'm sorry.'

'That's all right. What did he look like?' Soren said. He was reminded of the attempt to kill him before he left Auracia. Could there still be men looking for him on Amero's behalf?

'Sallow, long black hair, thin moustache, pointed tuft under his bottom lip. Anyone you know?'

Joris's description would have fit half the men in Ostenheim. Soren could think of a dozen people that matched it, none of whom had any reason to be looking for him.

'No. I don't think so.'

'Strange. Maybe he was looking for someone else. Well, I'll leave you to watch for the storm!'

All he left Soren to was the gut wrenching certainty that the incident in Auracia was not a one-off.

The following morning proved that Joris's prediction was correct. Dark clouds had gathered in the sky over the horizon, and the air had become noticeably colder. The clouds reminded him of the shroud over Vellin-Ilora and the memory made him a little uncomfortable, but there were new things to worry about now. The wind had shifted into the north and increased steadily over the night. Joris said he expected the storm to be upon them by midday. The western coast of the Middle Sea was still a long way off, and there was no hope of making landfall before it hit.

Soren spent all morning feeling useless. The sailors worked frantically, doubling up each of the lines and sheets used to control the sails so that if one broke there would be a backup. All of the rigging was checked for wear and reinforced where necessary. All of the cargo and loose items on board the ship were secured down and everyone on board enjoyed their last hot meal before the galley fire was extinguished. Everyone had a job to do but Soren, leaving him to watch the angry black clouds crawl across the sky toward them and wonder how nervous he should be. The sailors maintained their usual patter of fatalistic humour, but there was noticeable tension on board.

The first indication of the storm being close came with an increase in the sea state. Where before there had been a steady and regular pitching of the ship, now the waves were larger, more confused and the *Honest Christophe* felt as though she was being thrown in several directions at once. Soren's earlier hopes that he had become accustomed to a life at sea proved unfounded as the familiar nausea returned and he vomited that last hot meal back over the side.

The day darkened quickly and Soren felt as if he was back in Vellin-Ilora. The wind whistled through the rigging and spray started to break across the deck of the *Honest Christophe*. The crew were not chatting now; the fatalistic humour was replaced by silence and gritted teeth. Joris stood determinedly at the wheel, his face showing ever greater strain as he wrestled with it, struggling to keep control of his ship and ensure she remained on his chosen course.

As the wind continued to build, the whistling increased to a constant screech that made it impossible to hear even his own voice. Joris had one of his crew tie him to the binnacle so he could concentrate on the wheel and not have to worry about hanging on to the ship. Soren didn't need to be told twice when one of the crew instructed him to go below and lash himself into his hammock.

The next several hours were a nightmarish blur. Strapped into his hammock, Soren's body was flung back and forth with each violent pitch and roll of the ship. Sleep was impossible and, isolated in the darkness below the decks, he had no idea what was going on. He felt completely powerless, that his fate was out of his hands and that he had no control over whether he would live or die over the next few hours.

He vomited several more times, soaking the cloth of his hammock with foul smelling bile. Stinking bilge water sloshed around and was added to by waves that broke over the ship and washed down the companionway. The ship's timbers groaned and creaked in protest, and Soren thought she was going to break apart. Above all other noise was the howling of the wind as it tore across the decks and through the rigging. Soren's imagination ran wild; he feared that the crew had all been washed overboard and he was the only soul on board, being blown inexorably toward his death.

The nausea and the stench, the violent movement of the ship, the noise, the darkness and the fear all drove him to a state of near delirium as the storm seemed to go on for ever.

At some point, like a blessing from the gods, sleep came.

He was still strapped into his hammock when he awoke. From the swinging movement, it seemed to him that it was still attached to the deck beams of the ship. He was not floating in the sea, which had seemed a likely outcome the night before and something he was thankful for. The movement was less violent now, more regular and not straining the lines of his hammock with each swing. The sounds of the ship groaning and straining to hold herself together were also gone, as was the screaming of the wind across the deck. The stench of bilge and vomit was still there though, and each time he caught a whiff of it he wanted to throw up again.

He was hungry and exhausted by the strain of the night before, both physical and emotional. He slowly undid the ties on his hammock and released himself from his wet and stinking cocoon. He dropped his feet to the deck, which was awash with water; hardly a good sign. He slipped from the hammock and stood unsteadily. The cold water was a shock and sent a shiver up his spine. His nerves were still shaken from the night before and the gradual tolerance he had been developing for ship-board travel was completely erased. Each time one of the pieces of junk that was floating in the bilge water brushed against his feet and ankles, it gave him a start.

He moved from handhold to handhold as he made his way to the companionway. The fresh air drifting down from above was a relief and flushed the stench of below from his nostrils. He stumbled up the steps and out into the sunlight.

The initial shock of the water sloshing around aside, Soren's hopes had grown that the *Honest Christophe* was still intact and seaworthy. He was unprepared for what greeted him when he stepped up on deck. Captain Joris stood by the wheel, one hand resting on its rim, his other arm in a roughly tied sling. The otherwise calm day was disturbed by a constant clanking sound. Soren turned to see two of the crew working a crank on a pedestal beside the main mast. With each turn there was a sloshing noise and Soren could see water gushing from a pipe that ran across the deck and out of the scuppers.

The main mast was now no taller than the height of two men, ending in shattered splinters of wood. Some of the spars were lashed down at the side of the deck, while others were missing. The bowsprit was also gone, along with much of the rigging. The ship also seemed to be riding lower in the water than it had been the day before. Soren looked back to Joris, who had a grim look on his face. There were two fewer men on deck than there had been the day before.

'Can the damage be repaired?' Soren asked hopefully.

'Not while we're at sea. We can jury-rig some sails that'll keep some way on her, but we've sprung a few timbers below the waterline and there's not much that can be done about that without getting to a dry-dock or beaching. The only question is, can we get to a safe shore before the lads are too tired to turn the handle on the pump? That's the only thing keeping us afloat. You'll have to take your turn on that. I'm not much bloody use now, I pulled my arm out during the night. We lost two of the lads overboard. Never even saw them go; one minute they were on deck, the next they were just gone. First time I've lost anyone at sea,' Joris said.

Soren thought about Alessandra. Had that been how she had died? The notion gave him a pain in the pit of his stomach. Soren considered trying to console Joris, but didn't want to dwell on the subject of drowning. Changing the subject was all that remained. 'How far are we from the coast?' he said.

'No clue,' Joris said.

So much for trying to change the topic to something more positive, Soren thought.

'The storm blew us south. We could be as much as two hundred miles farther south than we were when we started. We're still drifting that way too. I'll take a sighting on the sun at noon to see how far east we went. The coast could be ten miles, or a hundred. There's no steerage on the rudder because there's nothing to put canvas up on to drive us forward. We'll rig up something to try and put a bit of way on her and just have to creep along and land wherever we land.'

The eastern seaboard of the Middle Sea was one continuous coastline, which meant as long as they made ground to the east, they would reach land eventually, assuming they could keep the *Honest Christophe* afloat for long enough.

Chapter 20
THE RED FLAG

THE WEATHER HAD GROWN noticeably hotter since the storm. They were pushed much farther south than Soren had ever been before, certainly far south of the Auracian border, and perhaps even far enough to be off the coast of Shandahar. The heat, not something that had ever bothered Soren before, became oppressive. Combined with back-breaking work at the pump, Soren was utterly exhausted and beginning to suffer from the many signs of exhaustion and exposure. While the Fount was stronger on the ship than it had been on Vellin, it seemed that it was not strong enough to sustain Soren through the constant exertion of working the pump on minimal food.

Most of the ship's food stores had been spoiled in the storm; sacks were soaked through with bilge water and casks had been smashed open by the violent heaving of the ship. Some dried foods remained, but they had to be strictly rationed and were not nearly enough to keep up with the energy expended keeping the pump going. Coupled with his bouts of seasickness, Soren realised that he had not had a proper meal — that he had kept down — since leaving the dining hall in Vellin-Ilora. Even when living on the streets, he'd managed to eat better than he had over the past days.

There was little chance to spare a thought for any of the things that he had discussed with Berengarius, the information he hoped would help him master the Gift. During the short breaks he took from the pump, he tried to see the blue glow by accepting it was there, but he could not. He didn't have enough experience to know how much there would be on the ship with only eight men including himself. There was definitely some, as he was faring visibly better than his crewmates who had to make do with the meagre rations.

The crew managed to jury-rig a few of the less damaged spars into a ramshackle mast and yard, and fitted a spare sail to it. It gave them a little forward momentum, but they still crawled along at a snail's pace. The main issue was the ingress of water between the damaged planking of the hull, which required the pump to be worked continuously, the men taking their turns in shifts. It was exhausting work, and as the day after the storm wore on the shifts had to be shortened several times.

Despite their efforts and several abortive attempts to staunch the flow of water, they were fighting a losing battle and only delaying the inevitable. The question that remained was if they would be able to delay the inevitable long enough to get to shore. With the rapidly deteriorating condition of the crew, Soren did not think their chances were high. The ship was moving too slowly; with all the weight added by the water, their small and inefficient sail was not able push them along quickly enough.

The rowboat that Soren had taken ashore to Vellin would perhaps have been just big enough for the eight surviving crewmembers to abandon the ship, but it had been smashed to pieces in the storm. The prospect of spending days in a small, open and overcrowded boat was not attractive, and Soren was relieved that it was not an option. Abandoning the ship would have been a worst-case scenario, if there was one worse than their current predicament. Captain Joris's entire life's worth was tied up in the *Honest Christophe* and what was left of its cargo. If she foundered, he would lose everything and Soren suspected he would rather go down with her than abandon her. They would simply have to struggle on in the hope that they had been blown closer to the eastern coast than they thought.

The sky remained overcast with the tail of the storm during the middle of the day, preventing Joris from taking a reading from the sun and getting a rough idea where they were. He tried, but despite his best effort could not get anything usable. The crew groaned as they went back to the pump, still no wiser as to where they actually were, and how far away safety was.

※

The evening continued much as the day had been, a constant and exhausting struggle with the pump in order to keep the ship afloat. The idea of jettisoning the cargo had been mooted, but it seemed to be an impossible task. Had the rigging still been intact, it might have been possible to put together a tackle system that would let them hoist the crates out of the hold and over the side, but their flimsy jury-rigged mast wouldn't take the strain, and they could not risk losing even the meagre propulsion it allowed them to generate. Hauling cargo out would mean even more strain on the crew, and less energy for the pumps. Keep fighting the ingress of water, or try to lighten the load. They could only manage one, but seemed damned either way.

The strain on the crew became increasingly evident as the night wore on. Despite wrapping swaddles of sailcloth around their hands when turning the crank on the pump, they were all suffering from blisters that had turned the palms of their hands into little more than raw meat.

With the arrival of stars in the night's sky, the crew gathered at the stern of the ship to watch Joris take a reading from the stars. They huddled around him in silence as he watched the sky, waiting for a large enough break in the cloud. Finally he raised his astrolabe and held it up to the stars, squinting along a line etched on its surface.

'We're well south, past the border between Auracia and Shandahar.'

It was not the crucial piece of information all the men were waiting for. Soren was holding his breath.

Joris lowered the astrolabe and looked at the markings on its side. His mouth moved in silence as though he was working something out in his head.

'Twenty-five, maybe thirty miles from the coast.'

The men cheered, although the voices were strained and tired. Without needing to be told, they returned to their station. Joris had said earlier that they were making two miles to the east every hour. If they were able to keep the ship afloat and move at that pace, there was a good chance they would sight the Shandahari coast late the following day.

This lifted the crew's spirits, but there was only so much the positive news could do for their exhausted bodies. The darkness hid the return of despair and exhaustion, with each man living within his own bubble of pain and fatigue, none wanting to let the others see how tired they were. The camaraderie on board amazed Soren. There was something admirable about it, but he feared it might be futile. They had to keep the *Honest Christophe* afloat for at least twelve hours. Soren would have been concerned if told they only needed two.

By the time morning came, the crew were in a pitiful state. The ship was lower in the water than at the previous sunset. That it was still afloat at all was due to the unfailing effort of all the crew. One man had pushed himself to the point where he could not continue. They carried him down to his hammock in a comatose state from which he showed no sign of recovering. Soren would never forget the pained expression on Joris's face as he watched one of his lads drop. He seemed haunted by the two that were lost during the storm.

Soren had been able to sustain a higher work rate for longer, but he was now also in a state where hauling himself up off the deck to return to the pump handle felt like more effort than he could manage.

They were all so exhausted that when Joris announced the sight of land, there was barely a reaction. Shimmering in and out of view with the pitch of the ship, it was still distant, but there nonetheless. It was only mid-morning but the heat was building steadily. The haze in the air made it difficult for dry, tired eyes to see, but after a moment or two propped against the bulwark with his hand shading his eyes, Soren saw it, a thin yellow line atop the crystal blue sea. He looked back to Joris with a relieved smile while two of the men finally managed to muster enough energy to react, clapping each other on the back and laughing. The remaining food was dished out and they returned to the pump with renewed vigour.

The gods seemed to be smiling upon them as the breeze increased and the *Honest Christophe* responded, pressing on toward the coast with a little more speed. All eyes were fixed on the shoreline. Even those on the pump turned their heads and strained to see how much progress they were making toward it from time to time.

Joris was the first to spot an approaching ship. It had already covered half the distance between them and the horizon before he noticed it. Soren was on a break from duty at the pump when the call came, so he hobbled over to the opposite bulwark to look for himself.

There was nothing out of the ordinary about it. From the look of the spread of white canvas, it appeared as though she had avoided the worst of the storm. It occurred to Soren that if she closed with them quickly enough, her captain might be convinced to tow them closer to the coast. There was something unsettling about the way Captain Joris had announced his sighting however.

'Is there a problem?' Soren said.

'Not right now, lad, but there might be,' he said. 'She's moving too fast to be carrying cargo. That leaves two possibilities. Warship or pirate. In Shandahari waters, there ain't much difference between warship and pirate, not to a vessel from the north anyhow.'

Soren felt a flutter of panic in his chest. If they were attacked, there was no way they could repel it. He marvelled at how the other men had been able to keep going for so long. Despite the advantages conferred by the Gift, albeit when the Fount was very weak, he felt as though he was near the end. With nothing but some biscuit, salt beef and water, they had managed to keep going. With the state they were in, a boatload of children would have little difficulty overwhelming them and taking the *Honest Christophe*. For a moment Soren wondered what effect the arrival of a large number of people would have on him. With a stronger Fount, how quickly would he recover? Quickly enough to fight? Even with the Moment, how many would he be able to cope with? He knew he was expecting too much from the Gift. He also knew, for the first time in his life, he was facing a fight that he was certain he could not win.

When the ship drew closer a red flag broke out at her masthead. Whether she was truly a warship or a pirate, on this day she chose to be a pirate. Being caught was a foregone conclusion.

With the men so weak, Joris gave orders not to resist; the only sensible choice. If they took up arms, they would most certainly all be killed. If they surrendered peacefully, like as not they would have the chance to fight again another day.

It was with a sense of frustration that Soren and the rest of the crew leaned against the bulwark and watched the predatory vessel tack its way up to them, too tired to do anything else and no longer caring about the bilge that was rapidly filling with water. The pirate was sleek and of finer lines than the *Honest Christophe*, having clearly been built for speed and agility rather than cargo capacity. As she grew closer they could see that her deck was crowded with men. Even had the crew of the *Honest Christophe* been in perfect health, they would have had little chance in repelling so many men.

It was a new experience for Soren, waiting for an enemy to come to him in the knowledge that surrender was his only option for survival. It felt strange, emasculating. Even as a youth living on the streets of Ostenheim, he had fought for every scrap in the belief that he would win out in the end. Now he didn't know what the next few hours would hold. It reminded him of the despair and isolation of the dungeon in Ostenheim. He had realised then that no matter how many friends you have, or how many people you have around you, you always face death alone — and it was no different now.

The other vessel drew up a short distance away, close enough to make out the individual features of the men on board. Its crew scrambled to furl sails and make the ship ready for combat. Others stood by the rail, all armed, watching their prey.

Grappling hooks were fired from small arbalests mounted along the bulwark. The hooks arched gracefully through the air towing ropes behind them. One of the crew had to dive out of the way to avoid being struck by one. The lines were pulled tight, and once the grapnels had gripped the wood of the *Honest*

Christophe firmly, the pirates began to draw the vessels toward each other.

Captain Joris made his way slowly to the back of the *Honest Christophe* and pulled her pennant down from the broom handle that had been serving as a flagpole since the storm. He did not want the pirates to be under any misapprehension; the crew of the *Honest Christophe* would not be resisting.

※

Chapter 21
THE PIRATE

THE TWO VESSELS BUMPED together with a muted thud. The pump had not been operating for some time now, and Soren wondered how long it would be before the *Honest Christophe* foundered. It amused to him think of the possibility of the *Honest Christophe* sinking and dragging the pirate ship down with her. That seemed too much to hope for, and would in a sense be cutting off his nose to spite his face. If the pirate ship sank Soren would almost certainly drown, for he couldn't swim. The Fount conferred many benefits, but he didn't believe breathing underwater was one of them. At least if the pirate vessel remained afloat, there was a chance he would be taken prisoner, brought to land and have a chance to escape at a later time. Captain Joris hoped that their early surrender would earn them this mercy from their attackers.

The pirates did not swarm aboard immediately, as Soren expected. For several moments after the two vessels came into contact with one another, they continued to scrutinise the *Honest Christophe* and her crew. It looked as though they were weighing up the possibility of there being a horde of armed soldiers waiting below deck to ambush them. She lay low in the sea and they were not to know that was because she had taken on a large quantity of water. They were clearly not stupid. However, they must have been aware of the storm, and Soren thought it like as not that they were out searching for ships just like the *Honest Christophe*, that had been crippled by the bad weather and would make an easy prize.

Eventually their caution gave way to necessity, and several of the pirates clambered aboard. One of them, brandishing a broad bladed sword, stepped forward. He was tall and slender with jet-black hair tied back into a ponytail. He had a narrow, pencil moustache that made his mouth seem thinner than it actually was, and wore a ruffled white shirt and a wide brimmed hat with a white plume, giving him a dashing, albeit sinister look.

'Who is master of this vessel?' he said, his voice gravelly and authoritative.

'I am,' Captain Joris said.

The pirate smiled and stepped toward Captain Joris, who made to hand the pirate his sword. Without warning or provocation the pirate hacked his sword into Captain Joris's neck and then again as the already dying Ventishman fell to the deck of his ship. Soren looked on with a mixture of shock and horror, too surprised, too weak and too late to do anything about it.

'Well,' the pirate said, 'now that we have that confusion cleared up, I am Sancho Rui, captain of the *Bayda's Tear*, and master of this vessel also. What is this ship called?'

'The *Honest Christophe*, sir,' one of Joris's sailors said.

'I see. The *Honest Christophe*. A Ventish vessel is she?' Rui said.

'Yes, sir, that she is,' the sailor said, his voice wavering with fear.

'What is it with Ventish merchants and calling their ships "honest" or "trusty" or "reliable"? You're hardly likely to call it "schemer" or "swindler" now are you? Am I supposed to believe it is an honest ship because it is so called?' Rui said.

Soren wasn't sure if he intended to be rhetorical, but the sailor answered nonetheless.

'I don't rightly know, sir,' he said.

'Don't rightly know, sir,' Rui said. 'Not much use, are you. Still, at least you have manners. The Code of the Sea demands that I spare your lives for not having resisted my attack. I think I've properly acquainted your former captain with my personal view on that code. Blasco!' He turned to one of the other pirates. 'Have the brave men of the *Honest Christophe* line up by the main mast, if it can be called that.'

The man Rui had called Blasco was shorter than Soren, but had the characteristically lean, developed physique of a well-fed mariner. He sheathed his sword and picked up a belaying pin, using it to goad the crew, including Soren, into a line by the jury-rigged mast.

When Blasco was done, Rui walked along the line, inspecting each one of them.

'When I stepped aboard this ship, it and everything on it became my property by right of conquest. You, the crew, ceased to be people, and became instead property. My property,' he said. 'This one and that one are too far gone. Throw them over the side.'

Blasco followed his captain's orders without hesitation or question. He drew a dagger and had the throats of both men cut before anyone could react. Soren had not known the men well, but a bond of comradeship had developed in the hours of hardship they had suffered, and he had grown fond of Captain Joris's decency. They had showed their character in returning to Vellin-Ilora, overcoming their genuine fears to keep their word. They were good men who did not deserve to die like that. Rage flushed through Soren, but he was too weak and exhausted to do anything about it.

Rui must have spotted the anger in Soren's eyes, for he had stopped close by and was staring at Soren intently.

'You look healthier than the rest,' Rui said. 'A once fat passenger? Or perhaps you were hiding food from your starving comrades. It matters not which, I can see that you are more interesting than the others. I shall be watching you.' He smiled in a cold, predatory way.

He turned back to his crew. 'By the looks of it this wreck won't be afloat for much longer. I want it stripped of everything of value that we can fit on the *Tear* before next bell. Feed these five and then put them in the brig. If they live we may be able to sell them for a few florins.'

As they were bundled over the side and onto the *Bayda's Tear*, Soren saw one of the pirates carrying the leather travelling case that he kept his Telastrian steel sword and dagger in. One part of him was angered by the thought of the pirate putting his grubby hands on it, but he was mainly relieved that they would not be lost when the *Honest Christophe* sank. He would have the opportunity to get them back, of that he was sure.

Chapter 22
THE BRIG

Soren had already spent far more of his life in confinement than he would have liked. On this occasion he had to share it with four other men, and there would have been little enough space for two. Two of the men brought on board the *Bayda's Tear* had not improved at all, even with the food and rest they had since being captured. The struggle to keep the *Honest Christophe* afloat had pushed them past the point of recovery. Soren didn't expect them to last more than a day or two, if Sancho Rui allowed them to live that long. He didn't seem to be bothered by the thought of hastening a couple of dying men to their death if it saved him the expense of feeding them.

The door to the brig was opened and a bucket of porridge was pushed in. The door was slammed shut again and Soren pulled the bucket into the central space between the captives. He loaded the ladle with the thick, gluey porridge contained within and handed it to the man to his left. He wasn't sure why he was seeing to the needs of the other men first, but he felt some sense of obligation. He had recovered quickly since arriving on the *Tear*. His body showed the signs of insufficient food, but the Fount had returned him to a level of health he could not have hoped for otherwise. The same could not be said for the other survivors from the *Honest Christophe*. The food was not enough, and they continued to waste away. Even if they weren't going to last much longer, Soren would try to do as much as he could to make their final hours more comfortable. He owed them that.

They were allowed out of the brig for a few minutes each day to use the heads, but after a very brief respite of fresh air they were bundled back into the darkness of the brig. There was little to do but to try and practice with the Fount. With five of them stuffed in the brig and a large number of men outside, based on Berengarius's logic there would be enough Fount there to work with. Berengarius had also said that objects like walls would dampen his connection to an accumulation on the other side, but Soren reasoned that as wood was organic it might prove to be less of an obstacle than stone or brick and allow him to sense or connect to what was on the other side.

It was all speculation, but he had nothing else to do and no reason not to try. He had called on the Fount intentionally on previous occasions, but in a clumsy way that had exposed him to danger. The Fount would have been strong on those previous occasions, and he realised now how lucky he was that he had not allowed himself to be overwhelmed and burned out. He had held his focus on it for only a fraction of a second, all that the circumstances of a duel had allowed, but in that blink of an eye it flooded him with energy. It had not been enough to push him into the Moment, but it was far more than he had needed, and caused his actions to go far beyond what he had intended. He was not able to control them and that bothered him more than he would care to admit.

While sitting in their tiny prison, his mind frequently drifted to Alessandra. It was painful to think of her, of the time they shared and the wonderful future he had hoped awaited them both. He forced his thoughts to those that might be of some use. In the past, stress or danger had opened his connection with the Fount without him knowing. It was this mechanism that he hoped to exploit. Having to focus all of his attention on the Fount was going to get him killed sooner rather than later, so he had to learn to control this method of connection as soon as he could.

Berengarius had led him to think about the Fount in a different way. Initially it had been a mysterious blue glow that caused him to question his sanity. As he saw it more frequently he came to accept that it was real, if completely unexplainable. The idea of being aware of it as a leap of faith rather than a process seemed to dictate against the approach he had been taking. Instead of trying to force his mind to see it as he had been doing he merely accepted that it was there and waited for it to appear. It had not worked thus far, but he felt it was worth persevering with. Each day, he fought against the tendency of his mind to wander and tried to relax, in the hope of making drawing on the Fount as effortless as breathing.

As the days passed in the hot, stuffy darkness of the brig he found his way back to the Fount. It was weak, but where before there had been nothing but darkness, Soren could now make out the shapes of each of his companions, outlined in the faintest of blue glows. On the previous occasions when he had connected to the Fount, the connection had ceased as soon as his concentration had broken. Now however, it was there when he looked for it. Rather than feel himself fill with its energy, he was aware of its presence.

That was the problem. It was not rushing in on him, but equally he didn't seem to be able to attract it. He began to grow frustrated. Although he had found a new and less involved way to see the Fount, he still felt as though he was as far from controlling the Gift as he had been when he set off from Auracia.

More days passed, each blending into one long, hot waking nightmare, and despite his best efforts he could not make the Fount bend to his will.

<hr />

Chapter 23
Isles of Spice

Interruption to their monotonous routine finally came when the rolling and plunging motion of a moving ship ceased and was replaced by the gentle rocking of a stationary one at anchor. Soren heard the sounds of cargo being hauled around and smaller boats banging against the side of *Bayda's Tear*. When the time came for their short daily release from the brig, instead of being bundled back in when their necessaries were completed, the pirates lined them up by the mainmast and their hands were bound.

Another man joined Captain Rui and the two of them surveyed the prisoners. The two weakest of the group, who to Soren's surprise had clung onto life, attracted the most attention. They were barely able to stand and wavered unsteadily as Rui studied them with the appearance of a man choosing between two pieces of fruit. The other man looked at them grimly and shook his head. Rui nodded to a crewman who cut their throats without hesitation and began to haul their corpses to the side to bundle them overboard. Even having already witnessed how Rui operated, the unflinching brutality shocked Soren.

While the barbaric act had been committed, Rui had watched him intently. He smiled when he saw the anger flare behind Soren's eyes.

'This one has spirit, Salicar,' he said to his companion. 'I saw it when I first took them and killed his captain. Every time he looks at me, I know that he wishes to kill me. I can't decide whether I should kill him first. But then again, what has Sancho Rui to fear from a slave?'

'He's the only one of them that will fetch a decent price,' the man called Salicar said. 'You might as well have killed them all when you captured them and saved yourself the bother of feeding them. The others will need a few weeks feeding and exercise before it will be worth bringing them to market. Even then, there won't be much profit to be had after the expenses.'

'There never is, Salicar. There never is.' Rui stared at his companion with a wry smile. 'They were in terrible condition when we took them. Take them ashore and do as you please with them. I know you will get me the best price that can be had. If you don't...' He gestured to the sailor bundling the corpses over the side.

Soren and the others were manhandled into a longboat and rowed ashore, where they were put sitting beside an ever-growing pile of plunder on the beach. Salicar's slaves had considerately erected an awning of palm fronds for them to sit under which Soren was grateful for, as the sun was very strong and the day very hot. He suspected that they would have been put to work like the other slaves were it not for the fact that they were so weak, and their new captor was motivated to achieve the highest price possible.

In spite of everything, it was a lovely day and a beautiful, exotic place, and Soren revelled in the change in circumstances from the dark, stuffy brig. The white, sandy beach was u-shaped and surrounded the cove that the *Tear* had anchored in. The land rose steeply up toward the main shoreline, creating cliffs at the cove's mouth. Once in the little bay, a ship would be hidden from view from anywhere other than the mouth. It was a perfect spot for a pirate to hide while unloading a cargo, or even to weather out a storm. Behind the beach there was a thick jungle of palm trees and lush vegetation. Doubtless there was a trail to be found that would allow the transit of the plundered loot, but from where he sat, Soren couldn't see it.

There was a rich scent in the air — Soren had noticed it as soon as he came out of the brig — that he initially thought was the relief of being back out in fresh air. It was still there though, and made him wonder where they actually were. There was no way to know if they were in Shandahar, or anywhere else; he had lost all track of time while in the brig. The smell in the air made him think it might be the Spice Isles, and their reputation as a pirate haunt bolstered his opinion. The Spice Isles were a chain of islands that stretched across the neck of the Middle Sea in the south, and marked the boundary between it and the Southern Ocean. The name came from the fragrant and exotic goods — spices, tobaccos and teas — that were produced there. The Isles were little more than a name to him before that day, so it was impossible to know if he was right.

He watched the ship as it tugged gently at its anchor line. He could see Sancho Rui moving about the ship and Soren did his best to burn the man's face into his mind. Rui had Soren's sword, and he wanted it back.

At first none of the men spoke as they sat on the beach, hands bound, waiting for the *Bayda's Tear* to be unloaded. They had seen the brutal way Rui treated anyone who drew his attention, and no one wanted to be on the receiving end. On the beach though, they were ignored. Soren was sure that any attempt at escape would be noticed, but otherwise they were left to their own devices.

'Where d'you reckon we are?' he whispered to one of the other sailors, seeking confirmation of his theory.

The sailor looked about nervously before answering. 'One of the Spice Isles. No doubt about it. No idea which one though.'

Soren was strangely pleased with himself for having come to the same answer. He leaned back on his elbows and started to experiment with the Fount.

It was far stronger here and at first it felt frightening, having become so used to it being very weak. With the thick jungle only a few yards away, not to mention the dozen or so slaves, countless insects, birds and unseen animals, it was as strong as Soren imagined it could be.

Each time he looked for it, everything around him became blanketed with a vivid, deep blue glow. With such strength, each time he connected Soren could feel the energy of the Fount pressing against him. He had to keep telling himself that one day the whole process would become second nature, as effortless as breathing, but for now it was intimidating and frustrating. He had not been able to draw on the Fount while on board the ship, either through lack of skill or because it was too weak. Now he was too afraid to do so, lest it flood in and kill him.

The pirate vessel was fully unloaded by the time the sun set. The slaves started loading the boxes onto a cart that had been hidden in the tree line during the day, while they put the smaller, lighter items into hempen nets that were carried by two slaves with a pole. Soren and the other remaining crewmen from the *Honest Christophe*, as well as several other unfortunates who must have been taken from other ships and held elsewhere on the *Bayda's Tear*, were herded on into the jungle like cattle.

In addition to the slaves who were enduring the backbreaking work of hauling plunder through the warm and humid night air, there were four armed men to help Salicar to maintain order. The slaves seemed to be thoroughly cowed and posed no threat. Those destined for slavery, Soren included, had their hands bound and were linked together by rope. It was hard for Soren to tell if the guards were old soldiers or pirates, but they had the look of men accustomed to enduring and inflicting hardship. Each of them had a sword strapped to their waist and carried small crossbows, but they did not pay much attention to the captives, only occasionally chiding the slaves to increase their pace.

Soren tried to work out what opportunity there was for escape should he be able to get free, but despite his best efforts he wasn't able to loosen his bonds. Being lost in a strange jungle in the middle of the night didn't fill him with enthusiasm, so he settled on waiting until they got to wherever they were going.

They trudged for some time through the jungle, tied in single file behind the cart that had been loaded to capacity and beyond. Each time the cart hit a rut in the trail Soren expected the boxes and crates to come tumbling off, but they never did. The trail had been slowly working its way uphill through thick tropical vegetation. After so long in the cramped confines of the brig, it was extremely tiring. It was not long before Soren's calves, thighs and feet ached. To make matters worse, each time the cart lurched into a rut, the rope that attached the captives to the back pulled taut and then went slack. It was a constant struggle to stay on his feet and he found himself wishing that wherever it was they were going was not too far away.

It was a great relief when Salicar called their motley little column to a halt in a small clearing. Even the guards looked pleased to have the rest. They at least had water skins to drink from. Soren and his fellow soon-to-be-slaves had no such luxury, but he was grateful for even just a few moments of sitting down. They hadn't been sitting for long when the background noise of nocturnal insects was broken by a clear, confident voice.

'Salicar Pah! As I live and breathe. Fancy meeting you here.'

Chapter 24
THE JUNGLE CLEARING

SOREN COULDN'T SEE THE source of the voice, but Salicar's reaction was clear to all. That he recognised the voice was beyond doubt. That Salicar was terrified of it was equally as obvious. He had been sitting mopping his brow, but as soon as he heard it, he jumped to his feet and began looking around anxiously for its source.

'Moving loot for Sancho Rui again, are you?' said the voice. The speaker appeared from the undergrowth, a tall man with a deep tan and dark hair. He had a thick moustache and a neatly trimmed beard, and stood with a soldier's bearing.

'That's none of your business, Ramiro,' Salicar said. 'Where I buy my merchandise is no concern of yours. I'm not party to the Accords; I have as much right to trade here as you do.' He spoke with the confidence of someone with four crossbowmen waiting on his orders, but he didn't manage to conceal his fear.

'Oh, but it is my business, Salicar, when you buy it from anyone who is not me, as the Accords state. As well you know.' Ramiro still appeared to be alone, but his confident manner said otherwise. He looked at Salicar's guards, who had all reached for their crossbows, and smiled. 'Well, it matters not. You and your men have five minutes to disappear. Without any of your contraband merchandise. Anyone that I can see after that is dead.'

'You've brass balls calling this contraband. Or have you bought letters of warrant from the Governor? Gone legit?' Salicar laughed, but Ramiro remained silent. 'I didn't think so. Brought friends then? I've brought mine.'

Salicar gestured to his four guards. He seemed to be emboldened by the fact that Ramiro hadn't done anything yet, other than make threats.

'Of course I brought my friends. Would you like to meet one?' Ramiro said.

On cue, a crossbow bolt shot out of the jungle and punched into the chest of one of Salicar's guards. He gurgled as he collapsed to the ground. Soren dropped flat to the jungle floor, curious as to how this was going to play out, but concerned by the prospect of being hit by a stray crossbow bolt. There was no way to know how many men the newcomer, Ramiro, had with him. He remained standing where he was, confident to the point of arrogance.

The whole situation could still be a well-played bluff, but Soren was not so sure that Salicar was the type of man to take that chance. He didn't have the carefree attitude that Sancho Rui or Ramiro had. He came across as a man of detail and money rather than action, and his decision would be made on the balance of risk and reward rather than the reckless pursuit of excitement.

Salicar licked his lips, his eyes flicking along the edge of the clearing into the dark jungle beyond. 'Well, Ramiro, I'm thinking that if you had enough men to take what you want, you'd have taken it by now. Why don't you and your friend fuck off.'

He showed more courage than Soren would have credited him with. Maybe Salicar was more afraid of Sancho Rui than he was of Ramiro. Still, from the expression on his face, Soren could see that Salicar was calculating everything, weighing up all of the information he had before saying or doing anything. Whichever it was, it took a certain amount of grit and Soren fully expected that more men were about to die.

Salicar and Ramiro stood in silence, staring at one another. Everyone else remained deathly still.

'Shoot him,' Salicar shouted, breaking the silence as he dived for the cover of the cart.

His guards made to fire, but a half dozen crossbow bolts flitted out of the jungle, none striking the guards, who dived for cover as soon as they realised what was happening. The cart bore the brunt of the crossbow attack, shuddering each time one of the bolts hit it. A number of the slaves fled into the jungle as soon as the volley was fired. It was probably the best chance any of them would have for freedom.

Soren had never been in a fight where he was not one of the combatants, and it felt odd sitting there while matters unfolded without his involvement. His hands were still bound, and there was a sense of helplessness that he found discomfiting. Nevertheless it was curious to be merely a spectator. He would have tried to escape there and then were it not for the fear of being mistaken for one of Salicar's men and attracting a crossbow bolt. His best chance to remain unscathed was to appear as slave-like as he could.

Salicar's men may have been used to fighting, but they had obviously not done any soldiering. Rather than work as a unit and fire at coordinated targets, they were shooting as individuals and Soren knew this spelled disaster. The attackers had been coordinated so far and if that continued they would kill off the guards and most likely Salicar.

Ramiro had drawn a sword and closed the distance to Salicar, who had also drawn his but he didn't look as though he was familiar with using it — nor did he look eager to do so.

Three men emerged from the jungle with swords drawn and moved quickly toward the cart where the guards had taken cover. Any of the slaves that had not already taken the opportunity to flee now did, leaving only Salicar's men and Soren and his unfortunate companions tied to the back of the cart.

With everyone distracted, Soren began to work furiously at the ropes binding his hands together. As the sounds of fighting filled the clearing, the knots started to loosen. He pulled his hands free of the rope but remained crouched down behind the cart with the other captives so as to continue unnoticed.

'Ramiro Qai! Did you really think I would be that foolish? That Sancho Rui would send his plunder through the jungle in contravention of the agreements signed by us in the presence of the Conclave?' a voice that was familiar to Soren said.

Sancho Rui appeared on the trail behind them with ten men at his side. Ramiro smiled broadly and lowered his sword; a grateful looking Salicar stepped back out of striking range.

'So that's what this is about. I should have known better.'

Sancho Rui nodded with a satisfied smile on his face.

'You couldn't swallow the fact that you didn't get it all your own way in the Accords,' Ramiro said. 'And of course you knew that you couldn't hope to best me at sea, so you created this little deception. Always your way, deception and cowardice when skill and bravery are found wanting.'

Sancho Rui's smile faded.

'I trust there will be no quarter?' Ramiro said.

'Sancho Rui offers no quarter, and expects none,' Rui said, his bravado clearly a contrived effort to refute the slight on his courage.

Soren was becoming irritated with the way Rui constantly referred to himself in the third person. The reasons for killing him seemed to keep mounting up. Soren also noticed that his stolen sword was strapped to Rui's waist. He had taste at least.

'Well then,' Ramiro said, 'I don't see any reason to wait around.' He pounced forward and slashed out quickly with his sword, a slightly curving single edged weapon. The attack took Salicar by surprise and was lethal. He dropped to the ground with little more than a grunt and Rui shouted for his men to attack. While Soren had been confident that Ramiro would kill Salicar and his men before, Ramiro was now heavily outnumbered. He was showing great bravado in facing likely death.

Soren's plan had been to wait until Ramiro killed Salicar and his guards before either making his escape, or killing whoever tried to stand in his way. With Sancho's arrival, Soren knew he had to play a more active role or end up tied to the back of the cart again.

Ramiro's men fired a final volley with their hand crossbows. Two bolts found their mark and the targets dropped. Sancho Rui's men charged forward, and the men that had been with Salicar made their move from the flank. It seemed as good a time as any for Soren to get involved. Soren grabbed one of Salicar's guards as he passed and smashed his head against the back of the cart. His body went limp and he dropped his sword.

Soren picked it up as the sounds of clashing steel rang in his ears. Ramiro and his men were backing up toward the tree line from which they had come, but things were not going to go well for them.

As Soren moved forward, crouched in as pathetic a fashion as he could so as not to draw any attention, he opened his mind to the Fount. The blue glow appeared, covering everything. He waited for a second, hoping that something would happen, but nothing did. The blue glow remained, coruscating benignly all around him, but he felt no different.

'What are you waiting for? Free us,' one of the other prisoners said.

Soren nodded, and putting aside his frustration, he cut each man free of the rope securing them to the cart.

'Let's get out of here,' one of the crew from the *Honest Christophe* said, as the other captives all scrabbled furiously to undo the knots that bound their hands together.

Soren made to follow but stopped. If he ran off now, he might not have another opportunity to get his sword back. He focussed his mind on the glow that he still saw, concentrating on it to the exclusion of all else, his old and distractingly dangerous method of drawing on the Fount. It hit him like a bucket of icy water, stronger than he expected, and he swore under his breath at the fact that the new method would still not let him draw on the Fount.

With the other captives gone there was nowhere for Soren to hide. Two of the pirates standing back from the fighting with Sancho Rui spotted him with sword in hand. They left their captain and rushed at Soren, striking at him from both sides, but Soren was able to parry their attacks and cut them down in one circular, sweeping movement.

Sancho Rui obviously spotted the speed and efficiency with which Soren had dispatched two of his men and backed away behind those jostling for the chance to get at Ramiro. Soren charged at him, intent on getting his sword back. Sancho pulled two of his men out in front of him and shoved them forward. It took them a second to spot Soren, but their orders were clear and they ran toward him. Soren cut through them like a scythe through dry grass. Sancho retreated further and screamed at his men, who broke away from Ramiro. They charged at Soren, who dealt with them in similar fashion to the previous pair.

Ramiro and his men stood where they were, visibly awestruck by the speed with which Soren was tearing their attackers apart. One moment they had been fighting for their lives, and the next a grotty looking captive was standing over the bloodied bodies of their foes.

The fight was intense but brief, but it had been long enough for Soren to exhaust the energy he had drawn from the Fount. Now that the effect was waning, fatigue would not be long in replacing it.

He looked around for Sancho, but not seeing him looked to the bodies at his feet, hoping that Rui had stepped back into the melee with the others and fallen to Soren's blade without him noticing. He wasn't there, and neither was Soren's sword.

Soren's disappointment was tempered with anger. He wasn't going to let Rui get away with his sword and he was equally keen to avenge Joris and his crew. He looked back down the road and along the edge of the jungle trying to decide which way Sancho had gone when the fatigue hit him. He felt dizzy and swayed on his feet as his arms felt too heavy to lift.

He heard the confident, assertive voice of Ramiro Qai say something, but he could not make out what. Strong hands gripped Soren and lifted him off his feet. Somewhere in his muddled mind it registered with him that he was being placed on the plunder cart, which trundled off a moment later.

Chapter 25
THE LAST BASTION

Soren woke just as the sun broke the horizon. He was swinging gently from side to side in a hammock, and at first he thought he was back on board the *Honest Christophe* and that everything else had been a vivid nightmare. As his sense returned, he remembered being loaded onto the cart in the jungle clearing.

He struggled against the shifting cloth of the hammock to sit up, and took a look around. The hammock was hanging from the roof of a covered porch at the front of a house in a small town. He could see the water over the rooftops and several ships at anchor out in the bay. The town was nestled between the sea and the jungle covered hills that surrounded the bay.

It was quiet. The day had not yet begun for the town's inhabitants and there were only a few people and animals shuffling about.

'You're awake.' Ramiro walked out of the house, accompanied by two other men.

'Where am I?' Soren said.

'You're in Valkdorf, and I am Captain Ramiro Qai. You are?'

'Banneret Soren.'

'Well, Banneret Soren, I didn't have the chance to thank you for your help in the jungle before you took your little turn. Things looked very bad for us until you joined in.'

Soren slipped out of the hammock and stood a little unsteadily. 'Valkdorf? Is that Ventish? Ruripathian?'

'Ruripathian,' Ramiro said. 'One of the few places that can still be called that from what I hear. This is one of their colonies, although I am given to believe that once the Governor has confirmation that the principality is no more, he'll declare himself Bayda of an independent island. That he's waited so long is something of a surprise.'

'I've not had news of the war in some time,' Soren said. 'Ruripathia is losing?'

Ramiro nodded his head.

'Did you get Sancho Rui?'

Ramiro smiled. 'Rui? No, we didn't go after him. Not today at least. As you were one of Rui's captives I could technically lay claim to you as being my property, but considering the service you've done me I won't make that claim. You're free to go.

'However,' Ramiro said, 'I'd ask you to give consideration to a proposal. I can always find a use for men as handy with a sword as you are. I'd be happy for you to join my crew. It's a good offer, so do not dismiss it lightly.'

'Your crew? You're a pirate?'

Ramiro and his men all laughed. 'Gentleman of the sea, but yes, I suppose you could call me that.'

Soren had no reason to believe that Ramiro was of a similar character to Sancho Rui, but had no interest in finding out.

'Thank you, but no,' Soren said. 'I'd like to get back to the mainland.'

'I suspected that might be your answer. You should have no difficulty in finding a ship to take you back, although it might take a week or two. The tavern, over there on the main square.'

He pointed toward the other side of the town. 'Most captains will visit it when they are here. That's the best place to find a ship. You'll find lodging there too.'

'Thank you for your help,' Soren said. He turned and started toward the tavern. He had only gone a few paces when Ramiro shouted at him.

Soren stopped.

Ramiro tossed a small coin pouch to him, and doffed his faded brown, wide brimmed hat. 'You have my thanks also. Your share of the plunder!' he said, gesturing to the pouch he had just thrown.

The other men laughed.

'If you change your mind, you know where to find me,' Ramiro shouted.

Soren nodded. As he walked, he took a look around. A solid looking, large stone building sat up on the hill a short way out of town. It was painted white, standing out from the green vegetation all around it.

The town square fronted onto the wharf, and was the only part of the town that he had seen so far to be cobbled. A number of larger, official looking buildings sat on the edge of the square, along with several warehouses closer to the shore.

The sun was above the hilltop as Soren walked across the square, and the air was warming rapidly. The gentle breeze was pleasant, carrying with it the unique fragrant quality that the Isles were known for.

Out of sight of Ramiro, Soren took a look in the little coin pouch. There were a few gold crowns inside; enough to allow Soren take a room in the tavern until he could find a ship to bring him to the mainland.

Chapter 26
A Chance Encounter

Soren was greeted by the fantastic smell of cooking food, and it reminded him of how hungry he was. It had been far too long since he last had a decent meal, and his mouth watered at the thought. He sat at the bar and waited for the tavern keeper to take his order, a large plate of sausages and eggs.

As he waited for his food, Soren looked around. After the bright warm sunlight outside, the tavern was cool and dim. There were a couple of men sitting at tables. Soren thought about Sancho Rui, and his sword and dagger. He wanted them back, but didn't see a way to get them. He could spend years chasing Rui around the sea without ever finding him. He could stay there to seek the pirate out in the hope of recovering his sword or return to Auracia to continue practicing the Gift and preparing for his revenge on Amero. It hurt to give up on his weapons, but he had higher priorities.

Hunger certainly made for the best sauce and he made short work of the large plate of food when it arrived. He ordered a second plate as another man walked into the tavern. He also sat at the bar and struck up a conversation with the barkeeper. Soren recognised the man's accent as Ruripathian.

There was something else that seemed familiar about his voice. Soren didn't want to draw attention to himself, so he tried to look at the man out of the corner of his eye. The Ruripathian was tall and slender with black hair tied back from his face, with a neatly trimmed moustache pointed at the ends, after the popular Ruripathian fashion.

On the occasion of their previous meeting the man had styled his facial hair differently, but Soren recognised him.

His name was Rodolfo Varrisher and he was one of a breed of merchant captains that were peculiar to Ruripathia. The seas around Ruripathia froze every winter and the challenge of bringing out the first and last cargoes each year had become a sport. When Soren was in Ruripathia, Captain Varrisher was fêted as the champion of dodging the sea ice. It was a position of some celebrity and the fame had gone to Varrisher's head. Soren remembered him as being obnoxious and arrogant and they had even come to blows. It was an acquaintance that Soren had no desire to remake.

Soren was faced with the difficult choice of finishing his second plate of sausages and eggs or leaving in order to avoid being seen by Captain Varrisher. The food won out and he hoped that as long as he remained hunched over his plate and kept to himself he could remain unnoticed. It had been some time since they had seen one another, and Soren's appearance was considerably different. He was scrawny, scruffy and filthy and far removed from how he had looked when he had been in Ruripathia, a well dressed, well fed Academy student with the world at his feet.

Varrisher turned his back to the bar and surveyed the taproom of the tavern. His gaze stopped on Soren, who willed himself to sink into the wooden bar counter.

'I know you, don't I?' Varrisher said.

Soren stopped mid-chew. It seemed his hopes were not to be realised.

'I don't think so, no,' Soren said. He kept looking ahead, hoping that if he avoided eye contact Varrisher might just leave him alone.

'No, I do. I'm sure of it. I'm Varrisher, Rodolfo Varrisher. We met once, at the Royal Palace in Brixen, three years ago or so as I recall. You're Tyro Soren, or were, you must be a banneret by now. I'm right, am I not?'

Seeing no reason to prolong what was clearly a futile subterfuge, Soren decided to come clean. 'Ah yes, I remember now. How are you?'

'I've been better to be honest, as appears to be the case for you too,' Varrisher said. 'The last time we met you were under the patronage of Duke Amero. I presume that's no longer the case?'

'No,' Soren said, 'we decided to go our separate ways.' He wondered if Varrisher would leave him alone if he was as rude and unforthcoming as he could be. He tried not to get his hopes up again.

'Well, I don't know if you've heard, I expect I'm the one bringing the news to the island, but Amero, the "Tyrant of Ostia" as he's being called now, is also master of Ruripathia,' Varrisher said.

This caught Soren's attention. 'Brixen's fallen?'

'Yes, two months past,' Varrisher said. He sounded dejected. There was none of the haughty arrogance that Soren remembered.

'The Royal Family?' Soren said.

While in Ruripathia, he had struck up a friendship with Princess Alys, the daughter of Prince Siegar, the hereditary ruler of Ruripathia. He hoped that she was safe, but if she had fallen into Amero's control, that was unlikely.

'I'm afraid I don't know,' Varrisher said. 'I was at sea when the war started. By the time I returned home the Ostians had blocked access to our ports. I tried running the blockade a few times, but our fleet had been defeated by then and there was little I could do; mine is not a warship, not for that type of fighting anyway. I carried dispatches to Venter seeking help, but they were unwilling, as were the Humberlanders, the Mirabayans and the Estranzans. No one wants to stand against Amero when he's not knocking on their front door.'

The conversation had already gone farther than Soren would have liked. He was sorry for what had happened in Ruripathia, and hated to think something bad had happened to Alys, but they all had their own problems, and Soren wasn't interested in hearing Varrisher's.

'When I got to Estranza, word had already arrived that Brixen had fallen. There didn't seem to be any point in going back, so I came here instead. My plan is to load up with spices once I've got some money together, take it back to the mainland — Venter probably — and try to set up my own trading company.'

'How long have you been here?' Soren said.

'On and off for a few weeks. You?'

'Just arrived.'

'I offered my services to the Governor when I first got here, but he seems to have plans of his own. When the war started all of our naval vessels were called back north, which left the Governor with a pirate problem. He seems to have negotiated a deal with one of them, which takes care of that. He doesn't want to upset things, so my ship and I are surplus to requirements. I was hoping to get work as a pirate hunter here to build up funds for my spice trading plans. No luck.'

Varrisher was being far friendlier than during their previous acquaintance, which came as a surprise. There hadn't been one boast or one slight against Soren in their conversation so far. It occurred to him that perhaps, despite his dislike of Varrisher, the man was just pleased to see a familiar face from a home and time that was now lost to him.

'You know, I feel I should apologise to you. I didn't behave well the last time we met.'

Soren had to control himself not to react with visible surprise.

'I won't make an excuse for my behaviour, but I'd only begun to establish myself as a captain and perhaps I was trying too hard to find a place for myself in court. It'd been going well enough, but when you arrived, I was quickly forgotten. I took that out on you at the time but I realised later that the court's interest flitted from novelty to novelty as often as the tide turns. After you it was someone else, and someone else after them. I'd just been the novelty of the day before you arrived, and in my naivety I thought that would last. So, please accept my apology,' Varrisher said.

Surprise compounded surprise. Soren had put up with barbs from Varrisher during his time at the Ruripathian court in Brixen. Their brief acquaintance had culminated in what had been described at the time as a friendly demonstration of differing techniques of swordplay, but had in reality been a duel that had descended into less than friendly behaviour. Soren had come out of it the better, but the apology seemed sincere.

'Apology accepted. Please also accept my apology for the part that I played,' Soren said.

'Excellent. It's all water under the bridge anyway, and now here we are sitting miles from home in a sweaty little shithole of a town. If it were later in the day, I'd drink to it!'

Soren couldn't help but laugh. Varrisher was right. The lives that both of them had seemed destined for when they had met previously were irreparably lost to them.

'Not quite where I expected to end up, but here we are,' Soren said.

'Well, I've told you my tale of woe, what misfortune brings you to Valkdorf?' Varrisher said.

Soren launched into an abridged version of the past few weeks, leaving out his visit to the Shrouded Isles and focussed on the events after the storm.

'It's interesting that you should mention Sancho Rui. What did you make of him?' Varrisher said.

'Arrogant, vicious, not as brave as he'd have you think. He murdered some good men from the ship I was on. Stole my sword. I'd very much like to have another meeting with him on more equal terms, but that's not realistic.'

Varrisher nodded. 'What are your plans now?'

'I'm going to try to find a ship that's headed for the mainland. The sooner the better,' Soren said.

'Rui's prohibited from landing on this island, which is the reason for the argument you got caught up in. Ramiro Qai made an exclusive agreement with the Governor and got all the other pirates to abide by it. The Governor turns a blind eye to Ramiro basing himself here and Ramiro doesn't harass the local trade. Anyone else gets their plunder confiscated if they're caught. It's the closest island to the mainland in the east, so it's always been a popular spot for the pirates.'

'Why's that?' Soren felt churlish for his earlier behaviour and wanted to try to make more of an effort.

'Ruripathia was never as hostile to pirates and their trade as other countries, so there are always plenty of buyers here for their plunder.'

'Rui and Qai both talked about "the Accords",' Soren said.

'After the Governor made his agreement with Qai, there was danger of a pirate war, so they sat down and signed accords that carved up the Isles between them, formed an organisation called the "Conclave", a guild for pirates. They're all allowed to stop here for water, but nothing more. How long ago did you see Rui?'

'A few hours at most, I can't say for sure.' Soren didn't want to mention the fact that he'd been unconscious.

Varrisher thought for a moment. 'Sancho Rui's been upsetting the order of things here lately and there've been rumours that trouble would flare up again. A few months ago he captured a

Shandahari ship, the *Gandawai*, that was on its way to Kirek in Shandahar. It was carrying a Shandahari princess and her wedding dowry. An absolute fortune in gold and jewels that boggles the mind. It's the biggest haul that anyone's ever heard of, and it's given Rui the wealth to start trying to muscle the other pirates off their territory.'

'Well, I hope they kill him. He's murdering scum and the fewer there are of his kind in the world, the better.'

'The Shandahari aren't too happy with him either. I've just come back from Shandahar myself,' Varrisher said. 'The Khagan of Kirek, the one meant to be marrying the princess, or "rala" as they're called there, has offered a bounty on Rui's head. A big one. I mean to claim it. It's big enough for me to buy a trade concession here in the Isles, fill my hold full of spice and sell it all for a fortune when I get to Venter. My lads are re-victualing my ship, *Typhon*, now and we set sail to hunt down Rui as soon as she's ready. With what you've told me, it sounds like we're closer to his trail than I'd hoped.'

'Good luck with it,' Soren said, suspecting that Varrisher had something more in mind.

'I could always use someone as good with a sword as you are. There'd be a share of the bounty in it for you, and after we have him, I'll drop you off at any port around the Middle Sea that you choose, with your sword safely back on your belt, of course. What do you say?'

Chapter 27
A Sailor's Life

THE SECOND OFFER IN a day — and the third offer in as many months to become a sailor. Even for someone who hated the sea it was attractive. Ramiro's had been tempting also, but Soren didn't want to be a pirate, or be associated with pirates.

His plan had been to return to the mainland and take work as a mercenary, or something along those lines that would allow him to practice the Gift in an environment where killing carried less severe consequences. He could easily do the same here, and the idea of being a pirate hunter tugged at his romantic, adventurous urges. A foolish notion, but it fit well with his desire to get his sword back. Then there was the matter of wanting to see Sancho Rui die. Amero could wait a few more months. 'How long will it take?'

'Every pirate hunter with a ship'll be after Rui now that there's a bounty on his head. As soon as I can bring him to action, I will. Any delay will let someone else grab him. I'm going to get him, and soon.'

The only factor that made Soren reluctant to agree was

that he had hated Varrisher from the instant he first met him and this opinion had held sway up until a few moments ago. Despite Varrisher's newfound affability, Soren was not entirely convinced.

'What would my share of the bounty be?' Soren said.

'As a banneret you'd be entitled to the same as an officer; one and a half shares after expenses,' Varrisher said, clearly sensing that he had Soren on the hook.

'How do we go about finding him? Are the Spice Isles a big place?'

'It only takes about five days to sail from one end to the other, but to be honest that isn't the difficulty. There are hundreds of islands, some no bigger than this room and Rui could go to ground on any of them. Any information we can get will help. You said you helped Ramiro Qai fight off Rui.'

Soren nodded.

'If Rui tried to kill him, Qai might be willing to share anything he knows with you. After what's happened, I'm sure he'll be as happy as anyone to see Rui dead. I don't know what we'll get from him, but it might be useful and anything that'll get us to Rui sooner is worth trying.'

'And if I agree to join you, you'll take me anywhere I want to go when we're done?'

Varrisher smiled. 'Absolutely anywhere. I'll deliver you to the court of the Mogul of Jahar if that's where you want to go.'

'I won't need anywhere as far as that; Auracia will do,' Soren said. 'But I have your word of honour on that?'

'You do,' Varrisher said.

'All right then. I'll join you.'

'Outstanding. Now, Ramiro Qai. Will you speak with him?'

'I'll give it a try. He seemed grateful for my help in the jungle.'

'Good. He keeps a house here, on the other side of town.'

Soren nodded. 'I know where it is.'

'His ship's still at anchor, so that's where we'll find him,' Varrisher said.

Soren finished mopping up the last scraps from his plate with a piece of bread and stood. 'Let's get going then.'

They walked across the cobbled square and toward the house. There were several tough looking men standing outside, a couple of whom had been in the jungle the night before. They were dressed in the sailor's uniform of baggy calf length trousers, loose shirt and waistcoat, and they were all heavily armed. As soon as they spotted Soren and Varrisher, they became alert and threatening.

'Whaddya want?' demanded one of them.

'I'm here to see Captain Qai,' Varrisher said.

'I'm sure you are,' the pirate said, 'but he ain't here.'

'S'all right,' one of the men said, pointing at Soren. 'He's the fella that was in the jungle with us.'

The pirate looked him up and down. 'Fine. I'll check with the cap'n. Wait here.'

He went into the house, leaving Soren and Varrisher to wait with the other pirates outside. They looked at Soren with a curiosity that was excessive for an ordinary visitor. Soren wondered what they had been told about the fight in the jungle. They didn't have to wait long. The first pirate reappeared.

'You can go in,' he said.

Both Soren and Varrisher made to go forward, but the pirate stopped Varrisher.

'No, just you,' he said to Soren. 'And you can leave the blade here,' he added, pointing to the broad bladed short-sword that Soren had picked up in the jungle and carried strapped to his waist.

Soren looked at Varrisher, who shrugged. Soren pulled the sword from his belt and handed it to the pirate, who took it and beckoned for Soren to follow him. They went into the house, leaving Varrisher to the pirates' hostile stares.

'Ah, Banneret Soren. Have you decided to take me up on my offer?' Ramiro Qai said. He sat at a small table in the centre of the room, a position that afforded him a view across the town from the single window. There was an open bottle containing a dark amber liquid sitting on the table. It was half full and accompanied by mismatched glasses.

'Please sit,' he said, gesturing to one of the other chairs.

Soren nodded and sat as Qai filled two glasses from the bottle. He slid one of them across to Soren.

'Ruripathian whisky,' he said. 'It's very good and the last of it that we're likely to see for some time.'

Soren took the glass, tipped it to Qai, and took a sip. It might have been good, it might not, but Soren wouldn't have known one way or the other.

'I'm not here to join you, I'm afraid.'

'Oh. I have to admit I'm a little disappointed. A man of your talent is of great value to a man of my profession. The question that remains is why you are here then…'

'I want some information on Sancho Rui,' Soren said. 'He has something of mine, and I want it back.' There was no need to mention the bounty, or Varrisher.

'Ah, I see,' Qai said, leaning back in his chair. 'I realise that you're new to these islands, and that you'll not be aware of how things work here. While it might appear to you that Sancho Rui is my enemy — and indeed, he is — there are certain, how should I put it, acceptable and unacceptable practices. If I were to give you any information about a brother member of the Conclave I would be in breach of the Accords of membership of the Conclave. You are aware of what the Conclave is?' Qai said.

'Yes, I am.'

'Cenceno, my bo'sun tells me that you're here with Captain

Varrisher. Captain Varrisher has spent the last few days here asking about Captain Rui and telling anyone that will listen that he's going to kill him and take his head to Shandahar. I assume he's made you a more attractive offer than I did. If I'm seen helping you with this in mind, it will not reflect well on me,' Qai said.

Soren silently cursed Varrisher. It seemed that old habits die hard and Varrisher still tended toward courting attention wherever he could get it. 'Our goals are the same for the time being, and I wasn't lying to you when I said that Rui has something that belongs to me. Varrisher's reasons are his own, mine are as I've told you.'

Qai looked thoughtfully at his glass of whiskey for a moment. He swirled the contents and took a sip. 'If I furnish information about a member of the Conclave to one outside of it, I breach my accords. Enemy or not, if I were to do this, the other members of the Conclave would view me with the same disfavour that they currently have for Sancho Rui. He's our problem and we will deal with him in our own way. That is the rule of the Conclave, one of the tenets of the Accords that we all signed.

'There's something else that I can tell you though, which can be considered common knowledge, but may not be known to you and Captain Varrisher as newcomers. It's no secret that the Conclave has divided the Isles up into territories, where each member of the Conclave has the exclusive right to operate. Rui is not happy that he cannot land in Valkdorf.'

'I know that it's considered the best place to unload plunder in the Isles,' Soren said.

'More so, with the war. The Ostians have always policed the coast as far as the border with Shandahar to protect their merchants. Now though, all of those warships are in the North, and the mainland coast is fertile ground much farther north than it ever was before. Rui was the first of us to realise it. Sailing back and forth between his territory in the western isles and the east coast takes time; time that could be spent plundering merchant ships.' Ramiro paused and smiled, not continuing until he was sure that Soren had heard what he had just said.

Soren realised what Qai was doing. The western isles. He hoped it would mean more to Varrisher than it did him. It was a circuitous way of doing things, but would allow Qai deny having informed on Rui. He nodded and smiled.

'If Rui had managed to kill me with his ambush, this island would have been free for all to use, at least until the Conclave could meet again and reassess the territories, when he would undoubtedly have claimed it. He's already done well cruising the Auracian coast but when he took a Shandahari ship recently, he put all of that to shame. With that much wealth he's a threat to everyone in the Conclave. For now though, I expect he will return to his own waters to plan his next move.' Ramiro paused again for a moment and smiled.

'I'm sorry I couldn't be of any help to you, Banneret. While I'm in your debt for the assistance you gave me, my hands are tied on this issue. I will demand my rights under the Accords from the Conclave, and we'll soon be seeking him out also. He's broken our accords and we'll kill him for it. I'll use all of my not inconsiderable influence to ensure this happens. If you get in our way, you will be shown no quarter.'

'I think I understand you, Captain Qai,' Soren said. 'Thank you for taking the time to see me.' He drained the last of the whiskey and left.

Varrisher was much in the same position, standing uncomfortably under the hostile gaze of the pirates, who regarded him with something akin to hungry intent.

'Well?' said Varrisher.

'Nothing, I'm afraid,' Soren said, as they started back toward the tavern but while they were still within earshot of the guards around Qai's house.

Varrisher cursed, but as soon as they were far enough away not to be overheard, Soren continued.

'He's headed for his base in the western isles. Ramiro as much as told me, but couldn't say it outright.'

'Well, that's better than nothing. West it is. There are still a lot of islands, and a lot of sea to cover, but at least we know what direction to go. Pirates tend to stick near the main shipping channels where there's plenty of prey, and men like Sancho Rui draw quite a bit of attention to themselves wherever they go,' Varrisher said.

Soren reflected that they weren't the only ones.

'I have to call in on Governor dal Sifridt — or the Bayda as I'm sure he'll be calling himself before too much longer. I haven't sailed much farther west in the Isles than we are now, so I'm hoping he may be able to help with some rutters — navigators' notes — and perhaps some warrants. Technically he's still an agent of the Ruripathian crown, whatever that may be now, and he might give me letters of marque, which'll come in useful if we encounter any of the western navies. Seeing as you're an Ostian, it might be better if you wait at the tavern and I see the Governor on my own.'

Chapter 28
THE CLOTHES MAKE THE MAN

Soren spent the rest of the morning wandering about the town. After having spent so much time locked in the cramped filth and stench of the brig on the *Bayda's Tear*, there was a great pleasure to be taken from the sunlight and fresh air, and the endless view across the turquoise and ultramarine sea.

The sounds of the port faded into the background as he sat by the wharf. He leaned back against a thick, coiled anchor cable and closed his eyes. It seemed that only a few seconds had passed when he heard Varrisher's voice. He was carrying a bulging leather folder.

'I was right, it's Bayda dal Sifridt now. He was very helpful though. He's as eager as anyone to keep the pirates under control. Doesn't want anything to threaten his new title I expect. I've letters of marque under his seal as crown representative of Ruripathia and under his own seal as Bayda of Valkdorf as well as some rutters that were confiscated from pirates. I don't know how reliable they'll be, but they're better than nothing.'

Soren felt a building excitement at the prospect of this new adventure. He was not fond of ships, but the idea of being a pirate hunter — of getting rich and visiting exotic places — was winning him over and pushing the darker thoughts from his mind. They were not forgotten, but they could wait.

'He also told me that a ship has just arrived with some Ruripathian refugees. I'm going to head out to it to see if anyone wants to sign on with the *Typhon*, but it shouldn't take long. Other than that there's no reason to dally here any longer. Each hour we remain lets Rui get farther away and harder to find. The *Typhon* should be fully provisioned by now. Is there anything else that you need to do before we leave?' Varrisher said.

'Well, I've nothing but the clothes on my back; it would be nice to have some more options in that regard. And I'll need a new sword. This... thing,' he held up the crude cutlass that Ramiro's bo'sun had returned to him after he left, 'isn't much better than scrap.'

Varrisher looked at the cutlass. 'Yes,' he said as he pulled a small coin purse from his pocket. 'The sword I can provide you with from the weapon store on the *Typhon*. There're plenty of decent Ruripathian blades there, I expect you'll find one that suits you. The clothes I can't help you with, beyond giving you some money and pointing you in the direction of the general store beside the inn. Make sure to get something suitable for life on board a ship though; fine city fashions don't tend to last long on a man-o'-war. The jolly boat will be waiting at the jetty in thirty minutes. Get what you need and come straight out to the *Typhon*.'

―――◆―――

Soren left Varrisher and made his way to the general store. Varrisher had given him far more than he thought he would need, given his expectations of what a store in a small town would have available. What greeted him came as a surprise; a shop stuffed with what Soren believed to be the latest fashions, and cluttered with crates likely to be containing more of the same.

'Can I help you?' a voice from the back of the shop said. A tired looking man came into view and made his way forward.

'I need some new clothes,' Soren said.

The man looked him up and down. 'Yes, you do. Did you have anything in mind?'

'I need some sea-going clothes. I thought two sets, and one set of shore clothes. Nothing too fancy.'

'Come this way, I'll show you what I have,' the man said.

He led Soren toward the back of the shop, which was a single story wooden building that was longer than it was wide.

'I have to say, the amount of stock you have comes as something of a surprise,' Soren said.

'A few months ago there was hardly anything at all. Things are changing fast here though and I intend to keep up.' He walked along the shelves, picking up things as he went. 'These should fit,' he said, handing the lot to Soren. 'You'll want to try them for size. You can go back there.' He gestured to a wooden partition that jutted out from the wall and had a curtain hanging from a rail at its front.

'So why all the stock?' Soren said, as he stripped out of the rags that he was wearing.

'Lots of refugees coming into Valkdorf. This is the only bit of Ruripathia left. The population has trebled in the last few months. I expect there'll be even more coming the way things are. Aristocrats are starting to arrive too. With plenty of money. If I don't meet the increased demand, someone else will.'

He stuffed a jacket past the curtain, which Soren took.

'Of course that fool Governor will have some questions to answer when there are enough of them here to take him to task. He's just taken to calling himself Bayda! Thinks this is his own personal kingdom. Gods help him if any of the royal family turn up here. Although I expect they'll go somewhere more civilised, Venter or Humberland maybe, if they managed to get out of Ruripathia that is. How do they fit?'

Soren walked out of the changing cubicle. 'Fine. I'll wear this set now if that's all right.'

'Thought you might say that,' the shopkeeper said. 'It's not a problem.'

He managed to get everything he needed well within his budget and made it down to the dock with time to spare. Varrisher was waiting for him in the jolly boat, along with two sailors who were sitting at the oars. Soren walked down the wharf and threw his bag of clothes into the boat ahead of him.

'Well, a few more days in the sun and you'll certainly look the part.' Varrisher shouted. 'Jump aboard.'

Soren stepped down into the boat. It rocked under his weight, putting him further off balance. He sat on the wooden bench beside Varrisher in as graceful a fashion as he could manage. The two oarsmen wasted little time in casting off and pulling away toward the ships at anchor in the bay.

Soren handed the coin purse with the remaining money to Varrisher, who weighed it as discreetly as he could before tucking it away. Soren turned his attention to the ships at anchor, wondering which was Varrisher's.

Chapter 29
THE TYPHON

The Typhon was a medium sized vessel of noticeably sleeker lines than the others at anchor. Varrisher told Soren that it had been a fast cargo ship before he'd decided to become a pirate hunter. It had been used for high value cargoes and a premium had been placed on speed and manoeuvrability rather than capacity. These were two qualities that made it perfect for Varrisher's new career path.

Soren was glad the sea was still relatively calm as they bumped alongside the *Typhon's* hull. Getting from boat to ship and vice-versa was a skill he had not yet acquired and he risked a swim each time he did it. Not a good first impression to make with a crew.

The oarsmen had shipped their oars and were busy stowing them when the crew on the deck above dropped a rope ladder down. Varrisher scaled it nimbly with a sure-footedness that Soren knew he wouldn't be able to match. He lunged for the ladder, hoping to keep the forward momentum going long enough to get a firm hold on the top of the bulwark above. All his sudden movement did however was push the jolly boat away from the side of the *Typhon* and it was a lucky grab of the ladder that stopped him plunging into the water.

He dangled from the ladder for a moment until his body stopped swinging, then started climbing. As he neared the top two pairs of hands reached over the top and took a firm hold of his arms, then hoisted him over the side.

The experience was embarrassing, although nobody seemed to take any notice. Nonetheless, Soren felt it would take a little effort to earn the respect of his fellow *Typhon*s after it.

Soren took a good look about to get a sense of his new surroundings. *Typhon's* transformation from fast cargo carrier to man-o'-war was clear from the rows of ballistae that lined the bulwarks of her upper deck. They were fierce, heavy looking constructions of wood, firmly bolted down to the deck. The bow arms were sprung with steel and the thick cords that would propel the missiles were covered with leather sheaths to protect them from the elements.

Varrisher spoke briefly with one of the other sailors, a squat, muscular man in a grey jacket of a similar cut to the one that Soren had just purchased. The squat man barked orders to several other sailors and a block and tackle system was quickly rigged up to haul the jolly boat on board.

Soren carried his newly purchased clothing in a burlap sack that, to his surprise, was dry despite his awkward boarding. Varrisher beckoned for Soren to follow him as sailors climbed into the rigging and dropped the sails from the yards. He could feel the ship come to life under his feet as the anchor broke free from the bottom, and the first of the lowered sails filled with breeze. The process had been fast and seemed effortless; Soren hadn't expected that they would get underway so quickly.

The *Typhon* was far more akin to a thoroughbred horse than the carthorse-like *Honest Christophe*. There was something exhilarating about the way it responded to the wind and for the first time he could understand the appeal of being a sailor. Varrisher had taken the wheel and Soren could see the pleasure that he took in pressing the *Typhon* against the wind to drive her forward.

As they stretched away from the shore, the previously flat sea took on a more rolling nature and the *Typhon* raced down the waves and clawed her way back up the other side as it pushed on across the water as fast as a horse at a canter. There was an immense sense of power in the vessel as it surged forward, its rigging taut and its sails full. Everyone aboard had a job to do but Soren, and he very quickly felt the odd man out as he stood on the deck concentrating on keeping his balance.

Varrisher had slipped into another world, and was all consumed by the marriage of wind, wood and sea. Soren felt uncomfortable interrupting him from his reverie so he tried to find an out of the way place close to a firm handhold and remained there.

The breeze grew stronger as the day went on and the *Typhon* felt as though she was beginning to fly at times. Eventually Varrisher relinquished the wheel to the squat sailor. He spotted Soren with the expression of a man who realises he has forgotten something important.

'I'm sorry,' he said. 'I was so eager to get going I forgot about you. There are more than enough experienced hands on board to manage the ship. I want you along for when the fighting starts, so I don't want you risking broken bones while you're learning to be a sailor. You're welcome to rest in my stateroom, or stay here and enjoy the sailing if you prefer. I'd also like you to do some weapons drills with the crew, but we can discuss that a little later.'

Soren realised that his knuckles were white on the tarred rigging he was gripping onto for dear life, despite enjoying the experience of the lively ship. He gratefully took Varrisher up on his offer and went below.

Soren awoke to the gentle rolling motion of the *Typhon*. He was sprawled out on the couch by the gallery window at the back of Varrisher's stateroom, where he had sat down intending to remain for only a few minutes. It was getting dark outside, so he had slept for several hours. He was still groggy, but he made his way out onto the deck, which was still a hive of activity. Soren felt guilty for sleeping while they all worked. When the time came to train them, he would have to prove his worth and ensure he had their confidence and trust before they went into a fight together.

He walked up the few steps onto the quarterdeck where Varrisher stood next to the sailor at the wheel.

'Ah, Soren, this is Sailing Master Rodin, my first mate,' Varrisher said.

Rodin nodded politely but didn't take his hands off the wheel.

Varrisher looked to the horizon and Soren followed his gaze. There was a sail that seemed to be heading in their direction.

'We spotted her about ten minutes ago,' Varrisher said. 'It's not Rui, I'm afraid. Judging by her rigging, she's a merchant through and through. Still, if we can get within hailing distance she might have useful information.'

'How long till we're close enough?' Soren said.

'Less than half an hour. If her master's worth his salt, he'll recognise us as a man-o'-war. What he won't know is if we're a pirate or otherwise. He might try to run, but if he knows what he's about he'll realise that'd be a waste of time. Pirates tend to go easier on those that don't cause them too much difficulty. Either way, I don't plan on chasing him.'

※

Varrisher's estimate proved to be accurate. As they came closer to one another, Varrisher had a number of signal flags hoisted. They seemed to have the desired effect as the merchant ship began to take in its sails and slow accordingly. Varrisher did likewise and the two ships coasted to within shouting distance of one another. Varrisher went to the bulwark with a speaking trumpet.

'*Typhon*, out of Valkdorf,' he shouted.

'*Fair Kateryn*, out of Callham,' a voice from the other ship shouted back.

'You're a long way south,' Varrisher shouted.

Soren vaguely recalled Callham being a port in Humberland, many miles to the northwest.

'First run of the season. Thought we'd try to get an early start.' He was being canny with the information he was giving out, obviously wary of the *Typhon*'s intentions.

'We're on the lookout for a ship that may have sailed past you. Corvette rigged, captained by a pirate called Sancho Rui,' Varrisher shouted.

'I've heard of Rui, but I've not seen his ship. We saw smoke coming from the last island back. Looked like it was coming from Martensport. We gave it a wide berth.'

Varrisher digested the information for a moment. 'Thank you, *Fair Kateryn*, a safe voyage home to you!'

The man doffed his hat to Varrisher. Varrisher barked an order to his crew and without missing a beat they were swarming up into the rigging to get the *Typhon* back under way.

'I know Martensport; we should be there not long after dawn. I'll show you to the weapons locker so you can pick something out. We may have a fight on our hands when we arrive.'

Chapter 30
MARTENSPORT

SOREN SLEPT SOLIDLY THROUGH the night. He awoke to the noise of commotion on deck, and the feeling of the ship at rest. He picked up the two swords that he had chosen from the weapons locker and tested their balance in his hand. One was a rapier. It was a mass produced weapon, but the blade was well crafted, and he reckoned it would serve him well.

The other was a short, broad bladed sword similar to the one that he had been using since the jungle, but of far better manufacture. He decided to take it too. In the event of having to fight in the cramped conditions below decks the shorter weapon would be more effective.

He went up on deck where the crew were securing the ship for sitting at anchor. They were not far from the shoreline and the smouldering ruin of the town that had been called Martensport.

'It wasn't much before, just a collection point for the local farmers to drop off their produce to be picked up by passing traders. No more than a dozen or so buildings, fifty, sixty residents. We should go ashore, see if there are any survivors. Maybe they can tell us if it actually was Rui who called here,' Varrisher said.

From the look of it, Soren doubted there would be anything worth finding, but disagreeing with Varrisher in front of his crew didn't seem like a smart thing to do.

The crew lowered the jolly boat into the water and Soren, Varrisher and two sailors got on board. They were not concerned about having a fight; there was no sign of Rui's ship and they didn't expect to find him or any of his men still there, if indeed it had been him that burned the town.

The sailors rowed them to the jetty, which appeared to be the only thing not touched by the fire. They disembarked, Soren being careful not to make a spectacle of himself, and made their way to the remains of the small town. There was very little left; every building had been put to fire, and few of them were made from brick.

'Have a look around,' Varrisher said to the two sailors. He turned to Soren. 'I don't expect we'll find anything, but you never know. We might as well have a bit of a poke around and then get back to the ship. If Rui stopped here then he'll have lost some of his lead on us, but there's no point in squandering any gains we might have made.'

Soren nodded and began walking toward one side of the town, looking into each of the still smouldering ash piles that were all that remained of the buildings. They had only been burned a few hours before. If it was Rui who attacked the town, everything of value that he could carry would have been taken, and anything else would have been burned. Including the corpses. He had not seen any, but like as not they were under the piles of ash that would have been their homes or places of work. It reminded him of the savagery of a barbarian attack he had seen several years before. There seemed little sense in all of that destruction.

'Captain,' one of the sailors called out. He was kicking through the ash on the other side of the town. Soren looked in his direction. A group of horsemen watched them from the tree line behind the village. There were about twenty of them. They might take it into their heads that Soren, Varrisher and the two sailors were the pirates who had destroyed the town and slaughtered its inhabitants.

'Ho there, friend,' Varrisher called, raising a hand in greeting and stepping toward them.

It was a risky move, but given the circumstances there weren't many options available to him. If the men chose to attack, they would most likely kill Varrisher and his two men before Soren could get close enough to help.

'Stay where you are!' came the response. It had the accent of a Ventishman, which was unsurprising as the island was a colony of Venter. 'Who are you and what's your business here?'

'I'm Captain Varrisher of the *Typhon*. I'm chasing a pirate and we wanted to investigate,' he shouted back, having stopped in his tracks as commanded.

The riders remained silent for a moment before three of them rode forward. As innocuously as possible, Soren started walking slowly toward Varrisher. The riders moved cautiously, but they didn't appear hostile.

'You will find nothing of interest. All of the survivors have been removed to safety and all that remains here is ash,' said the rider in the centre of the three. 'I am Captain Avert Hayck of the Carellen militia. We saw your ship sail into the bay and came down to investigate.'

He looked tall, although on horseback it was difficult to tell. He wore a military style tunic that looked at least one size too small — the same as the other two men with him, although theirs were too large — and he had a ruddy face topped with a mop of sweaty, straw coloured hair.

'How long ago was the attack?' Varrisher said.

'Yesterday, late in the afternoon and they were gone before dark. They were sailing out of the bay by the time we got here,' Captain Hayck said.

'Do you've any idea of where they were headed?' Varrisher said.

Captain Hayck looked at one of his companions and then back to Varrisher. 'The Commissioner's plantation isn't far from here. The survivors are there. They might be able to tell you more.'

Soren joined Varrisher. He made sure to keep his hand away from the hilt of his sword. Varrisher was obviously uncomfortable with the notion of going with them. It had been their intention to get back to sea as quickly as possible and there was still no reason to trust the bona fides of the horsemen. Settlers got funny notions after they or their ilk were attacked, and sometimes any stranger they could lay their hands on would serve for their version of justice. Soren had seen it before in the plains to the east of Ostia and had no desire to find himself on the receiving end of that type of anger-fuelled justice.

Varrisher looked to Soren who shrugged his shoulders. There was no way to tell if these men intended to do them harm, but with their greater numbers it would have been as easy for them to do it there rather than luring them into the jungle. They might find out something useful from the survivors of the attack.

'Very well,' Varrisher said. 'We'll come with you to the plantation.'

'We have no extra horses, so you'll have to walk. It's not that far, just out of sight beyond the promontory at the end of the bay,' Captain Hayck said, gesturing.

'First I need to send word back to my ship to let them know what we're doing,' Varrisher said.

Captain Hayck nodded. 'We'll wait for you by the trees.'

Varrisher called over the other two sailors and talked with them for a moment before they headed in the direction of the jolly boat, and Varrisher returned his attention to Soren.

'Well,' he said. 'What do you think?'

'I think it's worth the risk.'

'That's what I thought,' Varrisher said. 'I'm not sure we have any choice anyway. I suppose we'd best be getting on after them then.'

They walked over to the waiting riders who moved off at a trot when Varrisher and Soren reached them.

It took less than an hour to reach the plantation house, which sat on top of the promontory that Hayck had pointed out to them from the ruins of Martensport. It was a fine, stone building, with a white gravel driveway and was surrounded with lush green bushes covered with purple flowers.

The sound of the twenty horsemen on the gravel driveway attracted some attention and several people appeared from the gabled portico. Two were armed, two were servants or perhaps slaves, and one, with a thick moustache and slicked back, grey hair, was finely dressed, probably the master of the house.

'Captain, what do you have to report?' the finely dressed man said.

'It doesn't seem to have been a pirate ship, Excellency,' Captain Hayck said. 'I've brought her master to speak with you.'

At this cue, Varrisher stepped forward. 'Master Mariner of the Grey, Captain Rodolfo Varrisher. To whom do I have the honour of speaking?' he said, formally.

'Baron Pitir dal Froyt,' the finely dressed man said, 'Commissioner of Martensport. I was not aware gentlemen of the grey still existed.'

'Well, that's a matter of opinion,' Varrisher said, 'but it's not relevant to the matter at hand.' He said it politely, but there was an edge to his voice.

'Perhaps you might tell me what is of relevance to your being on Carellen then. But not here, it's getting unpleasantly warm. We can discuss it inside,' dal Froyt said.

Without waiting for an answer he turned on his heel and disappeared into the shade of the portico, followed closely by the two armed men. One of the men that Soren had taken for a servant or slave rushed forward and beckoned for them to follow. The other assisted Captain Hayck as he dismounted. The three of them followed the servant into the house.

Soren felt oddly self-conscious about his dusty shoes and sailing slops as they walked through the immaculately clean house. He regretted he had not had the chance to change into the shore-going clothes he had bought and realised how far he had come from the youth who had judged clothes by how warm they would keep him in winter. It was an odd feeling, but it proved the effects of an expensive education.

The servant led them through to a long room at the far side of the house. It was lined with large windows that provided a spectacular view of an ornamental garden and the sea beyond. The house was bright and airy, with a cool breeze passing through which was a pleasant change after the walk up to the house from the smoking ruin of Martensport. The Commissioner had sat down at a writing table in a comfortable looking chair that gave him full advantage of the view from the windows. There were no chairs for the others to sit, and no apology was made for the fact.

'Now, tell me, Captain Varrisher, what is it that brings you to Carellen so soon after a pirate attack,' Commissioner dal Froyt said. 'Hoping to pick at the scraps left behind?'

'Far from it. We got word that there was a lot of smoke coming from this island. I estimated that we were roughly twelve hours behind the pirate that we're tracking, so it stood to reason that he might have been involved in the attack.'

'You're a pirate hunter? I assume you have documentation?' the Commissioner said.

'I do,' Varrisher said. 'Letters of marque to sail under the flag of Ruripathia and also the Bayda of Valkdorf.'

'The Bayda of Valkdorf? Is that what Governor dal Sifridt is calling himself now?' the Commissioner said, with a chuckle. 'Perhaps I should take to calling myself something a little grander, eh, Hayck?'

Captain Hayck forced a smile but said nothing.

'Well, as you say, Commissioner, the continued existence of Ruripathia as a sovereign state is a matter of conjecture now. He wanted to provide us with as much legitimate authority to carry out our task as he could,' Varrisher said. 'Time is something of an issue, Commissioner, so I would appreciate any information you might have on the attackers so we can be on our way.'

'Do you have these letters on your person?' the Commissioner said.

'No, they're on board my ship. I wasn't expecting to need them considering the condition we found Martensport in,' Varrisher said.

The Commissioner sighed and drummed his fingers on the writing desk. 'Very well. Several of the survivors of the attack reported that they overheard the pirates talking about Caytown. They didn't know any more than that, but I would venture that with Caytown's reputation, it's not unreasonable to assume that it is the next destination of the savages that burned the town. From the descriptions given, I believe the pirate that attacked us was Sancho Rui, who I presume is the man you are pursuing.'

Varrisher nodded.

'I'm afraid that's all I can tell you that might be of assistance. The attack was particularly well timed. Martensport was the collection point from which all of the spice and sugar grown on this side of the island was brought for shipment north. This season's harvest was collected only two days ago, and there was a considerable amount of gold in storage there awaiting division among the plantation owners.

'I'm very eager that Sancho Rui be brought to a swift and

painful end and have already sent letters to the Governor of Carellen to issue warrants for Rui's arrest.' There was venom in the Commissioner's voice.

'Thank you for your help, Commissioner,' Varrisher said, 'I would ask your leave to continue our pursuit.'

Chapter 31
THE PURSUIT

Having never been involved in a naval pursuit, Soren was amazed by the unrelenting pace that Varrisher kept up. He'd slept only for an hour or two at a time since they had been at sea. Every time that Soren had gone on deck, Varrisher had been there, conferring with whoever was at the wheel, usually Rodin, or was helming the *Typhon* himself. He derived a manic energy from driving his ship on and eking every ounce of speed out of her that he could. He was never satisfied, and constantly called for minor alterations to the trim of the sails. Soren wondered how the crew tolerated the constant hectoring; no sooner had they made one change than another was called for. They did it though, without grumble or complaint.

The *Typhon* raised anchor no more than three hours after it had been dropped and once again she leaned into the breeze and pressed on like the thoroughbred she was. Varrisher had referred to the rutters he had been given to plot a course to Caytown. They were farther west than he had hitherto been in the Spice Isles, and he approached the matter of sailing in unknown waters with intense concentration. The town was on an island a little more than two days' sail away, but it was through waters that the rutters indicated were heavily populated with small islands. It was not so much the islands that were of concern to Varrisher as the shoals, sandbars and reefs lurking out of sight below the surface that were also common features.

Nonetheless, Soren was once again surplus to requirements, so he retired to the stateroom. The fatigue of the past few weeks still weighed heavily on him, and combined with the regular motion of the ship and the comfortable couch, he quickly slipped into a light, dozing sleep that was full of vivid dreams.

He dreamt that Alessandra was calling him, but it was dark and he couldn't find her. He was in a state of panic as he tried to work out where her voice was coming from, but each time he started to run in one direction her voice would come from somewhere else.

She screamed and he jolted awake, but the sound was still there. As the cloud of sleep departed he realised that the sound was an insidious screeching, grinding noise that reverberated through the timbers of the hull. It was dark outside, so he had been asleep for several hours. Soren wanted nothing more than to curl up and try to shake the sensations that he had been left with from his head, but something was going on and he couldn't ignore it.

Varrisher stumbled from his small sleeping compartment on the port side of the stateroom, doing up his doublet with the clumsiness of one who has just been pulled abruptly from a deep sleep.

'What's going on?' Soren said.

'Dunno,' Varrisher grunted, 'but it doesn't sound healthy.'

Soren followed him up the three steps out the doorway that led onto the main deck, before turning and ascending the final steps up onto the quarterdeck where the wheel was. Rodin was at the wheel with a grim expression on his face.

'What's happened?' Varrisher said.

'We touched bottom. A reef by the sounds of it, but we're sailin' free now,' Rodin said. He was usually a cheerful man, but his face bore no trace of good humour now.

Varrisher rubbed his face with both hands. 'All right, get some men down below to inspect for damage.'

'Already done, Captain,' Rodin said.

'I feared something like this would happen. We've been pushing on too bloody hard in unknown waters, when the one thing we did know was that the area is cluttered with sandbanks and reefs. It's lucky we didn't hit whatever it was at low water, otherwise we might still be stuck on the bloody thing.'

Soren didn't think he had ever heard Varrisher swear before, and part of him was curious to see how he acted now that things were not going his way. Would the Varrisher he had known in Ruripathia resurface?

A sound all too familiar to Soren disturbed the night's peace as the clanking sound of a ship's pump began to rattle across the deck. It sent a shiver down his spine as he thought of the night and day struggle to save the *Honest Christophe*.

'Well, that answers the question of if we've been holed,' Varrisher said. He went forward as two men came up the companionway steps, the opening of which was between the fore and main masts. They conferred for a moment before Varrisher came back up onto the quarterdeck.

'We've sprung a couple of planks,' he said.

Soren noted that Varrisher did not sound particularly concerned, but his own face must have betrayed that he was.

'It's a pretty common occurrence for ice runners, so there's no need to be too worried. I've dealt with worse before and lived to tell the tale.'

He still seemed remarkably calm, if anything revelling in the situation. Soren began to wonder if he was slightly cracked; too many years at sea, too little sleep. Whatever the reason, Soren didn't see how a large hole in the bottom of the boat was nothing to get too concerned about.

Varrisher could see that Soren wasn't convinced, so he elaborated. 'The ship's hull is specially designed to cope with being holed and still remain afloat. *Typhon* also has two sets of pumps, one of which would be more than enough to service an oceanman, so we're not likely to have a problem clearing any water we take on. The problem that we do have is a great bloody hole in the hull slows us down considerably, and best counsel is to avoid pootling about too much when you have one. I'm afraid we're going to have to beach her to repair the damage as soon as we can.'

'How long's that going to take?'

'We're lucky that we're on a flood tide, which means if we can find a suitable beach in the next couple of hours, we can hove down straight away,' Varrisher said.

'Hove down?' Soren constantly felt like an idiot when he was on board ships. Sailors seemed to have a language all of their own.

'A true mariner will never admit to intentionally running his vessel aground, so we just call it something different. Basically, we ground *Typhon* on a soft, sandy beach at high tide, take lines from the top of the mast, the halyards, secure them to some trees or rocks and winch them down so when the tide goes out, the damaged area of the hull is exposed and we can patch it up. I've sent men aloft to keep a look out for somewhere suitable and there are so many small islands hereabouts it won't be too difficult to find one.'

'That doesn't sound too complicated,' Soren said.

'Well that's the condensed version, but we carry everything we need to do the repair on board, so long as it's not too extensive.'

'And how long?' Soren said, trying to bring the subject back to his original question.

'We're at the mercy of the tide. We can only work on the

damage while enough of the hull is exposed, which will be no more than three hours or so at a time. I really won't know how many hours of work will be needed until I see just how bad it is. Two tides minimum though, which means we won't be floating off until tomorrow morning at the earliest. That's assuming we manage to find somewhere suitable before this tide turns. If we don't, you can add at least another twelve hours,' Varrisher said.

'Lots of uncertainty then,' Soren said, distracted by the dream he had been having, which still felt real to his groggy mind.

'Yes,' Varrisher said. 'Such is the way of the sea. I'm as keen to get my hands on Rui as you are. Right now my future plans are entirely dependent on getting the bounty on his head. Rest assured that we'll deal with this as quickly as we can.'

Ferrata had watched the docks at Auracia each day since returning to the city. It was the same tactic that he employed in Voorn, and he was beginning to see that it was flawed. However, when someone moved about as much as Soren did there were few ways to keep track of them.

One of the *Honest Christophe*'s sailors was less than guarded with his tongue after a few drinks, and Ferrata had been able to learn that Soren had been on the *Honest Christophe*, but had disembarked for the Shrouded Isles. The mention of the Shrouded Isles came as a surprise, and made Ferrata wonder if Soren had a death wish. Ferrata couldn't help but wonder what it was that drew him there, but it didn't matter.

All that interested Ferrata was the fact that they were collecting Soren on their return to Auracia. Another trip across the Middle Sea and now he was loitering by the docks in Auracia waiting for a ship to come in. Again. At least the weather was better. Several days overdue, even taking into account their detour, and it looked as though the *Honest Christophe* wasn't going to arrive.

With all of the stories surrounding the Isles, it was possible that neither Soren, nor the *Honest Christophe* would ever be seen again. This would make it very difficult for Ferrata to collect the bounty. Failing to kill an ordinary man would also be bad for Ferrata's reputation. Give me a duke and I'll give you a corpse, he thought, but an ordinary man? It explained why the price on Soren's head was so high at least, but it was frustrating.

As though the involvement of cursed islands wasn't enough, there was also talk of a ferocious storm that had swept down from the north and wrecked a number of ships, damaging several more. Ferrata was lucky that his ship had arrived in Auracia before it hit.

There was a third story, and that one was far more interesting. Of the ships that had managed to make it back to Auracia after the storm, several of them had spoken of being chased by a pirate ship that was preying on vessels crippled by the bad weather. If it was true, Ferrata rather admired the captain's initiative. It might also mean that Soren was headed for a pirate sanctuary in the Spice Isles, rather than providing food for fish, or whatever was on the Shrouded Isles.

So much uncertainty, so much frustration. He would think twice before taking another high price contract on anyone but the aristocracy or merchant elite, people whose greed tied them to a particular place.

Ferrata groaned. Another sea voyage was the last thing he wanted, but there was no rest for the wicked, and he most certainly was that.

Chapter 32
THE RECEDING TIDE

It was an hour before the call rang out from aloft that land had been sighted. The pumps still clattered away, spewing water over the side, but they didn't need to be worked nearly as hard as the one on the *Honest Christophe*.

The clear sky and full moon meant visibility was good. He could see a stretch of white sand not far from where they were. The small waves breaking on its shore twinkled in the moonlight. It seemed Varrisher deemed this spot suitable for their purpose, as the *Typhon* lurched as he steered directly for it.

The performance of the ship was noticeably worse since the holing. Varrisher had shortened sail to slow her speed so they took on less water, whilst still allowing them to make their way to a safe beach. She no longer felt as lively, lumbering each time her course was altered rather than pouncing as she had before.

They shortened sail until the *Typhon* was moving at a snail's pace, creeping ever closer to the shore. As the beach grew near, Varrisher called out for all hands to brace themselves. Soren was pitched forward as the ship made contact with the sand, but it was not nearly as abrupt or violent as he had been preparing himself for. Her momentum continued to drive her on until she came to a halt. It felt odd. Soren had become used to the gentle pitching of her deck but now she was held firmly in place by the sand.

'Lower the jolly boat,' Varrisher shouted.

There were a couple feet of water still surrounding the *Typhon*. Long planks of wood had already been brought up from the hold and secured to the larboard bulwark, ready to be lowered to carry out the repairs. The crew lowered lines from the masthead into the jolly boat, to be rowed ashore and secured to whatever could be found. This done, they set about removing everything from the hold of the ship. There was only the food and water for the crew and whatever sail cloth, cordage and lumber were required to effect running repairs. Nonetheless, it was back breaking work. It took several trips and the ship had to be unloaded before she lost the support of the surrounding water and could be winched down onto one side. Once this was done, all that was left was to wait for the tide to go out and allow the real work to begin.

The receding tide brought bad news. A neat rent had been sliced in the hull on the starboard side of the keel. It ran for several feet and had destroyed a number of the planks that curved toward the bow. Soren wasn't sure how severe this was in the grand scheme of things, but from Varrisher's expression he could see that this would not be a quick patch job. While Varrisher discussed the matter with the ship's carpenter, Soren sloshed forward through the warm, ankle deep water to have a closer look at the damage.

With the ship pulled down onto its larboard side, the hole in the hull was several feet above him. The boarding ladder had been laid over the side and Soren climbed up a few steps for a better view. Where the wood had been cut, there was a residue of a white shell-like material crushed into small pieces; the remains of the reef that had gouged the hole. He dropped back down into the ankle-deep water and made his way over to Varrisher.

'It's not good news,' Varrisher said, 'but that's evident to anyone with eyes. The carpenter reckons he can have us up and running in three days, but that will be a patch that will only get us to the nearest dockyard. If we want something that'll take us into a fight, he'd rather have a week to do it.'

'If we just patch it and head to Caytown, we might still be able to catch Rui,' Soren said.

'Yes, but he'll run as soon as he spots us and we won't be able to follow. The best we could hope for is that we could take him to task while he and his crew are still in town. That raises all sorts of other problems. If we start a fight in the middle of Caytown, we'll have the local militia to contend with. Pirate or pirate hunter, they won't give a damn. If we start trouble there, they'll be a problem for us. My plan was to identify if Rui was in the town and then wait for him to leave, preferably when his crew were too hung over and wenched out to put up much of a fight. With the type of wealth he has now, who knows how many island commissioners and militia commanders he has in his pocket. When we go for him, it'll have to be in a place of our choosing,' Varrisher said.

'And why won't the patch be enough for us to attack him?' Soren said, with growing frustration.

'Because it won't let us get close to him. Do you see the way all of the other planks curve smoothly into the bow?'

Soren nodded.

'Each of those planks needs to be carefully bent and shaped to fit properly. That takes time. Otherwise, the *Typhon* won't perform properly. We won't be able to sail as quickly, or as close to the wind. That'll give Rui too much of an advantage. I can't ask my men to go against Rui with a ship like that,' Varrisher said.

'He'll get away.'

'Not necessarily,' Varrisher said. 'Rui and his crew have been cruising for several months now. Caytown will be their first call to a friendly port in all that time. Even with all the plunder that Rui has brought his crew, if he suggests leaving Caytown before they've had their fill of booze, dream seed and women, he'll be face down in the mud with his throat cut before he knows what's going on. He won't do anything to interfere with his crew's fun. From what I've heard, he's as enthusiastic a participant as any of them. His crew won't be thinking of leaving Caytown until they've spent a big chunk of their share of the plunder.'

Soren couldn't fault Varrisher's logic. Rui didn't know he was being chased, so had no reason to run. With a great run of luck behind them it was hard to see he and his crew not taking their time to enjoy themselves.

'In terms of losing track of him, I'm not at all worried. My only concern is that the Conclave will have him assassinated at a card table or in a whore's bed in Caytown before we can get to him.'

'I'm no happier about the delay than you are. I need the bounty on Rui. I spent all my capital trying to garner support for Ruripathia in the war. What money I've left has barely kept the *Typhon* running, and the men've not been paid for a month as it is. Each time I use some of my spares, all of which are top quality, I'll not be able to pay to replace them. I need Rui's head, and I need it soon.'

Chapter 33
Wooden Swords

As it was evident that they were going to be stuck on the little island for more than just a couple of days, how to fill the hours became a relevant question. There were only so many men that could work on the damage at any one time, and Varrisher kept his ship in such an excellent condition generally that there were few other tasks that needed attending to.

Soren saw it as a perfect opportunity to establish his worth with the crew. Varrisher had already mentioned that he wanted Soren to drill them with small arms before they caught up with Rui.

He had Varrisher break out the arms and line the men up on the beach. Up until that point, Soren was only the passenger who'd nearly gone for a swim trying to get on board. Soren had very little contact with the other members of the crew. Most of them were Ruripathians and, being an Ostian, Soren had no idea how they would respond to him when having to deal with him on a regular basis. While lounging around in Varrisher's stateroom, he was out of sight and out of mind. Training the men on a daily basis, he would not be so easily forgotten.

They stood in their file, each holding a sword of some description, most of them being the short, broad-bladed cutlasses favoured on board ships. These would be fine for practicing guards, and to make sure they were comfortable and familiar with the weight of a real weapon, but Soren didn't want them cleaving chunks out of one another in the name of training. Later in the day he intended to have them make a batch of wooden weapons to train with, as the carpenter and his team were too busy to do it for them.

Varrisher left him to it and went to supervise the repairs. As soon as he turned his back on them, the men adopted a more relaxed pose.

'The Captain's asked me to take you through some weapons drills. I expect you all know who I am by now. I'm a banneret and I served in the Barbarian War.'

'What about the Ruripathian War?' one of the men said.

'No. I might be Ostian, but plenty of Ostians are against that war and have had to flee as a result. I'm just as much a refugee as any of you.'

There was a grumble, but no further comments.

'First of all, attacks.' Soren drew his sword and adopted a guard position. 'Copy my movements.'

The men did so, but with visible reluctance. He may have quieted them for the moment, but he was certain they resented him. It would be difficult to get past that but it wasn't his aim to get them to like him.

He took them through a number of attacks and guards, repeating the movements over and over until they gradually stencilled themselves into the men's memories. The process had been called 'doing the positions' at the Academy and there was no better way to ingrain the basic movements of swordplay. He kept the men at this until the sun was high, marking out that it was mid-day, or near enough as made no difference. He let them rest and get something to eat, and instructed them to come back with a wooden practice sword similar to the proper cutlasses they'd been practicing with.

While they went off to have their lunch and scrounge up some wood from which to make their practice swords, Soren lay on the beach watching the repair works proceed.

The remains of the damaged planking were being cut away in preparation for the repair. As interesting as it was, carpentry and shipbuilding was not something that could hold Soren's attention for long. He stared at the skin on the back of his hand, which was turning a dark golden shade of brown from the hot southern sun. He decided how to deal with the men's animosity. When they returned, he would pick out the one the rest looked to; the smartest, largest or strongest and thrash him in a demonstration.

When the men sat down to lunch, having cobbled together their practice weapons, Soren went and prepared his own.

They returned to the line they had formed that morning, all clutching the swords they made over lunch, all looking excited in the knowledge that making wooden practice weapons could mean only one thing. Soren gave the weapons a brief inspection. As he expected, they were all superior to his own. There were few sailors that could not turn their hand to working a piece of wood in a competent fashion. Nonetheless, his own was functional and would suffice.

He'd decided who his victim would be: he'd easily identified the member of the group that the rest deferred to and commanded him to step forward.

'In a moment I'm going to put you in pairs to practice what we worked on this morning against an opponent. First I'm going to give you a demonstration of what I want you to do.' Soren turned his attention to the sailor that he had pulled out from the group. 'Attack me!'

There was a chorus of cheers and encouragement from the crowd, and also one or two calls for acts of extreme violence, but Soren's chosen opponent came at him much as Soren expected; like a man trying to chop down a tree in a fit of rage.

He was a big man, by far the biggest on the ship, and Soren had seen him turn the anchor windlass on his own, a feat that was testimony to his strength. As seemed to be the case with all sailors he was nimble too. His attack was all rage and didn't bear even a hint of the techniques they'd been practising that morning. It was all that Soren could do to suppress a smile as he stepped out of the way, putting a gentle tap on the sailor's sword to help push him even farther off balance than he would have been anyway.

He thundered through the spot where Soren had just been, his weight too far ahead of his feet. Soren gave him a kick in the backside, which sent the sailor sprawling face first into the sand. One of the other sailors chuckled, but quickly stifled it under the glares of his comrades.

The big sailor pushed himself to his feet and moved toward Soren again, more slowly. His face was caked with sand and he blinked repeatedly to try and get it out of his eyes. His attack was more measured, just a swipe back and forth through the air that Soren stepped away from. As the sailor was about to step forward again to close the distance, Soren lunged forward, driving the tip of his sword into the sailor's sternum, knocking the wind from his lungs.

He collapsed back onto his backside, clutching his chest and straining to draw a breath. The sailor was less of a challenge than Soren had expected, even without drawing on the Fount.

'You,' he said, pointing at another one of the gathered sailors. 'When your friend is back on his feet, join in and help him.'

The sailor looked at the others but got no reaction. They all seemed surprised at the ease with which Soren had put down the big man.

His pride clearly injured, the big sailor got back to his feet, drawing in air more easily now. His friend moved around behind Soren, and Soren could see in the big sailor's eyes that a signal had been sent and understood. Soren spun on the spot in time to deflect a high to low slash aimed at his head, which even with a wooden weapon would have done damage, and knocked him senseless at least.

Soren parried the wooden blade while it was still well over his head and twisted again. The big sailor had followed in quickly, his comparative speed continuing to come as a surprise considering his size. Soren slashed and ducked, dodging the attack and connecting with his own wooden blade, a hit that would have opened the big sailor from belly button to spine had it been for real.

Soren wheeled around, continuing the same movement and thrust the tip of his sword into second sailor's chest, a strike that would also have caused a fatal wound.

'That's enough I think. Do you agree?'

They both nodded with a mixture of relief and embarrassment.

'Good. Everyone pair up. One partner attack, the other defend. Four attacking strikes and then switch around.'

They did as they were told without a sound. Instead of the wild and reckless strikes that had characterised their fighting before, they were cautiously attacking with the positions that he had shown them. There was a long way to go, but it was a start.

He walked around, watching and commenting where necessary. With his attention focussed on something else, he let part of his mind wander in the direction of the Fount. A shimmering, glowing blue mist formed around the men, brighter and denser around their bodies. Soren tried to keep his attention on what the men were doing, to remain aware of the Fount but stop his mind from focussing on it. It was encouraging, but like the sailors he had a long way to go.

Chapter 34
Caytown

The Typhon dropped anchor in Caytown Roads ten days later. As each day on the beach stretched into another, it had seemed to make sense for the carpenter to do as thorough a job as possible; one that would carry them to the completion of their goal and financial liquidity for Varrisher. When he finished, the carpenter had declared that the repair was as good a job as would be carried out in the dry dock of a shipyard, and Varrisher seemed to have enough confidence in his skill to agree.

Caytown was larger than Valkdorf and appeared far longer established. It reminded him of one of the smaller mainland cities. There were a number of ships in the harbour, bobbing at the end of their anchor lines. Varrisher joined him at the bulwark and surveyed the roads.

'Do you recognise any of them?' he asked.

Soren shook his head. 'No. I'm not sure I'd know the *Bayda's Tear* even if she were right in front of me; one ship looks much the same as another to me.'

'I thought that might be the case. The bad news is several of those ships are men-o'-war. I'm hoping that they're all Humberlander naval fleet rather than Conclave warships. Certainly some of them are; I recognise the pennant on that one.' He pointed out to the largest ship at anchor in the roads. 'That belongs to a Humberlander admiral. A complete prick. Anyway, we'll find out quickly enough one way or the other if Rui's been here when we get ashore. If they have, they'll have been throwing money around and it won't be too difficult to find trace of them. A ship's crew making landfall with plenty of money tend to draw quite a bit of attention. We'll go ashore and do a bit of poking around. If we're in luck, they're still here and I'll be able to work out which ship is the *Tear*. Once that's done, we just wait for them to sail and jump them as soon as we can.'

'I hope it's that easy,' Soren said.

Varrisher laughed. 'I do too, otherwise I'm going to have to hock the *Typhon* and sign onto another ship's list.'

They went ashore in the jolly boat, having to dodge the other boats that were busily moving to and fro in the roadstead. There was a queue of boats waiting for a free space at the stone quay. It was a bustling little port with a lively atmosphere.

'Taverns will be the best place to start,' Varrisher said. 'I'd suggest splitting up to cover the ground more quickly, but it'd look out of place to be sitting alone in a tavern eavesdropping. I think it'll look more natural if we work our way through the taverns together.'

'One drink in each, keep our ears open and then move on?' Soren suggested.

'Ha. From what I've heard about Caytown, we'll be in a pretty sorry state if we take that approach. There are more than twenty taverns and inns here, so we'll have to pace ourselves,' Varrisher said.

The jetty they landed at was for passengers only. Varrisher seemed to be correct in that one of the first sights they were greeted with was of an inn. It had a large sign above its door that would once have been bright and gaudy but was now faded, that announced it as being 'The Old Emperor Inn'. Both Soren and Varrisher had stopped to take in their surroundings, the inn and all the town's activity in particular.

'Seems as good as anywhere to start. I dare say this place gets a lot of trade from sailors straight off the boat. I doubt Rui's men are any different. Unless they have a particular favourite drinking den that is, in which case we could be here for a while.'

Varrisher was always the optimist.

They walked into The Old Emperor; they were men who had just stepped off their ship after nearly two weeks away from any type of civilisation so it was not difficult to behave like sailors glad to be ashore. It was not busy, but there were a few men sitting at tables partially concealed by wooden and glass screens that created little snugs.

They ordered ale from a bartender who seemed to be enjoying the quiet of the late morning trade. He brought them their drinks. Varrisher paid from his small coin purse, the same one he had given Soren to buy clothes. Soren felt guilty at having spent from it so liberally, not realising Varrisher's strained financial circumstances at the time.

'Can I get you fellas anything else?' the barman said.

'No, we're fine for now, thanks,' Varrisher said. 'Quiet in here today.'

'Yes, nice for a change though. It's been crazy for the last week. A ship came in and the crew were spending money like it was water. I've been here fifteen years and it's the first time that we've emptied the taproom in one night. They did that every night for a week.'

Nicely done, Soren thought. A casual comment and they had struck gold in their first inn.

'Sounds like it was pretty crazy,' Varrisher said.

'Aye, it was. The boss was glad of the business, but he was

just as glad to see the back of them. When there's that much ale being drunk it's only a matter of time before things get ugly. We got away lucky, just some broken stools and tankards but a couple of places weren't. They did some serious damage. There's still one of them locked up in the dungeon at the fort. He trashed a brothel and beat a few of the girls that work there. The Commissioner has a stake in the place and wasn't rightly pleased, so he had the sailor thrown in the dungeon. Usually a blind eye is turned to the bad behaviour of sailors bringing that kind of money into town, but I guess even here there are lines that can't be crossed,' the barman said. 'What ship are you lads from anyway?'

'The *Fair Christa*,' Soren said. It was the first name he could think of, coming to it by way of a jumble of the *Fair Katheryn* that they had passed at sea, and the *Honest Christophe*. Varrisher had already shown himself to be loose with his tongue; Soren wanted to make sure their intentions didn't reach the wrong ears and wanted to get in before Varrisher had the chance to answer.

'A Ventish ship?' the barman said.

Soren should have realised that a man working in a town that saw so much shipping passing through would have recognised the naming style, but it was better than him recognising the name itself.

'You lads don't sound Ventish.'

'We're not, just signed on for the voyage,' Varrisher said.

'Fair enough. None of my business anyway,' the barman said, before drifting off down the bar to attend to other tasks.

Varrisher looked to Soren and raised his eyebrows, before gesturing to the door with his head.

Once outside, Soren spoke 'Do you think Rui would have left one of his crew behind?'

'Maybe. If things had gotten too hot for him here, I don't think he's the type to favour loyalty over self-preservation.'

'True. Like you said earlier, a shipload of pirates with money to burn aren't going to go about their business quietly. We're pretty sure that the *Bayda's Tear* was going to stop here. The crew had plenty of cash, so there's a good chance this sailor in the dungeon is from the *Tear*. It's certainly worth looking into, and it's definitely better than having to drink anymore of that rotten piss-water.' Soren said.

Varrisher chuckled. 'It's not so bad when you get used to it. Let's go and find this fort.'

Chapter 35
THE PRISONER

THE FORT WAS IMPOSSIBLE to miss. It sat on top of an area of raised ground in the centre of the town that dropped steeply down to the water. They walked around the base of the hill, which became less steep as they moved further inland. The streets were narrow and cobbled, and lined with a mix of redbrick and wooden buildings.

A path led up the grassy hill to the gate. There were two guards standing outside, dressed in tarnished steel breastplates and shabby looking brown uniforms.

They leaned on long pikes and chatted idly. It took them a while to notice Soren and Varrisher approaching. When they finally did, they stood to attention and called out a challenge. Soren and Varrisher stopped a few paces away.

'I wonder if we might speak with one of your prisoners,' Varrisher said.

'Which prisoner would that be?' one of the guards called back.

'The sailor from the *Bayda's Tear*.'

The guards conferred with one another for a moment. 'You'd need the Lieutenant's permission for that,' the first guard said.

'And how do we get the Lieutenant's permission?' Varrisher said.

'One of us'd have to go and ask him,' the guard said, with a smile that revealed a mouth containing less than half the teeth it should have.

Varrisher sighed, the implication obvious. He took his coin purse from his belt and fished inside for two coins. From the way he had to poke around in it, it didn't seem there were very many left. He flipped a coin to each of the guards, who caught them with greedy hands. The one who did the talking tapped his fellow on the chest before turning and walking back to the gate. He knocked on it and a wicket door opened to let him in. Varrisher and Soren were left outside with the remaining guard who regarded them with a condescending gaze.

A few moments passed before the wicket door opened once again, and the other guard emerged.

'Lieutenant says you can come in,' he said.

Varrisher doffed his hat to the talkative guard and he and Soren followed the other inside the fort. He led them to a small guardroom to the side of the entrance archway, where a man sat at a desk that showed signs of a very recent and very hasty tidying.

'Lieutenant Swetway,' he said. He did not wait for either Varrisher or Soren to introduce themselves. From his demeanour, it seemed that he didn't care. There was a more pressing matter that he wanted to get to. 'Guardsman Fynn tells me that you want to see the sailor from the vessel *Bayda's Tear*.'

'We do,' Varrisher said.

Silence.

Soren could hear Varrisher swear under his breath as he reached for his coin purse again. An officer would be more expensive than a guard, so Varrisher took three coins out, possibly the last of those within, and placed them on the desk, one at a time.

'I thought you lads from the *Tear* had more gold than sense,' the Lieutenant said, without budging from his slouched position in his chair.

'Booze and whores,' Soren said, without elaborating further.

'Ah yes, the price does tend to go up when there's a lot of gold in town, even more so when places are being smashed up,' the Lieutenant said. He leaned forward and picked up the three coins.

They were gold crowns, so decent money for doing nothing — even for an officer, if this man could be considered such. He had not introduced himself as a banneret, so most likely he had been promoted from within the ranks by displaying more avarice and less incompetence than his fellows, while posted to a colonial town that no ambitious officer of proper background would even consider.

'Guardsman Fynn,' he said, as he resumed his slouch. 'Take these two gentlemen to see our prisoner.'

Fynn shuffled off down a corridor on the other side of the guardroom; Varrisher and Soren followed. The only illumination in the corridor, which went down a short flight of stairs before reaching a large vaulted room, was provided by oil lamps that gave off a warm, waxy smell that cloyed in Soren's nostrils.

'Your prisoner,' Fynn said, gesturing to a door with a small, barred window. Varrisher stepped forward and peered through the window. The door was wood banded with iron. The walls were thick and there were likely more guards than Soren had seen so far. If it came to trying to break this man out, he didn't fancy their chances.

Varrisher stepped back and gestured for Soren to take a look. He leaned forward and got a waft of the stench of sweat and piss. There was a man lying on a pile of stale, rotting straw against the wall of the tiny cell. His face was obscured, so Soren couldn't identify him.

'Can we go in?' Soren said.

'No,' Fynn said, 'you have to talk to him from here.'

'All right,' Varrisher said. 'Hey.'

There was the sound of straw rustling and movement from within the cell. A face appeared on the other side of the window.

'Yeah? What do you want?' he said. He had thick, unkempt black hair and a dark, swarthy complexion.

If the face had not been enough, Soren would have recognised him from the sound of his voice alone. It was Blasco, the mate from the *Bayda's Tear*.

'We want some information from you,' Varrisher said.

'Get me out of here, and I'll tell you whatever you want,' Blasco said.

'What's his sentence?' Varrisher said, turning to Fynn.

'He's for the chopping block. He smashed up one of the whorehouses that the Resident Commissioner owns, the "Sugar and Spice". Beat the piss out of a couple of the girls. Yon scallywag's captain wouldn't pay to put the damage right, so the Commissioner refused to let him go. The next time he sees the sea it will be from the casket they stick pirates' heads in on Headsman's Rock out in the bay.'

Soren took Varrisher aside and spoke quietly. 'His name's Blasco. He's one of the officers on the *Bayda's Tear*.'

Varrisher turned back to the cell window. 'Where's the *Bayda's Tear* gone?' he said.

'Told you already, fella, you get me outta here, I'll tell you anything you want to know,' Blasco said. His voice had become more animated in the few moments they had been speaking.

Soren knew from personal experience that seeing a chance of getting out of prison and away from an impending execution did that to a man.

'You'll give up Captain Rui if we get you out of here?' Varrisher said.

'Gladly. That fucker left me here to have my head cut off. Get me out, you won't be able to shut me up.' His voice was excited now. 'Favourite routes, hiding places, crew numbers. I know it all. Whatever you want to know.'

'Who do I need to talk to about getting him out of here?' Varrisher said, turning to Guardsman Fynn.

'It's the Resident Commissioner that had him put here; him that signed the warrant. S'pose it's him you need to talk to.'

Bribing two guards had cost two florins, a Lieutenant three crowns and he had only taken that reluctantly. How much, Soren wondered, did a Resident Commissioner cost?

Chapter 36
THE RESIDENT COMMISSIONER

THEY WALKED BACK DOWN the hill into Caytown. The Resident Commissioner's mansion was a striking white building in the centre of the town, surrounded by gardens filled with exotic trees, bushes and flowers. When they got there, they asked to speak with the Commissioner's private secretary. There was some deliberation before it was decided to only let one of them in. It seemed that the Commissioner was nervous about his personal security, perhaps more so now that he had imprisoned a member of Sancho Rui's crew and refused to release him.

Despite the departure of the *Bayda's Tear* a few days previously, it wouldn't be at all unlikely for Rui to have engaged an assassin for the sole purpose of addressing the slight against him by the Commissioner's defiance, rather than out of a desire to free his first mate.

They decided that Varrisher would go in to negotiate Blasco's release. Soren would have preferred to do it himself, but he had to tread carefully with Varrisher. He needed him and would have to let Varrisher have his own way from time to time to ensure that they remained on good terms. While they were getting along well,

Soren could not forget the man that he had met in Ruripathia and was not yet convinced by his apparent change of character.

While he waited, Soren went to the nearest tavern that he could find. It was not far — Caytown seemed to have more taverns than anything else — and gave him a view of the Commissioner's mansion. He bought a mug of ale and sat by a window overlooking the mansion so he would see Varrisher come out.

Time passed. People came and went from the tavern. A number of them were sailors and from a little idle eavesdropping, Soren discovered that a Humberlander naval squadron had arrived at Caytown a few days before to resupply, confirming what Varrisher had thought.

They had been patrolling the region to keep Humberlander shipping safe from pirate attack in the east and south, far beyond their usual patrol areas, now that piracy was on the increase as a result of the war and the dearth of Ostian warships. Their impending arrival might have also had something to do with Rui's sudden departure.

It was several hours before Varrisher finally came out of the mansion. Soren walked out of the tavern and waved to him. Varrisher looked drained as he made his way over.

'What's the tavern like?' he asked.

'Fine. Unremarkable.'

'It'll do. I'm starving. Let's get something to eat and I'll fill you in on my meeting.'

Varrisher tapped the last coin out of his purse. It was a silver florin, enough to pay for a meal for both of them.

Soren thought for a moment before taking a crown from his own purse and placing it on the table. 'I'll get this one.'

Varrisher nodded and smiled gratefully. He put his florin back in his purse. 'I met the Commissioner's secretary. Just as Guardsman Fynn said, it seems the Commissioner's taken a personal interest in Sailing Master Blasco. As soon as he found out what my business was, he said the Commissioner would be more than happy to release Blasco, and would do so promptly as soon as we pay him five hundred crowns restitution. He had no interest in negotiating a lower amount or an alternative.'

'Well… That'll take a while to put together,' Soren said, understating the impossibility.

'Agreed. I don't see any point in staying around here. There's no way we can expect to break Blasco out of prison and get away alive; there are too many guards and soldiers here. The only thing that I can think of is to go in and lie through our teeth to him in the hope that he will give us some information that we can use.'

'What are our chances of finding Rui without Blasco's help?' Soren said.

'It's doable, but it'll take a long time; there are a million and one places for him to hide. By now I'm sure there are other ships hunting him and he probably knows it. We could have done without the delay, but there's no use in getting upset about it now. Blasco's our best chance of getting to Rui before anyone else does.'

'Maybe we can bribe the guards to bring in some booze. If we can get him drunk, he'll be a bit freer with his tongue. We might get something useful out of him,' Soren said, unlikely as it seemed.

'Perhaps. I'll have to go back to the ship and see if I can scrounge up some more cash first, unless you have more where that came from.' He nodded at the crown that Soren had put on the table. 'Between bribes and buying a few bottles of something strong, I don't have enough on me to cover what it will cost. Perhaps I can sell some of the ship's stores to keep us afloat a bit longer; the money's all but run out.'

◆—◆

They finished their meal and walked back toward the ship in silence. While the ship could be run for some time without any more money, assuming the sailors were willing to forego pay in anticipation of a share of the bounty on Rui's head and a portion of the plunder they expected to take from his ship, there were many other things — bribes for the most part it seemed — that did require money. Money that they no longer had.

They were halfway back to the quayside when a group of men approached them. One was wearing a naval officer's uniform, while his companions were in the uniform sea-scrubs of Humberlander sailors.

'Gentlemen, I am Lieutenant dal Montesfort. Admiral dal Laucelin wishes to talk with you,' the Officer said.

'Dal Laucelin? What does he want?' Varrisher said.

'Perhaps you mistake my manners for giving you an option. You'll come with me, willingly, or by force. The choice is yours,' Lieutenant dal Montesfort said.

Soren reached for the hilt of his sword. Varrisher shrugged his shoulders and gestured for Soren to leave his sword where it was.

'Well, if we have no choice,' Varrisher said, 'I'd be delighted to remake my acquaintance with the Admiral. Lead on.'

'You come too,' the Lieutenant said to Soren.

Soren expected they would be frog marched back to the Commissioner's house, but were surprised when the Lieutenant and his men escorted them instead toward the quay. They stopped outside an inn and the Lieutenant gestured for Soren and Varrisher to enter. When they hesitated the Lieutenant nodded to his men, one of whom shoved Varrisher forward. Taking the cue, Varrisher opened the door and went in. Soren followed, realising any resistance was pointless.

It was an expensive looking place; far removed from The Old Emperor and the tavern they had just come from, and definitely not the type of establishment that either Soren or Varrisher could afford to patronise right now.

The Lieutenant and his men followed them in. 'This way,' he said. He led them through the foyer and down a corridor to a small salon at the back. There was another man sitting there reading through some letters whom Soren took to be the Admiral.

'Good afternoon, Captain Varrisher,' the man said.' A twist of tobacco twitched in the corner of his mouth when he spoke, but it somehow remained where it was.

'A good afternoon to you too, Admiral,' Varrisher said.

Soren noticed an edge to his voice that told him a pleasant afternoon was the very last thing Varrisher wished for the Admiral.

'You do recall me, I presume?' the Admiral said.

'I do,' Varrisher said, his voice cold and his demeanour verging on openly hostile

'And your associate? Who are you, sir?' the Admiral said.

'Banneret of the Duke's Cross Soren.'

'An Ostian! You do keep the most unlikely of friends, Captain Varrisher. I must say that I hadn't expected to see you in these parts, although with recent events I imagine a great many Ruripathians have fled to Valkdorf.'

'What do you want, Admiral?' Varrisher said.

'Sad days for your country,' the Admiral said, deliberately ignoring Varrisher's question. 'Trying times make the best of us consider work that we would not otherwise.'

'What exactly are you implying?' Varrisher said.

'You sail into a known pirate haven, albeit one enjoying the benefits of flying the flag of Humberland, in a heavily armed warship with a crew far larger than is needed for sailing alone. The evidence only points to one thing. Turning to piracy is a sad fate indeed for a former doyen of the Ruripathian navy.'

'I'm not a pirate, Admiral. Call me one again and you'll have to back your words with steel.'

There was a tense silence. Soren grimaced. Having things get ugly with the Humberland navy was the last thing they needed, and would mean they could forget about Rui, the bounty, the booty, and his sword. He was about to speak up in the hope of calming the situation when the Admiral responded.

'The only steel I'll back my words with is the steel of the manacles you'll be wearing in the town gaol.' He cast a glance at Soren. 'Both of you. And your crew.'

The Admiral removed the twist of tobacco from his mouth and stubbed it out on an ashtray. He smoothed his thick salt and pepper moustache with thumb and index finger before continuing. 'There is, however, something that you could help me with. Something that would make me overlook the highly suspicious nature of your behaviour and circumstances.'

Varrisher smiled ironically. 'You expect me to help you?'

'I thought that you might be less than agreeable, considering the particulars of our previous meeting. Before you reject the offer I'm about to make, I'll add an incentive for you.'

Varrisher remained silent, his jaw clenched. Soren was not sure what was going on, so he kept his mouth shut.

'My lieutenant informs me that you were trying to negotiate with the Resident Commissioner for the release of a crewmate from prison. He tells me that the Commissioner demanded an extortionate amount of money for the release of your friend.'

Varrisher remained silent, as did Soren.

The Admiral sighed. 'Very well. I'll continue. Help me and I'll have your crewmate released.'

It was a surprising development, and an attractive one. Soren wondered what the Admiral wanted in return.

'You're not the only people that the Commissioner, Canning dal Camperey, has tried to extort. Extortion is one of his more charming foibles. Embezzlement, murder, fraud, theft. The list is quite eye-opening. Were it not for you Ostians and Ruripathians scrapping, we would never have had to send a fleet out to keep our trade lanes clear, and like as not the

Commissioner would never have had his litany of nefarious deeds discovered.'

Soren wasn't sure he liked where the Admiral was going, and he couldn't see how they would be able to do anything the Admiral's men would not.

'"Discovered" is perhaps too strong a word, however. I've a list of crimes as long as your arm, both against the individual and against the state of Humberland. They could only have been carried out with the complicity and most likely the involvement of the Commissioner. I don't have anything that directly incriminates him, however.'

Soren looked over to Varrisher and raised his eyebrows. It looked as though this was where they were going to fit into the plan.

'I plan on bringing dal Camperey to justice, and to clean out this rat infested shithole of a town. The first problem I have is that the Commissioner is not an idiot and proof is thin on the ground. The second problem is the Camperey family are well connected, and although I suspect the reason Canning is down here is because his own kin know him for the deceitful little shit he is, I can't treat him as I have threatened to treat you: on suspicion alone.'

'What possible use can we be in this?' Varrisher said.

'I'm glad you asked, Captain, I'm glad you asked. Simply put, I couldn't give a fuck who dal Camperey bumps off in the middle of the night, or who he screws out of a few crowns. However, someone has pulled a stroke that I'm not willing to let go unanswered and it has his grubby mitts all over it.

'Two of my frigates called here a few weeks ago to take on fresh supplies from the crown dockyard. All crown dockyards are required to maintain stores and all supplies are requisitioned locally but paid for by the crown. All of those supplies are certified as crown property and fit for consumption as soon as they are.

'The supplies my ships took on were spoiled and half the crews died. All the casks were certified recently, and there was no reason for them to be anything but fresh ship's provisions.'

'Why do we need to know this?' Varrisher said.

'Because, tragic as it is, this incident gives me the chance to catch dal Camperey in the act. They're selling the fresh, crown purchased provisions to all comers and pocketing the profit. They replace the missing casks with whatever cheap crap they can get their hands on so the ledgers tally with what is in the storehouse and no one knows any difference; an old trick. You and your chum here are going to pose as smugglers with some black market casks of ships' provisions.'

'I can see a number of difficulties with that plan,' Varrisher said.

'No problems, everything is in place. I just needed someone that could pull off the role of smuggler. None of my officers are up to it. When I saw your ship sail into the roads, I thought it was my lucky day.'

'How will we prove we're smugglers?' Soren said. There were too many gaps in this plan and Soren had no desire to find himself with a knife in his back when it went wrong.

'I captured a ship a number of days ago, an oceanman not flying any flag. We investigated and found its hold full of casks of provisions looted from Ruripathia. They must have cleaned out an entire dockyard. They were on their way here to sell the casks. I want you to try and sell them at the dockyard. There are a lot of casks so it will be a big deal. Too big for dal Camperey not to be directly involved.

Soren could see that Varrisher's knuckles were white. Whatever had happened between Admiral dal Laucelin and Varrisher was clouding his thoughts.

'We agree. Release our man from the gaol and we'll help you,' Soren said, before Varrisher could ruin the opportunity, and potentially have them thrown into the cell next to Blasco.

Varrisher cast him an evil glance, but said nothing. Even in his anger he would know it was the opportunity they had been looking for to get back onto Rui's trail.

'We'll need some money for expenses too,' Soren said.

'Of course,' the Admiral said, with a smile.

Chapter 37
THE PLOT

Soren and Varrisher returned to the *Typhon* and spent the remainder of the day discussing how they would go about the task. They hashed out several ideas that would fit with the Admiral's plan, finally settling on a backstory that had Soren as an Ostian officer who had been able to steal the contents of a Ruripathian naval depot toward the end of the war. He had negotiated a deal with a captured Ruripathian naval officer to transport the supplies away before the Ostian army arrived to appropriate them, and thus they formed an unlikely partnership.

They would have to play a clever game though. Soren reasoned that if weaknesses in their bargaining position of their own creation could be revealed during the negotiation, it might deflect attention from any querying of their bona fides.

They would claim that while looking for somewhere to sell the supplies they had been directed to Caytown, where they heard ships' supplies could be bought and sold. After the large ports on the mainland, Caytown was one of the biggest, busiest, and second only to Valkdorf in lax application of the law. With a full shipyard — something Valkdorf lacked — it was an obvious choice for smugglers trying to offload a cargo.

With their backstory decided upon, Soren couldn't help but wonder what the history between Varrisher and the Admiral was. Varrisher still seemed to be angry so he decided to hold his tongue. These things tended to come out in the open eventually.

The next morning Soren went ashore headed for the part of the town fringing on what was known as the 'Deep Pool', a deep water basin that allowed larger ships to be brought alongside the dock for loading directly. The crown dockyard dominated the quay around the Deep Pool.

The dockyard was walled and the gate was guarded. Soren stated his business to a sentry who did not seem especially interested in the answers. The guard gave him directions to the Commissary's office. It was an orderly place, or at least had been when it was first designed and built. Now it bore the characteristics of somewhere that was poorly maintained.

The dockyard had a number of sign-posted sheds and brick warehouses. The directions he had been given brought him to a single story brick building that abutted onto a far larger warehouse, the largest that Soren had seen there. It bore a sign over the door stating it was the Commissary's office.

The door led to a small reception area with a counter that ran the length of the room. Soren cleared his throat and a short, slender man with yellowing grey hair in later middle age emerged from the doorway that led into the warehouse behind.

'Name of ship?' he asked.

'I, ah, well I'm not really looking for supplies,' Soren said.

'No? Then what can I do for you?' the man said.

'Are you the Commissary?'

'I am,' he said. 'Commissary Harris at your service.'

'My name is Soren. A friend suggested that I call on you. I've come into possession of a large number of casks of ship's supplies that I thought you might be interested in purchasing,' Soren said.

'Really. What's your friend's name?' the Commissary said.

Soren smiled as cryptically as he could.

'I'm sorry, but your friend was mistaken. I can only purchase provisions for the crown stores from certified suppliers. All supplies are cured and casked in the dockyard so we can be sure of their contents and mark them as certified. We have to be sure the casks we provide to warrant and naval ships are of the highest of standards, you see,' he said, with an oily smile. 'I'm afraid that I'm not interested.'

'Well, I'm sorry to have bothered you,' Soren said.

'No trouble at all, good day.'

Soren walked out of the dockyard not quite sure what to make of the conversation. They had not expected that the Commissary would take the bait straight away. If he had, he would have been a fool — and would have been caught out long ago. The Admiral made it clear that he was good at covering his tracks. The rejection meant that they would move on to the second phase of their plan.

Soren spent the rest of the day going around the private ship's provisioners in the town who provided casks to commercial ships that didn't have the benefit of a royal trade warrant and had to purchase their own supplies. They relied heavily on repeat business and the good reputation generated by word of mouth. To get a reputation as having supplied even one spoiled cask would be hugely detrimental to their business and Soren knew that they'd get short shrift wherever they took their offer. To sell their casks wasn't their intention, though.

He was confident that the Commissary's interest would be piqued by the offer Soren had made if he was in the business of fraud as the Admiral claimed. Being a shrewd operator however, he was not going to jump into an agreement with a complete stranger. They hoped that making some noise around town that they were trying to sell casks, and were not trying to sell them to anyone in particular, would give their story more plausibility.

Soren hoped this approach would be more believable than trying to portray themselves as seasoned smugglers. In fecklessly trying to conceal their naivety, they were hoping to direct the Commissary's appraisal of them to their own intentions. Soren had even dallied on his way out of the dockyard to give the Commissary long enough to find someone to have him followed. He had seen the same face more than once in different places along the dock front, always at the same distance and engaged in a mundane and out of place activity in an effort to look innocuous.

At the end of the day Soren was exhausted from traipsing up and down the docks, trying to draw as much attention to himself as possible while pretending to sell his looted casks. He returned to the ship, making sure to state his destination loudly to the steersman on the launch. There could be no doubt that he was going out to the Ruripathian rigged vessel that had arrived the day before, which again supported the story that Soren and Varrisher had concocted over a glass of cheap whiskey on the *Typhon* the previous night.

The following morning, Soren and Varrisher went ashore to take breakfast in The Old Emperor. They wanted to be seen, and now that the Admiral was covering their expenses there was no reason not to treat themselves. Varrisher thought it the best spot as it was busy and central. The crew had likewise been given some coin to go about town and enjoy themselves, and where possible make intentionally indiscreet whispers of their feigned reason for being in Caytown.

As they ate, sitting in the window seat of the inn, Soren kept a careful but surreptitious lookout for the individual he'd suspected of following him the previous day. There was no sign of him and Soren started to wonder if their ruse had been successful. He had hoped that there would be someone watching for their return, but only time would tell.

With breakfast eaten, they both ordered coffee and sat back to wait. The plan required the Commissary to seek them out. As strangers to the town, there was no way Soren could think of to make themselves seem legitimate, or illegitimate depending on the point of view, beyond what he had already done. While the squadron was at anchor in the roads, it was possible that the Commissary was exercising a little more caution than usual, but greed was a powerful and reckless motivator so Soren hoped that the bait would be taken.

He had visited all of the waterfront provisioners the day before, so perhaps the next step was to investigate what black market dealers there were, and seek them out. If the Commissary was corrupt, as the Admiral suspected, he would be in contact with those black market dealers — which would hopefully add to the veracity of their story. Beyond that, there was little more they could do but wait.

A boy of not more than nine or ten walked into the lounge where they were sitting.

'Oi. You. Get out,' the barman shouted.

'I've got a message,' the boy said, 'and I'm gonna deliver it, so you can fuck off.'

Hearing a young child swear never failed to make Soren chuckle, but the barman was less amused. He took a stick from behind the bar, before making his way toward the opening into the lounge. The boy looked around frantically, realising that he had to deliver his message fast. His eyes fixed onto Soren and Varrisher. He rushed over and threw a crumpled-up scrap of paper onto the table in front of them before running for the door. He dodged the barman's arm and disappeared out into the street.

Soren picked up the piece of paper and uncrumpled it. There were three lines of writing:

The Drunken Rover
Seven bells
Come alone

Nothing more. He looked at it for a moment before passing it to Varrisher.

'The plan worked then?'

'Looks like it,' Soren said.

◆—◆

Soren was at *The Drunken Rover* at seven bells. The tavern was similar in style to the others that they'd been in. Lots of ornate wood panelling and partitions seemed to be a style popular with Humberlanders. Soren took a seat and ordered a drink so as not to seem too conspicuous. Varrisher was waiting outside a short distance away with several men from the *Typhon*, watching over the doors in the event that Soren was bundled away to prison, or worse.

They had taken the *Typhon's* jolly boat ashore rather than the public launch, and it was waiting for them at the quay in the event that they needed to make a speedy return to the *Typhon*. The remaining crew had orders to be ready to get the ship underway at a moment's notice.

Soren made sure to arrive earlier than the appointed time and had to wait a while before a man entered the tavern and made his way over to the bartender. Soren saw the bartender nod toward him and the man scrutinised Soren for a moment before walking over and sitting down opposite Soren.

'Good evening,' he said.

'Good evening to you,' Soren said.

He sat staring at Soren in silence, which made Soren very uncomfortable. The man stood again and walked around the tavern, peering into every snug and corner. When he seemed satisfied that there was no one else there, he walked toward the door, giving Soren a polite nod as he passed, and left.

Soren was bemused. Had their ruse been rumbled?

A moment later, the door opened again and the Commissary entered. He walked over to Soren and sat down where the other man had been.

'Hello again,' he said. 'I apologise for my caution, but you must understand that I won't do business with every stranger who walks in off the street. Now that I've had a little time, I've been able to satisfy myself that there is something to your story. I'm told that since we last met you've been trying to sell your casks of provisions all about the town. Have you had any luck in selling them?'

'You're interested in them?' Soren said.

'That might be the case. Why don't you tell me how you came by them?' the Commissary said.

'Does it really matter?'

'No, but it does go some way to help me decide whether or not I'm interested.'

'Let's just say that they don't have any paperwork,' Soren said.

'Very well, in that case I'll have to proceed on the assumption that many, if not all of the casks are spoiled when deciding on a price.'

Soren said nothing but tried to make the face of someone who has realised they've made a mistake, but is trying to conceal the fact.

The Commissary beckoned to the bartender to bring him a drink. 'How many casks do you have for sale?'

'A dozen on board my ship in the roads,' Soren said.

The Commissary rolled his eyes. 'That's it? All this fuss for a few casks?' He made to get up, but Soren interjected.

'That's just a sample. We have a little over nine hundred tonnes on board an oceanman less than a day's sail away, but for the sake of ease, let's just call it an even nine hundred,' Soren said.

The Commissary's eyes widened, and Soren could see the greed in them.

'Very well. I'll need to see the casks that you have before I can make a decision on whether I'll be able to take your full stock, or just a portion of it. Are you planning on remaining on board your ship or will you be taking a room ashore?'

'I'm staying on my ship,' Soren said.

The Commissary nodded, standing. 'Have your sample casks delivered to the dockyard before dawn tomorrow morning. There'll be someone there to take delivery. I'll send word to your ship if I'm interested in making a purchase.'

Chapter 38
THE CASKS

Soren had a dozen casks from the *Typhon* rowed over to the dockyard in the middle of the night. As they had all originated in a Ruripathian naval dockyard, they were suitable for the job without the need to get some from the Admiral.

With the casks delivered, the next morning he visited the town's branch of Austorgas' Bank. The transaction would most likely be carried out by way of a draft on the bank's credit. In order to add further authenticity to the ruse, he wanted to call on the bank to confirm the identity of its manager, who he would later require to authenticate any draft.

Then it was time to wait again. Soren whiled away the hours by practicing his fencing on the *Typhon's* deck. Despite their initial misgivings, in their days training together on the beach while the ship was being repaired, Soren had earned the respect and trust of the crew, who now seemed to forgive him his nationality and lack of sailing skill. Now whenever he trained, he had no difficulty in finding sparring partners, and his exertions generally encouraged others not on watch to do likewise. They all knew that they had a fight coming, with a potentially big reward at the end of it. They wanted to ensure they were alive to enjoy it. Even Varrisher, who Soren had humiliated in a duel not long after they first met, seemed to have put the encounter down to experience. He had developed the humility, or at least the sense, to learn as much as he could from Soren.

Word finally came that evening, requesting that Soren go ashore for another meeting with the Commissary. Varrisher sent word to the Admiral that the meeting was taking place. The meeting was in *The Drunken Rover* again, but when Soren arrived he was directed to a private room in the back. The Commissary was waiting for Soren, accompanied by two other men. He stood when Soren entered.

'Mister Soren,' he said. He seemed a little less sure of himself than he had on previous occasions. 'These are my business partners. I'm afraid they'd rather keep their names to themselves, for understandable reasons.'

Soren shrugged his shoulders. 'So long as their money is good, I couldn't care less.'

'It's good,' Harris said. 'Please, sit.'

'Commissary Harris tells us that you've only been in Caytown for a few days,' one of the business partners said. He was older, well past middle age with a head of slicked back white hair. His clothes were of excellent quality and Soren took him as being the man with the finances to front the operation. Might he be the Resident Commissioner himself? The other was younger, with dark hair and a narrow, pinched face.

'Yes, that's correct,' Soren said.

'Have you ever seen me before?' the man said.

'I don't believe so, no.'

'Before we go any further, I wish to set out some of the terms I will require you to agree to. If we reach a deal, you may not return to Caytown. If you set foot ashore after our deal is concluded, you will be arrested on sight and thrown in gaol. Do you agree to this?' the man said.

Soren shrugged. 'I don't expect to be back here or to come into another load of provisions, so I've no problem with that.'

'Good,' the man said. 'Commissary Harris tells me that you have no paperwork or certificates of quality and content for the casks.'

'That's correct,' Soren said.

'Well, we've opened the casks that you had delivered and I can tell you that the contents of two of them were spoiled,' the man said.

That was a lie. The casks had been taken from the *Typhon's* stores and were good. It was a ruse to knock the price down, but Soren wasn't there for the money.

He shrugged his shoulders again. 'If you don't want to purchase them, what was your reason in bringing me here?' Soren said, feigning exasperation.

'I didn't say that we don't wish to purchase them. I only make my observation to explain the price that I'm willing to offer you,' the man said.

'Go on.' Soren maintained his air of exasperation.

'I'll offer you two crowns per cask,' the man said.

A legitimate cask of provisions would cost anywhere from five to fifteen crowns when sold for their full value, depending on the contents.

'Four crowns.'

The man smiled. 'Three, and not a penny more.'

Soren pursed his lips and tried to make it look as though he was weighing things up. 'Very well, we have a deal. Three crowns a cask, for a total of thirteen thousand, five hundred crowns,' Soren said.

Everyone at the table gave some visible reaction. It was a huge sum of money and thinking of it made Soren feel giddy. It was enough to buy a title, an estate, and finance a life of exceptional luxury. He couldn't help but wonder what their chances of fleeing with the money would be. He was sure the Admiral would hunt them down, and with Amero already sending assassins after him he had more than his fair share of that type of trouble. He pushed the thought from his head, however intoxicatingly tempting it was.

'Agreed. Excellent. That only leaves the logistical details. It will take us two days to assemble the necessary funds. I understand that the ship on which you have the remainder of your stock is some distance away.'

Soren nodded. 'A day's sail, give or take.'

'I suggest that we reconvene here, two days hence. I'll expect your ship to be at anchor in the roads by that point. Once my agents have boarded and inspected the cargo, I'll transfer payment. There's a branch office of Austorgas' here in Caytown. I can pay you in coin, or in a draft in your favour made on the bank. As an Ostian, I trust you are familiar with them.'

Soren nodded. He had spoken briefly with its manager, Grenvery Austorga, a minor member of the family, earlier in the day. It was what the Admiral wanted. The draft would increase the paper trail for him to follow. Soren had been instructed to only accept the alternative if it would be a deal breaker. Soren also suspected that the Admiral did not trust him and Varrisher with that amount of money in coin.

'I am,' Soren said, 'and I'd prefer payment by way of bank draft.'

'Good, that will ease the process somewhat. Gathering this amount in coin on such a small island could have proved troublesome. What's the name of the ship that carries the remainder of the casks?'

'She's called the *Spirit of Brixen*,' Soren said. 'I'll require an officer of the bank to confirm the authenticity of the draft. In expectation of this agreement, I called at Austorgas' today and spoke to the manager. He's known to me and I'll require him to carry out this task. He agreed to do so when I spoke with him.'

'Very well, I have no difficulty with that; I'm familiar with Burgess Austorga myself.'

In saying that, the man confirmed that he was a member of the small circle of high society on the island, which was a further indication that he might be the Resident Commissioner. The Admiral would have men watching the tavern to identify who went in and out anyway.

'I believe that concludes our business for this evening.' The man stood, as did his companion who had remained silent throughout the meeting. 'I would appreciate it if you'd wait a few minutes after we have gone before you leave,' he said.

'Of course,' Soren said.

'Excellent. The day after tomorrow then. Good evening,' the man said. He and the other unidentified man left leaving Soren alone with the Commissary.

Commissary Harris stared at Soren for a moment in silence. 'This is a big deal. If you're fucking about, I'll have you killed quicker than you'll know. Don't think I won't. This ship better be bursting with casks.' He left.

Soren waited for what he felt was a reasonable amount of time, pondering what Harris had said, before he left.

He hadn't gone far before he heard a whisper saying his name. He looked toward its source, a small alley running between two buildings, and saw Varrisher skulking in its shadows. He came out and joined Soren as they made their way back to the quay.

'Have the others left?' he asked.

'Yes, a few moments ago. Three of them. Why?' Soren said.

'I'm pretty sure one of the men who left a few moments ago was the Resident Commissioner's private secretary. I didn't get a look at the other fellow with him.'

'I suspect that he's the Resident Commissioner,' Soren said. 'The Commissary was there too, but the two new faces didn't introduce themselves. The older of the two did most of the talking, the one I took to be the Resident Commissioner, and he made it clear they were concerned about keeping their anonymity. They've agreed to the deal, subject to conditions.'

'Which are?'

'We can't come back to Caytown again, and we have to have the casks here in two days.'

'If the Admiral arrests Commissioner dal Camperey when this is all done we don't need to worry about the former. The latter shouldn't be a problem. How much did he offer?'

'Thirteen thousand, five hundred crowns.'

Varrisher let out a gasp.

'It wouldn't work, so forget it,' Soren said.

'No, you're probably right, but maybe we should just sail back to Ruripathia and see if we can loot a few dockyards for real. How's he going to pay that much?'

'He's borrowing it from Austorgas'. I expect they've been financing his scams all along. The profit margins are huge.'

'Good, well, hopefully we have him,' Varrisher said. 'I saw a few navy types lurking around while you were in the meeting, so I presume that the Admiral knows who was there by now.'

'So far so good,' Soren said. 'With luck, there won't be any problems.'

'We're nearly there,' Varrisher said. 'I don't like helping the Admiral, but it suits our needs and in another day or two we'll have Blasco, and be on our way again. I just hope no one else has beaten us to the prize.'

They sent a note across to the Admiral's flagship that night and were summoned. It came as a surprise to Soren in light of the

Admiral's concerns about them being seen with one another while the plot was unfolding. They went immediately, hoping that the cover of darkness would be enough to conceal their movements from any prying eyes.

The Admiral's ship was impressive, several times larger than the *Typhon* and bearing the brutish features of a ship designed solely for war. As soon as they set foot on deck, a young officer greeted them and brought them to the ship's stateroom. Admiral dal Laucelin sat behind a table in front of the gallery windows at the stern of the ship, still at work, despite the hour.

'Come in, gentlemen. Sit please,' he said. 'My lieutenant tells me there's been an interesting development.'

'Indeed there has,' Soren said. He recounted the details of his meeting at *The Drunken Rover*, including the particulars of the deal and the additional participants.

The Admiral's lack of surprise when they told him of their suspicions confirmed that navy men had been watching the tavern.

'That's good news indeed, gentlemen,' the Admiral said, when Soren had finished filling him in on all of the details of the meeting. 'I had hoped that this deal would be too large to be completed without the direct involvement of dal Camperey. For the amount of money involved, Austorgas' will require his signature on any finance agreements; one of his lackeys doing it won't provide them with enough security. That should be more than enough for me to put him on the headsman's block.

'I had worried that my plan was too big, that the size of it would scare dal Camperey off. However, it proves once again that greed is a powerful motivator.' He leaned back in his chair and laced his fingers over his belly, with a contented smile on his face.

Chapter 39
THE DEAL

LATE THE FOLLOWING EVENING, the *Spirit of Brixen* sailed into Caytown Roads and anchored a short distance from the *Typhon*. Soren went across to it shortly after it arrived. He sat drinking tea and chatting with the Admiral's flag lieutenant who had commanded her from where she had been waiting for a little over an hour. He reckoned that was roughly the time it would take to make a full inspection of the cargo had he any interest in so doing, and went back to the *Typhon* in the jolly boat.

There was another day to go until dal Camperey would have arranged his finances and there was little to do other than wait, time which was spent drilling the crew in close quarters fighting. It might have looked odd to someone watching from the shore, but Soren wanted to send a clear message that anyone trying to seize either the *Typhon* or the *Spirit of Brixen* would have a very hard fight on their hands.

A small boat rowed out from the quay in the *Typhon's* direction. When it arrived, its crew delivered a note from Commissary

Harris saying they were ready to proceed. Varrisher had gone ashore earlier with the intention of keeping an eye on everything. After Harris's threatening talk, Soren wanted to be sure that he wasn't walking into a trap.

With the Resident Commissioner of the island involved in the deal — and with so much money involved — there was no reason for him not to simply throw Soren into jail, seize the *Spirit of Brixen*, take its cargo and save himself thirteen and a half thousand crowns. Soren hoped the presence of a large crew on the *Typhon* and their constant, visible training on deck would dissuade dal Camperey from considering this option. It would attract a great deal of attention and would be costly in terms of lives. The message Soren had wanted to send was that it would be far easier to see the deal through in good faith and make a big profit, rather than cause a big fuss and risk everything.

Soren went ashore and walked straight to *The Drunken Rover*, arriving earlier than arranged. The barman recognised him and waved him on toward the back room where the previous meeting took place. Once there, he sat and waited.

The Commissary and the older of the two unnamed men, the one assumed to be dal Camperey, arrived together and after a cursory greeting they sat at the table opposite Soren. Dal Camperey held a leather folder that he placed on the table.

'I sent my men out to the Spirit to inspect her cargo a little while ago, as we agreed. They'll send word here once they've completed the task, which I don't expect to take much longer,' dal Camperey said. 'As soon as they've confirmed that there are the correct number of filled casks on board, I'll give you the draft and our business will be all but concluded. There'll certainly be no need for us to meet again. I'll remind you of your agreement not to return to Caytown once this deal is finished.'

'I haven't forgotten,' Soren said. He reckoned that he would have been arrested by now if dal Camperey was intending to seize the Spirit. That was one danger he no longer needed to worry about.

'Yes, well, my men plan to move the Spirit into the Deep Pool tonight under cover of darkness and begin unloading her. I hope to have this finished by daybreak and she'll be available to you again then,' dal Camperey said. 'Should you find her surplus to your requirements, Commissary Harris will be more than happy to put you in contact with a ship broker who'll be able to offer you a fair price with very few questions attached.'

'That's very kind of you, but I was hoping to use her to bring a shipment of spices back north with me. With the funds from this deal, I should be able to fill her near to capacity and double my money.'

'Very enterprising of you,' dal Camperey said.

There was a knock at the door and the younger of the unnamed men from the previous occasion, the one Varrisher had said was the Resident Commissioner's secretary, entered. He walked over to dal Camperey and leaned forward to whisper in his ear. Dal Camperey listened and nodded several times. Soren felt his tension increase. If something was going to go wrong, now was the most likely time for it to happen.

'Excellent,' dal Camperey said.

Soren breathed a sigh of relief with as much discretion as he could muster.

'My men put the count at four thousand five hundred and twenty-eight casks. It's rare that I do business with one who under-sells his cargo. I think you are better off returning to the spice trade after all. You're too honest by far.'

'Perhaps, but the casks are of little use to me sitting in the hold of the *Spirit of Brixen*. I've had to come a very long way to find a buyer,' Soren said.

'To the final point of our dealings then,' dal Camperey said, opening the leather folder in front of him. He spun it around and pushed it across the table to Soren. 'I trust you will find that this is in order. A bank draft for the sum of thirteen thousand, five hundred crowns made out in favour of the bearer. I presumed that you would appreciate names being left absent. It shouldn't present a problem if you intend to draw the credit here in Caytown in order to buy spices. Otherwise I would recommend you call at the bank to have the draft amended to your name.'

Soren forced a smile to cover his disappointment. It would have been better if dal Camperey's name was on the draft. As the Admiral had indicated, he was very careful about keeping his tracks covered. However, there was no way he could have secured a draft for such a large sum without taking out a loan from Austorgas'. There would be plenty of paper for the Admiral to chase, hopefully leading him to dal Camperey. It wasn't Soren's problem; he had played his part.

The draft was made out in the correct amount and although Soren had never seen one before, the writing was extremely detailed and elaborate, the paper thick and of high quality. There was no reason to suspect it as being anything other than the genuine article. Nonetheless, it would have looked suspicious to not require further validation.

'Everything seems to be in order, pending my final requirement of course,' Soren said.

'Burgess Austorga is waiting outside to validate the draft, as you requested,' dal Camperey said. 'If it pleases you, I shall have my associate show him in.'

'By all means,' Soren said.

The younger unnamed man left the room and returned a moment later with Burgess Austorga, the same man that Soren had met the day he had first called at the bank.

'Burgess Austorga — as we discussed, if you would be so good as to confirm the authenticity of the draft on the table,' dal Camperey said, gesturing to the page on the table in front of Soren.

Austorga leaned forward and scrutinised the document, making a show of examining several features in particular. 'Yes, this is the draft that I authorised this morning. Austorgas' Bank will stand by it.'

'Does this meet with your satisfaction?' dal Camperey said.

'It does,' Soren said.

'Thank you, Burgess Austorga. That is everything we require,' dal Camperey said.

Austorga nodded to Soren and left.

'That concludes our business,' dal Camperey said. 'Your ship will be ready for you at daybreak. You may collect her from the Deep Pool. I'm glad our transaction has passed so smoothly, and bid you farewell. Once again, I would be obliged if you remained here a few minutes before leaving.' He and Commissary Harris, who had been glaring at Soren suspiciously for the duration of the meeting, stood and left the room.

Soren leaned back in his chair and relaxed. The whole thing had gone off smoothly, and hopefully now they would be able to get their hands on Blasco, who through the intervention of the Admiral was still languishing in prison, rather than in a cage on Headsman's Rock.

He took a look at the draft. Thirteen and a half thousand crowns was a huge sum of money, and in its current form the draft could be cashed by anyone.

He placed it back in the leather folder and stood.

Chapter 40
A Warm Reception

THE FIRST THING THAT struck Soren when he left the room was the racket of a commotion outside on the street. Harris, dal Camperey and the secretary were standing near to the door. The noise outside was unmistakably that of a fight.

'What's going on? What's wrong?' Soren said.

Harris looked back at him, his face showing a mixture of fear and anger. 'You know bloody well what's going on,' he said. 'You set this whole thing up!'

'I don't know what in hells you're talking about,' Soren said.

Dal Camperey turned and gave him an enquiring look before speaking.

'When we went outside a naval officer with a shore party tried to arrest us. Do you know anything about this?'

Had the question been phrased differently, the answer might have been yes, but as it was, Soren had no idea that the Admiral had planned on arresting dal Camperey after the meeting.

'No, not a thing,' Soren said. 'Who's fighting them?'

'I took the precaution of hiring some men. With so much money involved, I wanted to be cautious. I expect they'll have dealt with the sailors before too much longer. Until then I recommend that we remain here.'

'And if your men don't win?' Soren let the question hang in the air for a moment. 'I think I'll take my chances.'

He made his way to the door and drew his sword. He nodded to dal Camperey and smiled at Harris who continued to glare at him.

He opened the door and stepped outside. There was a pitched battle going on between a dozen men outside. There were already several bodies on the ground, one of which had a crossbow quarrel embedded in his chest. Soren looked up to the roof and saw two shapes moving around. No sooner than Soren looked, one of them took what was clearly an unintentional plunge to the ground, three stories below. Soren flinched as the man hit the street with a sickening sound that was a blend of a thud, crunch and squelch. The result seemed most likely to be death and there were certainly no signs of movement.

There was another shape on the roof now, taking the place of the man who had fallen. He was taking a sword to the other shape up there, and as Soren's eyes adjusted to the darkness after the bright interior of the tavern, he could just about make out Varrisher. He must have gone up there when he realised trouble was brewing.

The fight was not going well for the naval Lieutenant or his men. Two had been killed by the crossbowmen while the others were now pressed back against the buildings on the opposite side of the street. It seemed that the Admiral had over-calculated his hand when deciding to try and arrest dal Camperey at that moment. As it was, the Lieutenant and his men would be killed and, tipped off, dal Camperey would make sure any trace of this deal was erased — or possibly flee. Either way, the Admiral's chances of success would be significantly reduced.

Soren grabbed the first man he came to and dragged him back

from the melee. The man didn't realise what was happening at first. When he caught sight of Soren's face he realised that something was amiss. Soren smashed down hard on the man's temple with the pommel of his sword. The man dropped like a sack of rocks, allowing Soren to join the fight.

Soren recognised the Lieutenant from the Admiral's flagship. He had two men remaining at his side, and the others were slumped on the ground. There were four of dal Camperey's men left. The first thing that struck Soren was that they fought well and that one of them showed the hallmarks of being a banneret.

The Lieutenant was struggling to fight off two of the men. He parried one strike but didn't react to a slash by the second assailant. Soren knew what was about to happen and moved forward. Without thinking about it, the world around him illuminated with the ethereal blue glow of the Fount. The attack began to slow as Soren reached forward with his own sword. He realised that he was drawing on the Fount as he both wanted and needed it for the first time, but with no conscious effort.

He struggled to not give it too much thought as he parried the strike aimed at the Lieutenant. It was the closest he had ever gotten to the type of control that Berengarius had spoken of, and it was hard not to be excited by the fact.

Soren pulled the Lieutenant's attacker back by the shoulder and ran him through before he had a chance to react. He shoved the body back toward where the first had fallen and as he twisted he felt woozy. The blue glow flashed bright, blindingly so, as he turned his attention back to the remaining two. He was hit by a wave of nausea and realised what was happening.

He slashed wildly at the closest man as he turned his focus to shutting out the Fount. He may have finally developed the ability to draw from it with no effort, but controlling the flow was still beyond him. He stumbled backward, dazed by the bright flash of light as he fought to maintain control over the energy that threatened to force its way into his body. He focussed all of his concentration on shutting it out, oblivious to everything that was going on around him.

———

'Are you all right?'

Varrisher's voice was close, but Soren wasn't sure where it was coming from.

'I think so,' Soren said. He felt a hand on his shoulder, but he was still unsteady on his feet. 'You?'

'Fine. There were only two of them on the roof. Not too much trouble. You turned the tide down here before you started to look dazed. Did you catch a bang on the head?'

'Must have,' Soren said. The lie was far easier than explaining the truth. He still couldn't see very well, and Varrisher's face was a blur even though he was right next to Soren. 'I'm starting to feel better now though. The Lieutenant and his men?'

'Over there. Safe. They captured the last of the men that attacked them. I don't think they were expecting that much resistance. As the Admiral said, dal Camperey seems to be a very cautious man. More cautious than they gave him credit for.'

Gradually Soren's awareness of what was going on around him returned. His vision started to clear and he was relieved to notice that the Fount's blue glow had disappeared. All of his limbs felt heavy and his eyelids threatened to remain shut each time he blinked.

The Lieutenant and his two remaining sailors had the surviving attacker pinned against the wall. One of the sailors punched him in the stomach.

'Where has the Resident Commissioner gone?' the Lieutenant said.

'You know I'm not going to tell you that,' the man said.

'I'll ask you one last time.'

'Fuck yourself.'

Soren walked over. 'Who are you?'

'None of your fucking business.'

'You know how to use a sword. If you're a banneret you've my word as a brother banneret that I won't let these men kill you.'

The man mulled things over for a moment. 'Banneret Narset.' There was reluctance in his voice, but he knew he was defeated and no man welcomed the death he was about to receive.

'I'm Banneret Soren, and you have my word you'll be treated fairly. Now, where's the Resident Commissioner?'

Narset looked at the Lieutenant resentfully before spitting a mouthful of blood onto the street. 'He was inside last I knew of it. If he isn't there now, I can't help you.'

The sailor punched him in the stomach again. Narset gasped and struggled for breath.

'No more of that,' Soren shouted.

The sailor nodded and stepped back.

'I take it he wasn't in there?' Soren said to the Lieutenant.

The Lieutenant shook his head.

'Well then, it seems he's gotten away,' Soren said. 'But we've fulfilled our part of the bargain, so it really isn't our problem any more.'

'You have the bank draft?' the Lieutenant said.

'Yes, I have it here.' Soren took the leather folder out of his doublet. He showed it to the Lieutenant before putting it back. 'I'll deliver it myself if that's all right.'

'Fine. No need for us to go after dal Camperey now,' the Lieutenant said. 'The Admiral feels the draft will be enough to trace the Resident Commissioner's involvement. The island isn't large; we'll find him quickly enough.'

'Good evening gentlemen,' the Admiral said, as he walked into his stateroom and took his seat behind the desk. 'You'll be glad to hear, I am sure, that my men have secured Resident Commissioner dal Camperey. He was fishing bags of gold coins out of an ornamental pond in the gardens of Commission House. His getaway money it seems. My men finished the job for him, nearly a thousand crowns all told. On the subject of money, I believe you have the bank draft,' he said, directing the statement to Soren.

'Yes,' Soren said.

'If you wouldn't mind.' The Admiral held out his hand.

Soren took the leather folder from his doublet and handed it over.

'Excellent,' he said. 'This is the key piece of evidence against the Resident Commissioner. This is enough for me to justify making out a crown warrant. Burgess Austorga has agreed that he will verify what funds were used as security for the draft, and also the name of the individual standing surety for it. If the answers to those questions are crown funds and Canning dal Camperey, as I believe will be the case, I have all I need to arrest him. By the time any of his friends at home, if he has any left after all of this comes out, find out about it, he will have long since departed this world.

'All that remains is for me to fulfil my part of our agreement. This warrant will secure the release of your man from gaol.' He slid a sealed piece of paper across his desk to Varrisher. 'The officer there is expecting you. Finally, Captain Varrisher, I wanted to say that I'm sorry for our difference of opinion in the past; it was not maliciously intended. My motivations were entirely based on what I felt was dictated by my duty. Humberland didn't have the resources to protect her own interests and aid Ruripathia at the same time. No one could have foretold the… comprehensive defeat your country suffered.'

Varrisher nodded, but said nothing and remained expressionless.

Chapter 41
The Sailing Master

They tied a sack over Blasco's head and bound his hands for the trip down to the docks and the row out to the *Typhon*. Soren hoped that his brush with death would make him all the more grateful when he realised that he had in fact been rescued, rather than brought to his place of execution. It was a cruel trick, but considering who he was and what he had done, Soren felt it was well earned.

Once they were all up on deck, they removed the hood, but left his hands tied. He squinted into the bright sunlight as he slowly became aware of the people standing around him.

'We've kept our part of the bargain, Blasco. You're out of prison, and as soon as you've finished helping us, you're free to go wherever you want,' Soren said.

Blasco looked at Soren and narrowed his eyes. 'You're that slave what was on the *Tear*,' he said.

Soren felt the overwhelming temptation to hit him, but restrained himself. 'You said you'd tell us anything we want to know if we got you out of prison. We have, and now it's time to start talking.'

'Free to go, y'say?'

'Free to go. Once you've helped us.'

'And what do you want to know?'

'We're looking for Sancho Rui, and you're going to lead us to him.' Soren said.

'What d'you want him for?' Blasco said.

'Just because we saved you from the headsman's block doesn't mean that we won't put you right back there if you don't help us,' Soren said. 'We've been through a great deal of trouble to have you freed and our patience is wearing thin. If you want to continue living, you don't have much time to impress me with your willingness to help.'

Blasco stared at Soren. He looked about and rubbed his chin. He was on a ship in the middle of the roads. If he made a run and jump, they would have him fished out of the water or killed before he had swum a hundred metres and he knew it.

'Fine,' he said. 'I've no love for him since he left me here to have my head taken off. I'll tell you what you want to know.'

Varrisher led them both into his stateroom and opened the largest of the charts from his rutters.

'Where's he headed?' Varrisher said.

Blasco stood over the map and studied it for a moment. He stabbed a stubby finger down on the chart. 'Here,' he said, 'although this chart isn't much use. There's a small cove on this island with a little town. Rui calls it Point Vermeil. It's not much, just a few warehouses, bunkhouses and the like. It's Rui's own little kingdom. It's almost impossible to see into the cove from the sea, so it's a perfect hiding spot for a ship. What's more, the entire area around is littered with reefs and sandbanks.'

'Same could be said for the whole of the Spice Isles,' Varrisher said, impatiently.

'Aye, but it's more the case there. The reefs come right up from the bottom with no warning, deep water, then suddenly you're aground. Rui knows the safe channels like the back of his hand, but for anyone else the waters are treacherous. He's gone back there because he knows that the Conclave are comin' after him, not to mention the bounty that was put on his head after he took the *Gandawai*. I suppose that's why you're after him.'

'Running and hiding, is he?' Soren said.

'From the likes of you, maybe. He's lookin' to fry some bigger fish though. He's been spoiling for a fight with the Conclave ever since they gave Valkdorf to Ramiro Qai. They were the two strongest, but that put Qai on top until Sancho took the *Gandawai* and became as rich as the rest of them put together. Fancies setting himself up as a Prince of the Isles, but first he has to get rid of the Conclave.

'He's been breaking the Accords every chance he gets in the hope that he could draw them out. Tried to kill Ramiro a few weeks back, but it didn't work out. His plan is to lure them back into dangerous waters that he knows. He'll run them up on the reefs and kill them at his leisure.'

'And you know these reefs, and how to navigate through them safely?' Varrisher said.

'Who do you think piloted the *Tear* while he was down below with one of his wenches? Of course I know them, and if you want to get to him without ripping the arse out of your ship, you'll need me to get you through them. Your charts barely even show the island, let alone the nasty stuff waitin' for you under the water. You've saved my life and I'm grateful for that; won't have it be said I don't pay my debts, but I've got nothing, so if you want my help, I'm going to need more,' Blasco said.

He was brazen, Soren had to give him that at least. 'We're listening.'

'When you kill Rui, I want the *Tear*. You can take what you want, just leave me the ship and enough lads alive to run her. I can make nice with the Conclave and take over what was his.'

Soren looked to Varrisher, who shrugged. 'Fine,' Soren said. 'It makes no difference to us. You get us safely into Point Vermeil, and the ship and whatever is left of his crew once Rui is dead is yours to do with as you please.'

Blasco smiled. 'Well then, let's get going.'

CHAPTER 42
THE HIDDEN COVE

'WHERE?' SOREN SQUINTED AS he scanned the craggy cliff face. It was covered with vegetation wherever a plant could gain a foothold, which made it even more difficult to make out the features.

'There,' Blasco said, pointing with his stubby finger.

Soren followed the gesture with his eyes, spotting what looked like a darker patch on the cliff. 'That's it?'

'That's it,' Blasco said. 'It curves, so you can't see in from any angle. Told you it wasn't easy to spot.'

Soren rolled his eyes at Varrisher who shrugged. Blasco was an odious man who had done little to endear himself to anyone on the *Typhon*, but true to his word he'd got them safely to Point Vermeil.

Varrisher made no effort to conceal the fact that he still didn't trust Blasco, and had posted men at various vantage points at the side of the ship and in the rigging to keep a keen eye out for any underwater hazards. He took the wheel himself, being guided by both Blasco's instructions and the eyes of his own crewmen.

Soren felt that the added incentive of being given the *Tear* if they were successful had been a gift from the gods, and was one that would not have occurred to him had Blasco himself not suggested it. Past consideration was no consideration and however grateful he might have professed himself to be for his life, Soren didn't believe for a second that Blasco would have kept his side of the bargain had it not been for the ship. He might even have betrayed them to Rui in order to try to regain his place as sailing master on the *Tear*, something that Soren and Varrisher had not yet entirely discounted. With the possibility that the *Tear* could be his, at least their interests coincided.

Despite the apparent safety provided by the near invisible cove and the reefs guarding it, Rui was not one to take his safety for granted and Blasco had told them of an artificial reef of metal spikes that could be lowered down into the water with pulleys to prevent any other ships from getting in.

'How are we going to get to him?' Soren said. It was early evening and the sun was low in the sky. It was warm and the fragrant breeze blew gently over the *Typhon's* deck. It was so serene it was difficult to imagine a fight there.

'Well, we can't sail in,' Varrisher said.

Blasco shook his head in agreement. 'There're sentries posted on the cliff top on either side of the cove's mouth. Sancho probably already knows we're here.'

'Why doesn't he come out?' Soren said. He already knew the answer; Rui was a coward, and wouldn't fight unless he had a clear advantage.

'Why would he?' Blasco said. 'He can wait, and hope that you'll either get bored and leave, or try to sail in. He doesn't know that I'm on board and that you know about the spikes.'

Soren walked over to the bulwark to get a better view of the cove's entrance. 'We wouldn't be able to fire an arbalest bolt in with a challenge to come out and fight.' He was running out of ideas, and his frustration was made all the worse by the knowledge that Rui could stay in there longer than they would be able to wait.

There were no suggestions coming from the other two, so Soren racked his brains trying to think of how he could get Rui out of his sanctuary. Then it struck him; Rui had cultivated a flamboyant image of a rakish, swashbuckling adventurer that was far removed from the reality. He was no more than a thieving murderer. The façade was not just for his general reputation, it was also for his crew. Captaincy was by election, not right, and he needed to keep his crew believing that he was all of the things he claimed to be. He couldn't allow himself to be shown up for a coward.

'I'll go into the cove and deliver a challenge to him in person,' Soren said.

'Are you sure that's a good idea?' Varrisher said. 'He'll probably just tell you to piss off.

'Challenging him to a fight's the only way to get him out.'

Blasco shook his head and was about to speak when Soren continued.

'No, hear me out. If I can get in there and make the challenge in front of his whole crew or a big portion of it, he'll have no choice but to accept it. He won't let himself be made look like a coward in front of them, and I'll make sure that's how it will play out if he refuses. To be certain it works, I'll tell them all that there's a chest full of gold crowns in our hold to try and tempt him out. I doubt his crew'll be too happy if they know he's turned down the opportunity to take a decent prize, regardless of how much they've already got.'

Varrisher shook his head. 'I don't know. What's to stop him taking you as hostage and demanding the money without fighting for it?' Varrisher said.

'I'll play to his vanity,' Soren said. He wasn't sure who he was trying to convince that the plan could work, Varrisher or himself. 'We're talking about a man who refers to himself in the third person. I don't think it'll be too difficult to turn his ego to our advantage, especially if I can make the challenge out in the open in front of his men. That's the only thing I can think of, but if you've got something better I'm happy to listen.'

'No, 'fraid I don't. I agree with you that it's the best we've come up with so far, but it's risky. How do you propose to do it?' Varrisher said.

'Have a couple of men row me into the cove in the jolly boat, hope the lookouts don't shoot us with crossbows and then try to make the challenge from the boat. If I'm shouting up to him on the *Tear*, everyone on board will be able to hear what I'm saying.'

'And if he's ashore?'

'Makes no difference,' Soren said. He was starting to believe that it could work. 'I'll issue the challenge to whoever's on the ship at the time. They'll have to relay it to Rui. Even if they try to capture me, I'll have advertised the challenge and he won't be able to hush it up.

'I'll tell him that if I'm not back on board the *Typhon* in half an hour, you'll sail. I'll say that if you do leave without a fight, you'll quite happily spread it around that Sancho Rui is a coward.'

Varrisher nodded. 'I wouldn't feel right if I didn't offer to go in on the jolly boat myself.'

'No, I'm happy doing it,' Soren said. 'If something happens to whoever goes in, better that it's me. I wouldn't have the first clue how to run the ship in a fight.'

Soren also reckoned he had a far better chance of fighting his way out of any trouble than Varrisher did. And he needed Varrisher to deliver him back to the mainland when it was all done with.

'I take your point,' Varrisher said. 'Anyway, if it comes to a fight, you're better suited to cutting your way out of it than I am!'

Soren smiled. Perhaps Varrisher's ego was less prone to bruising than Soren had given it credit for.

'There's no point in waiting any longer,' Soren said. 'Do you have any preference for when we ask him to come out to face us?'

'Not especially. Daylight would be nice though; it'll make dodging the reefs a little bit easier, even with Blasco's help, which I'm still not convinced about.'

'Fine. The sun's setting, so if I go in now, it's doubtful that he'll be ready to come out before daylight anyway. I can say that we'll be gone by sundown tomorrow if he hasn't emerged. Hopefully that'll ensure he won't simply wait until tomorrow night to keep the advantage of his crew's better knowledge of the local waters,' Soren said.

By the time the jolly boat was lowered, the sun had set. Ideally Soren would have liked Blasco with him to ensure they could find the entrance to the cove in the darkness, but the sailing master was too valuable an asset and too likely to be taken by Rui to risk bringing him in with them. If Rui agreed to the duel, Blasco's knowledge could be the difference between ripping open the *Typhon's* hull on a reef and successfully defeating Rui, assuming he kept to his word. Having him was an advantage of which Rui would be unaware, hopefully making him even more cocksure.

The *Typhon* had anchored in one of the channels that Blasco said would give the ship enough room to swing on her anchor line. It meant a short row to the entrance to the cove.

At first there was only the sound of wood creaking as the oars moved in the rowlocks and of water splashing as the blades dipped in and out. This continued until they grew closer to the island when the sounds of the nocturnal insects began to fill the air; a cacophony of strange and exotic sounds that reminded him of the jungle near Valkdorf. He scanned the dark cliffs for the gap as they went, their blackness barely contrasting with the inky blue of the sky and water. Even having already seen it, it was difficult to spot in the dark

'There,' Soren said. They had almost gone past it before he spotted it, and directed the oarsmen and the bo'sun toward it. They rounded the corner and rowed through a narrow gap in the cliff face that would only be barely large enough to allow a ship the size of the *Tear* to pass through. The blackness of the cliffs looming above them almost shutting out the sky gave way to an open cove, bright with moonlight, with a ship anchored at its centre. The *Tear*.

Soren hadn't known how he would react to seeing it again. He felt a flush of anger as he thought of how Rui had treated Captain Joris and his men. The *Tear* sat stern toward them as they rowed into the cove. Overhead, he could hear two separate voices call out above the constant droning of the insects. They had been spotted by the lookouts. If they were to be attacked it would in the next few moments. If not, what played out after would dictate whether his plan ended in him being rowed back out to the *Typhon* with word of his success or slowly sinking to the bottom of the cove riddled with crossbow bolts.

'Who goes there?' came a shout from the ship.

'I have a message for your captain, Sancho Rui,' Soren shouted, as he stood up.

'Who says he's captain of this ship?' came back the reply.

'Tell him Captain Varrisher of the *Typhon* challenges him to a ship-to-ship combat. We await Captain Rui's answer,' Soren shouted. He had to concentrate on keeping his balance in the small boat, but his oarsmen were aware of his less than seamanlike legs and had pressed the flats of their oar blades on the water to keep it steady.

There was little to be heard over the sound of the night, but Soren could just make out voices in what seemed to be a heated discussion on the *Tear*'s deck.

'Hold your position. Come any closer an' you're dead!' came the voice after a few more moments.

Soren sat down. He was still alive, which was better than his worst-case scenario. The oarsmen gently worked the oars to keep the jolly boat in position. The response came only a moment later, delivered by a voice that was both more authoritative and more irritated. Sancho Rui.

'Who are you?'

'Just a sailor with a message from my captain,' Soren said, standing once again.

'What's your captain's message?'

'Captain Varrisher challenges you to a ship-to-ship combat. He awaits you outside of this cove,' Soren said.

The sound of his voice and commotion that his arrival had generated had brought a number of shadowy figures to the bulwark of the *Bayda's Tear*. There seemed to be enough to ensure that any information Soren gave would reach the entire crew in short order. 'Captain Varrisher also bids me tell you that there's a chest in his stateroom containing five thousand golden crowns, the purchase money for a cargo of spice he is tasked with bringing north. That will be your prize if you can defeat him.'

'What's to stop me taking you and your crew mates there hostage for a chunk of that gold?' Rui said, which elicited a laugh from his crew.

'If we don't return in the next ten minutes, Captain Varrisher will continue on his voyage, making sure to inform everyone he comes across on his way that Captain Sancho Rui was too afraid to face him in combat. My captain bade me tell you that he will remain on station until sundown tomorrow at which point he will depart, again informing everyone that he meets that Captain Sancho Rui was too afraid to meet him in combat,' Soren said.

His success in striking the nerve he had been aiming for was evident immediately. Rui exploded with rage.

'Fuck your captain. What's to stop me from fucking killing you right now?' he screamed. 'Then going out and killing your fucking captain as well? Taking his fucking money? Sancho Rui is afraid of no man! Tell your fucking captain that I'll be out at dawn to cut his fucking heart out! Tell him I'm going to eat it when I am done killing you and every one of his fucking crew!'

Even in the dark, Soren could see the spittle flying from Rui's mouth, tiny silhouettes created by the light on the deck of the *Bayda's Tear* behind him. He smiled.

'I'll relay your message to Captain Varrisher,' Soren said. 'We'll await you at sun up.'

He gestured to the boatswain to get the jolly boat underway. They had a tough fight ahead of them, but Soren found himself looking forward to it.

Chapter 43
A Duel of Ships

Soren watched the Bayda's *Tear* appear out of the entrance to the cove a few minutes after the sun rose. The *Typhon* and her crew had spent the night at anchor beyond the distance over which a ballista bolt could be fired from the shore. Despite Rui's declarations of murderous intent, Soren and Varrisher were under no illusion: he would try to set the *Typhon* alight if the opportunity presented itself.

No one had slept well that night, least of all Soren. He was already awake when the call to station was made shortly before dawn. Varrisher wanted them all wide-awake and alert well in advance, so the anchor was raised and the sail set as soon as everyone was ready. They had been tacking up and down one of the channels between the submerged reefs in wait, but now that Rui was showing his nose Varrisher gave the command to go straight for him.

Soren stood next to him at the bulwark on the quarterdeck of the *Typhon*, feeling his excitement rise as they watched the distance between the two ships diminish. He had been a passenger on board for too long; now he would get to show his worth.

'How does this work?' Soren said. He had never seen a naval battle before, much less been involved in one. The capture of the *Honest Christophe* was as close as he had ever come.

'We'll manoeuvre to come alongside one another and we'll fire a volley with the ballistae to try and clear their deck a little. They'll probably try to do the same, so be ready to duck. Once that's done, all the sails will be taken in and we'll grapple the ships together. When we're close enough, it's over the side and at them. I'll leave some men up in the rigging to fire crossbows down at the deck, but we'll win or lose on what we do with our swords. That's where you come in,' Varrisher said. 'Until then, you should stay out of harm's way. It would be unfortunate to have come all this way only to be taken out of the fight by a well-aimed shot. That brings me on to the other thing that I need to discuss. If I should be killed, Rodin will take command of the *Typhon*. He's a good man; you can trust him. Whatever way the fight turns out, if *Typhon* is still floating at the end, I've instructed him to take you wherever you wish to go, as we agreed.'

'I'm sure that it won't come to that,' Soren said.

Varrisher nodded. 'I hope that I'm being overly dramatic, but it's often best to prepare for these eventualities before things get started.'

The *Bayda's Tear* was close enough for Soren to make out the individual features of the sailors on board when Varrisher ordered the ballistae fired. The ship shuddered as they launched their heavy, steel tipped bolts toward the *Tear* where they shot across the deck. Each bolt cut a swathe through the sailors massed there.

Rui responded in kind, but the *Typhon* carried fewer crew so her deck was less crowded. Soren counted a half dozen casualties at most, far fewer than Rui had suffered, but the speed and ferocity with which they had been killed still shocked him.

Varrisher moved to the wheel. He manoeuvred the *Typhon* aggressively, steering left and right on Blasco's instructions to keep her away from the reefs as the two ships continued sailing parallel to one another. The deck pitched with each turn but Soren found that his sea legs had finally become more reliable, on the larger ship's deck at least. The sudden and unpredictable movement made him feel sorry for the sailors who were up in the rigging trying to aim their heavy naval crossbows.

Blasco stood next to Varrisher at the wheel, frequently pointing to some unseen hazard lurking beneath the surface of the water. He was wearing a foul weather hat that obscured his features. His knowledge was an advantage to them, all the greater while Rui was unaware of it.

Rui had brought the *Tear* close to the *Typhon*, but maintained too great a distance to attempt grappling. It seemed that his plan was to run the *Typhon* onto a reef. Soren smiled at the knowledge that it wouldn't work. He wondered how long it would take Rui to figure that out.

Blasco directed Varrisher to steer the *Typhon* into another clear channel, forcing Rui to follow and hope that his opponent would blunder onto the next reef. He had clearly expected the *Typhon* to founder as he had already begun to turn the *Tear* to pounce on her once she had struck the reef. When it didn't happen, it left him out of position and even to a landsman like Soren it was obvious that he was uncertain what to do next.

Varrisher was not one to allow an opportunity to pass by. Soren had to admit that, although he might not have been much more than a competent swordsman, he was a superb sailor. After confirming with Blasco that there was room to manoeuvre, he called out a nautical term to his crew that was beyond comprehension to Soren, and turned the wheel hard over. The *Typhon* responded instantly and Soren was forced to grab onto the bulwark to stop himself from falling overboard.

The *Typhon* spun about in a circle tighter than Soren would have thought possible, and Varrisher aimed her directly at the *Tear*, her bow pointing toward the stern of Rui's ship. Soren's heart leapt into his mouth. Could Varrisher be intending to ram? The space between them was dropping away rapidly and it seemed to Soren that even if a ramming was unintended, it was now unavoidable. Just as he began to tighten his grip in preparation for impact, Varrisher called to the crew once more and threw the wheel over in the opposite direction. The *Typhon* turned sharply once again. Soren stared down the length of the *Typhon* toward the bow, his heart still in his throat as the side of the *Tear* raced past the *Typhon's* bowsprit, no more than inches away. He felt a wave of relief as clear air appeared, leaving the *Typhon* alongside the *Tear*, and well within grappling range.

The *Typhon's* momentum and the close proximity meant that a collision was inevitable, but it seemed to Soren that this was Varrisher's intention all along. Side to side, the *Typhon* and the *Bayda's Tear* slammed into one another with a thunderous boom and a jolt that would have thrown Soren off his feet had he not been still gripping the bulwark with fervour.

'Grapples away. Go at them, *Typhon*s,' Varrisher shouted.

Soren could hear the sound of crossbow bolts fizzing through the air and thudding into wood and flesh. Screams of pain intermingled with shouts and battle cries as the crew of the *Typhon* hurled grappling hooks onto the *Bayda's Tear*. As soon as the two ships were secured, they followed their grapples. Soren had been so caught up in the novelty of the naval combat that he almost forgot this was the moment when his own skills came to the fore.

He vaulted the bulwark, drawing his sword. The Fount appeared as soon as he desired it and he smiled as the mass of men on the deck of the *Bayda's Tear* were shrouded in a flickering blue glow. Movement began to slow, and for the briefest time Soren considered allowing his connection to remain open a little longer, to see if he could temper the flow to sustain his need and no more.

The memory of the fight outside *The Drunken Rover* was too fresh in his mind though, and he resisted the temptation. If things were going against them, he could always draw on it again.

He forced the connection to the Fount to close and waded into the fight. The *Typhon*s who had crossed over to the *Tear* had formed a pocket, pressing into the mass of Rui's crew. Varrisher had all of his men tie a strip of grey cloth around their heads or upper arms before the *Bayda's Tear* emerged from the cove, grey being the state colour of Ruripathia. It made life far easier for Soren in the heat of battle.

Soren pushed his way through the *Typhon*s to get to the enemy. He had the image of Sancho Rui's face burned into his mind and he was eager that Rui should fall to his blade rather than someone else's. Rui was the priority irrespective of his personal motivations. The *Typhon*s were outnumbered, but Soren reckoned that if they could kill Rui his crew would surrender.

Finally faced with the enemy, Soren was able to set himself to turning the tide in their favour. He had chosen to use a rapier rather than his shorter sword. He knew that the longer blade would be difficult to wield in a tight press of men, but with his elbows he cleared the room to move his arms and used the tip of his sword to clear the space in front of him.

The clash of metal and the shouts of fighting men filled the air, drowning out all other sounds. A pirate slashed his short sword at Soren's head. Soren parried it high and drew his dagger with his left hand. He pushed forward putting the pirate off balance and stabbed him in the guts. The pirate grimaced and Soren finished him off before shoving the body to the deck. Another man took his place before Soren had the chance to step over the body. His rapier was still held high so, as the pirate began a thrust to Soren's midsection, he cut down hard and split the pirate's head open.

He pushed forward into the space, slashing out with both sword and dagger to either side as he went, adding to his tally. It put him in the midst of Rui's crew. A man bumped into Soren as he tried to get through the mass of his own crew and at the *Typhon*s, not realising that he was faced with an enemy. Soren barely paid him a thought, lashing out with his sword. The pirate parried it away, which came as a shock to Soren, and grabbed his complete attention. The pirate countered and his blade came at Soren far more quickly than any of the previous pirates had managed. He countered it, but it was clear that the effect of the Gift was already ebbing, and was doing so quickly.

It seemed that the small draw he had made in the Fount was not enough to keep the Gift going for very long. Even without the extra benefit of the Fount, he was still more than a match for any of the pirates on the ship, but whether he would be able to have the impact on the battle that he wanted was another question. As soon as his desire to draw from the Fount returned, it appeared once more. He felt the rush of energy flood through his body. He scooped the pirate's sword out of his way with his dagger, then ran him through with his rapier.

He allowed the connection to remain open a little longer this time, revelling in the way his body grew exponentially stronger, while all around him slowed at a similar rate. At the first hint of light-headedness he focussed on blocking off the Fount.

Rui's crew were so focussed on getting at the group of *Typhon*s on the *Tear*'s deck, few even noticed Soren in their midst. Another pirate eventually did and attacked him with a wild sweep of his blade. Soren parried just in time to bring his sword back down to stop another attack from a second pirate. Now he was identified as an enemy in their midst, more pirates converged on him. The first pirate attacked. Soren knocked his blade aside and stabbed the pirate's neck with his dagger.

He kicked the body free and turned his attention to the others. He spotted Rui standing behind his men, trying to urge them to drive the *Typhons* from their deck. Soren cut down another pirate and rather than fight his way through to Rui, he dropped his shoulder and charged.

Soren had a big frame, which had once been well developed and muscular. The deprivations of his captivity had robbed him of some of this weight and natural strength, but he was still big and strong enough to barrel his way through a group of unsuspecting men. He drove forward with his legs until he stumbled out of the press of bodies and faced Rui.

Rui looked surprised, obviously not expecting to have to deal with an attacker himself. He reached for the hilt of his sword, which was still sheathed. It was Soren's Telastrian steel sword, which both delighted and infuriated him. He had hoped that Rui would keep it, it being most likely the finest sword that would ever cross his path, rather than sell it on, but seeing it at his waist fuelled Soren's anger.

'You've something that belongs to me,' Soren said.

'Sancho Rui takes what he likes,' he said as he finished drawing Soren's sword. He squinted slightly. 'I know you. You've been on this ship before.' He dropped into a low fencer's stance that looked very practiced as his eyes widened in recognition. 'Ah, of course. The slave who helped Ramiro Qai in the jungle. I knew I should have killed you when you were my prisoner.'

Soren had no interest in bantering with Rui, so he said nothing.

'I will put that mistake to rights now!' Rui said. He lunged forward and Soren parried the attack with a grinding clash of steel. He cringed at the thought of damaging his beautiful sword, but knew it was the sword he was holding that was going to take any damage.

Rui mistook Soren's hesitation for uncertainty and slashed left and right in a flamboyant but sloppy attack. Soren pushed the sword aside with his own vastly inferior blade and stepped forward quickly, punching his dagger into Rui's throat.

Rui gasped, his eyes wide in disbelief. His mouth twitched as though he was about to say something, but the only sound was a bubbling hiss, and that came from his ruined throat rather than his mouth.

There was a sickening squelch followed by a crunch as Soren cut through Rui's neck and spine.

'Rui is dead!' Soren shouted so loudly his words scratched at his throat. 'Sancho Rui is dead.'

He could barely hear his own voice over the din of the fighting, so to emphasise his point, he held the head aloft, trying not to cover himself in gore in the process. As he pulled Rui's head free from the body, something fell from around the stub of his neck and dropped at Soren's feet. He trapped it with his foot to inspect when he was done advertising Rui's death. He continued to display the head, its lifeless eyes staring out at the crew. Gradually they started to notice it, and the fighting waned.

When the noise had dropped to a manageable level, Soren shouted out again. 'Sancho Rui is dead! Throw down your weapons and you'll not be harmed.'

Varrisher had been fighting a group of Rui's crew on the quarterdeck of the Typhon. In the heat of the battle, Soren hadn't realised any had crossed over. Varrisher disarmed the men he was fighting and then hopped up on the bulwark where everyone could see him.

'We came here to kill Sancho Rui and we've done that. I've no interest in your ship or anyone else. Throw down your arms and we can all go our separate ways with no more killing,' he shouted.

The sound of grumbling started to grow from a low murmur to a confused discussion and was eventually joined by the sound of a sword hitting the deck. It was followed by many others, and then the sound of cheering coming from the *Typhons*. With a nod and a smile to Varrisher, Soren lowered the head. Only then did he bend down to pick up whatever it was that had fallen from Rui's neck. He moved his foot which had been covering it and gasped.

He recognised it straight away, but could barely believe his eyes.

It was a small silver amulet with a clear stone at its centre: a Ruripathian huntsman's amulet, a good luck charm of which there had certainly been more than one made, but few enough even still. It was also the only gift of value that Soren had ever given Alessandra. He reached down to pick it up, his hand shaking, his heart racing. The sight of it filled him with desperate, dizzying need for it to be hers, but part of him could not accept that this could possibly be the one he had given her.

His heart sped to a frenzy as his fingers came in contact with the cool metal. He savoured the touch, wanting the feeling of hope that it brought to last as long as possible. He gathered it and the chain that was attached to it into his hand and brought it close to his face, his knuckles white as he clutched it. With a deep breath he opened his hand. Etched on one side in the long dead northern language was the prayer that Jarod, the royal huntsman who had given him the amulet, told him was meant to be for good luck and to bestow protection on the wearer. It hadn't worked for Rui.

With another deep breath he flipped it over and there, in the neatly engraved letters placed on it by a silversmith in Ostenheim at Soren's request, was Alessandra's name.

The rush of joy he felt made him so lightheaded he had a moment of panic that the Fount was flooding into him. If the amulet was on board the *Tear*, Alessandra could not have been lost at sea. He swayed on his feet as a variety of emotions — hope, love, fear, desperation and others he couldn't even identify — rushed in on him in a confused jumble.

It was joined by a wave of panic as he looked down at Sancho Rui's headless corpse. Had he killed the only man who could tell him where she was, or if she was still alive?

✲

Chapter 44
The Amulet

Varrisher jumped down from the bulwark and made his way over to Soren as the crew of the *Bayda's Tear* were checked for weapons and herded to the front of the ship to be supervised.

'Well done,' he said. 'That went as smoothly as we could have hoped.' He noticed the expression on Soren's face. 'You look like you've seen a ghost.'

'I feel as if I have,' Soren said, holding the chain and amulet out in front of him and staring intently at it.

'What's that?'

'It's a Ruripathian huntsman's amulet,' Soren said.

'Huh,' Varrisher said. 'That's odd. Not something you expect to see in these parts. I wonder how it got all the way down here? I suppose Rui must have taken a Ruripathian vessel with a huntsman at some point. Plenty of refugees coming down to Valkdorf now. Must have made easy pickings for him.'

'Not this one,' Soren said. 'It was mine.'

Varrisher was still bemused by the strength of Soren's reaction to the small silver amulet. 'Of course, I'd forgotten about your hunting adventures. He took it from you when you were his captive?'

'No. I gave this to someone,' Soren said. 'She fled Ostenheim a few weeks before I did. I was looking for her in Auracia, but there was no trace of her ever having been there.'

'You think this might explain what happened to her?' Varrisher said.

'I do. I hope I haven't just killed the only person that can tell me how he came by this amulet,' Soren said, his voice strained. He handed the head he still held to Varrisher who took it delicately and with an appropriate degree of disgust.

In an effort to put his mind to something else, he knelt down at the side of Rui's corpse and began to prise the dead fingers from the hilt of his sword. Any joy he might have had in being reunited with it was tempered by the presence of the amulet. The matching dagger was still in its sheath on the belt around Rui's waist, which also belonged to Soren. He pulled them free roughly, angry at Rui and himself.

'If you know when Rui captured her, we might be able to work out where she is now,' Varrisher said.

Soren stood and looked at him intensely, desperate for any suggestion. 'How?'

'Even a pirate is going to have to keep logs of some sort. They probably won't reveal much, but it might be enough to work out where he next made landfall. It's not much, but it's a start, and gives you somewhere to begin your search. Also, we still have Blasco and a whole crew to question about what they might remember, the ships and prisoners they took and where they went to sell their plunder.'

It seemed so obvious Soren couldn't understand how he had not thought of it himself, but his emotions were in turmoil, and he wasn't thinking clearly, not to mention he was fighting off the after effects of the Gift. Varrisher's suggestion went some way to settling his mind and giving him hope. Having a way to move forward allowed him to focus on something that would be useful, rather than dwelling on the worst outlook.

'Get Blasco,' Soren said. 'I'm going to start looking through Rui's stateroom to see if I can find anything.'

Soren knew that Alessandra had fled Ostenheim roughly seventeen weeks earlier. The voyage south to Auracia would have taken eight days or so, if it had been anything like his own voyage south several weeks later. Rui's cruising waters had been in the south, which meant she would have been close to Auracia, a week or so into the voyage when he came upon the vessel taking her there, if that was what had happened. He couldn't expect that a pirate would keep a detailed log, but even they would need to keep financial records of some sort. Knowing roughly when Alessandra had been taken would give him something to go on. If Blasco could fill in any more detail, all the better. He had proved cooperative enough so far and had no reason to dissemble if he hoped to take possession of the *Tear*.

The *Tear*'s stateroom was no larger than that on board the *Typhon*; the ships were roughly the same size. Soren looked around, wondering where to start. On the starboard side there was a small cot on gimbals where Rui must have slept. On the port side there was an escritoire, which seemed like Soren's best hope.

He attempted to open the cover, but it was locked. After a cursory search for a key he pulled out his dagger and jammed it into the lock. It punched through the wood of the desk and he gouged out the metal lock. Barely able to contain his impatience he pulled the cover down into an extended desk.

There were some papers contained within, scrawled with clumsy script of the type he had produced when first learning to write, not all that long before. He scanned through them quickly, dropping each irrelevant document on the floor until the escritoire was empty and Soren still had no useful information.

He sat on the bench at the back of the stateroom and sighed. He felt rushed even though there was nothing for him to do. Varrisher entered with Blasco, who seemed very pleased with himself. Despite their agreement to give him the *Tear* when they had what they needed, he still had to win the support of the crew — which he had obviously been confident of doing. Now that they had the help that they'd needed, Blasco was once again in a precarious position. Soren had no qualms with threatening to go back on their deal about the *Tear* if Blasco refused to help him. In the mood that held him, there were few things, if any, that he would have qualms about doing to get the information he was looking for.

'I need you to tell me everything you know about the movements of the *Tear* over the past few months,' Soren said.

'Not sure I can help you,' Blasco said.

He was looking smug. Delighted no doubt about their victory and the ship that he thought was about to become his. Soren resisted the urge to punch him in the face.

Blasco saw the dark look on Soren's face. 'Now, see here. There's only so much I can do before I'll have lost the chance to get the lads to trust me again.'

Soren ignored him. 'About fifteen weeks ago, maybe sixteen, you took a ship bound for Auracia. There was a woman on board. She was wearing this, and Rui took it from her.' He held up the amulet. 'I'm looking for her, and if you don't tell me where she is I will kill you, every man on this ship, and I will burn the *Tear* to the water line.'

Blasco was shocked by the abruptness of the threat — but not nearly so much as Varrisher from the look on his face.

'There's no need for threats,' Blasco said, 'but you have to understand my point of view. Getting help to kill Rui is one thing; the crew respect me for that. Shows initiative. Ambition. They're about to agree to appoint me as captain. If I tell you where the ship has been and what the crew've done, I'll be peaching on them, and they'll string me up for that. If they think I'm telling tales that could put them on the chopping block, I won't last ten minutes after they find out, and they will. To tell the truth, you killing me will be quicker and less painful.'

They were at an impasse, and it seemed to Soren that threats of violence were not going to get him anywhere. He struggled to control the rage that was coursing through his veins. He didn't know what alternatives were left open to him. Blasco stood sheepishly in the centre of the stateroom, afraid. He wasn't trying to act tough or call Soren's bluff to assert his authority. It appeared that he fully expected to die in the next few minutes unless he was extremely lucky. Varrisher looked equally awkward.

Soren wondered if the rest of the crew would be of the same opinion as Blasco. If shipboard justice for 'peaching', as Blasco had put it, was so harsh, Soren would have to shed a great deal of blood in a particularly brutal fashion before he would get anything that might even be potentially useful. He had to ask himself if he would be able to live with that, although there was something inside him that didn't care, and that frightened him.

He felt his rage flare up again, but he took a deep breath to try to quell it. 'And all the crew will feel the same? Even if I start cutting them up and throw them to the sharks?' He managed to keep his voice calm and even.

Blasco nodded.

'Hold him,' Soren said.

Varrisher did as he was instructed, not quite sure what was going to happen next.

Soren took one of Blasco's arms and pulled it over to the table, placing Blasco's hand flat on it. Blasco resisted, but Soren was able to force it. He pressed his dagger down on the first knuckle of Blasco's index finger.

'Sure you've nothing to say?'

Blasco was breathing heavily through his nose and his mouth remained shut. He shook his head.

Soren pressed down harder, until a thin line of blood appeared on either side of the blade. Blasco began exhaling in sharp, staccato breaths, but still said nothing. Soren looked at him and held his gaze. He was not going to say anything. He slammed the point of his dagger down into the table. Blasco gasped in anticipation and sighed when he realised that his finger was still attached to his hand.

'Fuck!' Soren said. 'Fuck!'

He was still assuming that the *Tear* had taken the ship that Alessandra was on. There was no real way to know for sure, unless they had taken the names of those they had captured. Rui could even have bought the amulet at a market somewhere. Despite his overwhelming desire to find her and to extract any useful information from the crew of the *Tear*, torture and murder was not something he could bring himself to do. It was too much.

'Get out,' he said to Blasco. Varrisher released him and Blasco was out the door almost before Soren had finished speaking. Soren dropped his head into his hands.

'You really had me going there. I thought you were going to hack him to bits,' Varrisher said, as he made his way over to the escritoire and kicked his boot through the pile of papers that Soren had dumped on the floor.

'I nearly did,' Soren said.

Varrisher bent down and picked up one of the pieces of paper, and then shuffled through the mess on the floor to find several others written in the same hand.

'When did you say you thought your friend was taken?' Varrisher said, as he went through the pages he had picked up.

'I don't know. Maybe fifteen or sixteen weeks ago, give or take. Maybe not at all.' He walked over to the bench beneath the stern gallery window and slumped down on it.

'Well,' Varrisher said, 'these are receipts for ship's provisions. This is the most recent.' He held up a piece of crinkled paper and pointed to something on it that Soren couldn't make out from where he was sitting. 'This mark means that it was issued from a ship's provisioner in Caytown. This one is from about ten weeks ago. It's from a provisioner in Galat, a city on the coast of Shandahar. This one is from another ten weeks before that, Caytown again. The *Gandawai* was taken eleven or twelve weeks ago if memory serves. It seems that after they took her they stopped at Galat and bought stocks of fresh food and water. Although it doesn't say for sure, it stands to reason that they would have sold off any prisoners they had at the slave markets there. Prisoners take up space and cost money to feed. They also have a habit of dying when maltreated in cramped conditions and fed slop, so it makes sense to unload them and sell them off as soon as possible.'

The scenario that he painted was not one Soren was comfortable hearing but, as Varrisher said, it stood to reason. Slavery and gods only knew what else would have awaited her. He felt like he was going to throw up.

'When I first agreed to sail with you,' Soren said, 'you said that you'd drop me off anywhere I wanted. I'd like to go to Galat.'

'I did,' Varrisher said, 'and I intend to honour that agreement. Kirek is on the way to Galat, so it won't delay us stopping there to collect the bounty on Rui's head. I'd bring you directly, but you know how desperately I need to collect the money. Anyhow, I'm sure your share of the bounty will be of help when you go after your friend.'

PART III

Chapter 45
The Desert Kingdoms

Kirek was not what Soren had expected. To his mind, Shandahar was a desert filled with oases and nomadic tribes but that couldn't have been farther from the truth. The city was a mass of white buildings surrounded by a lush, verdant river plain. It was a large port, one of five along the Shandahari coast, each of which sat on the delta of the river that bore the same name as the city. Each river cut through the desert, a blue and green swathe in a sea of yellow sand.

The *Typhon* arrived in the circular harbour of Kirek six days after leaving Point Vermeil and the fight against the *Bayda's Tear*, just as Varrisher had predicted. The harbour was massive and allowed vessels larger than the *Typhon* to make fast to the octagonal quayside that projected into the centre of the harbour.

The ship dropped its sails before entering the harbour and coasted through the mouth under its own momentum. A pilot boat was waiting with a thick tow cable that was hauled on board. The cable disappeared into a building on the quay.

As they were being towed in, Soren watched small boats make

their way in and out of the harbour, powered by triangular sails and helmed by bronze skinned Shandahari.

Flocks of birds swirled about in the hot air, screeching and occasionally diving down to the water to retrieve one of the scraps thrown overboard by the passing boats. As they were drawn ever further into the harbour, the noise level grew. The sounds of sailors and dockworkers filled the air, shouting, laughing, cursing and hauling goods about the place.

Soren had encountered Shandahari before in Ostenheim. Like all the peoples of the Middle Sea, they were a race of maritime traders, famed for their fine, vividly coloured fabrics. Their ships regularly called at Ostenheim and Soren, who had spent much time watching the hustle and bustle of life around the docks in his youth, had always enjoyed experiencing the different cultures and exotic merchandise that passed through.

The hot weather was tempered by a cooling sea breeze creating a pleasant climate that was not nearly so humid and sticky as the Spice Isles. Gone also were the fragrant and exotic smells. Kirek smelt much like any other city that Soren had visited, albeit hotter. Between the colours, the weather and the prospect of being on the right path to finding Alessandra, Soren was in the best mood he had experienced for many weeks.

Once the *Typhon* was secured against the quayside, Varrisher was eager to call on the Khagan as soon as possible. Sancho Rui's head had been floating in a small cask of vinegar and Varrisher wanted to be rid of it nearly as much as he wanted the money. Soren and Varrisher left the ship and walked toward the city, along the causeway that connected the quay to the mainland, dodging the fast moving carts laden with goods destined for markets in both Kirek and in the other direction, to those that were a sea voyage away.

The city was characterised by white, flat-roofed buildings. Occasionally the monotone aspect was broken by ultramarine blue constructions that glistened in the sun as though their surfaces were wet. The streets were narrow and busy, filled with sounds and colours that fascinated Soren. Varrisher had been in Kirek before and led the way toward the Khagan's palace, seemingly oblivious to the visual feast on display.

Soren followed him as best he could, as his attention was constantly grabbed by the exotic and intriguing new city. They crossed a nondescript bridge over a river that was wide enough to allow two of the long, narrow boats that plied it to pass one another.

There were many small rivers running through the city, and they were crossed by dozens of the plain little bridges. The water flowed quickly, keeping the rivers free from rubbish and filth and keeping the hot city feeling fresh.

They were heading toward a large blue archway straddling the road, one of the blue buildings Soren had noticed when they first arrived. As they approached he could see that it was covered in glazed tiles of ultramarine blue and was decorated with gold and silver reliefs of fantastic looking animals that Soren had never seen before. It was the first time that he had been in a city that had never been part of the Empire. It was the most unique place Soren had seen.

Distracted, he bumped into a man who swore at him in a language that was entirely alien to Soren's ears. Soren mumbled an apology but the meaning didn't carry across the language barrier and the man continued with his angry utterances as he made his way on down the road.

They had to stop at the archway, which was guarded by several men in pale blue robes with enamelled armour and helmets. When they saw Varrisher and Soren approaching, they blocked the way and presented their spears.

Their challenge was completely unintelligible to Soren, but he could get the general idea from the context of the situation: 'Who are you, what do you want, piss off'. Varrisher seemed to get by in Shandahari and remonstrated with them for a few moments, gesturing frequently to the small barrel he held by an attached loop of hempen rope. He moved to open the barrel, which was enough to persuade the guards to let them through.

As they passed under the archway, Soren could see why there were no visible gates attached to it. They would have ruined the aesthetic appeal of the arch and were more than adequately replaced by the enormous metal portcullis that was hidden above them in the centre of the vaulted roof.

The arch led into a large walled compound that was filled with an ornamental garden. Despite Soren's previous conception of Shandahar being an arid land of deserts, the palace didn't give any hint that they might be short of water. The courtyard was dominated by two large fountains on either side that created several cascades and waterfalls that disappeared into metal covered drains in the ground. The courtyard was filled with trees and bushes and the sound of the flow of water and the shade of the lush vegetation created a peaceful enclave.

They walked through the garden toward the front of the palace where another guard was waiting. He demanded what Soren assumed was yet another explanation. Varrisher rattled off a few sentences of Shandahari interspersed with gestures to the barrel, which seemed to satisfy the guard. He led them up a flight of white stone steps and into the palace itself.

Professional curiosity drew Soren's eye to the guard's weapons and armour as they followed him. Like the men at the gate, he wore robes of pale blue material that had a smooth sheen when the light caught it a certain way. The guard also wore armour made of black enamelled plates that only covered the vital parts of the body, and the forearms and shoulders. Unlike the armour that the men at the arch had worn however, this man's armour was finely decorated in a neat pattern of muted golden swirls and floral curves. Such decoration would not come cheap, so Soren presumed this man was an officer or a member of a more elite group of warriors. The sword at his waist was slender and had a slight curve, not unlike the Ruripathian sabre.

The Khagan's throne room was more like a balcony than a room. It was long with a roof but no walls along its sides, merely a stone rail interrupted at regular intervals by stone pillars that supported the roof. Soren peered out at the fine view it gave of the city. The design allowed a breeze to pass through which kept it cool. There were a number of people there, most of whom were clustered at the far end around a dais that contained only one chair, on which a man sat.

The guard gestured for them to wait and went forward to speak with someone in the group at the far end of the room. After a moment he brought the man he had been speaking to back with him.

'You are Imperials?' the other man asked, in accentless Imperial that Soren had no difficulty in understanding.

'Well, yes I suppose so,' Soren said.

'I appreciate that the Empire has not existed for a very long time,' the man said, 'but in Shandahar we tend to refer to all those from the north as Imperials. No offence is intended and the reference is purely based on your common language.'

'None taken,' Soren said, trying to remember the basics of the etiquette classes he had taken whilst a student at the Academy in Ostenheim. It was easy to forget that he was no longer dealing with pirates and shipboard humour. 'I'm Banneret Soren of Ostia and this is Master Mariner of the Grey Varrisher of Ruripathia.'

The man nodded. 'I am Esqivel, First Jan of Kirek. I welcome you to the court of my master, His Magnificence the Khagan Raspa tai Kirek. Captain Barema tells me that you bring good news for my master.'

'We do. One week past we met with the pirate Sancho Rui and defeated him. I bring to your master his head as he requested,' Varrisher said.

Esqivel smiled. 'That is excellent news indeed. His Magnificence will be greatly pleased. He will be finished with his current business in a moment and will grant you audience. Until then, might I offer you refreshment? We have a great many foods and drinks here that I understand to be delicacies in the North. Some iced lemon perhaps?'

Esqivel shouted an instruction to a servant who disappeared down a narrow stairwell at the side of the room as soon as his name was called. He reappeared a moment later carrying a tray with two large glasses filled with a solid, pale yellow content and two small silver spoons. He presented the tray to Soren and Varrisher, who each took a glass and a spoon. They were freezing cold to the touch, a sensation that instantly reminded Soren of his time in Ruripathia — and no doubt reminded Varrisher of his homeland.

'The ice is brought down the river from the mountains as quickly as possible in large blocks packed in cloth and straw. Much is lost in transit, but when it arrives it is stored in a room deep under the palace that remains very, very cold no matter how hot it gets up here. The cook crushes it and mixes it with lemon juice, sugar and spices to produce this, which is a favourite of the Khagan. I think you will enjoy it.'

The Shandahari had something of a reputation for intrigue, the poisoning of rivals being a chief feature of that reputation. The thought was at the forefront of Soren's mind as he held the glass and looked at Esqivel, who was watching him in anticipation. If the reward for killing Sancho Rui was indeed as large as Varrisher had indicated, then poisoning them would certainly have made sense.

Soren thought it unlikely that the Khagan would have them killed before the identity of the head in the barrel had been confirmed though. He brought the glass up to his mouth and scooped some of the contents in.

The bitter flavour made his mouth tingle, but the edge was softened by a sweet aftertaste of sugar and spice. The ice crystals nipped at his teeth and the back of his throat, which gave him a pain behind his eye, reminding him of his worries about poison. It was so good that Soren would have found it difficult not to eat it all even so.

'It's delicious,' Soren said, as politely as possible. He had never felt comfortable speaking in the formal way necessitated by the requirements of etiquette as he had not been brought up with them; they had been rammed down his throat by a particularly unpleasant professor at the Academy and it was difficult for him to disassociate the two. The result was that he always felt stilted and awkward when presented with a formal situation. At least as a non-native speaker, Esqivel would be less likely to pick up on Soren's clumsy manners.

Someone at the front of the room caught Esqivel's attention. He nodded and turned to Soren and Varrisher. 'His Magnificence will see you now.'

Chapter 46
THE KHAGAN OF KIREK

They approached the Khagan, who was sitting in the single chair on the dais. He was thin, bald and clean-shaven, wearing robes of finely decorated cloth. He had an air of unquestioned power that Soren found disconcerting.

'My First Jan informs me that you have come to claim the bounty on the pirate Sancho Rui,' he said. His voice was deep and resonant, oozing authority. He was obviously not a man accustomed to having his requests denied.

'We have, Magnificence,' Varrisher said.

A servant came forward and took the barrel from Varrisher. Joined by another servant, they prised the lid off and hesitantly peered in, their faces contorting in disgust when they saw what was inside. For some morbid reason, Soren found himself oddly curious as to what the head would look like after over a week in the heat of the southern climes and if the vinegar it was steeped in would have any preservative effect.

The Khagan was not a squeamish man. When his servants confirmed that there was a head floating in the pungent vinegar, they brought the small cask to him and he reached in and pulled the head out by the hair without hesitation. He inspected it closely for a moment, the vinegar dripping all over the floor and filling the air with its tang. He said something to First Jan Esqivel, who gave a series of commands to one of the guards. The guard strode purposefully out of the room as the Khagan dropped the head back into the barrel with an unpleasant plop.

'It will take a few minutes to confirm the identity of the head you have brought us,' Esqivel said. 'We have someone who knew Rui and will be able to do so, as soon as the guards bring him here.'

'I noticed earlier that you were looking out over the city.' He walked toward the balustrade and gestured for Soren and Varrisher to follow. 'The city is built on the edge of the delta of the River Kirek. Several branches pass through the city, which provide us with the water used to fill all of the fountains and pools—' There was a commotion at the door that cut Esqivel off mid-sentence. 'Ah, the guards have brought our prisoner.'

The guard returned with a colleague and a man who looked as though he had seen far better days. He was shoved along the length of the room until he was only a few feet from the Khagan, who, once again showing his possession of an iron stomach, pulled the head out of the barrel of vinegar. He spoke in Shandahari, but Esqivel had moved to his side and translated his words into Imperial.

'His Magnificence asks if you recognise this face,' he said.

'I do, sir, that's Sancho Rui. Sure as anything and swear on my life,' the man said.

Esqivel spoke quickly to the Khagan who nodded and gestured toward Soren and Varrisher. He spoke to the guards who dragged the wretch out of the room and turned his attention back to Varrisher and Soren.

'His Magnificence is satisfied that you have indeed slain the pirate Sancho Rui and wishes to express his gratitude. We received word that he had been killed, two days ago, but we needed to be sure of his identity and that you were the ones responsible before paying the bounty. It is being put together as we speak, and His Magnificence wishes to offer his hospitality to the men who have done him this service. You will find there are a great many pleasures and comforts to be enjoyed in the court of His Magnificence and he wishes to extend these to you while you remain in Kirek.'

Soren cast a glance at Varrisher who seemed tempted by the idea; life had not been comfortable for either of them for some time, but for Soren it was not an option.

The question that remained was how they could refuse the Khagan's hospitality without angering him. Soren had no desire to end up like the man that had just been brought before them. He could make it clear that his refusal stemmed from his own injury at the hands of Sancho Rui, in the hope that the common complaint would ease the slight of his refusal.

'Tell the Khagan that I am most grateful for his kind offer of hospitality, but am unable to accept,' Soren said. He could see the change of expression on Esqivel's face and the one of disappointment on Varrisher's, so he continued quickly. 'I have also suffered injury at the hands of Sancho Rui. He attacked a ship carrying a friend of mine. I believe she may have been sold as a slave in Galat, and I need to go there to find her.'

Esqivel nodded, seemingly satisfied by the explanation. He turned to the Khagan and relayed the information to him. Soren tried to read his face, but the Khagan's expression gave nothing away.

He spoke in a commanding tone, but in the unintelligible Shandahari language and he had to wait for Esqivel to translate before Soren knew whether or not he had caused offence.

'His Magnificence says that he understands and sympathises with your position. He takes no offence at your wish to depart as soon as possible. He asks me to show you to the comfort and tranquillity of his courtyard while you wait for your reward to be brought to you. If you would follow me this way please.'

Esqivel led them back down to the courtyard, before leaving them to fetch the bounty. There were several servants waiting for them, carrying trays of food; various fruits, most of which Soren had never seen before, as well as a selection of sticky pastries that looked delicious. Soren had to admit that the temptation to remain was strong. There was something so intriguing and exotic about the city and its culture, with all its colours and unusual sounds, and that was not taking into account the food that was available there.

Nonetheless, he was uneasy remaining in the court of an all-powerful man who owed them a large sum of money. Perhaps to the Khagan it was merely a trifling amount and of no concern to him — this was the only comforting thought that Soren could muster and he wanted to get out of there as quickly as they could.

He picked up a few items from the trays that caught his eye, sat and began eating them. It would be as easy for the Khagan to have them killed by his guards as by poison. He had already shown that he wasn't squeamish; having blood let in his palace was unlikely to bother him.

Esqivel returned a few minutes later with two guards who carried a wooden chest between them. He opened it, revealing the very attractive lustre of gold coins. Soren picked one up. They were too small to be gold crowns, and were minted with a design that Soren had never seen before.

'Your bounty, as agreed,' Esqivel said. 'Please feel free to count it, although I assure you it is the full sum offered.'

Esqivel noticed Soren's curiosity. 'They are Gold Tremissi; we do not use Imperial currency in Shandahar, although there is a good deal of it in circulation. Each tremiss is worth roughly half an Imperial Crown.'

Soren nodded in appreciation and threw the coin back into the chest.

Varrisher stepped forward and ran his fingers through the coins. Faced with so much money, he seemed just as eager as Soren to depart as swiftly as possible. 'It appears to be fine,' he said.

Esqivel nodded and turned to Soren in the slow, purposeful manner that defined him. 'His Magnificence wishes to speak with you again. Captain Varrisher may leave if he pleases. Or wait if he would prefer.' He gestured for Soren to follow him.

Soren looked at Varrisher and shrugged. There was no reason to suspect danger, and the offer for Varrisher to wait or leave suggested that Soren would also be free to leave once he was finished speaking with the Khagan.

'I'll wait,' Varrisher said.

'He will not be long,' Esqivel said, gesturing for Soren to follow him.

The Khagan's hall had been cleared of people by the time Soren and Esqivel got there, with only the Khagan and two of his guards remaining. He said something to Esqivel when they reached the dais and then looked at Soren with his authoritative and penetrating stare.

It made Soren uncomfortable, and having denied the Khagan once already, he knew it would be dangerous to do so again.

'His Magnificence believes you may be able to assist him with another matter and wishes you to listen to his proposal.'

Soren tried not to show any reaction, but he was cringing on the inside. 'Of course,' he said.

'The reason that the Khagan placed a bounty on Sancho Rui was because Rui captured his ship, the *Gandawai*. The *Gandawai* was carrying, in addition to a great fortune in jewels, gold and cloth, the Rala of Serash, daughter of the Khagan of Serash. She was to be married to His Magnificence and the fortune on board represented her dowry. It was not pure happenstance that Rui came upon the *Gandawai*. He was given information of her voyage by the Khagan of Galat, His Magnificence's sworn enemy.'

If the Khagan was looking for an assassin, Soren would have to come up with a reason as to why he was not the man for the job, fast. He wasn't going to take on any job that would come between him and finding Alessandra.

'The Rala is currently being held in Galat. His Magnificence is given to understand that Galat is trying to negotiate a treaty with Serash using the Rala as an incentive. This displeases His Magnificence. He has engaged several skilled warriors to secure her freedom, but none have managed to achieve his task. He believes that the warrior who killed Sancho Rui may be able to succeed where those others have failed and asks that when you go to Galat in search of your friend, you also free the Princess of Serash and bring her here. He asks me to assure you that the bounty you have been paid for Sancho Rui's head will be but a drop in the ocean in comparison to the rewards he will bestow upon you should you succeed. Such is his desire for his betrothed to be brought to him that he bids me tell you that he will allow you name your price, and so long as it is within reason, he shall pay it. Land, titles, wealth, slaves, whatever you wish.'

Soren had to concentrate to stop his jaw from dropping.

CHAPTER 47

THE SEARCH RENEWED

THERE WAS REALLY NO answer that Soren could give other than yes. He was thankful that the task would not interfere with his search for Alessandra, so he agreed and Varrisher brought him to Galat. On the voyage north, Soren had outlined the content of his conversation, through Esqivel, with the Khagan.

After all they had been through together, he felt that it was only proper to give Varrisher the opportunity to accompany him on what was in effect an extension of their original agreement. If he was being honest with himself though, he was hoping that Varrisher would decline. Soren had always been a loner, which he knew was a symptom of being an orphan and growing up alone through dire circumstances. While being part of the crew of the *Typhon* had been an interesting experience, living and working in such close confines with the same people every day all day was not for him.

It came as a relief when Varrisher had become uncomfortable when Soren brought the issue up. He had been at pains to avoid causing offence, but outlined how he and his crew had agreed that once the bounty was collected they would return to the Spice

Isles to buy a cargo to bring north — and in so doing he would establish himself as a merchant. Once he had delivered Soren as agreed, that was the plan he would be pursuing.

Soren made it clear that there were no hard feelings, and the two parted as friends. It was with a degree of uncertainty that Soren clambered out of the jolly boat at the quayside in Galat and watched it being rowed back to the *Typhon*, alone once again. All he had for company was the sword and dagger strapped to his waist, a sailor's duffle bag at his feet and a purse of gold tucked away inside his doublet, the remainder of the spoils from his previous adventure safely deposited with the Austorgas' representative in Kirek.

Ferrata was confident he had reached the point where the man in front of him would be screaming loudly, were it not for the gag stuffed in his mouth.

In Ferrata's experience, threats of torture were never effective when dealing with the type of men his profession brought him into contact with. It might work with someone unaccustomed to the harder aspects of life, a clerk or craftsman perhaps, but a pirate would be rightly scornful, and possibly downright offended by mere threats of violence.

That was why Ferrata always began his information gathering sessions with a statement of his bona fides. It was not necessary to inflict pain as such, but rather to demonstrate that he was comfortable with matters that might make someone else squeamish.

He finished removing the man's second little finger — not as quickly as he might have, for pain did play a role — and cauterised the wound with the flat of a blade which was glowing a yellowy red colour.

Once the initial pain and then the stench of burning flesh

subsided, Ferrata spoke to the man, a swarthy looking pirate by the name of Blasco he had abducted from outside a tavern.

'Now, you're probably wondering why I've brought you here, and why I'm doing this to you.'

There was terror in the man's eyes, but also a sizeable portion of indignation. That might make things more difficult.

'I'm going to ask you some questions in a moment, and if I feel you've answered them honestly and comprehensively, I'll let you go, no worse but for the loss of a couple of fingers and a bump on the head. Do you understand?'

Blasco glared at Ferrata for a moment, then nodded his head.

'Excellent,' Ferrata said. 'Now. I'm going to remove your gag. There's no one nearby to hear you if you scream, so I would advise against it. If you do scream, I'll gag you again, remove another two fingers, and we can start over. Understand?'

Blasco nodded again, with no delay.

Ferrata gave the ropes securing Blasco to the chair he was sitting in a cursory check and then pulled the gag from Blasco's mouth.

'Now. I've been led to believe that you recently encountered a fellow called Soren. Tall, dark hair, good with a sword...'

Blasco said nothing.

Ferrata raised his eyebrows and lifted the gag up.

'Yes, I did,' Blasco said.

'Excellent. I need to know where he went after you parted company. I know he sailed east again, but after that. Where was he headed?'

'I don't know— No wait. Galat. I think he's going to Galat. There's a girl. He's looking for her. He thinks she might be there.'

A girl? There was a girl with a price on her head also. A small one, but a price nonetheless, and he had been told she might well be associating with Soren when he caught up with him. It was an insignificant sum compared to the one offered for Soren, but it would make the killing worth the effort if she was close at hand.

He stood and cut Blasco's throat with the blade he had used to remove the two fingers. It was time to find a ship heading for Galat.

Soren had packed his sea-going slops in the bag and wore his shore-going clothes when he left the *Typhon*. If he set foot on a ship again, he sincerely hoped it would be as a passenger and not a member of the crew — but preferably not at all.

Galat appeared similar to Kirek. It was made up of white, flat roofed buildings that were rarely taller than two stories, intermingled with blue constructions.

He walked through the town, which had the same fascinatingly exotic feel that he had found so appealing in Kirek: bright colours, strange sounds, interesting smells. While he would like to be finished with his business as quickly as possible, he had already learned the consequences of insufficient planning the hard way and had no desire to repeat the experience. An ill-conceived flight across the plains east of Ostia was unpleasant, but he reckoned that it would be a veritable pleasure by comparison to a similar flight across a desert. Freeing Alessandra only to lead her to her death in the arid sea of sand between the Galat and Kirek rivers would be counterproductive.

Nonetheless, the thought that she might still be in that city was intoxicating, and his heart began to race every time he allowed himself to dwell on it.

He began to look out for an inn, or the Shandahari equivalent. He spent some time wandering around, his difficulty all too evident. It was the first time he had ever been alone somewhere that he didn't speak the language. It was hot and he was tired, not to mention hungry, and his frustration grew as each minute passed.

Happily one thing that seemed common in Shandahar was the prevalence of food vendors on the street. Soren wandered past several, trying to see what was on offer without drawing the attention of the proprietors. Eventually he was overcome by the smell of the food and stopped at one of the stands. At first he simply pointed to food that he wanted, some type of heavily marinated meat that set his mouth watering each time he drew in a breath, but the vendor was quick to pick up on his ethnicity.

'Imperial? Yes?' he said.

'Yes,' Soren said. He pointed to the source of his temptation. 'How much for a portion of that?'

'Honey and spice marinated beef,' the vendor said, with a smile that revealed a remarkably good set of teeth as he scooped a ladle full from the pot. 'Two grossi, or about four Imperial pennies.'

'So, less than four pennies then,' Soren said.

The vendor smiled. 'Yes, but there is of course a premium for the service of exchanging a foreign currency.'

It was an outright lie. Imperial currency had been in use for such a long time, and used for trade over such a vast area that it was used interchangeably here as it was in most places that had contact with the Empire. Esqivel had said as much. This vendor was relishing the prospect of being able to inflate his profit, even if it was only by a small amount, probably for no more reason than the chance to do it. Soren almost felt bad to spoil it for him.

He handed over one of the gold tremissi that came from his share of the bounty. 'You have change for a tremiss?'

The smile dropped from the man's face, but he took the coin and rummaged about in a leather waist pouch, taking grossi out one at a time. He placed each coin down with a sullenness that made Soren smile. It had been a small battle, but he was victorious.

The vendor handed over the coins and the thin wooden bowl

he had filled with the marinated beef, along with a flat wooden spatula, both of which were designed to be disposable.

'You're a mercenary, yes?' the vendor said.

Soren nodded. He was always guarded with information, especially so when in strange places. There was no point in correcting the man's mistake.

'Lots of mercenaries around these days. Are you stationed up at the palace or have you just arrived?' he said.

'Just arrived,' Soren said. 'Where's the nearest inn?'

'Ah, I know of a—'

'The nearest inn,' Soren said firmly, not interested in whatever establishment his brother, uncle or best friend might be running on the other side of the city.

'Of course,' the vendor said, clearly offended by Soren's brusqueness. 'The nearest is only a short walk from here, but the directions will cost you two more grossi.' He smiled condescendingly.

Soren felt a flash of anger, not at the vendor, but at himself for inviting this. He handed over another two grossi.

The vendor smiled at having evened the score. 'That,' he said, 'is the nearest inn.' He pointed to a building no more than a dozen paces away.

Soren nodded in a belated display of manners, which might have saved him two grossi had he employed them earlier, before turning and walking toward the inn, eating as he went. The food was surprisingly good, the meat tender and the flavour rich and sweet.

From the price he paid to the innkeeper for a room for three nights, it seemed that the people of Galat had become used to northern mercenaries being in the city and having money, and had adopted a policy to fleece them as best they could. The room was small but looked as though it had been cleaned since its previous occupant had left, which was something at least.

He had no expectation that anything he left would still be there when he came back, so he only left those things that were of no value to him; the sailing slops that he hoped never to have to wear again, and one or two odds and ends that he could not conceive of being of value to anyone else.

With finding somewhere to sleep taken care of, he could begin his search. He would start with the docks. Hopefully someone there would remember the *Tear* having arrived with its notable cargo and be able to give him some information that he could use. The food vendor had mentioned foreign mercenaries being employed up at the palace. It occurred to Soren that it was worth investigating. A position there might carry with it enough authority to make his search easier, not to mention it would get him into the palace without drawing suspicion, allowing him to find where the Rala was being held.

After the docks, he would check the slave markets, although a young, attractive and foreign woman would not remain unsold for long. He had no expectation of finding her there; he simply hoped that someone would remember her, and remember to whom she had been sold.

Each time he thought of the task ahead of him, despair threatened to take hold of him. All he could think about was how impossible it would be, how unlikely it was that she would be remembered. The only thing that counted in his favour was that she was a foreigner and she was beautiful, two qualities likely to make her stand out in the mind of a slave trader.

Chapter 48
THE INTERPRETER

Soren returned to the docks and spent a few minutes getting a sense of how things operated. There was no sophisticated harbour system here, as there had been in Kirek; it was smaller and less prosperous. He looked around for a harbour master's office, or anyone who looked as though they had any authority.

He spotted a small, square hut made of panels of sun-bleached wood that had a window overlooking the harbour. It was no more than a box, but contained a single man. Soren made his way over and knocked against the open door frame.

'Excuse me,' he said. 'Do you speak Imperial?'

The man looked at Soren with a puzzled expression on his face.

'Imperial?' Soren said, hoping there might be a result.

The expression on the man's face didn't change. He returned his gaze back out over the harbour, disregarding Soren.

Soren sighed. The language was going to cause him problems. He'd hoped that in a port city, with so many ships coming in from what the locals still called the Empire, most people would have a working knowledge of the language as the street vendor had. He realised now that he couldn't rely on finding people who would be able to understand him and would have to address the issue. How he'd do so was another question.

There was only one other person in the city that he knew for certain could speak Imperial. Soren was reluctant to have to speak with the street vendor again, and certainly didn't trust him enough to ask him to interpret, but perhaps he could point Soren to a library or university where he would be able to find someone that would be worth employing.

He went back to where he had bought the admittedly delicious meal. The vendor smiled broadly when he saw Soren coming.

'Back for more?' he said.

'Perhaps later,' Soren said. 'I need to know where I can find people who can speak Imperial. A university or a library perhaps.'

The vendor said nothing, but continued to smile. Soren reached into his pocket, took out two grossi and placed them down on the counter of the vendor's stall.

'There is a library off the city's main square,' he said, pointing. 'Near to the palace.'

Soren didn't bother thanking him; the two grossi were thanks enough and he disliked being seen as an easy touch. He liked someone who took advantage of other people's situation even less. It would be unfortunate if he needed anything else from the vendor, but he doubted the man would turn down the potential to earn a few coins no matter how impolite Soren was.

He set off in the direction the vendor had pointed, wondering if the man might have sent him off in a random direction. Eventually he reached an open area, bordered on two sides by small rivers running through brick lined channels.

The palace was the first feature that caught his eye on the square. It was more austere than the one in Kirek, tucked away behind plain walls, although similar in that it was built from white stone and bore a number of features covered in the glazed blue tiles and relief work. There were no elaborate fountains or lush gardens however, again suggesting less wealth. To the left there was a two-story building with a colonnaded façade, the only one on the square that even remotely resembled a library.

The inside was dark and cool, a marked contrast to outside. A number of men in dark purple robes made their way around row after row of shelves. Unlike the libraries that Soren had studied in, the shelves were not flat surfaces holding bound books. Instead they were like slices of honeycomb, with tier after tier of small boxes containing rolled parchments.

A man approached Soren and spoke. It was unintelligible to Soren, but he didn't want to appear rude by interrupting.

He waited until the man finished and shrugged. 'I'm sorry. I don't understand. Do you speak Imperial?'

The man smiled and nodded. 'Yes. Can I help you?' He spoke carefully and slowly, like someone with a good knowledge but little practice.

'I hope so,' Soren said. 'I have some business to conduct in Galat, but I don't speak any Shandahari. I want to hire an interpreter, and thought I might find someone here. I'll pay well.'

'One of the junior scholars here might be interested in the work. I will ask around. When will you need them?'

'As soon as possible.'

'Very well. Come back in the morning.'

Soren returned to the library the next morning as instructed. The man he had spoken to was sitting at a desk near the door. When he saw Soren he stood and walked over.

'Good morning. If you would wait here a moment, please.' He turned and headed down between the rows of shelves toward the back of the library, returning a few moments later with a second man, who was also dressed in purple robes but was younger.

'This is Half-Scholar Erezaf. He is fluent in Imperial and also Shandahari, of course. He will require payment of one tremiss a day and will work from dawn until sunset.'

'Does he speak?' Soren said. From the way that the man was presenting Erezaf, he could well have been a mute.

'Only when commanded to, or questioned directly. At least until he becomes a Full-Scholar.'

Soren nodded. 'Fine, one tremiss a day is acceptable.'

They walked down to the docks in silence, with Soren leading the way to the office of the dock official he'd visited the previous day.

'Please tell him that I need some information on a ship that stopped here several weeks ago.'

Erezaf nodded and translated. The man in the hut listened and then spoke.

'He asks what ship,' Erezaf said.

'Her name was the *Bayda's Tear*. I believe she unloaded a cargo and a number of slaves.'

Erezaf translated once again. The man's face showed no signs of recognition. He spoke, but did not say much.

'He says he doesn't remember her.'

'Tell him she was the ship that brought the Rala of Serash to Galat.'

Erezaf nodded and spoke to the man again. They conversed back and forth for a moment before Erezaf turned back to Soren.

'He remembers the ship. There were a number of slaves, but

he does not know what was done with them after they were brought ashore.'

It was a dead end, but confirmation that the *Tear* had been there, and that it had unloaded slaves.

Chapter 49
THE SLAVE MARKET

Erezaf took Soren to the slave market, but reluctantly. He was glad that he had employed the young man, who was only a year or two younger than him. He would have struggled to find his way around alone — not taking into account his translation service, which was invaluable.

The slave market was in a separate annex off the main market square of the city, a short distance away from the square in front of the palace and library. A lane led off to a smaller courtyard in the centre of a cluster of buildings that was lined with holding cells. The smell was the first thing to hit him: of dense human occupation and less than sanitary conditions. Erezaf was visibly taken aback and had obviously never been anywhere near a slave market before. Soren hadn't either, but he had seen battle and death and the gore and filth that went with it. This wasn't so far removed from that.

Even with that experience, it was all that he could do to hold the contents of his stomach down at the thought that Alessandra had been there, treated like an animal to be sold on like a chattel.

He could only hope that her appearance would have made her more valuable and worthy of better treatment.

There were groups of customers clustered at various spots along the arcades lining the courtyard, variously inspecting their potential purchases under the supervision of one of the slave traders or haggling over the price after having found someone that met their requirements.

There was slavery in Ostia, but it was less visible than it seemed to be in Shandahar. He had passed by the slave market in Ostenheim many times and it was always busy, so the industry was certainly thriving. However, those slaves that were kept in the city were difficult to distinguish from free citizens and most were purchased for physical labouring outside on estates and in mines in the countryside. It was the uncomfortable subject that nobody in polite society spoke about. While people might ape their distaste at the idea, there were many nobles who derived some or much of their income from the work of slaves.

Soren had moved his coin purse to a prominent position as he walked into the slave market. He wanted them to see that he had plenty of money, and hoped this might make them a little more amenable to his questions, or at least lessen their suspicion until he found out what he needed.

Soren would not permit Alessandra to be subjected to that life if he could possibly prevent it, and he would not stop trying as long as there was breath left in his body. The question once again was how far he was willing to go to get the information he needed. His thoughts drifted to Blasco, and how close he had come to doing something he would have regretted.

He went unnoticed at first; there were more than enough customers to keep the slavers occupied. However, being avaricious businessmen, they were not likely to let a customer pass by without trying to tempt them to a purchase, particularly not a northerner, a group who had a reputation of having money and the desire to spend it. It was not long before one of them approached him, showing respectful deference.

'Imperial?' Soren said.

'A little,' the slave trader said. 'What are you looking for?'

'A girl,' Soren said.

Soren could feel Erezaf squirming behind him. He should have explained what was going on before they got there, but it was too late now.

'We have many girls here,' the slave trader said, gesturing to the cells that lined the courtyard, on two levels as Soren now noticed.

'I'm looking for something in particular,' Soren said. 'A northerner. An Imperial girl.'

'Ah,' the slave trader said. 'We are starting to get many requests for northern girls from the northern soldiers in the city. Something to remind them of home I think. Sadly we do not have any here at the moment, and it is unusual for us to get them. It does happen for time to time, but it has been a year at least. With growing demand, that might change. If you would care to check back? For now, I can recommend a Shandahari woman, or perhaps a Jaharan if you seek something a little more exotic.'

'A year?'

'At least. Perhaps longer. As you see, it might be a very long time before we have any. But there are plenty of others. I am sure we can find one that interests you.'

'Thank you, but no,' Soren said. 'I'm looking for someone specific. An Ostian, tall, slender, dark hair. I think she was brought here several weeks ago.'

The slave trader's demeanour changed instantly. 'If you are not here to buy, perhaps you should leave.'

Soren could feel Erezaf's tension from two paces away. The young man was deeply uncomfortable, and Soren regretted bringing him. He was getting more education that day than he was accustomed to, or would have wanted.

Soren nodded. There was no reason to believe the slaver was lying when he said they hadn't had any northerners there for over a year, even if he had reacted aggressively. Perhaps Alessandra had never been there, a thought that left him relieved. But if that was the case, where had she gone?

'Let's go,' Soren said, keeping his eyes locked on the slaver's, hoping to convey that he was not in any way intimidated by the slaver's aggressive stance.

Erezaf nodded in firm agreement, his relief at the prospect of leaving palpable.

They walked out of the courtyard and back into the market square proper. Soren continued to walk briskly, dragging Erezaf with him. It was possible that the slave traders would send someone to follow them, though unlikely. Angry relatives turning up looking for their kin was an occupational hazard for slave traders, and from what Soren had heard, it was a problem that was often dealt with very violently. He could not in good conscience send Erezaf off to make his way back to the library on his own.

He led them on a circuitous route of the city, with no particular direction in mind. He continued until he was sure they were not being followed — and he was well and truly lost. Only then did he tell the thoroughly confused and still frightened Erezaf that he could go back to the library. After paying him and getting directions back to his inn, they parted ways, but Soren very much doubted the young man would be inclined to work for him again.

There was a commotion at the inn, but Soren had walked through the door before he noticed it and turning around to leave would have drawn too much attention. He stopped in his tracks and the men causing the noise turned to look at him. The men regarded him for a moment before returning their attention to the innkeeper. They were not the slave traders, but they were also not Shandahari.

There were three of them, all soldiers judging by their bearing and clothing, and from the north. They wore loose crimson trousers and shirts, cinched tight by black enamelled armour plates. Seeing so many men from the north made him think of the night that he had been attacked on the streets of Auracia. But they had turned their back on him and were questioning the innkeeper intently. Soren heard an Ostian accent, which he found oddly unsettling.

These men must have been members of the mercenary force that Soren had heard mentioned. He had no idea what they were looking for, and really didn't care, so long as it didn't involve him. All he wanted was to get to his room without any hassle so he could think.

He flopped down on his bed and began to search his mind for any idea of what to do next. He thought about the mercenaries below, and the fear in the innkeeper's voice as he talked with them. If the Khagan was recruiting foreign mercenaries, becoming one might be of use. He had already decided to use that route to get into the palace and attempt to rescue the Rala, but he had not intended to do that until he found Alessandra. He was beginning to think doing so sooner rather than later was a better option. Perhaps the authority that the mercenary uniform would give him would help with his inquiries about Alessandra.

As sleep began to descend on him, it occurred to him that if the Khagan had seized the Rala, could others on the ship with her have been taken too?

Chapter 50
THE NORTHERN GUARD

THE SUN WAS STILL low in the sky, and the air was cool and fresh when Soren set off for the palace. It had an entrance arch of plain white stone with none of the magnificent adornments of the palace in Kirek. It had clearly seen better days, but had once been opulent. Where a palace was normally an expression of wealth and power, this one spoke of financial difficulty.

Soren was challenged in Shandahari when he got to the gate, but the guard issuing it was not a native.

When Soren answered in Imperial, the guard reverted to his mother tongue and directed him to the barracks where he was told that foreign soldiers were eagerly sought after for employment. He was told to ask for Captain dal Vaprio. When there, he was directed to a small office off the entrance archway.

'Captain dal Vaprio?'

'The very same,' the man said. He was sitting behind a messy desk but did not look particularly busy. His black hair was cropped, but he had a neat moustache and short, pointed beard in the Ostian fashion on a deeply tanned face. 'The "dal" part is very much a thing of the past, however. You are?'

'Banneret Soren. I was told you're the officer to speak to about getting work.'

'You were told correctly,' Captain Vaprio said. 'Please, take a seat.' He gestured to a rickety looking wooden chair beside Soren.

'Tell me a little bit about yourself,' he said. 'You're Ostian. Ostenheim?'

'Yes, Captain. Born and bred,' Soren said.

'Excellent. We're a bit of a mish-mash here, Ostians, Ruripathians, anyone who the Tyrant has tried to kill or dispossessed. It doesn't matter much down here, we're all foreigners — Imperials as they still call us — but it's always nice to meet someone from home. What year did you graduate from the Academy?'

'Forty-six,' Soren said. 'I had started at the Collegium, but unfortunately wasn't able to finish.' It was not entirely true, he had left prematurely of his own accord, but the statement implied another reason that Vaprio was quick to pick up on.

'Ah yes, bad times. I finished in twenty-five. Didn't stay on for the Collegium though; too eager to get out and see the world. Am I right in thinking you are not noblesse?'

'That's correct,' Soren said. They were straying onto potentially dangerous territory for Soren, but at least he was able to anticipate its approach.

'Sponsored?' he asked.

'Yes, by Rikard dal Bragadin,' Soren said.

Vaprio raised his eyebrows and nodded in approval. 'Impressive. I knew him in passing. A fine man. Tragic the way he died. I believe his son Pierro escaped Ostenheim before the Tyrant managed to get his hands on him. To Venter, I believe.'

'I'm glad to hear that. I didn't know that he managed to get out. But Lord dal Bragadin's only son's name is Ranph,' Soren said. He recognised it for the test that it was. He didn't want anyone to know, least of all Ostian exiles, that he had any past association with Amero.

'Yes, of course, Ranph. As I said I only knew the family in passing.' It was obviously a lie; Vaprio had been sounding him out. 'Do you have any combat experience?'

'I was with the Legion of the Eastern Marches during the barbarian incursions,' Soren said.

'Sharnhome?'

'No, I was in the city when that happened.'

'An ugly day. I was with dal Dura's Horse. I don't think more than a few dozen of us made it back to the city. Still, that's a story best left in the past. We've plenty of soldiers coming south for work. I've been here two months now myself. Not many officers though, so your arrival is very welcome.

'It's a cushy job that exists more out of paranoia than anything, as best I can tell, but the Khagan is hiring every northerner that can tell which end of a spear is the dangerous one. The pay is good, one hundred tremissi a month, around fifty crowns if you haven't gotten your head around the local coin yet, the food is excellent and the work isn't difficult. For the sake of propriety, I can only offer you a probationary commission to begin with, but assuming everything goes smoothly I'll be able to confirm it in a couple of weeks. If you make your mark here,' he said, sliding a ledger across the desk toward Soren, 'you'll be the newest Lieutenant in the Khagan's Northern Guard.'

Soren scanned the column of names, a mix of Ostian and Ruripathian with one or two others that were not so easy to pin down, before adding his own at the bottom of the list.

'Excellent. If you leave this office and turn left it will take you to the guardhouse. There you should find Lieutenant Veyt. Otherwise he'll be in one of the city's many whorehouses, but I would suggest the easiest thing for you to do would be to wait for him. He'll show you to your quarters, run you through your duties, and see that you have all your necessaries provided for. If there's nothing else, I will see you at mess this evening.'

Soren stood and saluted, which earned him a nod of approval. He followed Vaprio's instructions and was pleased to find Lieutenant Veyt where he was supposed to be. He was tall with fair hair and skin, the redness of the latter indicating it didn't agree with the strong Shandahari sun.

'Banneret Soren,' he said, offering his hand. 'Just signed on as Lieutenant.'

'Welcome. Banneret Veyt at your service,' Veyt said, jumping up from the seat he had been slouched in and shaking Soren's hand. The guardroom was more like the common room at Soren's house of residence in the Academy than the command centre for a military unit. Veyt was the only one there, lounging in the relaxed surroundings. 'You sound like an Ostian. When did you arrive in Galat?'

'Just yesterday, but it was late so I only came up here this morning. And yes, I'm Ostian.'

'Well, I think you'll enjoy it here. All of the rubbish from home gets left at the border, so it's a fresh start. I'll need to run through your duties with you first, then we can get you a uniform and supplies and show you to your quarters. You might as well sit; this'll take a few minutes.

'There are one hundred and eleven of us — twelve with you — not including Captain Vaprio who leads our little band. With your arrival, there are five Lieutenants and one hundred and seven guardsmen. Mainly Ruripathian and Ostian, but there are some strays that have blown in from elsewhere and the number grows every day.'

There might have been a lot of men in the Northern Guard, but there was little activity, and even less sign of discipline. There was a relaxed atmosphere, and Veyt's demeanour fit perfectly with it. A slack approach would suit Soren nicely as he attended to his own affairs.

'You've arrived in slightly more interesting times than normal.

There was a bit of a shit storm here a few months back, and since then things around the Khagan's court have been a little tense. Some big-name pirate landed his booty here, which livened things up. Don't think anything will come of it, but the Khagan's been hiring every foreigner that says they've done any soldiering. Doesn't seem to trust the local troops anymore.'

The mention of a pirate caught Soren's full attention. 'What happened?' Soren said.

'A ship full of important sorts was attacked by pirates. They unloaded their plunder here, which included a Shandahari princess — they call them "Ralas" here — and her whole household. The Khagan took the lot of them into his custody and he seems to have been using her as leverage to bargain with her father, the Khagan of Serash, which is on the next river to the north.'

Could that have included Alessandra? Was it possible she had been included in the household, or mistaken for being part of it when they were unloaded? Soren tried not to let his hopes inflate, but it was difficult.

'Things aren't as straightforward as they are back home,' Veyt said, 'or as they *were* back home. The Khagan has a lot of nobles in his court, called "Baydas", who you'll come across soon enough. They're a pretty powerful bunch and there's more than a few that fancy replacing the Khagan. Him taking the Rala into custody stirred things up with them, but nobody's made a move against him until they see what he does with her. His negotiations don't seem to have been going the way he wants though, and the Baydas are starting to act up again. That's what we're here for, to make sure they mind their manners.'

There was more tension than Captain Vaprio had led Soren to believe. He wondered how it would affect his plans, knowing they could either be a help or a hindrance, but would certainly impact them one way or the other.

'It's a complicated mess, but from what I've been told the

Khagan on the next river south has an interest in the Rala as well, and he's been causing trouble. He's tried to kidnap her a couple of times now. We dealt with the most recent attempt a week or two ago, so we're the favourite child right now. As a result, keeping a look out over the Rala has been added to our duties. That's brought its own problems. The local troops, the Bluecloaks, fucking hate us now even more than they did to begin with.'

Soren raised his eyebrows. 'It's complicated all right.'

'Try not to think too much about the politics,' Veyt said. 'I promise you, it'll drive you mad quicker than the bloody sun. Just follow orders, smile whenever one of the locals insults you and you'll do fine. Anyway, now you know why we're here. Our standing orders are to patrol the palace, to guard the Khagan and also the Rala. Not much to it. Those duties are rotated around and having you here now means it will be a bit easier for the officers.

'Keep an eye out for the Bluecloaks. There've been a few fights, just fists and no serious damage done, but best be aware of it and avoid them if you can. Smiling at them when they insult you seems to piss them off more than a punch.'

That was a complication that Soren could have done without. With the relaxed attitude the Northern Guard seemed to have, Soren had thought for a moment that he would have free run of the palace. Why couldn't things go easily for him, just once?

'The real prize duty is watching over the Rala. You'll never see a more beautiful woman, and most of her ladies are pretty easy on the eye too. You need to be careful though. The Bluecloaks'll have your head if you show too much interest, and they're just dying for the chance to kill one of us. I'll walk you through the three main duties that you'll be supervising as an officer, mainly from here, after lunch.'

Chapter 51
The Seraglio of Galat

Captain Vaprio had not been exaggerating when he listed excellent food as being one of the perks of Shandahar. Soren suspected that might be the case after having been pleasantly surprised by the bowl of food he ate the previous day, but it seemed that either Shandahari hospitality was superb or the Khagan was not afraid to show how highly he valued his foreign mercenaries. Either way, Soren loved his food and was never shy about looking for seconds.

All of the officers ate together and Soren was introduced to the other two Lieutenants, one of whom was also Ostian. Afterward, as promised, Veyt walked Soren around the palace. They went to the audience hall where the Khagan conducted his daily business. It was empty when they went in, leaving Veyt free to outline the required duties with candour, which for an officer amounted to little more than ensuring the appropriate number of men were present in the hall during their watch.

The next stop was the seraglio. It was centred around an idyllic courtyard garden surrounded by two stories of galleried buildings. It was the first example of true luxury and wealth that Soren had seen since arriving in Galat. Unlike the rest of the palace, it was well maintained and as luxurious as anything Soren saw at the palace in Kirek.

'Guards are restricted to this gallery when on duty here,' Veyt said, gesturing around him at the first floor gallery. 'I promise you, going down into the garden is a very bad idea. The punishment for being caught in the seraglio is death, and the Bluecloaks are chomping at the bit to kill a few of us. Do us both a favour and don't give them reason to.'

Soren nodded absently as he peered down into the courtyard to see if the women were as beautiful as Veyt had suggested. He almost didn't want to admit to himself that he was looking down to see if Alessandra was there, afraid of the disappointment he would feel if he did not spot her.

'I wouldn't even stare too long if I were you,' Veyt said. 'Some poor bastard, just an ordinary fellow off the street, sneaked in there a few weeks ago. The Bluecloaks got their hands on him. You could hear his screams for the rest of the day. At least they finished it before night; no one would have gotten any sleep otherwise.'

Soren nodded but continued to look down into the courtyard as surreptitiously as he could. There were a number of women moving about or sitting in the shade of the trees and bushes. It was difficult to make out anything more than their general shapes as they were too far away. There was no way for him to work out which of them might be the Rala and there was no one that resembled Alessandra. It had been so long that sometimes he struggled to remember what she looked like, unsure if the image he had in his mind's eye was a creation of his own, or an accurate memory. It terrified him to think he might see her and not realise who she was.

They left the seraglio and Veyt took Soren for the final part of his orientation, which was a tour of all the halls and corridors of the palace. He would have to make random patrols of them during his general guard duty hours. They were a web of corridors, passages and rooms underneath the current palace, which seemed to have been built on top of at least one of its previous iterations.

It was tedious walking through one nondescript corridor after another and Soren was certain there was no way he would remember it all. He breathed a sigh of relief when Veyt finally told him that the tour was over and brought him to the quartermaster to pick up the things he would need. He was fitted for a crimson uniform and the various pieces of armour plating that would go on over it.

The crimson cloth looked coarse, but was light, soft and extremely comfortable. The loose trousers and jersey were far more practical for the Shandahari climate than Soren's northern style britches, shirt and doublet, even if the latter had been purchased similarly far south. The armour was interesting, and far more complex than he had first thought when seeing it on other men. Instead of being two solid pieces that were strapped together, the breastplate was made up of a number of horizontal panels that moved smoothly over one another, allowing a greater deal of movement and articulation. The pauldrons and bracers were constructed in similar fashion, and each metal plate was enamelled in black.

The armour didn't cover nearly as much of the body as some of the heavy armours he had seen in the north, but it was broadly similar to the type worn by infantrymen on the battlefield.

He had the option to pick whatever weapons he wanted from the armoury, but he was content with what he had. All he wanted was to get out and recommence his search.

As Soren walked back to the guardroom with his new equipment, he began to think through the possibilities. There was a good chance Alessandra was at the palace; the facts as he knew them suggested that much. If so, there was one place that was much more likely than any other. The seraglio. Part of him was uplifted by the thought that he might be so close to her, but his enthusiasm was dampened by the nauseating thought of what she may have experienced. And he might be deluding himself with misplaced hope.

There was only one way to tell if she was in the seraglio, and that was by getting in for a look around. After what Veyt told him, that seemed to be easier said than done. Checking the kitchens and servants' quarters would be easily managed while he was on general guard duty, but those places were of secondary interest to him.

The Bluecloaks were the most obvious problem. They shared all guard duties with the Northern Guard and had been glowering across at him and Veyt during their tour of the seraglio, obviously looking for any opportunity for conflict. If Soren was caught trying to gain access to the seraglio, they wouldn't hesitate to attack him. With the Gift he knew that he would be able to fight his way through a good number of them, but would it be enough? If he was to attempt a smash and grab, he would at least need to be able to locate Alessandra, and also the Rala, and get to them quickly after breaking into the seraglio. However, Soren felt a cleaner, quieter approach was far more favourable and also more likely to be successful.

He had never sustained the Gift for more than a minute or two and every plan he could think of required him to use it for a prolonged period. Not even taking into account how he would be affected when he came out of it. He couldn't rely on Alessandra to carry him off to safety after he collapsed. From what Berengarius had said, he could potentially burn his body out from the effort to sustain it long before he got near the palace gates, let alone out of the city. For all its apparent advantages, the Gift was not the boon he hoped for.

Chapter 52
THE BAYDAS

Soren was counting the hours to his first duty overseeing the seraglio, but that did not come for two days. Before then he had to persevere with the monotony of standing guard in the audience hall and walk miles patrolling the passageways beneath. It gave him a chance to take a look at the majority of the kitchen and serving staff, none of whom could be mistaken for Alessandra.

As an officer he was only required to be present at the start of the watch and at the end with the occasional spot check over its course. For the rest of the time he could return to the guardroom and relax, but when he was assigned to the seraglio, he found himself pacing slowly around the gallery overlooking the courtyard for the duration of the duty, trying to look at every woman that passed through without drawing the attention of the vigilant Bluecloaks.

His men were in the prime of life, and the courtyard was filled with what were said to be the most beautiful women in Shandahar, yet they did not look. The only explanation was that they were concerned at provoking the Bluecloaks. If the perceived threat was strong enough to stop young soldiers from staring at attractive women, it must have been great indeed. He followed their example and tried to watch as discreetly as possible, only casting a glance whenever he spotted movement below.

He felt keen disappointment when the watch passed by without him seeing her, though he was aware he ought to know better than to build his hopes up. As the watches rotated, he would not be back at the seraglio for another three days, but there was nothing he could do about that. He would have to bide his time.

⁂

The following day, Soren's duty was in the audience hall. The Khagan had a steady stream of visitors all afternoon who had to be dealt with, mainly by an officious Jan who would scurry back to confer with the Khagan every so often.

The duty was mind numbingly boring and Soren was glad that he'd be able to sneak off to the guardroom for a break every so often. As with the other duties in the palace, this one was shared with the Bluecloaks. They occupied the other end of the hall, by the double doors through which everyone entering the room had to pass. Arguably it was a position of honour — the first place that an enemy would attack — but the truth of the matter was that until recently they had been stationed around the dais that the Khagan sat on. Now it was Soren and his comrades who drew that duty.

As his paranoia grew, the Khagan became ever more suspicious of his erstwhile protectors, and had shown ever more favour to the Northern Guard. This added fuel to the hostility between them and the Bluecloaks, and whenever they were around Soren could feel the tension in the air. The Bluecloaks were proud men and the disrespect shown to them by their leader angered them. That anger was directed squarely at the men that they saw as usurping their rightful place. Even a recent arrival like Soren could see that there was trouble fomenting, and it wouldn't take much to arouse it to the point of violence.

Later in the day, a large group of finely dressed and distinguished looking men entered the hall. From the deference they were shown by the Bluecloaks, it was clear to Soren that they were of some importance. Their clothes were decorated with scrolling embroidery that was of exquisite detail and quality.

Their arrival caused a stir at the dais. The Jan reacted as though someone had thrown hot coals into his trousers and after a brief but very intense exchange of whispers with the Khagan, he ordered everyone but the new arrivals and the guards out. When the room was cleared of those ordered out, the Bluecloaks closed the doors; the first time they had been closed since Soren began working at the palace. The Jan scurried forward to confer with the finely dressed men for a moment before returning to the dais, bringing one of them with him.

The Jan made an obsequious introduction, and the Khagan responded, the first time he had spoken aloud all day. That was as much of the conversation as Soren could work out. He looked to one of his men and shrugged his shoulders. The guardsman smiled and stepped forward.

'It's formalities, sir, always goes on for a bit when one of the Baydas comes in for an audience,' he whispered.

'You speak Shandahari?' Soren said, in as quiet a tone as he could manage.

The guardsman nodded. 'I've been here a bit longer than the rest. I came south to do security on the river barges near on a decade ago.'

'Any idea what this is all about?'

'That's one of the most powerful Baydas in Galat. He's been coming in every few days for weeks now to have a row with the Khagan.'

'What about?' Soren said. He tried to keep his voice low; disturbing the proceedings would not be well received.

'There's a noble lady being held down in the seraglio. She was brought in by a pirate a few months ago. The Khagan said he claimed her from the pirate for her own safety, but no one really believes that. The negotiations for her release haven't been going well for the Khagan, and his Baydas aren't too happy about it. This fella, Bayda Talan tai Azaf, is one of the Khagan's major rivals, and they aren't beyond bumping each other off down here to get what they want. He's probably using this as an excuse to drum up some support. If he gets enough, well the Khagan won't be Khagan anymore and we'll be out of a job. Maybe dead.'

'That's a cheerful thought,' Soren whispered.

'Aye, it is. Each time tai Azaf comes back in here, he has a few extra Baydas with him.'

Both voices were raised now and the Bayda repeatedly talked over the Khagan, a severe mark of disrespect.

'The Bayda just accused the Khagan of having the Rala of Serash kidnapped by pirates. Says he doesn't believe that it was a coincidence that the pirate brought her here. Says that he's brought the threat of war and ruin to Galat. Fighting talk,' the guardsman said.

The heated exchange ended and Bayda tai Azaf stormed out, followed by his supporters. The Khagan remained impassive until the doors were slammed behind him. Only then did his face betray a degree of strain. He left the hall with his Jan scuttling after him. Soren sent two of his guards to follow them and made his way back to the guardroom, his duty for the day done.

◆

He chose a route that took him near to the seraglio. If he was going to try to break the Rala out of it, he would need to know the passageways like the back of his hand. Each walk through the passages etched their layout a little more firmly into his memory. He couldn't risk straying too close and drawing attention to himself, but for the other corridors he could simply state he was doing a spot check and was unlikely to be questioned over that. He was keenly aware that tensions would be even higher now after the confrontation between the Khagan and his Baydas. He wondered how far the Khagan could push the Bluecloaks before their loyalty was completely lost. As his guardsman predicted, if that happened they could all end up dead. Soren was already suspicious of them, having seen how they behaved around Bayda tai Azaf. They paid him far more deference than they should. Trouble could come more quickly than anyone of them would like.

CHAPTER 53
FOOTSTEPS IN THE DARKNESS

Soren stood on the balcony overlooking the seraglio, coming close to the end of his duty. He tried to concentrate on watching the tops of the walls, casting the occasional look across the courtyard as though simply ensuring that all was well. He was always hoping to catch a glimpse of Alessandra.

The Bluecloaks also remained an ever-present menace. They spent as much time glaring across the courtyard at Soren and his men as they did attending to their duties. The two groups circulated around the balcony, always on the opposite side. There was one in particular that Soren had noticed glaring directly at him. He avoided eye contact, not out of fear, but complete disinterest. The Bluecloaks were always looking for trouble, but the intensity of their effort had increased since the Baydas had argued with the Khagan.

When his duty shift came to an end, he tried to ignore the feeling of disappointment that he still hadn't seen any sign of Alessandra, and made his way down into the passageways that led back to the guardhouse. He was starting to become a little more familiar with them and more comfortable navigating his way around the dark maze. The only danger was a lurking Bluecloak looking for a fight. Vaprio had told them all not to go around alone, hoping to avoid the eventuality where a lone Northern Guardsman proved too great a temptation for a Bluecloak, and disappeared.

On this occasion Soren had ignored the advice, just wanting to get away from the place. He felt his chest tighten when he heard a noise behind him, coming from a side corridor that he had just walked past. It could have been just a servant, the passageways were intended to allow them move freely about the palace without ever being seen, but his hand automatically moved to the hilt of his sword. He tried to place each foot a little more softly as he continued to walk forward, his ears straining to hear any sound behind him. He quietened his breathing as much as he could, but he heard nothing more.

He was beginning to relax, his hand loosening on the handle of his sword when there was a footfall behind him. He turned quickly, pivoting on heel and toe and drew his sword in the same motion. By the time he was fully facing the other direction, he had adopted a low, balanced fighting position, his sword held out in front of him. If a Bluecloak had decided to try his luck, he would pay for it. There was someone standing in the corridor, slight of build, but in the gloom it was impossible to make out if they were wearing the colours of the Bluecloaks, or if they were armed.

The person had stopped, but took a tentative step forward. Soren shouted a challenge and they halted again.

'It is you,' a female voice said.

Soren's heart began to race. So much time had passed that he could barely remember what Alessandra's voice sounded like, or if his memory of it was true. He strained to see better in the darkness. After so much frustration and disappointment, there was something inside that refused to allow him believe it was possible.

The woman was draped in cloth that concealed the shape of a feminine figure.

'Alessandra?' he asked.

'Soren,' she said.

He was so bemused at what was happening that he'd forgotten he still had his sword drawn. He sheathed it and stood straight. 'I hoped you'd be here, but I was beginning to think that I was deluding myself,' he said.

'I thought you were dead,' she said. 'Then I saw you in the gallery overlooking the seraglio a few days ago. I couldn't believe that it was you. I watched you all day today. Pacing up and down until I knew I wasn't mistaken.'

After so long searching, Soren had no idea what to say. He had never given any thought to what would happen when he actually found her. He had focussed all of his energy on the search.

'I've been searching for you for months,' Soren said. 'I was beginning to think that I'd never find you.'

'What made you think I was here?'

'The pirate, Sancho Rui. I found your amulet.' He fumbled in his pocket and held it out.

She nodded. 'I never made it to Auracia. He captured my ship when it sailed south to avoid a storm. Never thought I'd see that amulet again.' She reached forward and took it, dangling it in front of her eyes for a moment before putting it back around her neck. 'Maybe it is lucky after all.' She smiled.

They had parted under such strained circumstances without ever having the chance to properly deal with the matters that had initially driven them from one another. Once the first wave of emotion of having finally found her had passed, he found it was replaced by an uncomfortable awkwardness. He didn't know whether to rush forward and take her up in his arms or to shake her hand. 'I've come to get you out of here,' he said, realising that he still didn't know how he was going to go about it. Soren could just about make out her smiling in the darkness and felt an incredible sense of relief.

'You have a plan?' she said, in the slightly amused, teasing tone that she had so often adopted when he had acted thoughtlessly. It helped him relax a little.

He hesitated for a moment as he struggled to think of something that would sound at least a little plausible but was left wanting. 'No, not yet,' he said. 'I've only been here a few days and my focus was on finding you. Now that I have, I'm sure that I can come up with something. How did you know where to find me?'

'I've been sneaking out and looking around the passageways for some time, trying to work out how to get away from here. I know what routes the guards take when they go off duty. But I need to get back to the seraglio now or I'll be missed. I'm safe there for the time being,' she said. 'It's dangerous to leave. If I'm caught outside of it, it's very bad. There's someone else here also, I won't leave without her.'

Soren was about to ask her who, when there was a sound from the end of the corridor from which Soren had come.

'I have to go,' she said, with genuine fear in her voice. 'I'll sneak out again and find you when I can. Make your plans.'

He could make out a smile before she rushed forward and gave him the lightest of kisses, disappearing back down the other corridor. The scent of her perfume lingered in the air after she had gone, and the smell was warm and comforting. He had been so surprised by her kiss that he had not responded, and chastised himself for ruining the moment.

There was still the matter of the approaching noise, heavy steps and certainly those of a man. His desire to avoid running into a Bluecloak was still strong, so he continued on his way with haste.

Chapter 54
THE CURIOUS BEASTS

HE RAN THROUGH THE events of the day over and over as he lay in his bunk that night, until everything blurred together with his dreams. It was difficult to be sure that he had actually found Alessandra and not imagined the whole thing. He needed to come up with some way to get her, the Rala and Alessandra's friend out of the seraglio, the city and to safety.

The harbour was too obvious. As soon as it was noticed that the Rala was gone, the harbour would be closed. It might be an option if he decided to free Alessandra only, as her disappearance was unlikely to cause as much of a fuss. The only option that he could see if the Rala was with them was to make their escape by land. There would be many routes out of the city, and with the Rala, he could be going north to her father's Khaganate or south to Kirek, increasing the possibilities again. The thought of crossing a desert on foot did not fill him with joy, so preparations would need to be made.

He would have dropped the notion of rescuing the Rala were it not for the offer the Khagan had made. The money would give Soren and Alessandra security for the rest of their lives. It was too good an opportunity to pass up so he had to at least try.

Living in the close confines of the seraglio, Alessandra was bound to know the Rala by now, at least to see, so he didn't have to worry about trying to identify her any more. One item off a list that was growing longer and more complicated by the minute.

He hoped that Alessandra could take care of getting them out of the seraglio itself. Having sneaked out into the warren of corridors beneath the palace once, she should be able to do it again, and bring the others with her. That came as something of a relief, as getting them out had been Soren's greatest problem. The Bluecloaks presented too much of a danger for it to be done any other way, so he hoped she would go along with this plan

Once out in the corridors, if they were discovered, Soren could take care of it more discreetly and in a fashion that would not bring the whole garrison down on them. Getting out of the palace would be most easily done at night, while he was on duty. He could make sure the northern guardsmen under his command were somewhere other than the route he would take and direct Alessandra to lead the others out of the palace to somewhere they could wait for him to slip away. With luck it would be morning before anyone noticed that anything was amiss, and they should be many miles out into the desert.

All that remained was to arrange supplies, find somewhere that he could store them, and if possible, find someone who would be willing to guide them through the desert. He was a competent navigator, having spent several months leading cavalry patrols through the featureless grasslands on Ostia's eastern frontier. He had never been into the desert though. Local knowledge might be the difference between dying in the expanse of sand and having a pleasant journey through a foreign land.

Although it was almost evening, Soren was eager to begin right away. His duties were done with for the day and while it would be noticed if he was not present for the evening meal that all of the officers usually shared together in the guardroom, there were a great many diversions in the city that could easily explain his absence, and that were often responsible for the absence of others.

◆

He changed out of his uniform and went straight toward the market square, casting a wary eye toward the alley that led to the slave market when he arrived. He was quite confident that if he strayed too close, his appearance would be noticed and trouble might follow. Not what he needed.

On the walk down from the palace he had considered taking a room at the inn he had stayed at on his first night in the city. He'd need to store whatever supplies he gathered — and it could work as a place for them to meet after Alessandra had gotten out of the palace. However he didn't think it could be relied on.

He wandered around the market for a while to get a feel for what was on offer, which was pretty much everything imaginable. Cloths of every colour, foods of every smell and objects of every shape. He decided the easiest approach to finding what he was looking for was to ask.

He approached a merchant with a large stall that had a good selection of sturdy looking work wear and equipment laid out on his counter. Being larger and more prosperous looking than those around him, Soren hoped that he might have experience with foreign trade and speak some Imperial as a result.

'Do you speak Imperial?' he asked.

'Yes, yes, a little.'

'I'm planning a journey into the desert. What will I need to bring with me?'

He already had a fair idea of what would be required, but there was no harm in getting the advice of someone who was familiar with the desert.

'Water,' the vendor said, with a broad smile. 'Lots of it.'

He supposed he had invited a glib answer, but he did wonder if being a smart arse was a cultural aspect of Shandahari traders, or if it was just the people he chose to speak with.

'Most people who want to go across the desert join a caravan. It's the safest way. You pay them and they will take care of everything else, food, water, baggage. You will need good desert boots though,' he said, gesturing to a selection of tough leather boots on his stall. 'Suitable clothes too.'

'Thank you. I'll think about the boots and clothes.'

A caravan. It made sense, but he would just have to find one that would be willing to take them along, that would also be leaving at a time that fit in with his plans. While it was definitely worth investigating, it was unlikely that Soren would be able to fit in with someone else's timetable for leaving the city.

He found a passer-by that spoke Imperial, and got directions to the main city stables located near the landward gate in the city wall. It stood to reason that this would be a likely place for a desert caravan to start off from.

The stables were large, busy and smelly. There were many horses, but their numbers were easily equalled by camels. Soren had seen them in the menagerie in Ostenheim a number of times when he was younger so they were not completely unknown to him, but he had never been this close to one before. With two humps on their back and shaggy golden-brown fur, they looked comical to Soren, and to see them being used as anything other than a menagerie attraction was decidedly odd.

He approached a man giving out orders to various stable workers while doing very little himself. That could only mean he was in a position of authority. After establishing that the man could speak Imperial, Soren discovered that caravans left the city nearly every day, most often from those stables as Soren had thought. He was assured that there would be no problem in finding a place on one so long as he had the coin to pay his way.

The caravans left early in the morning, before the sun came up. The stable master told him that they made their way through the desert from one oasis to the next. Not the most direct route, but the one most likely to be survivable.

The timing was not ideal. The disappearance of the women from the seraglio would be noticed first thing in the morning. If he sneaked them out of the palace during the night, they would have to wait for several hours before the caravan left and wouldn't be as far from the city as he would have liked by the time their absence was discovered. The alternative was to hire a guide and camels so they would be ready to go whenever he was. There were benefits and drawbacks to both, greater safety and anonymity with a caravan, greater flexibility and speed with a guide.

Further inquiries got him the name of a guide, Sharbo, who worked out of the stables and owned five camels, enough to take them south without having to hire more. Soren's experience with the street trader made him wary of a guide recommended by a complete unknown, stable master or not. Being robbed and abandoned in the desert was not an attractive eventuality. His concerns were such that joining a caravan seemed a far more sensible option.

However, he wasn't going to dismiss the option out of hand, and spoke to Sharbo, who seemed to know his business, and had the look of a man accustomed to travel, discomfort and hard work. Looks could be deceiving, but Soren had few options and had to make a decision based on his gut feeling.

For a suitably large payment — not all up front — Soren got Sharbo to agree to wait at the stables, ready to go at short notice, from dusk until dawn for the next five days. The guide thought it odd, but the money on offer was enough to quell his curiosity.

With the bare bones of a plan in place, Soren headed toward the harbour, concerned that he was going to lead them all to a miserable death in the desert.

There were two ways out of the city and the territory that it controlled. While Soren had discounted the sea, there was no harm in laying as confused a trail as he could. It was a hassle, but it might give them a few more hours before pursuit began in earnest.

He started making inquiries at the docks about the ships in the harbour, and where they were headed. For the most part the men he tried to talk to shook their heads blankly and walked away, but there were a number of northern vessels there too and Soren was able to speak with some of the sailors from them. Most importantly, plenty of people saw him make his enquiries.

He found the names of several ships that would be sailing north over the next few days before returning to the guardhouse. He had no idea when his plan would be carried out, but he could return when he had a better idea of timing and make the fake purchase then.

Chapter 55
THE BLUECLOAKS

THREE DAYS LATER HE was wandering idly around the palace and the passageways beneath it, ostensibly on roving guard duty — which amounted to much the same thing — counting away the minutes. He had still not heard anything else from Alessandra. His plans were in place and he was starting to wonder if he should try to get a message to her. The guide was storing the clothes and boots that Soren bought, and would put together rations for a half dozen people for the journey. Keeping the details as vague as possible made it difficult not to arouse suspicion, but he couldn't see a way around it.

Alessandra had made it clear to him how difficult and dangerous it was to get out of the seraglio when they'd spoken, so he wasn't overly worried that she had yet to try, just impatient. If she'd been caught sneaking out, he would have heard about it.

He had two men of the Northern Guard with him as Vaprio had changed his advice on not going about the palace alone to a standing order. Soren arranged for a dozen other similarly sized patrols to make their way around the palace, all following different looping paths that would intersect every so often so they could update each other on how things were going. He planned to make one more circuit of this route before returning to the guardhouse to check on things there. As they approached an intersection with another corridor, he could hear raised voices.

He was not expecting to encounter one of his other patrols there, and the Bluecloaks were not supposed to be in that part of the palace. If it was Alessandra, it could make for a difficult job of explaining things to his men. He beckoned for them to stop and slowly walked forward alone. The voices were still too muffled to discern, and Soren tried to work out what was being said.

He reached the intersection of the passages and peered around the corner. An Ostian sergeant of the Northern Guard was squared up to a member of the Bluecloaks. He was alone, which would require an explanation, but that could wait until the situation was dealt with. The Bluecloak was not.

'What's going on here?' Soren shouted, hoping that he would be able to raise his voice enough to be heard over the ever-rising voices of the Ostian and the Shandahari.

The sergeant reacted and stepped back in deference to his superior officer, ending his tirade of abuse at the Shandahari guard.

'Haven't a clue, sir,' he said. 'This fucker bumped into me and started shouting.'

The Shandahari was still talking loudly and aggressively, gesticulating furiously. There were two other Bluecloaks with him, but with Soren's arrival and the men behind him, they were now outnumbered.

'Does anyone speak Shandahari?' Soren said to his men.

No one spoke up; one man shrugged apologetically.

'Imperial?' he asked hopefully in the direction of the Bluecloaks. Even if they did, he expected they would be too objectionable to want to discuss things in a reasonable way. The Bluecloak who had been arguing with the sergeant continued his diatribe unabated, with Soren recognising one or two of the words as fairly commonly used insults.

What to do now? If the Bluecloak didn't back down, or just shut up, then Soren couldn't see any way out of the situation that didn't involve a fight. The only way to deal with that type of aggression was to mirror it, and hope that the other party would back down.

He stepped forward quickly and summoned up as much anger as he could muster.

'Shut your fucking mouth,' he screamed at the Bluecloak. 'Back off!' He gesticulated aggressively with his finger, but stopped short of poking the Bluecloak in the chest.

One of the other Bluecloaks muttered something and the one doing all of the shouting glanced back over his shoulder. He was smiling when he returned his gaze to Soren. Soren could quickly see the reason why. Another four Bluecloaks were making their way down the other corridor, wiping out Soren's advantage.

The Bluecloak reached forward and shoved Soren, which was crossing a line and they both knew it. Soren's hand instinctively went to his hilt while with the other he gestured for the Bluecloak to stop. The Bluecloak looked back to his comrades for support and seemed satisfied, for when he turned back he shoved Soren again.

Soren grabbed him by the wrist and twisted it hard, pulling the Bluecloak off balance. Without really thinking about what he was doing, he smashed the heel of his hand into the Shandahari's face. The Bluecloak dropped to the floor like a sack of rocks.

The speed and aggression with which Soren had acted took everyone else in the corridor by surprise. The Bluecloaks shouted and all went for their weapons. Soren drew before any of them out of an instinct of self-preservation, but regretted doing it the second that he had; there was no backing down now. There was a series of rasping sounds as swords were drawn from their scabbards, both in front and behind. Any chance to diffuse the situation seemed to be well and truly gone. As naturally as his hand had gone to the hilt of his sword without his thinking, he suddenly felt the tingle, and saw the faint blue glow of the Fount. As he could see from its dimness, down there in the bowels of the palace it was weak, but with the dense pack of nearly a dozen men there would be enough to give him an edge.

Someone shouted in Shandahari and pushed his way forward, shoving men and drawn blades out of his way as he went.

'Put your sword away,' he said. 'My men will do so as well, as soon as you have.'

The Gift made his voice sound slurred and Soren felt an instinct deep within him crave a fight, tempting him to ignore the Shandahari's offer. He knew accepting it was the only way to avoid several deaths, but Soren had no reason to trust this man. He pushed his own increasing desire for battle aside and reasoned that if he ordered his men to put away their weapons, but kept his own drawn, he could hold the Bluecloaks back for long enough for his own men to get back in to the fight.

'Put them away, lads,' he said.

Behind him he could hear some grumbles, but more importantly the sounds of weapons being resheathed. The Bluecloak that had come to the front nodded and issued what Soren took to be a similar command to his men. They began to put their weapons away.

Once Soren and the man who appeared to be in charge of the Bluecloaks were the only two who still held weapons, Soren put his sword away. He never took his eyes from the man opposite him, and didn't relax until the Shandahari had put his blade away also.

When they were both no longer holding weapons, Soren spoke. 'You should teach your men some manners.'

The Bluecloak looked at him disdainfully, but said nothing.

He gave an order to his men and two of them moved forward to recover their comrade from the floor. The Bluecloak in charge watched as his man was scraped up off the floor and helped away. Only then did he return his attention to Soren.

'You should fuck off back to whatever northern hole you crawled out of,' the Bluecloak said.

'Perhaps if your Khagan had any confidence in you, he wouldn't have need of us,' Soren said, feeling his hand drift back toward the hilt of his sword.

The Bluecloak sneered at him and turned back to his men. They all shuffled off down the corridor leaving Soren and his men alone. He ordered them all back to barracks. He knew that he would have to make a report to Captain Vaprio and didn't want them to have another run in with the Bluecloaks without him.

◆

'It's not the first time, I doubt it will be the last,' Vaprio said, after Soren had finished filling him in on what had happened. 'From your description I think the Bluecloak that you spoke with was Captain Gulan. He's been quite happy to let any confrontations run so long as they don't get overly violent. Sooner or later one will get out of hand, though, and someone will be killed.'

'Doesn't sound like a situation that the Khagan can allow continue,' Soren said.

'He doesn't intend to. The Khagan's given orders to have Bayda tai Azaf arrested. He's all but lost control of the Bluecloaks, and if he doesn't move against tai Azaf soon he won't be able to. His last outburst was too much for the Khagan to stomach; the challenge to his prestige is too great to allow go unchecked. With Azaf out of the way, the other Baydas will fight amongst each other for a while before one of them emerges as the new leader. That should give the Khagan enough time to finish his negotiations over the Rala. If they work out well, he expects they'll put him in an unassailable position. If not, well, I doubt he's giving much thought to that eventuality.'

Soren nodded. The politics were so ruthless, and so similar to Ostenheim; powerful men happy to kill one another to climb to the top of the pile.

'With no unified voice,' Vaprio said, 'the Baydas won't be a threat, and the Bluecloaks will have no alternative but to stay loyal to the Khagan, at least for the time being. I dare say one or two of them will join tai Azaf on the chopping block though, your new friend Gulan among them.'

The thought of the sneering Captain Gulan meeting his end was a warming thought. 'When do we arrest tai Azaf?' Soren said.

'Now. The order's only just come through, but it has to be done right away, before tai Azaf can catch wind of it. I'm taking Veyt with me, and twenty men. I want you to keep an eye on things here. We'll be bringing tai Azaf back to the guardroom initially, so try to keep the Bluecloaks away. I'd like to have tai Azaf secured in here before they catch wind of what's happened.'

Sitting around while knowing that there was something important happening, something that he could make a useful contribution to, was difficult for Soren. Boredom had never been something he took to well, but under the circumstances it was even more agitating.

Vaprio and his men left the palace as discreetly as they could, hoping not to draw any attention from the Bluecloaks. They left in small groups, the intention being to meet up outside the palace and continue on to tai Azaf's residence.

Time passed and minutes became hours. Soren started to grow concerned. The mission should have taken no more than an hour from start to finish, and he expected that they would have returned by then. He got up from the desk that he was sitting at and stretched. His legs had grown stiff from the idleness and he felt awkward as he made his way out of the guardhouse to look down the avenue to the palace gates.

There was still no sign of them returning, but otherwise everything seemed to be normal. There were two figures clad in crimson standing by the blue archway as there should be and there was nothing out of the ordinary. Perhaps the Bayda's house was farther from the palace than he thought? He went back into the guardhouse, flopped into an easy chair and allowed himself to doze.

When he woke, it felt as though the guardroom had been hit by a storm. Lieutenant Veyt was shouting for him to get up and arm himself.

'We've got to get out of here,' Veyt said. He was rummaging through the shelves and stuffing things into a bag.

'What are you talking about?' Soren said. He was still a little groggy from the nap.

'The arrest was a fucking disaster. Azaf knew we were coming. He had half the Bluecloaks guarding his house.'

No wonder things had been so quiet during the afternoon.

'Vaprio's dead. So are most of the others that came with us. I managed to fight my way clear and get back here.'

'I don't see the problem. There's enough of us here to keep the palace secure,' Soren said.

'My arse. We've lost ten men already. One watch is off duty so there's about seventy men here at best. There are five hundred Bluecloaks, so if even half of them have gone over to Azaf, we're done. That isn't even counting his own retinue.' Veyt continued to shove things into a duffel bag. 'No, it's time to move on. The Khagan made his own bed, now he's going to have to lie in it. If we stay here, we're as dead as he's going to be.'

Soren took a moment to digest what Veyt was saying. Five hundred bluecloaks who very much hated the Northern Guard;

it was hard to dispute his logic. Some of them would remain loyal to the Khagan, but the Northern Guard would be caught in the middle.

'Well? Are you coming?' Veyt said.

'No, not yet, but I won't be far behind you.'

Veyt shook his head. 'It's your neck, but good luck. There's one thing I'd say to you though; don't let yourself be taken alive.'

It was chilling advice, but Soren didn't doubt its value. 'Good luck to you too.'

Veyt didn't waste another moment. Whatever Soren decided to do, sitting in the guardroom wouldn't get it done.

He ran toward the seraglio. He didn't pass another person on the way. Word had obviously spread to the other men of the Northern Guard; there were none to be seen, and no sign of the Bluecloaks. Once he got into the palace, there were a few people moving about, all in a hurry and a state of anxiety.

With every guard gone for one reason or another, the way to the seraglio was clear. After a cursory glance around the gallery to ensure there were no bluecloaks still lurking there, Soren leaned over the balustrade.

'Alessandra!'

Several of the women in the courtyard below looked up, startled by the unprecedented disturbance.

'Can you get Alessandra?' he said.

One of the women nodded and left her seat. She walked out of view while the other women present slipped away also. As he waited, his anxiety increased. This was too great an opportunity to allow slip by. If a coup was carried out successfully, Soren wouldn't have another opportunity. As it was, with all the confusion they could be miles into the desert before anyone noticed they were gone.

He felt great relief when the woman reappeared with Alessandra in tow.

'We have to go now,' Soren said.

'What? I'm not ready,' Alessandra said.

'It doesn't matter. There's trouble coming; it might be here already, but all the guards are gone and we won't have a chance like this again. We have to go. Right now.'

'All right, give me a moment.'

'Wait, I need you to bring someone else. There's a princess here, a Rala. Do you know her?'

Alessandra smiled. 'I'll bring her too.' With that she disappeared out of view leaving Soren to wait and hope that she wouldn't take too long. Each second seemed like an hour and Soren found the image of a half dozen bloodthirsty Bluecloaks charging around the corner hard to keep from his thoughts. If Soren were leading the coup, he would have placed the same significance on capturing the Rala as on the Khagan. Tai Azaf would expect her to be safely secured in the seraglio however, so if Soren was lucky he would not come looking for her until he had the Khagan in custody and the palace secure. Either way, Soren knew he had to move fast.

Alessandra appeared in the courtyard with another woman — presumably her friend. Taking the Rala with them carried too great a reward to not at least try.

'The Rala? Where is she?' he said.

'Nice to see you too,' Alessandra said. 'This is her, Rala Roxendi tai Serash.' She gestured to the other woman who bore an expression of puzzlement on her face.

'Your friend?'

Alessandra nodded. 'Meet us in the corridor where we talked the last time.'

He didn't have the chance to argue, as she took the Rala by the hand and led her to the opposite side of the courtyard and out of sight. Soren moved off, hoping that he could remember a direct route back to that spot. There were so many corridors, so many twists and turns that even now he was not as familiar with them as he'd have liked.

He had reached the lower level when he heard the first sounds of fighting, so evidently some of the Bluecloaks had remained loyal. That was good news; the longer the fighting went on, the longer confusion reigned. Each minute it lasted would allow them get further from the palace without notice.

Alessandra and the Rala were waiting for him when he got to the junction in the corridors.

'What's going on?' Alessandra said.

'The Baydas are trying to overthrow the Khagan. The Northern Guard have taken a beating and the survivors have scarpered. We need to do the same.'

Alessandra nodded. She muttered something to the Rala that sounded like Shandahari and they set off.

It was a relief when he came to a turn in the corridor that he recognised. They were not far from a stairwell that led to the entrance hallway on the ground level. While it meant they were nearly out of the palace, the next few minutes were going to be the most dangerous.

They reached the bottom of the stairwell and Soren drew his dagger. He told Alessandra to wait and made his way to the top in a low crouch. The stairs were wooden and he felt his heart skip a beat each time he placed his foot, waiting for the creak that would give them all away. He felt one begin to protest at his weight so lifted his foot and stepped past it. The top drew closer and daylight invited him ever forward. Once at the top he peered out into the hallway.

There were three Bluecloaks standing by the doorway that led further into the palace. The doors had been kicked off their hinges and lay haphazardly on the ground. The men appeared relaxed; they didn't perceive any threat. He couldn't get to them without being seen, and it was unlikely that he would be able to get

Alessandra and the Rala out without attracting their attention. He would have to bring them to him.

He gestured to Alessandra to wait out of sight. She moved out of view, dragging the Rala with her. Soren pressed down heavily on the step that had threatened to creak on his way up. He heard the men in the hall raise their voices and footsteps coming in his direction.

Soren crouched and pressed against the wall. A dark shape appeared silhouetted against the daylight at the top of the stairs. Soren grabbed a handful of cloth and wrenched the Bluecloak forward. He stabbed him through the throat and allowed the body to continue to fall down the stairs. He heard more footsteps now — more than one pair — moving faster.

Another shape appeared and Soren heaved him forward also. Once he was clear out of the way and cartwheeling down the stairs, Soren lunged forward and stabbed the final man in the chest, twisting the blade as he pulled it out to be certain it had done its job. He ran back down the stairs to deal with the Bluecloak he'd sent tumbling down.

As luck would have it, he had broken his neck in the fall and lay as dead as his comrades.

Alessandra and the Rala peered around the corner.

'It's safe, come on,' he said.

They came out from their hiding place, wide eyed at the gruesome scene.

'Let's go,' he said. He took Alessandra by the hand and led her and the Rala up the steps.

The hallway was clear and from there it wasn't difficult to get out of the palace and into the city. The confusion and chaos following the overthrow had proved to be their ally and he could only hope that the situation would continue long enough to put in some distance between them.

Chapter 56
BEST LAID PLANS...

Soren kept up a fast pace as he led them away from the palace. He headed straight for the stables, where he hoped his guide would be waiting. It was only late afternoon, outside of the hours of their agreement, though.

Soren recognised the stable master as soon as they arrived.

'Stay out of sight,' he said to Alessandra. 'I'll be back in a moment.'

'Wait,' she said. 'This isn't the harbour.'

'We're not going there. It's just too risky. Once they discover that the Rala is gone, it'll be the first place they look. That's assuming they didn't send troops there as soon as the coup started to prevent anyone important from fleeing the city.'

'You're planning on taking us across the desert?'

Soren nodded.

'Have you been out in the sun too long? They send the really bad criminals out into the desert here. They think it's worse than execution.'

'I know it isn't ideal, but if we're not well out of the city by the time things here have settled down, I can guarantee that a quick execution will be the best we can hope for. Please just trust me. I'm hoping a guide I spoke to will be here, but if not we can start off alone and if we push hard for a few hours we should catch up with the caravan that left this morning.'

'And if they refuse to take us?' She raised an eyebrow.

The Rala watched them both, her face a picture of bemusement.

Soren opened his mouth to answer, but had no reply. 'I'll go and talk to the stable master. Wait out of sight until I'm back.'

'I'm looking for Sharbo. Is he here?'

The stable master shook his head. He had spoken to this man the previous time he called to the stables, so Soren knew he spoke Imperial.

'Where is he?'

'He took his camels up river for grazing. He'll be back at dusk.' The stable master spoke in a dismissive tone, and clearly wanted Soren to go away and leave him in peace.

Soren's heart sank, though he had not allowed his hopes to get too high and had a fall back plan.

'Did a caravan leave here this morning?'

'Three did. Same as most mornings. North, south and upriver.'

'How much for three camels, food and water to get us to Serash?'

The stable master smiled, and gave Soren his full attention.

'You'll only need water and food to get you to the first oasis, a little over a day. There will be plenty more there to buy.'

Soren was headed in the opposite direction, but he hoped laying a little misinformation might be of help. The danger it created was that the next oasis south was farther away than the next one north. As reckless as Soren was with his own life at times, he was not happy to risk Alessandra's.

'My companions are elderly, so we'll be slow. I'll need three days of supplies for three people.'

Soren went back to the women, proud owner of what he felt confident were the three most expensive camels in Shandahar.

'The guide's not here, and we can't wait for him to get back. I've got us supplies and camels to take us into the desert. If we ride hard we can catch the caravan by the first oasis and follow them the rest of the way.'

'You're sure about this?' Alessandra said.

Soren was going to lie, but she deserved his honesty. 'No, but there's no other option.'

'All right,' she said. 'Let's get going then.'

They reached the oasis a little after midday the next day. It was tiring, but riding in the relative cool of the night had helped, as had the fact that the desert had been, for the most part, hard baked earth and stone rather than sand as Soren had feared it might be. The constant passage of caravans had left a trail that was easy to follow, even in the dead of night, and they were aided by the clear desert sky and a nearly full moon that lit the way.

The drawback of the clear sky was the cold, which Soren had not expected to be so severe. The stable master had suggested taking extra blankets for his elderly companions, and Soren was glad he had.

Despite the cold and their obvious discomfort, neither woman complained. They bore their hardship in silence, with the occasional short conversation. Alessandra seemed to have developed a good grasp of Shandahari. Soren was too concerned with remaining on the correct trail and with what might be following them to get involved in any chat. He also felt awkward around

Alessandra, now that there was time for conversation about things other than the escape.

The haste of their departure, and Soren's eager purchase of supplies and camels, would leave the stable master in no doubt of who they were when the Bluecloaks arrived at the stables looking for them. He could only hope that they'd be directed north, but if they had any sense they would send men in all directions. It was what Soren would do in their position. Their entire escape was based on the slim chance that the fighting and confusion in the city would give them enough of a head start for it not to matter. There was more than one route after the first oasis, so getting beyond there increased their chances massively.

The oasis was a shady grove of trees surrounding a pool of freshwater, sheltered by low scrubby hills all around it. It was busier than Soren expected, as a number of routes coalesced on it from all along the Galat river. It boded well for their chances of finding a caravan that would agree to take them the rest of the way to Kirek, now that there was more than one to choose from. There would be several days of travel between oases from that point on, and many trails going in different directions — not all of them to Kirek. To continue on their own would be madness.

There was a genial atmosphere at the oasis, the hardship of travel and the dangers of the road creating a common ground between the caravaneers. Some were excited at the prospect of their journey being near completion while others were buoyed up with the excitement of being near the start of a new adventure.

The pool was surrounded by dozens of camels, making long nuzzing sounds between drinks. It was an odd noise, and to hear so many of them together was bizarre. The people ranged from merchants and travellers to heavily armed guards who remained vigilant while the others relaxed.

Soren had left Alessandra and the Rala to rest in the shade of one of the palm trees while he had a look around. There were two small mud brick buildings that were in poor repair to the side of the oasis, at the edge of the line where the trees ended and the desert began. A well had been dug to the side of the pool to keep the water used by people separate to that used by the camels. Soren walked over to the well to freshen their water skins.

There was a short queue of men waiting their turn at the crank that raised and lowered a leather bag down into the water. He tried to make conversation with one or two others in the hope of finding a caravan that would take them the rest of the way, but all it resulted in was dismissive shakes of heads. Having filled the water skins, he returned to the palm tree where Alessandra and the Rala were resting. If Alessandra was as comfortable speaking in Shandahari as it seemed, she would be able to negotiate better than he.

They were both asleep when he returned and while he felt a little uncomfortable waking Alessandra when she was obviously so tired, there wasn't the time to wait around if they were to stay ahead of any pursuers from Galat. He gave her a gentle shake.

'I need your help finding a caravan to take us south. Can you translate for me?'

She rubbed her eyes and thought for a moment. 'I should be able to.'

Alessandra woke the Rala and spoke to her quietly. The Rala nodded and sat up, wrapping a blanket around her and casting a glance in the direction of their resting camels.

'She'll keep an eye on the camels,' Alessandra said. 'But let's not go too far; I don't want to leave her on her own here.'

Soren nodded and they walked to a nearby caravan.

'Ask them if they're going to Kirek,' Soren said.

Alessandra nodded and rattled out a line of impressive Shandahari to the man looking after the caravan's camels.

Soren wondered if he would have been able to pick up as

much of the language in the same amount of time. As it was he could recognise a couple of curses, but nothing else.

'You are Imperials?' the man said.

Soren couldn't help but smile to himself. He had tried to talk to at least a half dozen men on his way to and from the well, and not one was able to understand him. Now that he had woken Alessandra, the first person they approached was able to speak Imperial.

'Yes, we are,' Soren said. 'Are you headed south? To Kirek?'

'Yes,' replied the caravaneer. He stood arms akimbo. 'Why do you ask?'

'My friends and I are looking for a caravan to travel with. We'll need some provisions but can pay well.'

The caravaneer scratched his chin and gave Soren a good looking over, obviously trying to decide if he was chancing his luck or if he would actually be able to pay his way.

'How many of you are there?' he said.

'The two of us and one other.'

The caravaneer looked at Alessandra for a moment and mulled it over for a moment. 'The other? Man or woman?'

'A woman,' Soren said.

'You are welcome to come with me. If you can use those swords at your waist, all the more so. I don't have any provisions to spare though, and my cargo is of little value. If theft is your intention, know that my two sons and I are excellent swordsmen and will have little trouble dealing with one man and two women.'

Soren smiled. 'We won't cause you any trouble, we just need a guide south.'

'Fine. You will be able to buy what you need over there.' He pointed to the mud brick buildings that Soren had noticed earlier. 'Salted and dried meat mainly, but if they have any fresh fruit, get some of that also. Those water skins should last until the next oasis, but this is the last chance to get food. Make sure you have enough.' He scratched his chin again, looking at Soren's clothes and weapons. 'My price is one hundred tremissi.'

Soren thought about it for a moment. He knew he had no real alternative, but didn't want to appear too eager. 'Fine,' he said. 'Half now and half when we arrive in Kirek.'

'That is acceptable. My name is Shirma. I leave in three hours. Make sure you have everything you need by then. I want to be clear of the oasis before darkness falls.'

'I'm Soren.' He handed over fifty tremissi, before he and Alessandra went to the building that Shirma had pointed out. Inside there was a trader sitting amongst a number of crates and sacks. Soren didn't bother trying to speak to the man, he had frustrated himself enough for one day. He peered into several of the open containers and decided on what he wanted. Alessandra took care of the negotiations. She made a good job of haggling on the price, and they paid less than Soren expected, it being the last place to get supplies on the route south.

Chapter 57
THE LAST BANNERET?

BEING ANOTHER TWO DAYS away from Galat helped Soren relax. While they still had a long way to go to get to Kirek, each day put them closer to its territory, and ever greater safety. Soren wouldn't be able to completely relax until he was within Kirek's walls though.

The next oasis was very much like the first, albeit much smaller. They were resting there for the hottest part of the day and would continue on once it began to cool in the evening. The desert had become sandier as they continued south and it now looked much as Soren had envisioned it would. The going got tougher as the ground underfoot grew softer, but Alessandra and the Rala didn't slow or complain.

They were the only ones at this oasis, which hammered home the sense of isolation of being out in the desert. When they first left the previous oasis, they had been part of a steady stream of traffic; a long line of camels loping through the desert, nuzzing and groaning as they bore their passengers and cargoes south. One by one the various trains began to peel away toward wherever it was they were headed leaving the caravan that Soren was travelling with all but alone. Some way behind them was another party, barely visible in the distance, but other than that they were as isolated as if they were in the middle of the sea.

While travelling, there was always something to occupy the mind even if it was just as simple as concentrating on remaining on the camel's back. Now that they were resting in the oasis, there was little to do but talk and Soren found himself wondering what to say to Alessandra. She and the Rala talked, but he had been feigning tiredness to avoid being drawn in.

He desperately wanted to talk to her, but when the opportunity came he could never think of anything to say. It seemed that so much time had passed since they were last together. Their relationship had been troubled and despite a reconciliation shortly before they were forced to flee the city, there still remained much that they would have to talk about, sooner rather than later.

Eventually she broke the silence.

'What happened after I left you at the Duke's camp?' she said.

'They shredded my banner and I was arrested. I was thrown into the castle dungeons until they got around to deciding what to do with me. During that time, Amero took over. I expect I would've been exiled or as good as for not stopping the Duke's assassination, but I was too close to the heart of Amero's plot to be allowed to live. I was to be executed once he took power. He came down to the dungeon to tell me himself. Gloating bastard. If it wasn't for Ranph, that's the way it would have ended. He brought me out of the dungeons and put me on a ship to join you in Auracia.'

'I never managed to get there,' she said.

'No. I realised that, eventually.'

They both laughed and Soren relaxed a little more.

'And you? How did you end up getting captured by Rui?' he said.

She nodded. 'The captain of the ship I was on was trying to

avoid a storm. Sailed us right into Rui's path. He took us captive before sinking our vessel. He took the ship that the Rala was on a few days later. She's a good woman. When we got to Galat, she disguised me as part of her retinue. If it wasn't for that, gods only know where I'd be now.'

The thought made them both pause.

'How did you end up meeting Rui?' she said.

Soren explained part of his story, leaving out the part about the Shrouded Isles. It was easier not to mention it than have to construct lies. He might tell her one day, but there was no need then.

'You killed him?' she said.

Soren nodded.

'Good.'

'We stopped in Kirek on the way to Galat, where I was asked to see what I could do about freeing the Rala.'

'That's why you were asking for her?'

Soren nodded. 'I said I'd see what I could do, but that I'd other priorities.'

She smiled and reached forward, taking his hand.

·—·

Shirma had a policy of two rest periods a day. One was for an hour in the middle of the night, the other was for a few hours covering midday, the hottest time. At first Soren had difficulty sleeping when they stopped, but as the distance between them and Galat increased and he relaxed more, the fatigue of the past few days began to catch up on him.

He sat and closed his eyes for a moment, intending to get something to eat after a moment's respite, but when he opened them again, the sun was in a different position overhead. There was a commotion on the other side of the oasis, but not so much that he was bothered to look at first. He was able to disregard it as another caravan having arrived while he slept. They were most likely the group he had seen in the distance behind them when they had left the first oasis. As the dullness of sleep dropped away, his caution returned. He propped himself up on his elbows to see who had arrived.

They were not a trade caravan. Each of the camels bore saddles and personal equipment rather than the large bundles of merchandise that Shirma's were carrying. The men were going about the business of watering their camels and securing them, but there was something about the way they were doing things that put Soren ill at ease. They didn't have the practised efficiency that Shirma had when doing the same with his own animals. The way they behaved around their camels was familiar to Soren. It was similar to the way he behaved around them; wary and unsure.

There was no hiding the fact that they were at the oasis; Shirma's camels were far too large and noisy. Soren didn't want to alert them to the fact that he was suspicious of them. They could easily have been men fleeing the city after the coup, possibly other Northern Guardsmen in disguise, which would explain their unease around the camels. Moving as quietly as he could, he freed his blades from their scabbards. He gently shook Alessandra awake and shushed her as she began to question him.

'Men have arrived at the oasis,' he whispered. 'I don't know if they're going to cause us any trouble, but I'm not going to take any chances. I need you to wake the Rala as quietly as you can. Both of you hide over there. I want you to make sure I'm between you and those men at all times. Do you understand?'

'Yes.'

She still sounded groggy, but he was satisfied that his instructions had registered. Once she was moving to carry them out, he went to Shirma and relayed the same information to him. Unlike Alessandra, he protested a little, as did his sons. Instead of the fearsome Shandahari warriors that their father had intimated them to be, they were little more than boys and Soren was not willing to put them at risk. Soren's suggestion that they hide seemed to be an affront to their pride, but they agreed readily enough when he reworded it into a request to watch over Alessandra and the Rala.

The camels provided a screen between him and the new arrivals to the oasis and he intended to take advantage of that. He could be the best swordsman in the world and in possession of a gift not seen for a thousand years, but a crossbow bolt in the back would have the same effect on him as it would any man. Additionally, the men had not yet shown any outwardly hostile intent; all Soren had was suspicion and fear.

Two of them started to walk over. Soren kept his weapons concealed, not wanting to provoke a situation that could be otherwise avoided. They weren't wearing blue uniforms, which came as a relief, but they could as easily be bandits, and as much of a threat.

The simplest explanation was that they were ordinary travellers. That didn't provide a reason for their awkwardness around camels though.

'Ho there, friend!' shouted one of the men as he drew closer.

Imperial. It confirmed part of his suspicion. He didn't recognise the man, but he hadn't been in the Northern Guard long enough to get to know all of the men. The man's comrades, there were three of them, watched from twenty or so paces behind, giving Soren reason to fear that there would be a hail of crossbow bolts coming in his directions at any moment.

'Ho there!' Soren said, with as much friendliness as he could muster.

'You're name wouldn't be Soren by any chance?' the man said.

'Afraid not. My name's Henn,' Soren said. 'Will you join me for some tea? It's Shandahari, but it's not all that bad!'

The man didn't respond, but continued to smile, scrutinising Soren. His gaze dwelled on Soren's sword for just a moment too long and Soren knew that there would be violence.

'My name's Macchio Ferrata,' he said, standing arms akimbo. 'Am I right in thinking the bunch of Shandahari soldiers we killed were after you?'

Soren said nothing.

He smiled. 'Reckoned they were. Couldn't have them getting in the way you see. I've been tracking you too bloody long to let someone else get to you first!' He gestured to his three comrades.

They rushed forward, while the man named Ferrata remained behind, watching.

Although dressed in loose fitting Shandahari clothes, the men all carried rapiers. Two of them came at Soren right away, one from either side, while the third tried to flank around and get behind him.

They were good, almost excellent, and Soren was out of practice. He allowed them push him back with each attack, parrying until he found his rhythm and also to try to prevent the third man from getting past him. The blades flashed blindingly bright in the noonday sun, as he continued to defend himself. He hardly noticed the blue tinge that everything had taken on, nor the way the men slowed. One second, everything was happening quickly, and the next he had all the time he needed.

Parry and riposte sent the first man into a gurgling heap on the ground. In the same movement he drew his dagger to parry the blade of the second, and then cut him down with ease. The third man hesitated. Soren threw his dagger, which found its mark in the centre of his chest.

Soren took a deep breath and turned to look at Ferrata. He hadn't moved, still standing with his arms akimbo and an ironic smile on his face. The blue glow still flickered, over the trees, over Ferrata, over Soren's own limbs.

'His Grace said you were good, but I knew that from the size of the bounty.' As though irritated by the thought of having to get his own hands dirty, he shrugged his cloak back from his shoulders and drew his own sword and dagger.

With speed that Soren had never seen from another person before, Ferrata came at him, blades flashing through the air. Soren instantly regretted having thrown his dagger as he parried and retreated, but there was no way to know that this man would be such a threat. They exchanged blows for a little longer before Soren felt himself draw on the Fount again. He felt all of the sensations that went with it, the slight dreaminess, the indestructible feeling of energy and strength, but still Ferrata did not slow.

Soren parried and shoved Ferrata back, taking two paces himself to increase the distance between them. What was different about this man? Then it dawned on him.

'You have it too, don't you?' Soren said, breathing heavily and still not able to believe the only answer he could come up with to explain Ferrata's speed.

'Have what?' Ferrata said, as he crouched low and prepared to attack again.

'The Gift.'

'No idea what you're talking about.'

He lunged forward but Soren parried and leaped to the side. Soren countered, hoping to take the initiative, but no matter what he did, or how fast he thought he was, his blade couldn't find a way through Ferrata's defence. He backed away for space to catch his breath, gasping for air after the previous exchange. His left hand felt wet, as though it was dripping with sweat. He looked down at it and was shocked to see it glistening with bright red blood. He tried to lift his arm but he couldn't; it wouldn't respond. There was a gaping rent in the sleeve of his tunic, but he couldn't feel any pain, and he hadn't even noticed being wounded.

Ferrata looked at Soren's wound and shock at its discovery with relish. 'You're good. The best I've fought, but it's not good enough. Not for what I'm getting paid to do for you. There's another ten crowns on top if I get the whore as well.' He gestured with his head. 'I presume she's one of those two hiding behind the trees.'

He had been edging forward as he spoke, and by the time he finished speaking, he was within striking distance.

Soren's concern for Alessandra was such that he was almost caught off guard. He gathered his wits in time to fend off the attack, and realised that the gamesmanship betrayed the fact that Ferrata was not as confident of victory as he was trying to make out. As reassuring as this was, Soren wasn't confident either. No matter what he did, he couldn't find a way through.

He launched his own barrage of attacks, a mixture of cuts and thrusts, trying to find any opening, but failing each time. Despite his frustration, he found it oddly fascinating to fight someone so good, so fast. Possibly his equal. Possibly his superior.

Now there was a numbness spreading through his left arm and into his body. He might be able to continue fighting at the height of his ability until the end, but blood was streaming from his fingertips, and he knew that once he had lost too much, he would drop.

And then Alessandra would be left to Ferrata. He breathed in deeply and allowed the Fount rush in with the force of a breaking wave. He felt refreshed and uninjured, his skin tingled and his senses were sharp. His sword felt like an extension of his arm as he stepped toward Ferrata, as though his sense of touch continued along its metal edge. He saw a look of unexpected concern on Ferrata's face and realised how things must seem to him, Soren injured one minute, fine the next. Ferrata's movements slowed so much it seemed he was almost frozen.

Soren attacked with such grace and speed it felt as though he was in a dream, completely detached from his body. It acted almost without command and it was difficult to give any attention to Ferrata, so intoxicating and fascinating was the sensation rushing through him. He could feel his blade contact with steel, flesh, bone and viscera as though it was the edge of his hand doing the cleaving. He could feel the pulse of Ferrata's heart slow as the blood coursed from his body. He felt more alive, more powerful than he ever had before. Then he felt nothing.

CHAPTER 58
HOPE

THE FIRST THING THAT he became aware of was a rolling sensation, and at first he thought that he was on board a ship. As his eyes took in his surroundings, he realised that he was still in the desert, and he began to recall what had gone before.

He was sitting on the back of a camel, strapped into position. The rolling sensation was caused by its unusual, loping stride. He looked around him. There was another camel in front of him and another behind. His sight was still heavily blurred, but the rider behind looked up at him and began to move forward.

He heard a woman's voice, and then a man's. The camel lurched to a stop and then crouched down on its knees. He felt more than one pair of hands hauling him off the camel.

'Soren, can you hear me?' said a woman's voice.

'Alessandra?' He recognised the voice, but there were so many thoughts and memories that he couldn't sort one from the other.

'I'm here, Soren,' said the voice.

Alessandra's. Definitely Alessandra's.

'Where are we?' he said.

'We're safe. Don't worry, just rest.'

He felt some water splashing against his lips and drank it down, its coolness soothing his throat. His heart raced when he remembered Ferrata, but he realised that if both he and Alessandra were alive, Ferrata must be dead. Darkness embraced him once again.

―――

The gentle movement beneath Soren when he woke was familiar and had become more of a comfort than a dislike in recent days. He stretched his legs but his feet hit the wooden bulkhead at the base of the bed he was lying in, stopping him from going far enough for the stretch to have been of any use. He hopped out of bed and wobbled slightly. Soren instinctively moved to put his left arm out to steady himself but it didn't respond. He was still not used to the fact and regularly forgot; something that caused problems on board a moving ship. The day before he had felt pins and needles in his left fingers and this made him hopeful that feeling and the ability to use the arm would return. Alessandra told him to be patient, and he was trying, but it was difficult.

He pulled on some clothes and went out on deck. Alessandra was standing in the spot that she had made her own since coming on board several days before, staring out across the sea.

'Good morning, my love,' he said, embracing her with his right arm and kissing her on the neck.

She took his hand and pressed back into him with her shoulders. He loved the way her hair smelled. They both looked out to the horizon in silence for a moment.

'Do you think he'll send anyone else?' she asked, voicing the concern that blighted them both.

It was the first time she had mentioned it, the first time she had considered him recovered enough to cast his mind to things other than rest.

'I don't know, but we can go anywhere we want now. And anywhere's fine with me, so long as it's with you.'

Duncan is a writer of fantasy fiction novels and short stories that are set in a world influenced by Renaissance Europe. He has a Master's Degree in History, and is particularly interested in the medieval and renaissance periods.

He doesn't live anywhere particularly exotic, and when not writing he enjoys cycling, skiing and windsurfing.

You can keep up to date with Duncan at his website, duncan-mhamilton.com, or by signing up for his new release emailing list by clicking here.

Made in the USA
Charleston, SC
28 November 2013